MIDNIGHT QUEEN

THE CRIMSON CROWN BOOK II

KAYLEIGH KING

For the ones who dance in the *darkness*

Her courage was her crown and she wore it like a Queen.
-Atticus

PLAYLIST

Make Me King - The Haunt
Queen - Jax Anderson
Venus Sunrise - Lia Maria Johnson
Dust to Dust - The Civil Wars
Peace and Quiet - Elenowen
Fly (Acoustic) - Meadowlark
Purify - Roniit
Bare - WILDES
Be Still - The Fray
The Yawning Grave - Lord Huron
Empty - PVRIS
Where It Stays - Charlotte OC
Never Let Me Go - Florence + the Machine
Dust to Dust - The Civil Wars
If I Die - Ed Prosek

CHAPTER 1

Silas

For centuries I'd lived without a beating heart.

I'd grown accustomed to the silence that has resided in my chest and I'd come to accept the emptiness I felt there. The hollow, echoing cavity that was once the home to the organ that kept me alive is now where my black corrupted soul lives.

I was at peace with what I'd become, and I wanted for nothing, but then I found my sun and, for a second, I had a heart once more.

My soul was a little less dark and my skin a little less cold. She became the very thing I didn't know I needed or wanted. She was my everything. She made me feel human, something I haven't been in a very long time.

I had her in my grasp, and before I was able to hand her the battered, broken pieces of what was left of the man I used to be, she was ripped away from me.

Just like that, I've lost my sun, and I'm once again without my heart. The darkness she kept at bay is flooding back in and the anger that has filled my body since I knew she was gone is like a hurricane. It's been five hours since Quincey was abducted from my home, and with each passing second, the turbulent winds and wrath grow stronger. At this rate, no one will survive them. And I'm okay with that.

I will tear the world apart until there is nothing but ruins left, and I will rip the hearts out of the chests of anyone that dares get in my way of finding my own.

It's as if the monitor in front of me knows what I'm missing, and it mocks me with the sound of the steady heartbeat. It's a heartbeat I'm thankful for, but it's not the one I truly want to hear right now.

"Mr. Laurent." A voice pulls me away from watching the monitor. The steady rising and falling lines have kept me company for the hours I've waited. I hate waiting. It's not in my nature to be patient, but if I have any hope of finding her, I must be willing to wait for them to get here. "The doctor is here if you'd like to talk about Mr. Greyson's condition."

"Duke," I correct her instantly. "His name is Duke." He's my best man and he's currently lying unconscious in a hospital bed with a tube down his throat because of a choice I made a hundred years ago.

The nurse with the hideously unflattering purple scrubs nods her head. "Right, Duke." Her eyes behind her red-framed glasses look at the man in the bed. He appears weak in this state, not like the strong and capable soldier he is. "I know you were very upset when you wanted to talk to the doctor earlier and he wasn't available," she says warily, eyes cutting back to the door of the hospital room.

The cracked and splintering glass of the sliding door is currently being held together with bright orange tape. While they were shocked I'd thrown the chair, I was more surprised the glass hadn't completely shattered into pieces on the ground. The orange tape now acts as a warning sign to anyone passing by that danger is lurking behind it.

Without acknowledging her comment, I step away from Duke's bed for the first time since he's been out of surgery and stalk past her flinching frame into the brightly lit hallway. The fluorescent lights in the ceiling make my sensitive eyes burn and the lingering pain in my head worsen. The damage my body endured from the explosion was healed by the time I opened my eyes on the forest floor. But the dull ache in my head hasn't diminished. I need to feed but haven't done so yet. How can I ease the pain in my body when Quincey is missing, Duke is injured, and Ira is dead?

A man wearing a white coat raises his head from the tablet he's reading through when I approach. "Hello, I'm Dr. Richardson. I've been—"

I hold up my hand, silently instructing him to stop talking. "I don't care who you are, I only care that you're going to be able to fix Duke. If you're not, I need you to tell me now so I can make the necessary arrangements and get your replacement on a plane. There is no shame in admitting you're in over your head, but if I find out that you had any doubts about your abilities and operated on him anyway, I will destroy you myself. Do I make myself clear?"

The doctor balks, his lips parting in dismay. "I'm not sure who you think you are, but you can't talk to me like this."

With a threatening step forward, I tilt my head, scanning his smaller body like a predator looking at the weakest link in the herd. "I know *exactly* who I am, but it appears you don't. That's a deadly mistake. Almost as deadly as lying to me and telling me you're capable of helping Duke." With another step, I corner him against the sterile white wall behind him. "Tell me now if I need to find someone else. This is the only time I'm going to give you this opportunity. After this, every mistake you make moving forward is a mark against your life."

He swallows hard, the column of his thick neck moving as he tries to find his words. "I'm the best neurologist in the state, sir." *Sir.* Good, he's a quick learner. "Your friend's injuries are nothing new to me. I've already established a plan for him and if all goes accordingly, he will make a full recovery."

"You say this, but he's in a coma with a ventilator breathing for him," I remind him tersely.

"In the accident, Mr. Greyson—"

"*Duke*." Duke hates being called by his last name. It reminds him of his father, which is something he doesn't enjoy. He always said he'd change his last name if it wasn't the name he shared with his sister.

"In the accident, *Duke's* head slammed into something hard. Either the windshield or steering wheel, we aren't sure, but because of this, there is swelling in the brain. To get the swelling to go down, we've placed him in a medically induced coma. This will give his brain the time it needs to heal," the doctor explains quickly. Only a couple times does he trip over his words.

"Will he have any lasting effects from the brain injury?"

"We won't know until he wakes up and we won't wake him up until the swelling goes down. At this point, it's all just a waiting game."

More fucking waiting.

With a stiff nod, I move away from the doctor, granting him back his personal space. "I will be leaving here shortly, but I will have someone sitting in the room with him and they will be reporting back to me with updates."

He straightens out his white coat. "We have strict visiting hours here in the intensive care unit."

"I wasn't asking for your permission. I was being courteous by letting you know what will be happening," I sneer before turning back down the hallway toward Duke's room.

The sun will be up in a few short hours, and I can't remain here, but I can't in good conscience allow Duke to stay here alone in this vulnerable condition. I've lost enough people tonight and, as it is, I barely got him out of the destroyed car in one piece.

I have no idea what lengths Gideon is willing to go to but based on the carnage he inflicted on my home and my people tonight, I think it's a safe assumption he won't stop until he sees me ruined.

A bold move on his part. At one point, he was my right hand. He knows what I'm capable of. He knows what his fate will be when I get my hands on him. If he thinks he's earned a quick death, he's wrong. I'm going to make him beg me for the peace of death, and each time he does, I'm going to prolong his life so he can feel each agonizing second.

Gideon Rolfe is a name I haven't so much as thought about in over a century. Once my business was done with him, he'd ceased to exist to me. I thought by allowing him to live after he changed the human he'd fallen in love with that I was doing him a kindness. My act of kindness is now coming back to haunt me.

I stop in my tracks when I find Della standing in front of Duke's room with a balled-up tissue held against her mouth and nose. Fat tears roll from under her glasses as she looks on at the man she's cared for like a son. Her head turns in my direction, and she drops her hand from her face. "Silas." Her bottom lip wobbles.

"Della," I reply. I don't know what I'm supposed to tell her right now to comfort her. Even if I did possess the ability to console someone, I'm not sure I'd have the words right now. I can't think straight. "Is it finished?"

She was given a task that, under normal circumstances, I never would have asked her to do. It wasn't fair of me, but I was out of choices. It's a job that normally would have fallen to Duke if he wasn't in his current indisposed state.

Della's gray hair that is usually pulled into a neat updo is down, the curly ends wild around her shoulders. Her face is completely bare of any makeup, something I don't think I've ever seen in all her years of service to me. "Yes, the team finished up and then I came straight here." Her voice croaks as she speaks. "It's all cleaned up. There isn't a thing out of place or a drop of evidence. You'd never know that there was a shoot-out on the property or that..." she chokes on her words. "That Ira died in that room."

I've lived through wars and plagues. I've seen more carnage and death that anyone should ever have to see in a lifetime but walking into Ira's bedroom to find his cold body lying in a pool of his blood is a sight I won't soon forget. My friend of over sixty years was not supposed to leave this earth like that. He was never supposed to be caught in the middle of the wars I fight in the shadows.

Neither was Quincey.

It was equally horrifying to discover that she was missing from my home. I should have been there with her. Had I not insisted on staying in the city to work, she would be safe, and Ira would be alive.

I vowed to keep them both safe and I failed them both.

"They took his body, I'm not sure where." More tears fall. "Silas, how did this happen to him? How did any of this happen..."

I had Ira's body collected and taken to a nearby morgue. It is where he will remain until we can give him the proper burial he deserves.

"Della, I can't talk about Ira. We will mourn him when I have Quincey back. I cannot focus on anything other than that." I don't care if that makes me sound cold and apathetic to what's happened to Ira. It's what needs to be done. "We will feel the weight of his loss later." I can't allow myself the luxury of feeling anything other than anger right now. The anger will keep my focus sharp and mission clear. Bring her home.

With a tight, reluctant nod, Della agrees, "Okay." She releases a long breath and wipes her face in a desperate attempt to get herself together. "How are we going to do that? Where would this *Gideon* have taken her?" After getting Duke into the ambulance, I'd returned home to find my home and life in disarray. The unfortunate phone call to Della to inform her of what had transpired is one I never wanted to make.

It physically hurts me to say these words, "I don't know." And that's why I've called them in. It's not easy for me to ask for help, but I'm asking it from each of them. It's not just me they'll be helping. It's everyone in a hundred-mile radius because if Quincey is killed, there is no telling what carnage I will inflict. Stopping me will be damn near impossible and that's another reason why I've called *him* in after all these years. He may be the only one strong enough and willing to stop my destruction. "But I've made a few calls."

CHAPTER 2

M y mom always said that monsters were real. I always believed that not only was she full of cheap tequila, but that she was also full of shit.

I learned the hard way that I was wrong.

So, so wrong.

Monsters are real and I gave my heart to one.

I knew it was dangerous to do so, but just like I did with the monster, I looked the danger in the eyes and laughed. I thought having the monster at my side I would always be safe and that he would always protect me. He promised me he would, and I believed him with every fiber of my soul.

Mom was also wrong. She told me that all the monsters were evil. I've seen the good in the midnight eyes that will haunt me until my last breath. Those eyes send cold tendrils of fear down the strongest of men's spine, but not mine. I don't fear them; I find peace and safety in those dark orbs. I'd give anything to be staring into them right now instead of the stained ceiling above me.

It's either the ceiling or the metal walls. The shackles around my wrists and ankles keep me from sitting up or moving from the hard table I lie on. I'm freezing. The pretty dress Della had picked out for me has been removed from my body. I don't remember this happening. It had to have been while I was drugged.

There are events in life that you have to assume will only occur once. The odds of them happening more than that are just so highly unlikely you don't consider them a possibility. Like getting struck by lightning more than once, I thought the chances of me being drugged and abducted *again* were slim to none.

But I was really fucking wrong.

Though as I lie here in nothing but the matching panties and bra I'd put on for my date with Silas, I have the sneaking suspicion that it's not going to work out as well for me this time around.

The room is cold. A steady breeze of cool air flows over my exposed skin, causing goose bumps to rise and my body to shiver. I feel like I'm in a walk-in refrigerator.

I want to cry and scream, but I refuse to break and show how scared I am. If Ira can be brave in his terrifying last moments, I can be too. For him, I will be.

My chest physically aches as it constricts with emotion. Ira was the sweetest soul I've ever met. The world he lived in for the better part of sixty years could have hardened him like it has Silas, but he remained gentle and sweet. We were all blessed to have him in our lives.

Ira didn't deserve the ending he got, but much like me, he was treated as a pawn on this sinister chessboard. He was used and then thrown away like his life meant nothing. Each second I spend strapped to this table, the more I'm afraid my fate will be the same.

I squeeze my eyes shut when angry tears threaten to fall. There have been many events in my life that I've been angry over, but none of them have consumed me with the amount of rage I feel now. I don't like to live in anger. It's exhausting and it's not in my nature to do so, but right now, it's like a dark fog seeping from my pores.

With an irritated snarl, I yank at the chains. The cuffs around my wrists dig painfully into my skin, but I force myself to ignore the discomfort and keep pulling. Even when I feel my skin break and blood drip down my arms, I keep yanking. I try to shift my feet to gain more leverage, but the chains are so taut on my ankles that I can't move them a single inch.

Out of breath and wrists hurting, I stop and stare back up at the ceiling. As my chest heaves, I try to anticipate what's to come.

Or *who's* to come.

I didn't recognize the man who'd been waiting for me in Ira's room, but I know I should be afraid of him. I know from the look in his eyes and Ira's blood dripping down his chin that he's one of the monsters my mom tried to warn me about. The fact he's a vampire isn't what scares me most. It's that he's willing to go against Silas. Anyone who is willing to go against their king is either criminally insane or they have nothing to lose. Both options don't bode well for me.

There's a loud clanking noise, like a latch being pulled before the metal door slides open. The cold air that had been circulating in the small room hurries out as warmer air brushes against my skin. I want to curl into it, but the sound of footsteps at the doorway has me holding my breath and freezing in place.

When the room goes pitch black and I can't see farther than an inch in front of my face, my heart thuds against my rib cage. Another switch is flipped somewhere in the room, but this time, an ominous red glow illuminates the space. Adrenaline rushes through my veins like a coursing river as I anticipate what's to come.

"What makes you so special?" A voice suddenly bounces off the metal walls of the small room. I can't see him, but I recognize the odd tone. It belongs to the man that used his teeth to rip out Ira's throat. I hate it almost as much now as I did then. "What could be so special about you that the great and mighty Silas Laurent would go against everything he stands for?"

Now is not the time for a snarky or sarcastic remark, but I've always struggled with my lack of filter and that's why instead of staying quiet like I should, I'm saying, "I like to think it's my dazzling personality and quick wit."

Finally, Ira's killer steps closer to the table, the parts of his face that aren't hidden by a curtain of dark shoulder-length hair are illuminated by the red light. He doesn't look like he could be older than thirty, but that means nothing when you're a vampire. For all I know, he's been this age for a very long time. His clean-shaven face is pale, but the skin under his hooded eyes is dark with heavy circles. It's like he hasn't slept in a hundred years.

His dry, cracked lips pull in a sneer, exposing his slightly crooked teeth. So far, his fangs are tucked safely away, a small gift I'm thankful for. "I never thought I would see the day that Silas fell for a human." He then smiles to himself. "Don't get me wrong, I'm thankful he did because it gave me the leverage I've been waiting for." When he speaks, there isn't any emotion in his tone. It's robotic. For some reason, I find this scarier than if he were screaming in my face. Even when he smiled, it looked like a rehearsed act. Like doing it wasn't something that came naturally to him. "For a hundred years, I've waited for Silas to make a mistake. I knew it would happen eventually. All I had to do was be patient and my moment would come." Calculating eyes slide down my exposed body. "I would have waited another hundred years if it meant I got this glorious opportunity."

Nervously, I lick my bottom lip. "What opportunity? I have no idea what you're talking about or who you are or what it is Silas did to you."

I haven't been in Silas's world long enough to learn just how deep and dark his secrets run. He told me his past was full of blood and death. I believed him when he said it, I was just naive and believed I'd never have to face his past indiscretions myself. That I would be paying the price for his crimes.

His head shakes in slow, stiff movements as he trails a cold finger down my bare thigh and then down my shin. I've never minded Silas's cool body temperature. In all honesty, I've never given it much thought, but as my captor touches me, I'm reminded of the fact that he's truly not alive. At least not in the way I am. "That's the unfortunate part of all of this. You did nothing wrong." His voice is just barely a low whisper. "I'm afraid to inform you that your only crime was falling in love. It's a shame to be punished for something that's so natural and such a *human* thing to do, but alas, it will cost you everything. Just like it did her."

I try to jerk my leg away from his unwanted touch, but the chains keep me stuck in place and at his mercy. "Her? I don't know who you're talking about."

His head lifts from where he'd been staring at my body to look at the dark corner behind him. For the first time since he's entered the room, his eyes reflect emotion. The cold emptiness residing in them is replaced with longing.

"Margret." He sounds like he chokes on her name as he says it, like her name pains him. "Much like you, Quincey, she was punished for something that wasn't her fault. In our world, the innocent are always punished for the sins of the wicked."

He talks to me but still doesn't look at me. Something else has caught his attention. Searching the dark corner for what's holding his gaze captive, I find nothing there. It's empty, just like it's been since I woke up in here.

Finally, he blinks slowly as if he's clearing his vision before continuing trailing his finger down my leg. This time, he stops where the shackle ensnares my ankle.

"He took Margret from me and now I'll do the same to him," he vows. "He works in the shadows, taking and doing as he pleases. For a century, I too have been confined to the shadows. Nothing but a ghost. My name and my existence have been long forgotten, but I'm going to remind everyone who I am. And I'm going to remind them that their king isn't as untouchable as he wants us to believe."

I stare at my captor, waiting for the punch line of the joke to come, but it never does. Gaping in disbelief at the man, I question, "Surely you're not this stupid. You can't honestly think you can go against Silas and win." It's true I've only gotten glimpses of just how ruthless their king can be, but I know there is a reason that he's been able to maintain control all these years. He hasn't given his kingdom any other choice than to bow to him.

He doesn't respond. Instead, he pulls a key from the pocket of his dirty, ripped hoodie and undoes the shackles around both my feet. In a moment where I should be feeling relief, all I can feel is dread. He's not releasing me because he plans on letting me go. No doubt this man has a plan up his filthy sleeve. "Up until this point, Silas has had very few—if any—weaknesses I could exploit. I tried destroying his business and his empire, but honestly, it was futile. He has so much money and resources that any damage I caused could be effortlessly repaired. It was more of an annoyance to him than anything. I thought about taking the woman who works for him, but then you showed up and I saw how he saved you. I knew then that you were my answer—my perfect revenge."

I don't know if it makes me feel better that I now know the face and voice of the man who is responsible for me being chased and almost raped that day in the cemetery. The men who'd attacked me had said something about waiting for Della to come that day, but I'd been sent in her place.

The chains from my ankles fall to the ground with a loud ruckus. In stiff, measured movements, he backs away from the table and reaches for a lever on the wall. Before I can so much as take a breath or plead with him, there's a loud buzzing noise and the red lights flash.

The chains around my wrists pull tight and my heart begins to race.

By my wrists, my body is slowly lifted and moved off the cool surface of the table. I dig the soles of my bare feet into the smooth metal and try to stop myself, but it's no use. My shoulders and wrists ache as my body is hoisted into the air. Like I'm on some kind of track system, he drags me to the center of the room. My feet dangle a foot off the ground. My legs kick out into the empty air while I pull at the chains again, but just like earlier, the metal doesn't give. All I end up doing is hurting myself more.

The flashing lights stop, and the loud buzzing silences. Once again, the room is eerily quiet. Frantically, I look around for the man and my stomach drops when I see him setting up the tripod.

"What are you doing?" I demand, but whatever bravery that's remained in my voice up until this point is gone. My demand sounds more like a whimper—a plea.

"Silas made me watch as he killed Margret. I'm going to make him do the same. I'm going to make them *all* watch." He gives me another one of his cold smiles and presses the button on the side of the camcorder. A small, blinking red light joins the other red lights in the room. Stepping in front of the camera, he pushes the hair out of his face so that every angle is visible. Standing straight and with one last deep breath, he calmly declares, "My name is Gideon Rolfe and I have something that belongs to Silas Laurent."

CHAPTER 3

Silas

I never thought I could relate to the woman who sits on the bench outside of the hospital with her head in her lap. Sobs rack her body so violently, her entire frame shakes. I do not know who she is, but I understand her pain. While I don't have tears, I do have her desperation. In between her cries, she pleads with a man who kneels in front of her. I don't know what it is exactly she's begging for, but I know that just like me, she'd give anything to have it.

Quincey Page was supposed to be a means to an end. She was going to be another person I would use until they no longer had anything to offer me. She was never supposed to be more than that, but she is.

She is worth more than anything to me, and Gideon saw that. I knew my world was too dangerous for her, but I allowed myself to bring her close. I corrupted her light with my shadows and sins.

If I had the strength to take it all back, I would, but I can't do that. The second my lips touched hers, and I tasted her sweet blood, she was mine. The fragments of what's left of my black soul claimed her.

The only thing strong enough now to take her from me is death itself.

I turn away from the blatant and unashamed display of emotion when my cell phone buzzes in my pocket. Ducking my head, I shift back and move to the side of the building where there are fewer people to overhear any conversation I may have. I don't want to move too far away from the entrance of the hospital. He should be arriving soon, but then again, he's never been one to be punctual. Either way, I want to make sure I'm outside to greet him before we move inside and return to Duke's room.

Pulling my phone from my suit jacket, I check the caller ID, a small wistful piece of me hoping Quincey's name will be miraculously sitting there. Instead, the name that is lit up across the screen instantly causes a bitter taste to form in my mouth. On any given day, she is the last person I would like to converse with, but now, even the notion of hearing her voice is enough to make me almost crush the phone in my palm. Keeping my composure, I decline the call and return the now silent device to my pocket. The grinding of my molars is the only sign of my frustration.

Annoyed, exhausted, and restless, I step away from the building but stop when the scent hits me. It's a scent I've been held prisoner to for the better part of four centuries.

Blood.

Being that I'm currently at a hospital, an establishment that is constantly full of spilled blood, my first instinct is to write it off as an injury in the emergency room. But when I instinctually take a deep, greedy lungful of the intoxicating scent, I know without a doubt this blood is fresh and the source of it isn't inside the hospital.

My gums tingle, my sharp fangs threatening to descend as my throat burns with hunger. I should have asked Della to bring me some of the blood I have stored at the house, but at the time, my own discomfort was not of the utmost importance. It still isn't.

Turning my head, I narrow my eyes in the direction of the blood as it calls to me and my hunger. In a city like New Orleans, where the threats aren't just bloodthirsty monsters like me, but humans as well, injuries aren't uncommon. I should ignore it and wait here like I'd planned. What's happening on the busy streets is none of my concern tonight, but the voice in my head orders me to pay attention to what's happening.

The last time I'd ignored my gut, I'd ended up in the predicament I'm in now. I won't do it again.

With one last look behind me to check for any prying eyes, I take off through the dark alley. I move faster than any other being on the planet. My body is nothing but a fleeting blur moving through the shadows of the night.

Following the scent, I weave between narrow alleyways until I reach a poorly lit parking garage a few blocks behind the hospital. The scent is much stronger now and the sound of soft whimpers is no longer lost in the bustle of traffic and people milling about.

The whimpers aren't ones of pleasure or joy, they are ones of pain. Again, I know what's happening inside the structure is none of my business, but the knowledge that if Quincey were here with me now, she wouldn't hesitate to charge inside to investigate, and that keeps me from walking away.

It's been a long time since my motives haven't been purely selfish. Everything I've done, every move I've made, has benefited me in some way. Quincey is the opposite. Every choice she makes, she contemplates how it will benefit others. Her selflessness and bleeding heart are what drive her. Those things are what make her so wrong for me, but also what draws me to her.

Ultimately, that's why I stalk inside the building. For *her*, because this is what she'd ask of me if she were at my side. Where she is *supposed* to be.

Staying close to the concrete walls to ensure that I'm still concealed in the shadows, I follow the scent of blood and soft cries that belong to a woman.

A car door slams, before a gruff-sounding voice shouts, "I warned you! I told you this would happen if you kept asking questions. Your job is to show up on time, look pretty, and shut the fuck up!"

In movements too quiet for the humans to hear, I finally round the corner and the pair comes into view. What I see has my chest tightening to the point of pain as the anger I'm barely keeping at bay rushes forward.

The woman might be considered pretty if her face wasn't bruised and covered in blood. Her nose is broken, and her lip is split. Even though she holds a balled-up shirt to her face, blood still flows from the wounds. Her heavy makeup streaks down her face as she fights to keep her tears at bay, but the man caging her between the black sedan and concrete wall isn't helping her efforts.

While I observe, I'm vaguely aware of the buzzing coming from my phone again, but I'm too focused on the sight before me to bother answering it. The fact that I also have a fairly good idea of who is calling me makes me less inclined to stop what I'm doing and talk to her.

He waves a hand as he continues to yell, the movement makes the brunette woman jerk back and her eyes widen with fear. "The only time I want you to open that mouth of yours is if you're sucking dick," the balding man orders. "Do I make myself clear?"

She tearfully nods her head.

"Are you sure? I would hate to teach you another lesson." He reaches for her, his fingers locking down painfully on her bony shoulder. It's only now that my eyes lock on his knuckles. Just like her face, they're also bleeding and covered in abrasions.

My world tilts, and in that moment, the dark-haired woman's features melt away and they're replaced with Quincey's soft angelic ones. The balding man disappears and reappears as Gideon. It's a face I never thought I'd see again, but he looks exactly as he did a hundred years ago. Gideon grins as his fingers tighten on Quincey's shoulder until she cries out in pain. The rational part of my brain knows that she isn't in this parking garage with me, but in the same breath, I'm reminded of what Gideon could be doing to her as I'm here, unable to help her.

That thought is what finally breaks the chains on my monstrous side.

One second I'm standing in the shadows, a safe distance away from the pair, the next I'm behind the man with my hand wrapping around the back of his neck. I'm vaguely aware of the woman letting out a startled yelp, but I'm too focused on the prick in my grasp.

In one fluid motion, I lift him off the ground with one hand before I'm slamming his body into the hood of the black luxury sedan. Something he can only afford because of the women he mistreats. There is no doubt in my mind that there are more girls just like the one here tonight.

The metal of the car crunches as his body collides with it. The pained sound he makes appeases the monster within. It grins, sharp teeth bared, when the satisfying scent of his victim's blood mingles with the humid air.

With him still disoriented and in pain from the blow his body took, I yank his swaying body back into a standing position.

Turning my attention briefly to the woman, I instruct, "Go to the hospital and have someone look at your face." She stays locked in place, her swollen eyes staring at the injured man in my grasp. I need her to leave because I know what's coming next and I don't want an audience. "Why are you still standing here? Go now." The tone of my voice leaves no room for argument. When she hesitates again, I repeat with an impatient roar, "*Now!*"

With a scared squeaking noise, she finally grabs her discarded purse from the ground and flees. I don't watch as she leaves, but I wait until the sound of her cheap high heels clicking against the cement are just a distant noise. Not once does my grip loosen on the fucker's neck. His erratic pulse thuds against my fingertips as his pounding heart pushes blood through his veins.

He tries to move away from me, but it's no use. Like a bug caught in a spider web, all he can do is wait for his end. One that is coming sooner than he may suspect.

"Do you think you're powerful?" I coldly ask him, my voice eerily calm. "What about now? Do you still feel invincible?"

When he doesn't answer me in a timely manner like I wish he would, I whirl him around and shove him into the concrete wall of the garage. His brown eyes are wide and dazed as he finally faces me. Just like he'd done to the woman, his face is now bleeding. His nose, one that is already disproportionately large for his face, is now crooked and bleeding. His lips part as if he's attempting to form words, but it appears he may have lost the ability. Fear is useful like that. It makes my victims lose their faculties—makes them easier to hunt and kill.

I've always said I prefer to be respected, but when I can't get that, I'll gladly take their fear. Right now, I'm going to savor it.

"You didn't answer me," I sneer at him. The burning in my gums intensifies as my fangs finally descend. His eyes instantly lock on them, and his olive skin blanches to a ghostly hue. "Does it make you feel powerful to make women bleed? Do you get off on their tears and their cries?"

He shakes his head in small jerky movements. "I-I didn't—"

Before he has the chance to finish lying to me, I grab the collar of his shirt and yank him roughly toward me. "I don't much care for liars, and really, there isn't any reason for you to lie to me. Your fate has been sealed." I drag my eyes over him, analyzing him. "At this point, I'm being ill-mannered and simply playing with my food."

A whimpering sound comes from his throat as he chokes on his fear. "What are you?" he whispers.

I am death. I am the monster that people pray to their saviors to keep away. I am the reason children fear the dark. And I am just a man who's had his light stolen from him.

"I'm many things," I finally tell him. "But tonight, I'm simply your lesson. You have no idea what that girl means to someone. She could be their entire world—the reason they breathe—and you *harmed* her. Spilled her blood. It's a shame they aren't here to punish you themselves. I am more than willing to step up in their place though. I've been itching to get my hands a little dirty tonight."

Control. It's something that I pride myself on. How am I supposed to hold any authority over my subjects if I allow my carnal side to dictate my moves? I need to keep a clear mind and think thoroughly through each decision. Tonight, rationality and restraint have failed me. The second I discovered her missing, the chains on my control have been loosening.

And now, that side of me has been set free and the monster is rearing its ugly head.

"No one loves her," he chokes out. Not once do his eyes drift away from the sharp points of my fangs. "She's just a whore. Cheap pussy."

"Those are truly an unfortunate choice of last words."

My sinister smile is the last thing he sees before I'm yanking his head to the side and exposing his throat.

It's been a long time since I've killed while I've fed. For years, I've stuck to blood bags and designated feeders, like the women working at Rowena's, but tonight I'm craving the sensation of my prey's heartbeat slowing.

His fingernails claw at my suit jacket as he tries to fight me off, but I don't budge. He cries out, the sound echoing through the empty building and fueling the beast inside. There is a way to feed without making it painful, but he doesn't deserve to feel how euphoric this could be. He deserves to feel each agonizing second as I take everything from him.

With each greedy pull from his arteries, strength fills my deprived muscles and bones. Newfound energy rushes through my veins and my body comes alive with power. I'm not sure if I forced myself to forget how intoxicating the rush is that comes from hunting and killing my prey, but as I ingest every drop his body has to offer, I'm quickly reminded of the delightful sensation. While I drink from him, my mind fills with illicit thoughts of my next kill and that's when I also remember just how addictive it is.

Eventually, he stops fighting me and goes slack in my arms. I don't stop feasting when his arms fall limply at his sides or his knees give out. I easily keep him held up and at the height I need him at.

It's only a matter of minutes before his veins are dry and his heart matches mine. Still and forever silent. With my hunger sated but my anger still burning inside of me, I drop the body. It lands on the oil-stained ground in a crumpled heap.

My eyes are locked on the single drop of blood that trails slowly out of one of the puncture wounds on his neck. The crimson trail calls to me, despite the large amount I'd just consumed. My jaw clenches, my fangs still burning with an uncontrollable hunger.

The hard part isn't losing control, it's finding the strength to regain it.

Regret for what I've just done begins to shine through as the bloodthirsty haze begins to disperse. It's not regret for the fact I've just taken a life. No, this man's life meant nothing to me, and my city is better off without him. It's regret for the mess that I've just made. Typically, I would not have thought twice about the carnage, but that was solely due to the fact I knew I could trust Duke to clean it up. Something I'm realizing I've taken for granted.

I'm slowly coming to terms with the fact I've taken a lot of things for granted. I foolishly believed that the power I wielded would keep the things that mattered to me safe, that my years establishing my ruthless reign would keep my enemies at bay. It appears I was wrong, and I've grown too soft. Somehow too lenient. Once I'm able to think past the aching void in my chest, things will be changing. If they thought I was merciless before, they will learn it was child's play.

Slow clapping from somewhere behind me finally forces my attention away from the body and my thoughts. My spine goes rigid as each of my senses goes on high alert. It's not till the familiar scent of tobacco and whiskey washes over me do I relax. No matter how many years go by, it's always the same.

Taking a step away from the corpse, I use the back of my hand to wipe away the blood lingering on my mouth. "You're late," I tell him while casually straightening my black suit jacket.

He makes a scoffing noise. "On the contrary, I do believe I'm just on time. Had I been here earlier, I would have missed the show. A truly marvelous show at that." I don't have to look at him to know there's a grin on his smug face. "And that would have been quite the shame. You know how I find you so much more tolerable when you let loose a little bit. Had I known this was all it took for you to relax and have some fun, I would have taken the girl myself."

The girl.

Quincey.

The low, ominous growl is his only warning before I'm spinning on my heels and rushing toward him in a blur. Even though he's a vampire himself, he isn't granted enough time to dart out of my reach. My hand wraps around his throat as I slam his back into the wall with such force the concrete splinters and chunks of it fall to the ground.

In a fashion true only to him, a slow, lazy grin grows on his face as I snarl and bare my fangs.

"I would be very, *very* careful how you talk about her to me." My warning is low, my voice threateningly calm. "I'm hanging on by a fucking thread and I do not possess the patience or desire to entertain your games right now, Lorcan."

My warning is completely ignored, and his smile only widens. "That was more of a test to see just how much this girl means to you," The Irishman's sable eyes shine with humor as he observes me. "You didn't offer much information when you called, but I figured she meant a great deal since you were desperate enough to call *me* in." He pauses, like he's expecting me to divulge more into this conversation, but when I remain silent, he says, "It's been a long time, Silas."

With one last threatening squeeze to his tattooed jugular, I release him and back up a foot to give him his space. It has been a long time, but even after all these years, I haven't lost tabs on the elusive vampire before me. Like me, he may operate in the shadows, but I rule them. Everything that happens in my domain, I'm aware of. Or I thought I was until Gideon slipped through the cracks.

I grit my teeth as I fight against my instinct to keep my secrets close to the vest. Willingly admitting information about my private life coming unnaturally to me. "Quincey means more to me than you'll ever be capable of understanding." She means more to me than I thought was ever possible. I crave her more than I've ever craved blood.

He eyes me expectantly like he's waiting for the punch line of a terrible joke, but when it doesn't come, he simply states, "*Interesting*."

"Like I said, I don't have time for games. I need an answer. Are you going to help me, or do I need to find someone else?"

Stepping away from the wall, he calmly dusts the shoulders of his leather jacket. He takes a beat before answering, like he's considering his options. "I'll help," he finally agrees. "But it's double my usual rate *plus* an inconvenience fee since you called me while my cock was down someone's throat. *Nothing* kills a hard-on faster than seeing your name come across my phone."

I stare at him blankly, unamused by his latter comments. "Might I suggest not looking at your phone when you're otherwise *occupied*? It's in poor taste."

He shrugs his shoulder nonchalantly. "I like to multitask."

Pushing back the annoyance, I tell him, "I'll pay you whatever you want on one stipulation." This was a conversation I was going to put off having, but now might be my only chance to discuss my bargain without the worry of eavesdropping ears. "I need you to promise me something and no matter what's to come, you must keep your word, Lor."

I don't know if it's the shift in my tone or the heaviness that's suddenly in the air, but the amused gleam in his eyes vanishes. "I'm listening."

CHAPTER 4

Silas

Della doesn't look up at us when we enter Duke's hospital room. Her eyes, full of unshed tears, stay locked on the injured man, her bottom lip quivering as she fights to stay composed. The only time I've witnessed Della cry is the day Ira disclosed that his cancer was terminal. Even then, after a moment, she composed herself and she was back to her usual self.

The events of tonight have finally broken the steel mask she wears.

For her, I wish someone was here that could tell her everything would be okay. I know if Quincey were, she'd know what to tell the distressed woman. Quincey is the person anyone would want at their side during something like this. Her kind heart and warm energy can bring peace to even the most distraught souls.

I've experienced it myself.

Lorcan stops behind me, leaning his shoulder against the nearby wall while his eyes flick between the comatose man in the hospital bed and the crying woman. It's not like him to be quiet, but he hasn't spoken much since he agreed to keep his promise to me in the parking garage. I never doubted he would.

As he watches, he still doesn't say anything, but I know that his mind is full of chaotic thoughts. There are many things I can't relate to when it comes to Lorcan Reid, but his never silent mind is something I can sympathize with. Continuously being five steps ahead of everyone requires a great deal of planning and thinking. It's been many years since I've known peaceful slumber.

"Della, is she here yet?" I inquire quietly, finally drawing her attention away from Duke.

She hesitates to answer, the heavily tattooed vampire behind me catching her off guard. "No, not yet—or at least not that I'm aware of."

"If she were here, you would know." If it weren't just for her vibrant hair colors, her personality would alert you to her presence.

"Who is this girl again?" Lorcan asks at the same time my phone starts buzzing again in my pocket. My hands ball into fists at my sides as I let the phone call go unanswered. "And why are we waiting for her?"

"Just like you, Rory is the best in her field."

She's truly a savant. I'm lucky to have her on my payroll and not on an enemy's. Who knows what kind of damage she could have helped them inflict on me.

Della crosses her arms and turns her body to size up the vampire that is easily a foot and a half taller than her. Her features pinch as a scrupulous look crosses her face. "I don't know you," she tells him. "What exactly could you—*a stranger*—have to offer that Silas would need you?"

Lor's head cocks to the side, the corner of his lip tipping up in possible amusement. "I would hardly call myself a stranger. If I had to make a guess, I would say I've known Silas longer than your crotchety arse has graced this green earth." Lorcan has a unique ability of concealing his ferocity in a veil of humor. People tend to focus on the humorous pitch in his tone and are completely oblivious to the underlying threat. A critical mistake many have fallen victim to. "As for what I have to offer—that depends solely on who's asking and what day of the week it is," he offers as vaguely as possible.

"I'm asking and it's a Friday," Della responds without so much as a second of hesitation. "If you haven't noticed, things are falling apart around here. People have *died*." She chokes on the last word, like her body refuses to speak it aloud. "We can't lose anyone else. I need to know that you're here to help and not to cause more problems. We're already drowning in them, there is no need for you to come in and add."

Most people would be put off by Della's abrasive attitude, but not Lorcan. There's nothing he likes more than a good fight, verbal or physical; he lives for the conflict. Another thing that makes him good at his job.

I know he'd love nothing more than to bicker back and forth with my housekeeper, but we don't have time nor the energy for this now. Releasing an exasperated sigh, I shake my head at the pair. "That's enough. Della, Lorcan is here because while Duke is incapacitated, I need someone I can rely on to step in and assist in some of the tasks Duke would have otherwise handled. And his additional skill set will make him invaluable when retrieving Quincey."

Della's wrinkled lips purse as she considers this. Her head tilts back so she can make eye contact with me as she points out, "You said *rely* on. Not trust. Do you not trust this man?"

Lor chuckles, a wide smile breaking across his face. "Don't you know the golden rule? You should never trust a vampire."

Truer words have never been spoken. It doesn't matter how old they are, or how in control they may appear. Beneath the perfected surface is a bloodthirsty monster who is always hungry and lustfully thinking about their next kill.

Della jerks back and her eyes dart to the hospital room door to assure no one is lurking about that may have overheard Lorcan. The word vampire is something that is used very sparingly in my household.

Those who are privy to my secret rarely use the term. It's something we all know to be true, but seldomly speak of it. I can see how Lorcan's blatant use of it would catch Della off guard.

"We are in public," Della scolds him like a petulant child. "Mind your mouth."

What she doesn't understand is Lorcan has never seen any shame in being what he is. He would shout it from the rooftops and tell every person he meets in a crowded bar if he knew he could get away with it.

Lorcan's eyes drift to where I stand. "Does your entire staff act like this?"

"No," I grit out just as there's a raised voice coming from outside the hospital room. As if we'd rehearsed it like choreography, all three of our heads snap in the direction of the open door at the same time, each of us on high alert.

When the irate voice cuts through the silent intensive care unit, I relax.

"I don't know who the fuck you think you are, but if you don't let me go, I'm going to claw your eyes out of your big, dumb heads!" Rory threatens.

Lorcan's brow raises. "Are you sure about that?"

Two men wearing matching black suits come into view. I recognize them immediately as some of my hired security. Off the top of my head, I couldn't tell you what their names are. I know they've worked closely with Duke, and for the time being, I can trust them enough with smaller tasks. Such as collecting someone for me.

Their faces are completely impassive despite the thrashing woman they carry between them. They hold her just far enough off the ground that her feet can't touch, meaning her legs kick all about as she tries to get free of the grip they have on her arms. Her lilac hair is wild, covering her face and eyes.

One of the men addresses me. "She wasn't at her apartment like we'd originally thought. It took us a minute to find her location and well, when we did find her, she didn't make it easy—"

Scoffing under her breath, she cuts him off, "You dense motherfucker. *Of course*, I wasn't going to make it *easy* for you. You showed up and ordered me into some random car. I'm sorry for not wanting to be one of those poor girls on *Dateline*."

She still thrashes in their arms, not yet staying still long enough to discover I'm in the room. I'm subtly aware of the amused look on Lor's face and the completely unimpressed one Della wears as they watch on.

The guard remains stern, despite the girl's outburst. "As I was saying, I'm sorry for our tardiness, sir."

"*Sir?*" she repeats as she shakes the purple hair out of her face and finally looks at me. In an instant, all the fight leaves her body, and she relaxes in their hold. Her hazel eyes widen in alarm and her face blanches just a fraction. "*Mr. Laurent.*"

"Rory," I greet. Aurora 'Rory' Amos is barely old enough to order a drink legally, but she's smarter and more talented than most of the people I've met on my time on earth. You would never assume that the young girl standing before us, dressed in the shortest black leather skirt I've ever seen and revealing cropped shirt, is the same girl who was capable of hacking into my state-of-the-art tech company. She's a prime example of why we can't judge solely on appearances. You never know what someone is capable of when no one is looking. "I do wish I could tell you that I'm sorry for pulling you away from your weekend plans, but something has happened that I need your assistance with—"

"Emphasis on *weekend*," she tersely interjects. "I am an *employee* of yours. Nine to five. Monday through Friday. *Those* are the hours I work for you. My time outside of those hours needs to be respected. You have no right to order me around when I'm not on the clock."

She couldn't be more wrong.

My face hardens, my head cocking to the side at the courageous human. "There appears to be a misunderstanding between us. When you hacked into my servers and put my billion-dollar corporation at risk, I had a choice. I could either hire you and put your skills to use or I could eliminate you completely. Ultimately, I decided that a talent like yours is valuable and it would be such a waste to not use it to my benefit. That being said, I'm not opposed to the other option. Especially if you become more trouble than you're worth." I take a slow step forward and instantly she attempts to shrink back, but the hold the guards have on her keeps her in place. "As an employee of mine, you work when I need you. Day or night. Weekends or not, you are at my mercy. Your time belongs to me. Do I make myself clear, Rory?"

The room falls eerily silent, everyone holding their breath as they wait for her answer.

The internal battle she's having with herself is clearly written across her face. She doesn't want to back down, but just like everyone else, the threat against her life keeps her in line. "Crystal clear," Rory bites out between clenched teeth.

The room takes a collective breath, and the tension dissipates.

At my subtle nod, the guards drop the hacker to her knee-high boot–clad feet and take a step back.

Rory glares when she finds Lorcan staring at her exposed, tattooed skin. Much like himself, Rory is covered in various black and gray tattoos. Hers are done in a style I can only describe as Gothic, many of the images are dark in nature. "Who the hell are you and what are you staring at?" she questions, sounding completely unimpressed with the blond vampire.

Lorcan's lips pull in an amused smirk while his eyes flicker with interest. "I like you." His light-brown eyes swing in my direction. "I like her."

"No," I warn with a tight, terse shake of my head.

Straightening her rumpled clothes—or lack of clothes—Rory's inquisitive gaze darts between the people in the room. "So, what am I doing at a hospital? I know I've done some questionable things in the past but hacking into a hospital's system is low even for me…" For the first time since she's entered the room, she finally looks behind the three of us. I know the second she recognizes who currently lies unconscious in the bed. Her face falls, lips parting in a silent gasp, and she staggers back on her heels. "Duke?" she utters softly, her focus locked on the man. Blinking slowly, like she's in a daze, she slips between Della and me to stand at the base of the bed. "What happened?" she asks, her voice sounding stronger. "What the *hell* happened? I talked to him on the phone before I left the office for the night, and he was *fine*." Her hands, various rings on each finger, wrap around the footboard of the hospital bed.

As calmly as I can muster, I find the ability to explain to her what's happened without my wrathful venom seeping into my words. "After the phone call where we discussed your findings on Gideon Rolfe, our vehicle was hit with an explosive. Duke was driving. We believe—*no*—we *know*, it was set by the same person who is responsible for the various attacks on my businesses and the assault against Quincey." At the time, the fear I felt when I couldn't get to her was all-consuming, suffocating even, but it pales in comparison to what I feel now. "They ambushed my estate. People who have worked for me for a very long time were murdered." Beside me, Della sucks in a ragged breath as she fights back her sobs. Once again, she presses the tissue she's kept balled in her hand to her mouth to muffle the sound.

Rory looks to the upset woman. Her tough exterior fractures and sympathy seeps through the cracks. She puts on a good front, but she's more sensitive than she'd like people to know. "So, you need my help finding whoever did this to Duke? Those files I found earlier were from many years ago, I don't know if I'm going to find anything else in them that can help you. And as I told you, that Gideon dude is well over a hundred years old. He's dead." When no one confirms her statement, she repeats it, this time with her confusion clear in her voice. "He's dead, right?"

"He sure as hell is going to wish he was," Lor mumbles under his breath, because on top of lacking impulse control, he's also missing a filter.

Rory's head snaps in his direction. *"What* did he just say?"

Having a conversation such as this in the middle of an intensive care unit is unwise. I never wanted to introduce Rory to the darker parts of my world. She was merely to deal with my human-based dealings, but unfortunately, I don't see a way around it. Not when Quincey's life is depending on us. I will tell her everything when the time is right, but now isn't it, so I steer the conversation back to Rory's earlier question. "Yes, Rory, I need your help finding the person behind all of this because of what's happened to Duke." I feel my monster surge forward as I prepare to tell her, "But more importantly, I need him found because he's taken Quincey from me."

"Shit," she curses, her fingers digging into her lilac hair, an overwhelmed look on her face.

"The computer equipment from your office is being brought to a different location as we speak. I have video surveillance I need you to look through." The camera feeds from my home are kept heavily encrypted, and usually Duke is the only one who has access to them, but tonight, Rory will be the exception.

Rory's head nods, but her unfocused eyes make me think she's not truly hearing me. She proves me wrong when she offers, "Maybe we'll get lucky and see a license plate or something."

I look to the guards that have been waiting silently by the door. "Bring the car around. We're leaving." When they both turn to leave, I remember something important. "There's a body in a parking garage three blocks north of here. One of you needs to take care of it."

"But don't worry." Lorcan claps one of the guards on the back with his tattooed hand. "There's hardly any blood, so it's an easy-peasy cleanup for you." With that, he saunters out of the room with the usual cocky swagger that makes me want to remove his head from his shoulders.

"What the *actual* fuck?" Rory whispers under her breath, completely dumbfounded by the situation she's found herself in.

Not acknowledging her comment, I take her upper arm and I pull her away from Duke's bed. Her feet firmly plant on the linoleum floor, refusing to move from his bedside. Not looking at me, she asks, "He's going to be okay, right?"

"He won't be alone here as Della and a guard will be staying at his side. I have no intention of leaving him vulnerable." I've lost enough tonight. Until the threat of Gideon is taken care of, everyone will be on high alert.

When Rory's face drops and she reluctantly follows me out of the room, I realize she wasn't referring to Duke's safety here at the hospital.

CHAPTER 5

Silas

Over the years, I've purchased various safe houses across the state. They were precautionary investments on the off chance I became stuck in a city or town working on business and couldn't make it back to my home before sunrise. Each one has been fitted with sunlight-proof windows, allowing beings like myself and Lorcan to roam throughout the day. Before such inventions, we would have been confined to a basement cellar until sundown. The luxury residences are much more ideal.

Normally, I would have returned to my estate, but the idea of returning to that property without Quincey is an unsettling thought. She's left her mark all over the previously dark home. In the grand scheme of things, the changes are small and insignificant. They're just little adjustments here and there that let her presence be known. Like the lamps that have been kept off for so many years have been turned on, illuminating the shadowy hallways and rooms. I know if I went there tonight, those lights would be dark once more.

I had found peace with the darkness. It welcomed me with cold, open arms, and it's been my home for centuries. It wasn't until she came into my life that I remembered how much I long for the light.

I'm also not prepared to enter a home that still has the scent of Ira's spilled blood lingering in the air. I'm afraid the combination of her absence and the evidence of his death will be too much. My control has already slipped once tonight and it's still hanging on by a single thread.

Rory has sat silently, spinning the silver rings on her thin fingers the entire ride. She's trying her best to not look at me or the blond vampire that sits behind her in the rear seat. Lorcan had the option of sitting in the front seat but opted to sit directly behind the human. I wasn't sure of his reasoning at first, but it dawned on me halfway through the ride. Lorcan finds humor in making people uncomfortable. He's simply entertaining himself by making her squirm.

Even if she hasn't turned her head to look at him, it's evident she's aware of his heavy stare on the back of her head. Her spine is rigid, and her heartbeat is erratic.

Not wanting to allow him to add to her increasing emotional distress, I scowl at Lor, shaking my head in a silent warning. His response is to shrug his shoulders nonchalantly and slouch lower in his seat. I would be more irritated with his attitude if he didn't direct his attention to the window next to him.

The sound of my phone dinging in my pocket has me turning around. I pull the device out, expecting to find another unwanted phone call, but instead it's a text message confirming the mess I'd made in the parking garage has been taken care of. I don't require or ask for further detail. As long as the evidence is gone, I don't care how it was cleaned up.

"Is that the hospital?" Rory speaks up. "Is Duke okay?"

My head cocks to the side as I evaluate the girl. She meets my gaze but chews anxiously on her bottom lip. The dark purple lipstick she'd once had on is faded and splotchy. The heavy eye makeup has transferred to the skin under her eyes. She looks like a little girl who's gotten into her mother's makeup, and I'm reminded of just how young she is. "Interesting," I observe. "I wasn't under the impression you cared what happened to Duke."

"I don't," she snaps instantly, sitting back in her seat with her arms folded. "I was just curious."

"You two have shared more hateful words than nice ones in the time you've known each other," I continue, regardless of her dismissive remark.

She lifts a shoulder. "Yeah, he likes to annoy me. Press my buttons."

Clearly incapable of keeping his mouth shut, Lorcan leans forward, his arms resting on the back of each of our leather seats. "Yes, baby, I do believe they refer to that as foreplay and from what I hear, it's very important."

Rory glowers at him, "I don't like you."

He smirks at her, a devious look in his eyes. "Give it time, I grow on people."

"Yeah, like mold grows on bread." She reaches her hand out and presses it to the middle of his face, shoving him back into his seat. "Get away from me, you giant tattooed leprechaun."

Lor's head falls back as he laughs at her. "Are we giving each other nicknames already? Keep this shit up and I might just fall in love with you."

"Please don't," Rory grumbles, a grimace on her face.

Before I can open the door of the moving car and escape this madness, the black SUV turns onto the lamppost-lined street. This safe house is in the middle of a residential neighborhood, many of the houses are full of young couples starting their families. The street is often covered in various chalk drawings and children's toys lie in the neatly trimmed yards. This is the last place someone would expect to find me and that's precisely the reason I purchased this particular house.

The house is opposite of my usual taste in real estate, further perfecting the disguise. White brick with black trim, and the front door is painted a god-awful, cheery yellow color. Duke laughed for days when he first saw the house, stating how ironic the whole thing was.

I don't bother to wait for the driver to open my door when the car stops, instead I get out and close the door in Lorcan's face before he has an opportunity to climb out behind me. Through the glass window, I hear him grumble, "So fucking rude."

"Her equipment is already inside," the guard explains, while gesturing to Rory. "We tried to set it up exactly as it was at the office, but I'm not sure we did it right."

"I can assure you, even without looking, you didn't." Rory offers him a tight, fake smile. "Lead the way, no point dillydallying out here."

Lor nods. "Yes, best we get inside. Don't want to get caught out here with our arses hanging in the wind when the sun rises."

It's clear she's confused and wants to ask questions, but the hacker remains quiet and follows the guard toward the house.

Following behind everyone, I make it up the first three steps on the front porch when the sound of a car door slamming is quickly followed by a voice calling my name. "Silas!"

Instantly, every one of my muscles tighten and the anger in my chest intensifies. She shouldn't be here. Correction, she shouldn't be within a twenty-mile radius of me right now. I can't deal with her right now. I thought ignoring her phone calls would get the message across, but no, she's somehow found a way to track me down here.

"Who's the redhead?" I'm vaguely aware of Lorcan asking, but it sounds like he's a mile away with the thundering in my ears.

"Silas, I tried calling—" she begins to say again, but before she can finish her statement, I'm standing in front of her, our chests just a mere inch apart. She jerks back a step, but I instantly fill the space she'd just created. "Silas—"

On the porch, Rory asks frantic questions, her voice going up multiple octaves. I'm not sure what Lorcan tells her, and right now, I'm not sure I care. All my concern for keeping my vampire side concealed has vanished. Rory argues with Lorcan and the guard, but after a moment, they finally manage to get her inside the house.

"Rowena." My voice is an angry snarl. "You have an uncanny ability to show up where you are least wanted. Please do tell me what I've done to give you the impression I desire your company so I may rectify that oversight."

Completely unfazed by my comment, Rowena's painted lips lift in a coy grin. "On the contrary, I believe I'm exactly where I'm supposed to be. If you'd only let me speak, I could explain—"

"No," I cut her off. "I don't want to hear what you have to say, Rowena. I thought by ignoring your phone calls that would be evident to you, but it appears you're more ignorant than I originally thought."

"Silas," Rowena scolds. "I think you really should listen to what I have to say."

"Why would I do that? I didn't care what you had to say when I tolerated your company long enough to fuck you. I couldn't spare a single fuck to give you now." I pause, a thought dawning on me. "How did you know I was going to be here?"

No one should know about this location. Ira was privy to a lot of my secrets, but even he didn't know about my other properties.

Her eyes roll. "You're not conceited enough to think you're the only one with spies stationed around the city, are you? They're the reason I know about this quaint little house of yours and they're the reason I know things even you don't know, Silas."

Shaking my head, a hateful smile on my face, I take a step back. "I find that incredibly unlikely, Rowena."

"You're always so sure of yourself," she drawls slowly in an appeasing manner before she asks a question that has my world stuttering to a halt. "Do you know what's happening to that human *pet* of yours?"

I feel as if I've been sucker punched in the gut as the blood in my veins runs cold. "Rowena." My tone is eerily calm and controlled, a startling contrast to how I feel inside. "If you had anything to do with this—"

"Don't be ridiculous, Silas," Rowena interjects. "Much like you, I prefer to work in secret. I'd never do something so...*publicly*. If I'm being honest, I find the whole thing over the top and *tacky*. And it's all over some simple human girl as well." Her tongue clicks in disapproval. "Why would I waste my time for something so inconsequential?"

Lorcan, who has appeared at my side, threatens, "If you don't stop talking in circles, I'm going to make it so you never fucking speak again, *red*."

Rowena eyes the Irishman up and down like he's the most interesting thing to come into town in decades. "No need to be crass," she chastises after a beat, her painted red lips pursing. With one last lingering look in his direction, she turns back to me while her manicured hand digs into the pocket of her black trench coat. "Maybe next time you'll think twice about ignoring my phone call." Tapping a few keys on the device, she unlocks it before tossing it to me. "Maybe consider checking your email as well. I can only assume you were sent the same link as the rest of us."

"Link?" Lorcan repeats at the same time. I turn the phone in my hand and glance at the screen.

Rowena's head bobs. "Yes, a private web browser link. I almost didn't click on it, thinking it was just spam, but the subject line caught my attention."

I've witnessed war, I've experienced famine, and I've lived through plagues. I've seen the worst in humanity, and I've done things that most would find appalling, but now, as I stare at the screen, none of those events have prepared me for what I feel now.

Foolishly, I believed that not knowing where she was or what was happening to her was going to be the worst of it. I thought that once I knew, I'd be able to focus on my next moves and with a clearer head, I'd be able to make plans. But I was wrong.

One of the many things I pride myself in is my ability to be multiple steps ahead of everyone, but with Gideon, I've fallen behind and I'm completely blind to his moves.

Though, even if I had been ahead of him, I don't think I ever could have predicted this.

Quincey, my heart, is suspended from the ceiling of a room illuminated in red light. Metal cuffs sit tightly around her wrists and blood drips down her forearms. True to her character and despite her situation, she hasn't given up. She fights and pulls at the chains, further explaining the wounds. Her toned, bare legs kick out into the air, desperate for some kind of perch, but it's no use. My stomach drops and my silent heart constricts at the sight of her almost bare body. The possibilities of why he's removed her clothing running wild in my mind.

"Is this live?" Lorcan, who watches over my shoulder, asks the woman I'm considering tearing to pieces in the middle of this picturesque residential street. Over the years, I've grown tired of Rowena's meddling and bothersome presence. Her showing up here may be the nail in her metaphorical coffin.

"From what I can tell, this video is a livestream of what's happening," Rowena explains as she reaches for the phone. Her fingers, fingernails painted the same color she wears on her lips, pinch the device and attempt to pull it away from me. Unable to look away from where Quincey dangles helplessly from the ceiling, I refuse to let go. Rowena releases an annoyed huff. "I'm trying to show you another video. It was the one in the email. The link to the live stream was under it."

Begrudgingly, I let go and let her take the phone back. My fingers twitch at my side as I wait impatiently for her to find the other video. "Who else was this email sent to?" I question. "Who else can see her like this?"

Clicking something on the screen, Rowena passes the phone back to me. "From what I've heard through the rumor mill, most of the high society were sent links. Vampires with any semblance of power or status. Which means many, if not all of them, are currently members of the council."

The council.

Council is a loose term for what it truthfully is. Over two hundred years ago, I had a group of vampires attempt to take control from me, stating they didn't agree with my methods. In a false attempt to appear more civil and accommodating, I established a council of sorts where vampires could air their grievances or give their opinions on various subjects. They falsely believe that I take their viewpoints into consideration when making my decisions, but if they feel like they've been heard, they remain civil. Due to this, there haven't been any more attempted uprisings, and that's all that matters. I will entertain their fictional power as long as it continues to keep some sense of order.

I don't respond to her, instead I press play on the video she's loaded on to the phone. Just like the livestream, Quincey hangs from the ceiling. Her powder blue eyes are round with fear as she watches something or someone across the room. The camera shifts and adjusts a bit before Gideon himself walks into the frame.

Long gone is the stately man I knew. The exquisite clothing and borderline obsessive behavior regarding his appearance are no more. His clothing is ragged and stained. His hair is longer than I've ever seen it, but it's not his clothing or change in hair that is most noticeable. It's the loss of all emotion in his previously expressive eyes and face. The man I once knew and trusted with my life is no more. Replaced with a shell of a person.

He turns and says something to Quincey, something I can't quite make out before he faces the camera. In a calm, even voice, he declares, "My name is Gideon Rolfe, and I have something that belongs to Silas Laurent." For just a moment, Quincey goes still and hangs limply as she waits for what else he's going to say. Looking directly into the camera, as if he's speaking to me directly, Gideon continues, "You've made yourself the self-appointed king. You take and kill as you please, regardless of whom it might cause pain. I've waited a very long time to even the score, to get my justice for what you did to my Margret." He pauses, looking at the woman who hangs behind him. "My patience prevailed and I'm now able to return the favor. You murdered the love of my life in front of me and now I will do the same."

I'm aware of the redheaded vampire standing in front of me, glaring holes into my skull. My affection toward Quincey was something I never wanted to air publicly, as I didn't believe it would be safe for her. Rowena is already aware of Quincey's existence due to her *coincidentally* walking down the same street we were on. My behavior was suspicious at best, and no doubt alerted Rowena to my interest in the human. But Gideon declaring she's the love of my life leaves no unanswered questions or debates to be had.

I will never confirm those feelings aloud to Rowena, or anyone for that matter. That admission is reserved solely for Quincey. She is the only one besides myself that owns my secrets. She is the only one who I would reveal everything to with one simple "*please*". Things I've never disclosed to Duke or Ira, I would trust in the hands of Quincey.

"I'm not the only one you've angered, Silas. In all my years in hiding, I've heard the whispers. Your entire kingdom doesn't worship you like you believe them to." Not once when Gideon talks does his face display what he's feeling, nor does his tone fluctuate with emotion like it should. It stays completely flat. Monotone.

Gideon is wrong in his belief that I want to be worshiped. I don't wish to be prayed to or adored by the many. I've never wanted that. My only wish is to walk into a room and immediately hold everyone's attention. I want them to know with a single look in my direction and without me having to speak a single word that I am in charge. By doing that, that's how I maintain order. Had I not intervened and controlled the vampires, history would be a lot darker and a lot bloodier.

Gideon moves closer to Quincey. Once he's close enough, he reaches out to trail his gnarled fingers down her sternum. With an angry snarl, Quincey kicks in his direction. Her foot collides with Gideon's gut. Her success is meaningless in the end. A blow such as that does little to wound a vampire.

Gideon's hand wraps around her ankle to stop any more attacks. "Unfortunately," he begins, his focus on the finger he's begun to trail up her exposed calf. There isn't a single outcome where Gideon makes it out of this with his life but watching him touch her—*touching what is mine*—confirms that his demise will not be easy. "I can't grant everyone the same level of revenge as I will be receiving, but do not fret. I've found a way to make it fair. Shortly, you will be receiving an additional message from me. Inside will be a link to a private online auction."

"He's a twisted little fuck, isn't he?" Lorcan mutters to himself.

"I think it's only fair that I share my newfound prize with the rest of you." Gideon drops Quincey's leg and takes a step back from her. "Have you ever wondered what the blood of Silas's woman tastes like?" He reaches into the back pocket of his dirty jeans. At the flash of metal reflecting off the red lights of the small room they're in, my fingers tighten on the device, causing a crack to form across the glass screen. "Highest bidders will get to find out just how sweet she is." He twists the knife in his fingers a few times before lifting it to Quincey's hip bone.

I want to look away, but I'm frozen in place as I watch him press the end into her perfect flesh. Any other time, I would have been proud of the way Quincey is able to keep her reaction subdued. The only sign she's been injured is by the way she presses her lips into a flat line and her eyes briefly squeeze closed.

Meanwhile, I feel like I'm going to start slaughtering people at will.

Blood pools from the small wound, slowly dripping toward the waistline of her lace panties. As if he's making eye contact with me before he does it, Gideon looks back at the camera before pulling her panties down an inch and swiping the stream of blood up with his tongue.

A menacing snarl escapes my lips as my entire body begins to shake with rage. Lorcan places his hand on my shoulder, a gesture I assume is supposed to show his support, but only angers me further. Shaking his hand off me, I take a step away so I can focus on the video.

For the first time since he's stepped on screen, Gideon grins at the camera once he's licked all the blood from her body. "Delicious. How does it feel that while I savor every second of my short time with her, you'll be helpless to just watch? Or that you'll have to watch as I auction away her precious blood until there isn't any left?" The forced grin widens. "I will make you watch as she cries out in pain and begs for you to save her."

"Silas!" Her voice cuts through my very core. It feels like a lifetime since I've last heard her speak my name. It seems so foolish now that I refused to allow her to call me by my first name when I first brought her home. My name on her lips is my lullaby, soothing the rough edges of my bitter soul. "Don't watch." Quincey's voice cracks, despite her attempt to be strong. "I don't want you to see this. *Please* don't watch."

This is a prime example of why it wouldn't matter how many times I try to atone for my sins or beg for forgiveness for my transgressions, I will never be worthy of her tender heart or her love. In a moment where her concern should be on herself and her life, she's worried about me. Me. The sole reason her life is even in danger.

"He'll watch," Gideon declares arrogantly, as he shuffles toward the camera. Getting close to the screen, he speaks directly to me. "He won't be able to stop himself."

And like that, the video ends and I'm stuck staring at a black screen with a white icon to start the whole thing over again. There's no need for me to view it a second time, every second has been burned into my memory. I take a moment to compose myself before speaking. "When was this filmed?"

When she doesn't answer fast enough, I look up to find her scrutinizing me. A look of displeasure is written across her usually poised face. Slowly, she shakes her head. "It's probably for the best you didn't answer your phone. If you had, I would have missed out on seeing your reaction in person. I thought hearing your reaction would be enough, but I was wrong. I needed to *see* that miserable look on your face. It confirmed *everything* I needed to know. Truthfully, I'm a tad disappointed as I was still holding out hope that I was wrong, but it appears I was right all along." Her dark green eyes come alive with spite. "A human, Silas? Really? You're reacting this way over a worthless *human*? Do you understand how weak this makes you look?"

My step in her direction is halted when Lorcan is suddenly behind her. In a flash, he's wrapped her long red braid around his hand. He roughly yanks her head back until her entire jugular is exposed, a shiny serrated knife lies across her porcelain skin. "If he doesn't pry your head from your neck now, I might just take it myself. I've been itching for a new trophy to display. Your head might just be the thing to complete my mantel. You're pretty enough, I suppose. With any luck, I won't grow tired of staring at it like I have the others."

I want her head, but I have no desire to keep it displayed. I don't want a single piece of Rowena in my home—alive or dead. I'd rather drive to the swamps and let the gators feast on her.

Rowena's painted lips pull back in a hiss, white fangs exposed. "Get the fuck off me. Do you know who I am?"

"A dumb cunt who really doesn't know her place in this world," Lor offers without a second of hesitation. This is the first time he's met the female vampire, but his deduction of her is immaculate.

The Lor I'm seeing now is the reason I called him. The man who makes inappropriate jokes and lacks a filter is the disguise the killer underneath wears. *This* is the side I find most tolerable. Cool and calculating. Merciless when he needs to be. All attributes that make him an excellent hired gun.

"Might I remind you I could have kept this information to myself. He'd have no idea that his precious human was being auctioned off like a goddamn prized pig if it weren't for *me*."

Stepping closer, I snarl, "You didn't bring this to my attention because you wanted to help. You're very skilled in manipulation, Rowena, but everyone sees through your tricks. You're predictable."

"And you're pitiful," she spits. "Everything you've created will be threatened and for what? *Her*? You can't be serious."

Lor chuckles like he finds everything about this comical. "You really are an idiot, red."

"You should know to watch your words when you're in my presence, Rowena. They've always gotten you in trouble in the past and my tolerance for you is quickly depleting." I don't have time to properly deal with her now, but someday soon, she's going to be reminded of her proper place in my world. "You're scarcely on my list of priorities, and tonight you're even less so. I will deal with you at a later date. I suggest you leave now while I still feel inclined to allow it." Sliding my eyes to the blond vampire, I add, "Or before Lorcan decides to have his fun with you."

At my nod, Lorcan lets her go with the slightest shove. "It was a *pleasure* making your acquaintance." He gestures with the knife in an overall dramatic bow. "Hopefully, we'll have a playdate soon."

She shoves away from him with an angry huff. With wild angry eyes, Rowena threatens, "What do you think will happen when the rest of them find out about your affections for the human?"

"Go ahead and tell them, Rowena. Tell them all about her, but when you do, make sure they all know that she is under my protection and that if someone so much as steps in her direction, I will make the pits of hell look like a vacation compared to what I will do to them," I warn venomously. "She is mine, and everyone will soon be reminded of what happens to those who touch what belongs to me." I don't much care to hear what her retort will be. Without giving her the chance, I turn and head back toward the house.

But Rowena's never been one to know when to quit. Calling after me, she says, "I hope you understand how pathetic this all makes you look. She's a fucking human, Silas. You deserve more than her. She's not worth it."

Stopping in my tracks, I look over my shoulder at the hateful woman. "And you're worth nothing."

This time when I walk back to the house, I don't stop.

Lor catches up to me and in a low voice, he asks, "Did you fuck that?" Even if I felt inclined to answer, he doesn't give me the chance. "There's no way it was enjoyable. It'd be like fucking a lizard in designer clothing." His whole body shivers at the thought. On a dime, he switches the topic of conversation. Once again, his dark side is tucked neatly in place. "What are you thinking? How are we going to find where Gideon is holding Quincey?"

"I'm going to put my hacker to use."

CHAPTER 6

Silas

R ory paces back and forth in front of the dining room table. Her lips move as if she's having a silent conversation with herself, and her hands shift restlessly at her sides. The guard who'd brought her inside leans against the wall watching her, but not saying anything. He doesn't ask questions about the things he sees while on my payroll. As long as the checks keep clearing in his bank account, he doesn't care. That's what is so great about the men Duke finds and hires.

They don't ask questions.

Rory is the same way. Her ability to sweep everything under the rug and pretend it's not happening is something I appreciate about her. Many times, she's been tasked with looking into things that pertain more to my underground businesses. Each time, she's simply nodded her head and asked when I needed it back by. Easy as that. Based on her anxious movements and panicked facial expression, I don't believe it's going to go that way tonight.

The guard looks my way, and at the subtle wave of my hand, he walks away without a word.

Standing at the doorway, I give her the opportunity to address me first, but when she continues her pacing, I say her name.

Her head shakes and her mouth moves faster.

"It appears we've broken the poor girl." Lorcan's amused voice comes from behind me. "What a shame, I truly did enjoy her company."

Ignoring him, I step closer and say her name louder, my tone demanding her attention, "Rory." Finally, her steps falter and her head snaps in my direction. "Sit down." I motion to one of the wooden dining chairs with my chin. When she remains frozen in place, I stare pointedly at her. "*Now.*" In stiff movements, she pulls the chair away from the table and sits down. Her eyes continue to dart between the two men in the room, a nervous look in them. It's as if she's finally seeing us.

"Under normal circumstances, this is something I would have revealed to you in a more... *graceful* way," I start. "There is never really an easy way to explain this. Everyone handles the information differently. Della fled town for a month before she showed back up at my door one night after she'd come to accept it. Quincey, brave to a fault, vomited on her shoes after learning my secret. Ira shrugged and told me he already knew. He then promptly went back to trimming the hedges. "Unfortunately, for purely selfish reasons, I can't permit you the adjustment period that is usually needed in this situation. We don't have time for that—*Quincey* doesn't have time for that."

"You're—" she sputters. "You're both..."

"Incredibly dashing vampires," Lorcan throws out casually.

Rory's jaw drops, head shaking. "There's no such thing. They're not real."

"I do wish, for your sake, you could have gone the rest of your life thinking that, Rory," I sympathize. "This is a dangerous world and it's much safer for you if you're able to maintain your distance from it all. Dragging you into this is wrong."

She springs from her chair and teeters on her high heels as she rushes toward the exit on the other side of the room. "Then don't drag me into it. Just let me leave!" she begs.

I shift in front of her, blocking her escape before she can so much as get five feet away from the table. Rory gasps, hand coming up to cover her mouth to muffle the sound. She turns on her heels and darts around me. She makes it to the other doorway that Lorcan stands in front of.

Being the degenerate he is, he grins at her, fangs fully on display. "Where are you running off to so soon?"

She makes a noise in the back of her throat, frightened, before dashing around the room. Only when she has the six-foot-long wooden table between us does she stop. Like a caged animal, she frantically searches for a way out of the room, but between Lor and me, she's been cornered.

Not feeling too inclined to chase her around a table, I stand on the opposite end and wait, stone faced, for her to make her next move.

"Please let me go. I won't say anything to anyone, but please don't keep me here."

Not that long ago, Quincey said almost the exact same words to me. At the time, I had selfish reasons for keeping her with me. And now, knowing how it would end, I would do it all over again.

I was unable to grant Quincey's wish to be let go then, and it's the same for Rory now. "I'm sorry, I can't do that. *Yet.*" I emphasize the last word. "When I have Quincey back, I will let you walk away. I'll give you the money for a plane ticket to wherever you want to go, and I will give you whatever money you need to start your new life. You'll never be contacted by us again, but I can't let you leave yet. Not when she's out there and you have the ability to help her."

Rory holds her ground, shaking her head. "No, find someone else. I want to leave right now. I don't even *know* Quincey. What happens to her doesn't affect me."

The room falls eerily quiet. The only sound coming from Rory's erratic heartbeat. Keeping my face composed, I turn the phone I've been carrying over in my hand. I wait for the live feed to connect, my heart sinking when Quincey's suspended body comes into view. Teeth clenched, I turn the phone and show Rory. "This is what's happening to her as we speak. Gideon has plans for her and if you don't find out where he's streaming this video from, he's going to kill her." Rory's face blanches further. "And then I'm going to kill *everyone*."

I've already watched a wife die and the rampage I went on was devastating for many, but if I'm forced to watch it happen to Quincey, the damage I'll inflict will be catastrophic. My only hope is that someone is there to stop me in time. When a black heart like mine is shattered, no one is safe from the deadly shrapnel.

"Please," she begs, sounding too young to be in this situation. "Find someone else. I can't do this and it's unfair of you to ask me to, especially now that I know you're—" Rory chokes on the word as she nervously glances in the direction of Lorcan. I don't bother following her stare, but whatever she sees causes her to take another step back.

"I apologize because there seems to be some miscommunication between us right now. Do you really think I became the man I am today by *asking* for things? *Asking* is a common courtesy that I've never felt inclined to participate in. I've been as accommodating with you as I can thus far, Rory. Believe it or not, this is me being patient, but if you think I won't chain you to a computer until you start doing your fucking job, you're wrong."

"I don't—" she starts, but I'm just as quick to cut her off.

"He's going to drain her of her blood and then he's going to auction it away like it's a cattle auction. All while doing this, he's going to film it so those with animosity toward me can join in on the *fun* of watching her die. She doesn't deserve any of this." *It's all my fault.*

Rory watches the screen I still hold up, her frightened face falling the longer she stares at Quincey's battered, exposed body. "Gideon did this? He's like you?" she questions, her voice shaky.

"Yes," I confirm. "And now he's attempting to get even with me by hurting those around me."

"Then he's the one who hurt Duke?" she summarizes.

I nod. "My assumption is I was the intended target of the explosion, but Duke was in the car with me when we were trying to get back to the estate to stop all of this."

"Does Duke know what you are?" Her chin lifts, hazel eyes locking with mine. "Does he know you're a vampire?"

"Of course, he's my right hand. I trust him with this information, and I trust him to have my back in every situation." If he were here right now, he'd be by my side, leading the charge to find Quincey.

"And he trusts you," she whispers, mostly to herself.

I don't reply, not wanting to speak on Duke's behalf. Duke's been with me through enough things that I'd like to think he trusts me, but then again, can one ever fully trust someone like me? Trusting me is like trusting an unstable explosive. Quincey put her trust in me, and she's currently paying the price for it.

Rory squares her shoulders like she's preparing to go to battle. "Fine. Where are my computers? I'll need you to send me everything you have. Every link that's been sent. I'll work as fast as I can to find where he's streaming the video from. But once I have an address, I'm getting the fuck out of here. This is the last thing I will do for you, after that, I'm done. I quit," she declares, while glancing between us vampires. "And if either of you so much as gets within five feet of me, I will shove a number two pencil in your heart and then your neck."

Lorcan chuckles. "Are you going to bathe in holy water too? Sorry darling, wooden stakes don't—"

I cut him off by raising my hand. If the idea that stabbing us with a wooden stake gives her peace of mind, fine. I'll send someone out to get her a real stake instead of a flimsy writing utensil. I will walk into a church for the first time since I was a young man in France and collect holy water for her myself. I don't care what I must do to ensure she does what I need from her.

"Your equipment is in the den." I gesture to the French doors that can be seen through the dining room doorway.

With her head held high and false bravado working its way through her system, Rory marches toward the doors. When she reaches Lor, who blocks the exit, her eyes narrow in challenge.

Lor smirks and looks the young hacker over. "I really do enjoy you. You're *feisty*."

"Funny you should say that, seeing as I have a history of setting fires. If you don't want me to set your bed aflame while you're in it, I would recommend moving aside, *Irishman*."

Without skipping a beat, Lor huskily tells her, "I have no issue with you setting my bed on fire, just as long as you're in it too. Preferably naked, but I'm not picky. I know how to work around clothes."

"*Lorcan*," I growl in warning. "Let her pass."

With one last long perusal of her body, Lorcan steps out of the way and allows Rory to pass.

Without waiting for us to follow, she marches into the den and immediately slams the door behind her. The audible sound of the lock clicking in place follows suit.

Lor cocks his head, staring at the door before asking, "She knows a simple lock and a door made of glass isn't going to keep us out, right?"

CHAPTER 7

All I ever wanted to do was to help people. I chose a career path that gave me that opportunity, but it had one major downfall. I've seen a lot of death.

I've heard the wail of a mother as her child dies in her arms. I've heard the pleas and prayers from my patients' families to continue CPR. I've seen the doctors' faces break when they realize there is nothing else they can do to save their patient. I've held thin, frail hands as the remaining bits of their life escape them in that last shallow breath.

And in those moments of immense tragedy and grief, there's always that one person there to remind everyone of the little fucker called *fate*.

Sometimes it's referred to as God's plan or destiny. Kismet even, but in the end, it all means the same thing; no matter the paths you follow or the people you meet, your future has been planned and there is nothing you can do to change it.

So often I've heard *'everything happens for a reason'* or if we want to get even cheesier, *'it was written in the stars'* is always a classic standby.

Many times, I've seen sayings like those bring comfort to people, but right now, as my shoulders and wrists burn in excruciating pain with each breath, pulling air into my lungs becomes more labored, I'm cursing the people who ever created such bullshit nuggets of so-called *wisdom*.

If they are right, and everything has been established for us. That means it doesn't matter how hard I worked my ass off or how badly I wanted to help people, none of it would have made a difference. I still would have ended up here; in love with a vampire and hanging from a ceiling, waiting for my kidnapper to come back and finish the job.

That sentence alone is hard to wrap my head around, but the vague concept that this has always been my fate is even harder to accept.

Holding back a grimace, I look at the camera that still sits across the room, pointing at me. I don't want to give whoever's watching the feed the satisfaction of seeing me in pain, but more importantly, if Silas is watching, I don't want him to see it either.

To the bitter end, I will be strong. It's how I've made it through my life up to this point, and I will face this how I always have; with a brave facade and a will that can't be broken.

I know my plea to Silas for him to not watch has fallen on deaf ears. Gideon was right, Silas won't be able to stop himself. He will consider looking away as a sign of weakness—defeat—and that isn't in his nature. *Losing* isn't an option for him and that's how I also know he's doing everything in his power to find me.

It's a rare and extraordinary honor to be cared for by Silas Laurent. It's a skill that doesn't come naturally to him as he's spent many centuries closed off, never getting too close to anyone. When you know you'll outlive everyone you meet, I can see how he'd think developing relationships was a pointless endeavor. That's why when he allows people into his life, it's that much more special.

I've seen firsthand the lengths he'll go to make sure his people are safe and well taken care of. Just as I know this, I also know the wrath and vengeance he'll inflict on the people that threaten him. I was there when he put his fist through a man's chest, and I watched as he tore a head clean from someone's shoulders. Both of those acts will be a mercy for what Silas will do to Gideon.

The same clanking noise as before comes from the metal sliding door as Gideon reenters the room. I'm not sure how long he's been gone, the dark, windowless room messing with my semblance of time.

He shifts a black duffel bag to one shoulder after sliding the door shut behind him. "Have you been entertaining our viewers?" he asks as he checks something on the camera. "You should know you're quite popular, Quincey. I have many people making offers. They're bidding more than I ever could have hoped for."

I lift my head, my stiff neck groaning in protest. "*Of course* they are. You should know by now that Silas enjoys the finer things in life. Fancy cars, exquisite art, beautiful property." Lifting my mouth in a smirk, I add, "Grade A blood."

"You're arrogant," Gideon scolds.

"And you're *fucked*," I snap back, my hands tugging at the chains. Pain shoots from my fingertips to my shoulders. The human body isn't meant to hang from its wrists. I know by each passing minute, more damage is being caused to my nerves, but that doesn't stop me from continuing to taunt Gideon. "Silas is going to make you regret the day the first thought of your plan danced its way through your sick mind."

Gideon laughs his cold, robotic laugh. "You think I would ever grant Silas the gratification of killing me himself?" Shaking his head, he shifts across the small space to wrap his hand around the lever on the wall. "I've always known that once I had my revenge, I would go join Margret." Just like earlier, his emotionless eyes drift to the dark, empty corner of the room. "This is just my unfinished business before I'm finally at peace and with her once more."

Without warning, he pulls the lever and I'm plummeting to the ground. My body, stiff and numb in places, isn't prepared to catch itself. Instead, I crash to the floor, covered in various dark stains, in a disoriented heap. Everything hurts. Every ligament in my arms screams in pain, the joints protesting when my arms drop from the position they've been held in for so long.

Before I can fully bring in my next breath, a hand is wrapping around my long, tangled hair. My scalp prickles and a hissing sound escapes my lips as I'm dragged back to the table I'd woken up on. My knees burn as the skin is scraped off them in the process.

"As you can imagine, I'm on a bit of a deadline here. The clock is ticking for all of us. Ticktock, ticktock." Gideon grabs under my arms and I'm dumped onto the metal surface on my back. My fight-or-flight instincts kick in and I instantly try to swing my legs off the table in a desperate attempt to run. The hand that had momentarily left my hair returns, this time, my head is roughly yanked back to the table. The back of my skull collides with the metal surface. Pain radiates through my head, and for a minute, my vision blurs and my world tilts.

Taking advantage of my dizzy and disoriented state, Gideon makes work of chaining my hands and feet back in place. "That's better," he mumbles to himself as if he's proud of his handiwork. "You look good in chains, Quincey. Our viewers agree," he offers over his shoulder while he repositions the camera closer to the table.

"Beg Silas to save you," he goads me, the smile that I hate stretching across his face. "Beg him to find you and make all of this stop."

Locking eyes with the man, I shake my head. "No."

He stares me down for a minute like he's waiting for me to give in and look away, but when I continue to hold his stare, his lips flatten into an unamused line. "You can pretend to be strong, but eventually I will make you cry for him. You will break and you will beg for him to come in here like your knight in shining armor."

"Silas isn't a knight," I snarl. "He's a fucking king."

One second, Gideon is standing at the end of the table, the next he's so close to my face I can feel his breath across my cheek as he snarls, "He made himself king, but he's not God." This close to my face, I can make out just how unwell this man is. In his eyes, the exhaustion and sorrow he feels are reflected. They're the only proof I have that this man feels anything at all. "I was his ally—his *confidant*. I helped him maintain his power, but how does he repay me for my service? By *killing* her. He could have turned a blind eye and let us leave, but no. He's always lacked mercy."

The way Gideon talks about Margret's death, it's as if in his head, he views Silas's actions as rash and unfair, but I know Silas. Silas doesn't work impulsively. Every step he takes and every choice he makes are carefully thought out. It takes a lot for him to deviate from that path. "You keep saying he killed her, but you've never said why," I argue. I know Silas's history is painted red, but I know he'd never kill a woman without cause.

Gideon jerks back like I've slapped him.

"You're filming this because you want your story to be known, but you're leaving out a crucial part, aren't you?"

He doesn't answer, his face remains like a piece of marble.

Not giving up, I continue to push, "Why did he kill her? He had to have a reason—"

"Stop talking," Gideon warns, voice darkening.

Even though I know angering the vampire who appears to be experiencing a psychological break isn't a wise idea, I don't heed his warning. If he wants to make Silas the monster in his tale, that's fine, but he better tell the whole fucking story. "What happened, Gideon? You said before Margret was punished for something that wasn't her fault—"

There's a flash of silver and the same knife he used to cut my hip reappears. The shiny serrated blade is pushed to my throat by a surprisingly shaky hand for a vampire. "Don't say her name."

For a moment, I forget how to breathe and every single one of my muscles freeze in place, the fear of being cut momentarily taking me over. Slowly, I force myself to relax. Letting out a long breath, I lift my chin, giving him even better access to my jugular. "If it wasn't her fault, was it yours? Is it your fault that Margret is dead, Gideon?"

For the first time since I woke up in this room with him, varying emotions cross his face. His marble mask shatters, exposing the man underneath. First, it's like he's in physical pain from my words, but the pain quickly morphs into visible anger.

"I warned you!" he roars, his voice bouncing off the stone walls. "I told you not to use her name!"

Wonderfully and recklessly fearless, that's what Silas once called me.

In this moment, I'm not fearless. With every breath I take and each beat of my heart, fear works its way through my body. What's keeping me strong is my anger. Anger for what's happened to Ira and anger that someone would use me to hurt Silas.

Despite the nerves and alarm bells going off in my head, I ask a question I know he's not expecting to come out of my mouth. "Did she say your name when Silas took her life?"

I feel the blade slide shallowly into my neck when he presses it harder against my flesh. "No," Gideon grits out. "Silas didn't give her the opportunity. He acted too fast." The knife trails down my throat before stopping right under my collarbone, directly over my heart. "But I will. I'll give you ample opportunity to say his name, Quincey."

I feel nothing at first, just pressure, but then white-hot pain comes. My mouth opens in a silent gasp, air getting caught in my constricting throat and my back arches off the metal table in a poor attempt to escape the agony as the blade slices into my chest.

Blinded by the pain, I forget the promise I'd made to myself; don't let him see you break. My weak and shaking hands ball into fists at my sides, my nails digging into my palms. Forcing my mouth shut, my teeth grind together as I force myself to remain silent and still, but I'm unable to stop the hot tears that fall from the corners of my eyes.

Pausing in his task, granting me a small reprieve, Gideon looks down at me. "Say his name," he taunts.

Swallowing the ball of emotion trapped in my throat, I choke out a hoarse, "*No.*"

And then the pain returns.

CHAPTER 8

Silas

When I was in denial of my affections toward Quincey, I'd watch the security camera feeds from the estate so I could feed the addiction that had started to form.

Most of the time they were just clips of her talking with Della in the kitchen while the housekeeper cooked. Her eyes watched everything Della did with keen interest. Other times, she'd be sitting in the courtyard reading a book to Ira by the roses she'd insisted I'd plant for the dying man.

I observed everything she did, from the way her lips lifted in soft smiles when she listened to Ira tell stories or how her head would fall back as she laughed during her banter with Duke.

Often, I found myself fighting my own smile. Her joy and bright personality are contagious like that, but now, watching the footage we're streaming through the large television, I long to see one of her smiles or hear her laugh.

Her overly expressive face is guarded and closed off. The bright spark that's always sat in her powder blue eyes is diminished. Her sun-kissed skin looks pale and the dark circles under her eyes tell me just how exhausted she really is.

Despite all of this, she never once cowers to Gideon. She boldly meets his eyes, appearing unimpressed with his scare tactics.

"She's strong," Lorcan comments from the armchair he's sprawled in. "I like it. You need someone strong willed to put up with your bullshit."

Perched stiffly on the cream-colored sofa, with my elbows resting on my knees, I don't look away from the screen as I explain, "She shouldn't have to be *this* strong. She should have been untouchable." My estate has always been safe from my enemies. The security teams I've hired over the years should have been able to protect whoever resides within those four walls. "My security failed me—*failed Quincey*—last night."

"They were outgunned and outmanned," Lorcan attempts to reason to pacify my misplaced anger. I'm not sure who Gideon had found to inflict the devastation against my team, but I'm irritated they weren't on my payroll first. If Duke was awake, I'm sure he'd have a guess as to who the group was. His background in private security and time in the military makes him privy to that kind of information. "Maybe you should hire more vampires as security. They can at least take a bullet."

"I don't trust enough vampires to task them with protecting my important assets." When you're at the top of the food chain, people are always vying to bring you down. Allowing vampires close would put them in a position to find weaknesses they could exploit.

"Your *assets*? Is that what she is to you?"

"No," I manage to grit out, annoyed he's asking questions he already knows the answers to. "She's the only thing on earth that could get me to walk away from it all."

Before she was taken, I knew there was an expiration date on our time together. I knew sooner or later I would have to leave her behind.

That's what is required in my lifestyle. I knew it would be hard to do, but in the end, I truly believed I would be strong enough to leave.

It took her being taken from me to realize I'm no longer capable or *willing* to live without her. She's permanently engraved herself in my life and the void I feel now that she's gone is unbearable.

When I have her back, if she asks me to walk away from everything, I would do it without a second thought. I'd pick her over the power and money. She's worth more than both anyway.

Lorcan is quiet for a second while he ponders my words. I don't look at him, but I can feel his heavy stare on me. "I truly can't wait to meet the lass Silas Laurent would abandon everything for. She must be something incredibly special."

Before I have the chance to confirm his sentiments, the sight of an irate Gideon holding a knife to Quincey's throat has me leaping off the couch and stepping closer to the mounted television screen.

"Don't say her name," Gideon warns Quincey, the knife pressing harder into her flesh.

"Is he talking about the woman you killed?" Lorcan asks, now standing at my side, his posture alert.

Don't push him, I silently plead to Quincey. Her strength thus far has made my chest fill with pride, but right now, if only for a moment, I want her to do as he says. If it means she stays alive, I don't care what she must do. I just need her to buy Rory enough time to find her location.

"I didn't kill a woman," I snap at Lorcan. "I killed a monster disguised as the woman he loved." Margret came back, just like my wife did. Devoid of all empathy and humanity. Her only care was her next meal. If she hadn't been eliminated, the number of lives she would have taken would have been in the hundreds. Gideon was too weak to do what needed to be done, so I stepped in.

And that's what Quincey is trying to get Gideon to admit. She doesn't know the full history of what happened, but she does know *me*. She knows I wouldn't kill Margret on a simple whim.

My stomach sinks when she asks him, "Did she say your name when Silas took her life?"

Beside me, Lorcan hisses out a harsh curse while I'm completely frozen in place, my eyes locked on the stream of blood coming from the nicks Gideon had slid into her skin with his blade.

"No, Silas didn't give her the opportunity. He acted too fast," Gideon tells her, all while dragging the knife lightly down to her left collarbone. "But I will. I'll give you ample opportunity to say his name, Quincey."

The world around me stops existing when the knife slices into her perfect skin. Everything falls away but the sight of my heart being carved.

Gideon stops cutting long enough to tersely order, "Say his name." A malicious grin on his face.

Tears fall from her eyes, disappearing into her hairline. After a moment of tense silence, she refuses to do as he wishes. "No."

Wordlessly, he brings the knife back to her chest, and begins to cut another deep line through one he'd already made. In a matter of seconds, he's carved a perfect X into her previously perfect skin.

As if I'm standing in the middle of the ocean, waves of rage collide with my body. The power behind them is almost strong enough to make me lose my footing. I'm one blow away from giving in and allowing myself to drown.

Blood pools from the wound he's made. Smiling down at his handiwork, Gideon smears the blood across Quincey's chest. Like a deranged artist, he paints her skin red.

He lifts the hand now covered in her blood to his mouth. Taunting me, he once again looks at the camera while lapping at his fingers. "You found yourself a sweet one, Silas. No wonder you keep her around. She's simply delectable," he goads. "Think about all the people who will get to try her next. I've already had many offers. I wonder just how much I can make off her."

Hand still bloody, he reaches for Quincey's face. She winces when he harshly turns her head to force her to look at the camera. "Call to him, Quincey. Tell him to come and save you."

Her movements are hindered by his hold, but still, she manages a jerky shake of her head. Her face looks paler now, her eyes almost dazed from the pain.

"Very well." Gideon roughly lets go of her, leaving bright red fingerprints on her jaw and cheeks. "You're only hurting yourself, Quincey," he scolds before moving to the other side of her chest. "But at least this way, you'll be symmetrical."

Just like he did before, he begins to carve another X into her skin.

She tries hard to be strong. I can tell by the way her jaw clenches and her eyes squeeze shut that she's fighting like hell to remain quiet, but my brave girl can only take so much before she has no other choice.

The sound of her crying out in agony slices through me like a sword, rattling me to my very core. I haven't felt true pain in a very long time, but right now, as I helplessly watch him disfigure her body, it's all I can feel.

"That's it," Gideon encourages wickedly. "Now cry out to him, Quincey."

Her lips press into a flat line as she refuses his order once more. The tears that fall from her eyes streak through the blood he'd left on her cheek.

Not liking her stubborn silence, Gideon snarls at her as he digs his finger into the fresh wound he'd just caused. Once again, she screams.

My body turns around on instinct, as if my subconscious is trying to protect me from what's happening on the screen. Shoving my shaking hands into my hair, I yank on the strands before forcing myself to turn back.

"*Say. His. Name,*" Gideon orders close to her face, saliva spraying as he speaks.

Quincey slowly blinks her eyes, clearing the tears from them. She opens her mouth, her plump bottom lip wobbling. My body locks in place, and the air in the room becomes heavy as she works up the ability to speak again. "Silas," she hoarsely says. My chest constricts at how broken she sounds.

"That's it." Gideon grins in triumph, but the achievement is short lived.

"Silas," Quincey whispers. When she says my name, it usually has a calming effect on me, but now it causes a spot in my chest to ache. "Everything will be okay. Don't watch. Please don't wa—"

Gidcon's open palm collides with her face, effectively cutting off her plea to me. The force of the blow even makes Lorcan wince. "Stop trying to protect him. He doesn't deserve it." The knife falls when he reaches out for her. His bloody hands wrap around her shoulders, and he violently shakes her battered form. "He doesn't deserve anything!"

The back of her skull collides with the metal table from the force of his shaking.

A low, rumbling growl has started to form in my chest. It's like a tornado siren sounding before the storm touches down. I can feel Lorcan tense up beside me, prepared for whatever is to come.

With one last violent shake, Gideon shoves away from Quincey. She smiles hatefully up at him despite her now split lip. "I did as you asked. I said his name. What's a girl got to do to make you happy, Gideon?"

Many times, I found myself annoyed because of her smart mouth. I was unaccustomed to such obvious disrespect, and it appears Gideon wasn't prepared for it either.

"Do you think Margret would approve of what you're doing?"

"Don't," Gideon warns lowly.

But of course, she doesn't listen to him. "Do you think she'd like that you're *hurting* me?" She's trying to keep her tone even, but I can hear the ache in her voice when she speaks. The blood from her chest wounds runs down her shoulders and into her lace bra. The metal table beneath her has pools of it forming.

As if he's in pain, Gideon roars loudly before he moves away from the table. With his speed, he's nothing but a blurred shape. When he passes in front of the camera, he must bump into the stand it rests on. The footage wobbles and shakes for a second before finally crashing to the ground.

Dread wraps its cold arms around me in an unpleasant embrace when Quincey's body is no longer in frame.

"I told you to stop," Gideon seethes off camera. "Why can't you just do what you're told?"

The sound of something unzipping has my hands balling into fists at my sides.

"What is that?" Quincey questions, her voice pitched in slight panic. "What are you giving me?"

"I think I've heard enough from you today," Gideon coldly says. "It's time for you to close your eyes now."

The chains clang against the table. I can't see her, but I have to assume that she tries her best to fight off whatever he's doing to her. The commotion stops and the faintest whimper fills the silence before she whispers, "No, I don't want to sleep." Her words are slow and sluggish like she's been drugged.

"Sweet dreams," he offers.

I wait, my whole body shaking with an uncontrollable wave of emotion as footsteps slowly approach the fallen camera. When Gideon's face comes into view and Quincey isn't shown again, my spine goes rigid.

"That's enough for today, don't you guys think? The sun is now rising, and I must retire for a little bit." The robotic grin returns to his face. "Your girl is truly exhausting, Silas." He lifts his hand to the camera, showing off the blood that still stains it. "But at least she's tasty. My buyers are going to enjoy her."

And with that parting comment, the feed goes black, and my vision goes red with anger.

My body moves before I know what I'm doing. One second, I'm standing in front of the television, the next I'm at the front door.

CHAPTER 9

"**S**ilas!" Lorcan yells my name, but he sounds a thousand miles away. "Stop!"

Rationality has abandoned me, and I'm being driven by something uncontrollable. His warning goes ignored as I wrap my hand around the door handle. I've barely had a chance to turn it when hands come down on my shoulders and I'm yanked away from the door.

My body is thrown backward with such force, I collide with the long table that sits behind the couch. The wood splinters from my weight and I fall to the ground, surrounded by all the broken decor that had been residing on the surface.

"Are you bloody insane?" Lor questions me, completely appalled I'd think about opening the door. "Do you want to be burned to a crisp?"

Back on my feet, my fangs descend as I'm taken over by the deadly combination of rage and desperation. I face him with a low snarl. "Get out of my way, Lorcan."

He stands in front of the door, his feet planted. "Not happening,

Silas. Your head isn't on straight right now and you're not thinking clearly. If you were, you'd know that going outside in the *sun* isn't the wisest idea you've ever had."

"This is your last warning, Lorcan. I have to go." I'm not in the same room as her right now, but I can smell the blood Gideon has spilled. I've committed the scent to memory and I'm choking on it now.

"You won't make it five steps off the fucking patio." Like two predators standing off, we each refuse to break eye contact. "And then what? Who's going to save her?"

Not hearing the answer I'm looking for; I charge at him. Having anticipated my next move, he mirrors me and rushes toward me. Our bodies collide in what should be a bone-shattering impact.

Lorcan attempts to push me back and away from the door while my arms wrap around his torso. Lifting him off the ground like he weighs nothing, I throw his body into the wall across the room. The picture frames that had been carefully positioned on the wall crash to the ground when his body slams into it.

Falling to the hardwood covered in drywall debris, Lorcan's sable eyes glow with anger when he turns his attention back to me. "You can't save Quincey if you're dead!" he attempts to remind me. "And if you think I'm going to go out of my way to find her, you're very fucking wrong."

I can hear what he's saying, and it all sounds reasonable to the sensible side of my brain, but the monster that is rarely released from its confines is in the driver's seat. To him, Lorcan is standing between him and saving his woman.

"Outside of you, she has no one. Hell, even your human friend—Duke, was it?—he's even down for the count." He swiftly clambers to his feet. "Are you really going to let Gideon win this? That's what you'll do if you walk out that door right now."

"You don't understand," I roar so loud the UV-protected windows rattle. "This is all my fault. She's being tortured because of actions taken a century before she was born. I was supposed to protect her from all of it, and now she's *bleeding*!" My hand points in the direction of the blank television screen. "I have to find her."

Lor nods his head. "You're right, this is all your fault, but if you walk out that door, you're giving up the opportunity of ever making it right. How are you going to beg for her forgiveness and make all of this up to her if you're nothing but a pile of ash? Use your fucking head, Silas. You're too bloody smart to behave like this."

Blinded by the helpless feeling, I return to the door.

This time, Lorcan's body slams into mine like a freight train. Together we fly across the room, crashing into an antique standing lamp before we collide with the bookcase.

Glass embeds itself in my skin, but I don't feel the pain that should accompany it. Rolling from my side to my stomach, I attempt to climb to my knees but a hand wrapping around the collar of my shirt pulls me back down into the clutter.

"Honestly, Silas." Lorcan huffs. "This behavior is starting to become embarrassing."

My hand reaches for something in all the shambles to use as a weapon against Lorcan. My fingers brush against a hard object. Pulling it toward me, my vision, blinded by rage, momentarily clears long enough for the title of the book I'd grabbed to come into focus. Instantly, my body freezes, and I stop fighting off the Irish vampire.

The book I hold is a first edition copy that has never meant anything to me. Just simply another thing I've collected over the years to fill my various bookshelves. I've never paid it any attention until Quincey found a copy of the same book in the library at the estate. I don't know why she picked this specific one, but it's one of the many books she'd occupied herself with while she watched over Ira.

It's the very book she was reading before Ira revealed to us he'd orchestrated the whole plan to bring Quincey into my home—into my life. Even on his deathbed, he was concerned for me and knew what I needed, even when I was too stubborn to see it. He knew that Quincey was the missing piece in my life. Ira knew his days of being my compass were numbered but was at peace knowing that Quincey would be there to take his place.

Or she was supposed to be.

The chaotic monster that had been controlling me just seconds ago vanishes. My mind goes quiet for the first time since I was shown the footage.

Defeated and exhausted by the excruciating weight of the guilt sitting on my chest, I slowly twist my body into an upright position. I feel Lor's wary eyes on me as I rest my arms on my knees and drop my head.

I break the heavy silence after a few moments. "Before her, I'd forgotten how to dream," I utter quietly. "And now my dreams are filled with nothing but her face—her laugh." Her laugh is like a song, the lyrics written especially for me.

Lor doesn't say anything, just allows me to speak.

"If Gideon takes her from me," I force myself to say. "His torment won't stop when her heart does because I will still see her in my dreams. It will be a special kind of hell to dream of her—to see her so vivid and alive—then to wake up only to remember she's gone. That she's *dead*."

Lor releases a long breath before placing his hand on my shoulder. This time, I don't shrug off his attempt to show support. I'm too numb to care. "Nothing I say now will bring you any comfort because I know the only thing capable of doing that is Quincey herself."

The sound of a door slowly squeaking open stops me from having to respond to Lorcan.

Ever so slowly, Rory's lilac-colored hair peeks out from the doorframe. When she sees the destruction that has happened outside of the office she's been holed up in, her hazel eyes go wide. "I might be able to help with that..." she trails off as she emerges farther out of the room and the full extent of the damage becomes visible. "Is the vampire

WWE match over, or do you two need to go a few more rounds? I was trying to wait you out, but now I'm worried that this poor house isn't vampire proof." Reaching out to the wall I'd thrown Lorcan into, Rory pulls one of the loose pieces of drywall off. "I was eavesdropping—sorry, not sorry—and it sounded like you'd worked your shit out, but if you need more time, you two know where to find me." She backs up in the direction of the door she'd just come through.

Climbing to my feet faster than a human would, I move toward the hacker. Rory instinctually takes a step back from me and her almond-shaped eyes widen.

Granting her some space, I force myself to stay where I am. "What do you mean you can help?"

As if she's proud of herself, Rory's mouth lifts in a cocky smirk. "Remember when you had me looking into the people who attacked Quincey in the Quarter and I told you whoever was behind it was talented because they cleaned up after themselves really well?"

"Yes, you said they were good, but you were better, if I remember correctly."

"Exactly. Well, the person who was tasked with clearing up Gideon's digital footprint and paper trail is the same person that created the website that's currently streaming the footage of Quincey."

I stare at her blankly, confused. "I don't see how that's helpful information."

"Hackers and computer nerds like myself all learn the same things, but we spend years perfecting our work. Because of this, we all create different ways of doing things—we develop signatures in our code. If I study code written by someone else long enough, I can learn their little quirks, and more importantly, their mistakes. I studied Gideon's guy's work for days—I know this hacker's work backward and forward now."

Lorcan, who's busy pulling drywall and glass from his clothes and hair, pipes in, "Riddles, dear, you're talking in riddles."

Rory shoots him an annoyed look before continuing. "I was able to get into the website fairly easily, but when they turned off the video stream, the connection was broken, and I couldn't track the video any longer."

The small balloon of hope that had started to inflate inside of me deflates at this. "Again, how is this helpful?"

With an exasperated sigh, Rory points between both Lor and me. "This will go a lot faster if you'd both stop interrupting."

Lor waves his hand dramatically. "Very well, the floor is all yours, madam."

"I was able to get into the code and implant something called phishing software. Essentially, the website still looks like Gideon's, and when Gideon logs back in, he'll be none the wiser that I'd been there fucking shit up. The only difference is, when he logs in, he'll be on *my* network, and I will be able to access all the information on the website. *Including* the location the video is coming from."

The weight that has been crushing my chest for the hours since she's been gone lessens. "All we have to do is wait for him to log back on and just like that, you'll know where they are? It's that easy?"

Rory's face scrunches. "I wouldn't say it was *easy*. What I just did usually takes people twelve hours to do. I was just lucky that Gideon fucked up by using the same tech guy on both things, and I'd already figured him out."

"How do you know it's a man?" Lor asks.

Rory shrugs. "Only a man would be arrogant enough to implant his screen name multiple times in his code. Plus, there was no finesse or flair in his work. Boring as hell if you ask me."

Lorcan looks her over once again, that same sultry look in his eyes. "Yeah, I was right, I might fall in love with you."

"And I might shove a clove of garlic up your ass," Rory snaps back, completely unmoved by his aimless flirting.

He doesn't mean a word he says to her. Lorcan would flirt with a brick wall if he could figure out a way to fuck it. He's never been overly particular about who receives his affections, anyone who crosses his path is fair game in his book.

"Don't threaten me with a good time." Lorcan winks at her before turning his attention to me. "Finding where he's holding Quincey has always been half the battle. We have to assume the people who took out the guards at your house are still lingering around protecting him wherever he is. We'll need more than just us to go get her out."

I've lost two teams of security in the past twenty-four hours, one at my house and one at the docks where my product was being kept. But the good thing about having assets all over the world means I have various teams located everywhere that I can bring in. "Wherever Gideon's keeping her isn't protected from the sun, or he wouldn't have had to excuse himself. We have until nightfall to get people here."

Nodding, Lorcan picks another piece of debris off his clothing before stepping over a pile of books and shattered glass. His tattooed fingers point around at the mess that's been created throughout the room. "I'm not cleaning this shit up."

CHAPTER 10

Quincey

My lips are sticky with homemade lemonade and the air smells like roses. Lifting my face toward the brightly shining sun, I let it warm my skin. The light breeze moving through the courtyard shifts my hair around my shoulders and keeps me from overheating in the thick Louisiana humidity.

I could stay out here forever reading my book and enjoying the sun.

Sitting with my feet crossed underneath me on the picnic blanket Della had found in a linen closet, I read the final page of my book.

Reading the ending is always a bittersweet moment. Part of you wishes that the story would continue forever so you can continue to escape into the world within the pages, but the other part of you longs for the characters to get their happy ending.

And as we know, happily ever afters are often only found in the pages of fairy tales.

My heart sinks when my eyes drag over those two final words. The end.

Unsure of how to feel about the ending, I slowly close the book, my mind replaying that final scene repeatedly in my head.

"So?" a voice asks. "What was their ending like? Did they get everything they deserve?"

Shielding my eyes from the sun, I look up into the face that instantly brings me so much comfort. Like always, his gold-framed glasses are as crooked as his infectious smile. Pondering his question for a moment, I answer, "I'm not sure. They seem content, but there's so many unanswered questions. Their story doesn't feel... finished."

Ira sits down on the blanket next to me. "The best stories are the ones that never end, my dear. Just because they're no longer the ones telling their story doesn't mean it's over. As long as someone is out there telling their tale, they'll live on forever." He opens the book I'd dropped and points to the last two words printed. "Those words mean nothing. They're just a stopping point in the journey. There will always be another chapter to add."

Resting my head on his shoulder, I close my eyes. "I will always tell your story, Ira."

"And because of you, I will continue to live on, Quin." Ira's wrinkled and sunspot-covered hand reaches for mine. His grip feels stronger than I remember it ever being. The look of pain I'm accustomed to seeing on his face is gone.

I gesture to the book beside me. "Are you content like them?" The last chapter in his story didn't end the way it was supposed to.

"I will be," Ira offers vaguely with a soft pat on my hand. He falls silent, and when I lift my head to check on him, I find him staring at the red roses that had been planted for him. "You'll take care of my roses, won't you?"

"Always."

In comfortable silence, we sit together on the picnic blanket, just enjoying the sun and the sweet scent of flowers. I don't know how long I sit with him before he turns and kisses me on the forehead. "He's here."

Confused, I tilt my head at him. "Who's here?"

Looking over my shoulder, Ira's smile grows. "It's not very often the sun and moon cross paths, but when they do, it's a sight to behold."

Following Ira's gaze, I see the silhouette in the open doorway of the house. Even though he's concealed in shadows, I would recognize his form anywhere. "Silas," I breathe, elation filling my chest. The joy I feel is short-lived when I'm reminded of the sun beating down on my skin. "What is he doing?"

Ira stands to his feet, and I quickly follow. Grabbing my face between his two hands, Ira places one last kiss on my forehead. "I believe he made you a promise. I always told you Silas was a man of his word." Turning on his heels, he begins to leave but pauses a couple feet away. Looking over his shoulder, he says, "The princesses in fairy tales have to fight for their happily ever afters, Quincey. Fight for yours."

I turn to check that Silas is still there, but when I look back to Ira, he's gone. I'm about to search for him when Silas's voice washes over me like a soothing balm.

"Mon Soleil."

I shiver at the nickname, every inch of my body growing warm. Incapable of ignoring it, all worry of Ira diminishes, and I find myself turning back to where Silas stands in the shadows. "Silas, what are you doing? The sun will burn you."

My heart skips a beat and icy cold fear dumps over me when Silas steps out from where he's concealed. The bright afternoon sun shines down over his perfect face. I hold my breath when he tilts his face up toward it, as if he's greeting an old friend.

When his face, too handsome for this world, breaks into a smile, the air I hold in my lungs is knocked out of me at the sight. I'm not sure I've ever seen something as beautiful as Silas basking in the sun.

Stunned in place, Silas closes the distance between us. Acting on their own accord, my hands reach out for him. Trembling fingers run over his perfect bone structure, the neatly trimmed facial hair brushing against my fingertips. "How is this possible?"

He ignores my question; instead, his hands gather mine up and he lifts them to his mouth. His deep midnight eyes hold me hostage as he places a kiss to the inside of my wrist, right where my pulse beats erratically. "Open your eyes, my love," he rasps against my skin.

"I don't understand." I can feel panic start to form in my chest. "What's happening?"

Dropping my hand, he reaches for my face. Thumbs soothe over my cheeks as he says, "You are so beautiful in the sunlight."

The courtyard disappears. Ira's roses melt away and the warmth of the sun turns frigid, my skin instantly breaking out in goose bumps. My heart longs to be back in the courtyard when I open my eyes and find myself still trapped in the freezing cold room.

My head and vision are still cloudy from the drugs Gideon had injected into my arm in his fit of anger. I'd begged him not to do it, the idea of being unconscious and vulnerable making me panic, but now I'm not convinced it wasn't the ideal option.

I would take the warm dreamland I'd escaped to over the coldness of this room any day. At least while I'm asleep, I'm blissfully unaware of the damaged state my body is in or that there is a ticking stopwatch on my life.

There wasn't any fear or dread, only peace. Right now, I'm longing for the peace I found in my dream.

Correction, I'm longing for the kind of comfort only Silas can provide me. I want to feel his lips on my wrists instead of the metal shackles that still dig into them. I want him to brush the tears I'm powerless to stop off my face and, most of all, I want to hear him say the nickname he's gifted me with once more.

Hearing him say it in the dream wasn't enough for me. If I am to die tonight, hearing him say my name once more is my final wish.

The cuts are just deep enough that they haven't fully scabbed over. Blood still trickles from them. Everything hurts. Each breath I pull into my lungs causes the cuts on my chest to strain. My skin has been painted crimson from all the spilled blood. The fabric of my bra is caked with so much blood, the fabric is glued to my skin. My mouth waters as I fight back the urge to throw up because of it.

I attempt to shift my body into a more comfortable position, but the options are slim given my chained limbs. It's only when I try to move my arms do I realize they're no longer positioned above my head, but instead they are now at my sides.

The remaining drug-induced fog clears from my head when I look down to find the needles embedded in my veins on either arm. Crimson tubing leads to the blood bags that are slowly being filled.

My stomach sinks at the sight of my body being depleted. Gideon was vocal about this being his plan from the start, but there was a small part of me still clinging to hope that all of this would be over before he got around to actually doing it.

I believed Silas would find me in time.

I attempt to lift my head to get a better look, but with each movement, the wounds on my chest strain and cause blinding agony to shoot through my body. Reluctantly, I drop my head back to the metal.

"What did you expect, Quincey? You told the knife-wielding maniac vampire that you have grade A blood," I hoarsely scold myself.

"You were right." Gideon's voice suddenly comes from the dark corner of the room. He moves toward me in a slow, lazy shuffle. "I've told our viewers just how scrumptious your blood truly is. They're all very eager to get their hands on it." He pats the camera with the glowing red light on it as he passes. "Sorry, we started without you. I tried to wake you, but that sedative seemed to have worked better than I expected." Coming to a stop by my head, he looks down at me with unblinking eyes. I feel like every time he enters this room, he's further gone. It's like he's grasping on to the remaining pieces of his sanity. "Did you sleep well? Pleasant dreams I hope."

When his finger swipes across my jaw, I turn my head and try to bite him, but he moves before I can sink my teeth into his digit. Tauntingly, he waves the same finger in my face while making a *tsking* noise.

"My dreams were great," I snap at him. "I dreamed that Silas set your body on fire and while you burned into nothing, I roasted a marshmallow like I was a goddamn Girl Scout."

"I'll give you points for creativity," he offers dryly while he checks the bags that are filling with my blood. "You'll only be able to fill six of these before your body begins to shut down and you'll lose consciousness. There simply won't be enough blood in your system for your heart to pump to your brain. The good news is it shouldn't be painful for you." Just like so many times before, his eyes drift to the corner he'd been standing in just a moment beforehand. "And then I'll be ready to reunite with her."

I stare at the corner, trying to figure out what it is he's seeing, but just like before, it's empty. "I'm sure she'll be thrilled to see you and catch up after all these years apart. Tell me, Gideon, are you going to start with this story—*our* story—or are you going to start somewhere a little less gruesome?"

"Margret already knows this story," he corrects me instantly. "We don't have secrets."

It doesn't go unnoticed that he's no longer using past tense when he talks about her. He's speaking of her like she's still here with him.

Eyes drifting back to the shadowed corner, the dots start clicking in my head. Returning to look at his haggard face, I play along. "Honesty is good to have in a relationship. Lies bring nothing but trouble in the long run."

If rotations in the psych ward during nursing school taught me anything, it's if you can't beat the crazy, join it. For some patients, it was better for us to play along with their delusions instead of arguing their existence.

As it is, I'm too tired to argue or verbally spar with him right now. The emotional exhaustion and the accumulating blood loss are starting to deplete my energy.

"I never kept secrets from her—I told her everything," he says, switching back to past tense like he himself can't keep what he's saying straight. "She accepted everything about me."

"Of course she did," I sigh. "She loved you. When you love someone, you accept everything about them, even the flaws they see in themselves."

I see all the sides of you, Silas. Some of them I enjoy more than others, but I accept all of them. That's what I'd told Silas when I'd learned his secret. He tried so hard to convince me to be afraid of his monster side, but I hadn't listened. Instead, I kissed him until he believed me.

Gideon's brows pull together. "Even knowing what he's done, you can still accept him?"

I'm saved from having to answer the question when loud, abrupt pounding at the metal door makes my body jerk in surprise. I just barely catch the startled sound from escaping my lips.

A low ominous snarl comes from Gideon before he moves to the door in a quick flash of movement. His pale fingers almost rip it off the tracks when he slides it harshly open. "I told you I didn't want you on this side of the building," he snarls at someone I can't make out from my angle.

A voice I don't recognize answers, "I know, but there's a problem."

Gideon silently stands there for a second before his head turns back in my direction with an accusatory look.

On reflex, I roll my eyes at him. "Well, don't look at me. I didn't do anything." I huff. "I've been otherwise occupied if you haven't noticed."

Without a word, Gideon stalks out of the room, closing the door behind him with just as much force as he opened it.

I don't know what's about to happen, but I can feel it in my gut that things are about to get ugly. There's a shift in the air that causes my heart rate to shoot up and fingers tremble with anxiety. In an attempt to still my shaking hands, I ball my fists, but the action causes pain in my injured wrists.

Closing my eyes, I force myself to remain calm, which is hard to accomplish when nothing about the past day has been calm. With slow, steady breaths, I think of my dream and the way Silas looked in the sunshine. If I focus hard enough, I swear I can smell the intoxicating cologne that always clings to his skin.

The calm is once again ripped away from me when the deafening sound blasts through the room. You watch explosions happen in movies or television shows all the time, but you never consider just how loud they are in real life.

The chains that hang across the ceiling above me clang as the building shakes from the loud boom. My body tenses up. With each beat of my heart, anxiety pushes its way through my veins while I wait for what's to happen next.

An eerie silence falls over the building, and for a moment, all I can pick up on is the sound of my blood rushing in my ears and the steady flow of cold air circulating through the room.

But then I hear them.

Just like when Silas's home was ambushed by Gideon's men, the air fills with the sound of gunshots. One after the other, they fill the air. They're not as loud as the explosion, the thick metal door of the room making them seem muffled, but I'd still recognize that sound anywhere.

It's the same sounds that filled me with dread and fear just a day ago, but now, they have the opposite effect on me. Instead, I'm filled with hope and triumph.

He's here, Ira had said in my dream. I thought he meant that Silas was in the courtyard with us, but now I think my subconscious was trying to tell me that he was *here*.

He found me.

The smile that breaks across my face is one I wouldn't be able to fight, even if I wanted to. Even Gideon barging into the room with a wild look in his eyes can't make my smile fall.

"*Uh-oh.*" I pretend to sound concerned. "Sounds like you're in trouble, Gideon."

Gideon's lips move as he mumbles something incoherent to himself. He charges for me, and instantly, I attempt to jerk away from him, but just like before, it's no use.

Without acknowledging me, he makes quick work of removing the needles and tubing from my arms. He doesn't bother to reach for the bags that have been filling with my blood—it's as if they don't serve a purpose for him anymore.

"You shouldn't let that blood go to waste," I taunt. "Have a sip before he comes for you. A last meal of sorts."

Again, he keeps his head down and he continues to talk to himself. I'm starting to think I'm witnessing the remaining pieces of his mind break. He already had nothing to lose when all of this started, but if his head is cracking like a fucking walnut, things are going to get interesting for everyone.

He moves to the end of the table at a speed I struggle to keep up with. Cold fingers make quick work of releasing my ankles from the shackles.

"What are you doing?" I question when he moves on to the ones locked around my tender wrists. When the metal is peeled away from my skin, the scabs that had adhered to it are torn away, causing the wounds to open again. I hiss out a breath when the blood begins to drip. "Are you giving up and letting me go because you know you've lost?"

That does it.

Gideon's eyes snap to mine. Trouble sits behind those orbs now. Shaking his head, he says, "I haven't lost yet, Quincey." Wrapping his hands around my biceps, he yanks me off the table. My knees give out and I almost fall to the ground when he puts me on my feet for the first time since I've been here. "Get up!" he yells. "We've got a date with the king."

Half holding me up and half dragging me, Gideon leads me out of the room that's been my prison and into the chaos that waits for us.

CHAPTER 11

Silas

Warm blood sprays across my face when the guard, who's chest my fist is currently buried in, violently coughs. His eyes are so wide, I'm surprised they haven't fallen from his skull. More blood drips from his gaping mouth as I rip my arm from his body. He falls to the ground next to the other guard I'd ripped apart just seconds prior.

The black shirt I wear is soaked through with blood, the fabric sticking to my skin, but I don't mind getting my hands dirty right now.

Each person who dies by my hand tonight is a victory. I don't care that these guards are just doing the job they were hired to do. They're attempting to keep me from my woman and that is reason enough for them to die.

Twenty of my own guards have been brought in from all over North and South America. It's amazing what can be done in a short amount of time when you have more money than God. A few strings were pulled, and multiple wire transfers were made, and just like that, I had a small army at my disposal before the sun set.

While Lorcan and Rory had slept on and off all day long, I'd paced the confines of the safe house. I felt each agonizing second pass by as I waited for everything to come together. With the live feed disconnected, it had been unbearable to not see what was happening to Quincey all those hours. My mind had come up with each worst-case scenario and by the time the alarm on Rory's computer went off, I was once again prepared to walk out the door into the daylight to find her.

When the footage appeared again and I was able to confirm that Quincey was still alive, the uncontrollable beast inside of me settled and my rationality returned. She was pale and covered in dried blood, but she was breathing, and for the rest of my days, that's all I will care about.

As long as Quincey Page's heart continues to beat for the both of us, the world can burn for all I care. Nothing else matters.

A man screams in agony off to my side. Turning my head, I find Lorcan burying his fangs deep into his jugular. Fighting—*killing*—is what Lor lives for. It was what he excelled at as a human, and as a vampire, he's perfected the skill.

On the two hour long drive here, Lorcan had bounced in his seat like a child on his way to Disney World. A few times, I considered kicking him out of the vehicle and telling him to meet us at the meat packing plant where Gideon is holed up.

The plant hasn't been used for those purposes in a long time, but someone has been paying to keep the utilities on. I would bet a large sum of money that this property is owned by one of the many shell companies Gideon operates. If Rory were willing to do more research on the matter for me, I'm sure she'd uncover it, but the hacker was true to her word and so was I.

As soon as the address for the industrial building came up on her screen, the purple-haired human was running to the exit before I had a chance to thank her. She'd walked out the cheery yellow front door with her middle finger raised at Lorcan before disappearing into the night.

A gun goes off too close for comfort, making my eardrums ring. A millisecond later, my temple burns as the bullet grazes my skin. With a deadly growl, I turn on the shooter. The triumphant look they had been wearing vanishes the second I'm wrapping my hand around their throat.

"You missed," I snarl before I crush their windpipe with my hand. They fall to their knees, lips turning blue as they attempt to pull air into their lungs, but it's no use. It's a function their body is no longer capable of. I don't stick around to watch them slowly suffocate. Instead, I push them to the concrete and step over their suffering form.

Another guard rushes at me, pistol raised. The bullets rip through my chest and torso, but they don't slow me down. So long as my head remains on my body, I cannot be killed. I move toward him and rip the gun from his hands. Before he has a chance to reach for the other one strapped to his thigh, I've positioned myself behind him. Kicking his legs out from under him, he falls to his knees, and I twist his arm so violently it rips from his body. The sound of his screams is sweet music to my ears.

Letting him go, he reaches for the place his arm should be with his remaining good hand. I'm not sure if it's the shock or the pain of what's happened but his eyes roll back in his head as he loses consciousness.

Without a care, dismembered arm still in hand, I walk away from him and stalk toward the building Quincey's being kept in. My men had been smart by setting off the explosive. It drew out all of Gideon's men and one by one we're taking them out, clearing a path to her.

Out of the corner of my eye, I see one of Gideon's men huddled behind some discarded crates. A large rifle sits pressed to his shoulder. I'm in front of the barrel, blocking his view through the scope before he can pull the trigger.

He's just lifted his head when I swing the severed arm still in my grasp at his skull. I slam it into his face with such force, I hear bones break. Whether it's from the arm or the man's face, I'll never know. And frankly, I don't care. His head whips back and before he can recover, I'm dropping the arm and grabbing his face in my hand. With a flick of my wrist, I snap his neck.

Lorcan appears at my side, a shit-eating grin on his face. "Did you just use a severed arm like a baseball bat on that guy's head?"

Wiping my bloody hands on my pants, I shrug.

"That's fucking brilliant. I'm a little jealous I've never done that before."

I gesture at guards that are still alive. "There're plenty of arms still out here. Pick one and have fucking at it." Lor keeps pace with me as I continue to walk toward the building.

His sable gaze looks around at all the candidates before swinging back in my direction. "This is my Christmas." With that, he takes off back into the fray. Less than five seconds later, a scream splits through the air, letting me know he's found his victim.

Continuing toward the dark building, my body hums with anticipation. Like an addict who hasn't gotten their fix, my body craves to have her near again.

When the soft footfalls come from behind me, I don't slow down or turn around yet. These guards have no idea who they're up against or that no matter how quiet they try to be, they'll never be able to sneak up on me. I wait until they're just close enough before whirling around. They lift the gun in their hand, intending to shoot me in the face, but before they can so much as blink, I've taken the weapon from them and tossed it aside.

My lips pull back in a snarl and my fangs drop. "Now what are you going to do?" I taunt.

Frantically, he pulls the knife from his tactical belt. His hand shakes when he thrusts it toward me. Laughing, a noise that sounds cruel even to my ears, I take the knife with the same ease I took the gun. "You never stood a chance," I mutter before thrusting the knife through his eye and into his brain

I'm just about to pull the blade from his skull when the scent washes over me. It's faint and blending with the scent of all the spilled blood out here, but it still hits me like a semitruck. My muscles lock and my chest seizes as my head snaps in the direction of the building.

"Lorcan!" I manage to call out. I release the knife hilt, completely forgetting what I had been doing just seconds prior. Glancing around the dwindling battle, I find him standing in the middle of a handful of recently fallen men, with a severed arm in his hand. Blood is sprayed across his face and when he laughs manically, his white teeth are coated red.

He looks like the very thing people have feared and written stories of for centuries.

In a second, Lor is at my side. He uses the back of his hand to wipe the blood from his chin and mouth. He's just about to drop his hand when his body goes stiff and his head snaps up, nose flaring. "What is *that*?"

The possessiveness inside of me doesn't want to admit it, but he needs to know. "Quincey's blood," I grit out between clenched teeth. "She's close."

I wasn't naive enough to believe the sweet scent of Quincey's blood would only affect me, but I had made it my mission that no one else would ever find out. It was my *job* to ensure she was never injured—that her blood was *never* spilled.

Looking between the building and me, his pupils dilated, Lor says, "Well fuck, now I get why you like her so much." He makes no effort to hide the greedy inhales he takes of the air. "If I had a woman that smelled like that, I'd never let her leave my bedroom. I'd be fucking and feeding all day long."

Without warning, my fist darts out and connects with his sternum. Grunting, he doubles over but instead of making sounds indicating he's been hurt, he simply laughs.

"Go through the back. I'll go through the front. If you find her before I do, do whatever it takes to ensure she makes it out of this building alive." Lor nods his head in understanding before starting to walk away. He only gets five feet before I'm calling out to him one more time. "And Lor? I'm trusting you to stay in control when you're around her. Keep your fangs to yourself."

His eyes roll in his head. "Contrary to popular belief, I have excellent control. Have you ever heard the term organized chaos? That's what I am." He takes off before either one of us can say anything else.

I know that Lorcan has mastered his control. If I didn't, I never would have asked him to come assist me. The problem now is there isn't a single fiber of my being that trusts Quincey's life in anyone's hands but my own. The past twenty-four hours have broken something in me.

The front doors are unlocked and open without protest. With my senses on high alert, I move through the dark building. Compared to the gunshots and fighting outside, it's shockingly quiet within these walls.

Or it would be if there weren't two heartbeats beating wildly just behind the next set of double doors.

This is the problem with hiring humans to fight vampires; the humans will never have the advantage of surprise. We can always sense when they're close.

Smirking silently to myself, I grab a nearby abandoned cart. Giving it a harsh shove, it bangs through the stained double doors. Almost instantly, the room it has rolled into lights up with bright flashes as two automatic guns go off.

I move to stand by the doorjamb, concealing myself until my next victims make their appearance.

I'm so close to where she is, and every instinct is telling me to charge in aimlessly and find her. It takes a great deal of restraint to continue thinking strategically—a feat that is getting more difficult the closer I am to her. The scent of her blood is so heavy in the air that I can taste it on my tongue.

Two guards barge out of the doors, large guns raised and ready.

They move as a team, completely in sync with each other. It's obvious each of them is skilled at their job and it's truly a shame that such talent will go to waste now.

One second, I'm standing behind the swinging door they'd just kicked open, and the next I'm slamming one to the ground. Their weapon skids across the ground as my hand circles around the second guard's throat. With ease, I lift him into the air.

His gloved hands drop his gun so he can claw at his neck, trying to free himself, but my grip doesn't waver. His face grows redder with each passing second.

In my peripheral vision, the first guard attempts to crawl on his stomach toward his discarded gun. His fingers just brush against the hilt when my foot presses into his skull. "I wouldn't do that if I were you," I warn him, momentarily ignoring the man I'm still strangling.

"Rot in hell," the guard spits back as his hand darts for the gun once more.

"Didn't you hear?" I ask, my head cocking to the side. "I'm afraid I'm the king there as well." With that, I press the sole of my Italian leather shoe into his head harder. Slowly, I increase pressure until he screams in agony and his skull begins to crack. I don't stop until the red soles of my shoes are stained with blood.

The man I hold up makes a wheezing sound in his throat when he watches his coworker's brain matter leak onto the concrete floor.

"I suggested he stop. He chose to not listen," I explain simply before, without any remorse, I throw the man at the nearby wall. The sound of his spine breaking follows behind me as I march through the now clear double doors.

Not bothering to be quiet, I allow the doors to bang against the walls. The sound echoes through the silent cavern of the building. I don't want to sneak up on Gideon. No, I want him to know I'm coming for him. I want him to feel the same fear he's made Quinccy feel.

"Are you hiding from me, Gideon?" I call to him; my tone has a deadly edge to it. It's one that holds the promise of my wrath. "You made a spectacle out of all of this because you wanted everyone to remember your face, but yet you hide it from me now?"

I'm met with more silence, which only feeds my anger.

"Get out here and face me, you fucking coward!" My roar bounces off the walls and travels down the dark corridors.

The only source of light comes from the open windows at the top story. The moonlight casts shadows on the equipment that has sat unused for years. There's a thick layer of dust on everything that isn't covered with torn plastic sheets.

"A *coward?*" His voice cuts through the quiet air, making my steps come to a halt. "I am anything but a *coward*. A *coward* never would have dared go against you." Movement from the upper floors of the building catches my attention.

With narrowed eyes, I search the walkways that connect the different sides of the buildings like suspended bridges. The rusted metal creaks under his weight when he walks out of the darkness and into the moonlit walkway.

A low growl forms in my chest and my limbs begin to vibrate with a mixture of adrenaline and fury. My fingers, already stained with blood, twitch at my sides, yearning to rip into his flesh.

Gideon reaches into the darkness for something that is still concealed from my view. "If I was a coward, could I have done the things I've done to *her?*" With a rough yank, he drags Quincey onto the walkway with him.

Two emotions fight inside of me like two violent opposing forces when I finally lay my eyes on her. The relief is like ice water being poured over the uncontrollable flames that have burned bright since she was taken from me. But in the same breath, seeing her only makes my anger grow.

I thought I was prepared to see her in the state he's left her in. I foolishly believed that the footage was an accurate enough depiction of the damage he'd caused, but I was wrong. Seeing with my own eyes the way he's carved into her like a butcher and depleted her of the joyous light that usually shines beneath her skin makes the darkness in my soul only grow.

It settles in me like a heavy fog and makes everything else melt away but them.

She stumbles forward from the force in which he pulls on her weak form. My silent heart drops in my chest and I instinctually take a step forward, prepared to catch her if she were to stagger too far.

Quincey's hands catch the rust-covered railing in time to halt her momentum, but I still don't relax.

"What do you think of my masterpiece?" Gideon asks, sounding proud of himself. "We think she looks beautiful." What does he mean by *we?*

Something inside of me splinters when Quincey's blue eyes lock with mine. They could bring me to my knees right now if I'd let them. Her split lips part like she's going to say something, but she never gets the chance. She cries out instead when Gideon's hand wraps around her tangled and blood-stained hair.

He drags her backward until her back meets his chest. Smiling gleefully down at me, Gideon forces her head back, exposing her delicate throat. "You took Margret's head from her shoulders. Should I do the same to Quincey?"

With a snarl, I take a menacing step forward, but he's quick to shake his head at me. "I wouldn't come any closer if I were you, Silas." Gideon trails a finger down Quincey's face, a gentle gesture that makes me feel homicidal. "So angelic..." he purrs into her ear. "Do you want to see if she can fly like one too?"

"Silas," Quincey cries to me. She's been so brave, but it's becoming very clear to me by the way her voice breaks that she's exhausted all her strength. My sweet sun has nothing left to give. "Please."

She once begged me to let her go, to spare her life, but now she's begging me to save it.

"Now you call for him?" Gideon chuckles hatefully. "A shame you couldn't have done that when the cameras were rolling." He moves them forward until her bare stomach is pressed into the railing.

Each movement he forces her to make causes her pain. She whimpers and her bottom lip has begun to tremor as if she's fighting back tears.

Wanting his attention off her, I call to him. "Gideon, if you don't let her go, there aren't accurate enough words to describe what I will do to you." His gift of immortality will turn into a curse. For the rest of his infinite days, he will spend them in agony because of me. Each day I will make him regret the day he laid a single finger on Quincey.

His dark eyes glance down at me and with a curious cock of his head, he ignores my threat and asks, "Do you regret it now?" When I don't answer his question, he elaborates. "Do you regret taking her from me now that you know what it feels like to have the very reason you exist taken from you?"

While he talks, he squeezes Quincey tighter, making her cry out. The crazed monster inside of me beats against the cage I keep him in, desperate to get to her. If I thought I could get up there before he dropped her over the ledge, I would be sprinting to her. I'm fast, but not that fast.

I've never been one to offer false niceties, and I'm not about to start now. "No, I don't regret taking her from you," I tell him honestly. "I would do it once more without a moment of hesitation if you were to force my hand *again*. After all these years, you still haven't accepted the role you played in her death, Gideon."

He remains quiet for an excruciating long minute before he sighs, "Unfortunately, that was exactly the answer I expected you to give." He shakes his head like a parent who's disappointed in their child. "I have one more question for you, Silas."

"And what's that?" I bite out. My insides feel like a rubber band being stretched too far. It's going to snap, and all hell will break loose with it.

"What do you want more? To see me dead or to save Quincey? I think I know the answer to this one, but the unfortunate thing is you can only choose one. If you save her, I'll be long gone, but if you come after me..." Gideon trails off, glancing over the ledge he stands on. "Well, let's just say I don't think she'll be as pretty once she hits the concrete." Grinning at me, he continues, "I'll give you till three to decide."

Quincey cries out as he shoves her front half over the ledge. His fingers still intertwined with her hair are the only thing that keeps her in place.

"One..."

I stay silent and still, my face devoid of all emotion, a task that is exponentially hard now, but I'm not about to show him my cards just yet. For the first time since he reappeared in my life, I'm once more five steps ahead of him. Just like it should be.

"Two..."

Tears fall from Quincey's eyes. They fall three stories and land just feet in front of me, indicating the place her body will land. "*Silas,*" her cry for me makes my chest ache, the hollow place where my heart should beat, constricting.

"Three..."

And then he lets her go.

CHAPTER 12

Quincey

"*Are you going to catch me?*"
"*Always.*"

He made me that promise like he was making a vow and I believed him with every fiber of my being. There wasn't a single hint of doubt in my soul that Silas would *always* be there. That single word etched itself into my heart that night like a scar, a permanent reminder of his oath. An oath that carries so much more weight when his *always* is infinite.

He promised this to me when I told him I was falling for him, it never once occurred to me when he said it that one day, he would have to literally watch me fall before him.

When the man you've fallen for is a vampire, you believe nothing else can take you by surprise. Up until this point, I figured I was numb to both shock and surprise, but when I'm sent hurdling over the paint chipped railing, I feel both of those emotions with such force, the air is sucked out of me.

My mouth opens, but the trapped air in my lungs prohibits me from screaming. My mind knows there's no point in attempting to grab onto something to halt my descent, but my arms haven't quite caught up. They thrash at my sides, desperate to find something that might save me, but unfortunately the only thing that's in my path is the stained concrete floors three stories below.

Which is a sight I have absolutely no interest in watching barrel closer to me. With my eyes squeezed shut, I crash through the air. I know I'm falling at a much faster speed than my mind is leading me to believe, but the second my bare feet left the walkway, time slowed down to a crawl.

The three seconds it takes me to fall feels like an eternity. I keep waiting for the impact to come. From that height, I know I won't die on impact, which means I will feel every excruciating second as my fragile body breaks.

The pain never comes because when he said always, he meant it.

The first time I touched Silas and his arms wrapped around me, trapping me to his body, I felt nothing but all-consuming fear. It was the same kind of fear I felt when I woke up chained to the table. It's the kind of fear that makes your entire body shake and your heart pound against your rib cage so violently, you're almost sure the organ bruises.

But it's different now.

Despite the disorientation from the fall, the second his arms wrap around my body and I'm brought against his chest, the dread and panic are washed away. I'm met with nothing but peace. And *safety*.

Feeling his arms around me feels like coming home.

For a very long time, the idea of 'home' didn't bring happy thoughts. It made me think of the broken place I grew up and the damaged people who raised me. There were rarely happy memories made there. Even when I moved to Boston, the apartment I lived in was just a place I rested my head.

But now I know why none of those places ever felt right.

They weren't *him*.

Silas is my home.

The impact of my body colliding with his finally dislodges the trapped air in my lungs and I greedily breathe in air that smells of him, further soothing the fear inside of me.

Every time I so much as flinch, everything hurts, but I'll gladly take the pain right now. My arms move on their own accord, snaking around his neck in a hold that should be too tight for anyone to find comfortable, but I don't care.

I've yet to open my eyes to look at him. Just feeling him is enough right now.

He must feel the same way because he tightens his grip on my shaking body and brings me closer. It's as if we're both trying to settle the chaos of emotions inside of us by getting as close to each other as we can, but it still doesn't feel like it's enough. The thin fabric of his shirt even feels like it's creating too much space.

With a shuddering breath, I drop my head to his shoulder in a mixture of relief and overwhelming exhaustion.

My heart skips a beat when his lips skim across my temple. "*Mon Soleil.*" Silas says my name like it's a prayer. He speaks so quietly that if I wasn't so close to him, I would have missed it.

It doesn't matter the circumstances or how bad things appear, hearing him say those words will always bring a smile to my face. My lips lift, causing the split in them to pull, but it's okay because this is exactly what I needed to hear. Hearing the name he's given me is the last thing I needed to confirm that he's truly here with me.

Needing to see him, I lift my head from his shoulder. The expression that is written across his face makes me feel like I've been sucker punched in the stomach. I should probably be more alarmed by the blood that's sprayed across his handsome face, but that hardly holds my attention.

Silas is skilled at many things but keeping his face bland and emotionless is something he excels at. Right now, he's failing at it, allowing me to experience each of the emotions with him as they appear on his face. Those midnight eyes of his that I'm obsessed with are filled with an unimaginable amount of pain as he looks down at me.

There are a million different words that I could string together right now that could help soothe him, but what comes out of my mouth is, "So, I'm going to need a rain check on our date. Something else came up that I couldn't say no to."

His eyes widen like he's caught off guard by my words, but slowly, I watch as the harsh lines of his troubled face lessen. Releasing a long breath, he drops his forehead to mine.

"Thank you for keeping your promise," I whisper, my throat suddenly tight as emotion clogs it. I don't want to cry. Not here. This place has taken enough out of me already. I'm not willing to leave any more of myself in this building.

Silas shifts my weight so he can hold the side of my face. He gently lifts my head, encouraging me to look into his dark eyes. "For lifetimes, I've lived without you, but I have no interest in ever doing so again." His fingers thread into my tangled hair. "There was nothing that could have kept me from you. In this life or the next, I would have found you again, Quincey."

Silas's words are like a pain reliever. They wash over me, taking the sting of my wounds with them. Who am I kidding? I don't need his pretty words and sweet anecdotes. I just need him with me. And I *really* need him to take me away from here.

"I don't want to be here anymore. Can we go home now?" My voice cracks despite how hard I'm trying to keep it together. "Please, just take me home." The house I once viewed as my prison is the only place I want to be right now.

He soothes his thumb over my face. I haven't seen a reflection of myself, but if I look as bad as I feel, I'm sure I'm quite the sight to behold right now. All I want to do is cleanse my skin of this horror show and sleep. I want to sleep for a week and allow my head to be filled with sweet dreams like the one I had of Ira.

"You've been so strong. We are almost done here, my love. Just stay with me a moment longer," he encourages. "We just have to take care of one more thing." His face sharpens at the last line. He doesn't have to elaborate any further—I know who he's talking about.

Tilting my head back, I peer up at the walkway I fell from. The man who will be the star of all my nightmares moving forward is nowhere to be found. "Where did he go? He said if you chose me, you'd lose your chance at catching him." Panic builds in my chest, the unhinged look in Gideon's eyes replaying in my mind. "Silas, we can't let him go. It's not safe for anyone if he's free—"

Silas hushes me gently, cutting me off. He opens his mouth to say something else, but he stops and his head whips in the direction of what I assume is the back exit. "Don't worry, we found him."

A door opens and quickly slams shut somewhere in the building. The all too familiar clicking of chains follows close behind, along with a dragging sound. A low voice I can't quite make out bounces off the concrete and metal walls.

The plastic that covers one of the doorways is harshly torn away and the silhouette of a tall man appears. At first, I think it's Duke, but the man is a few inches taller than him. Unsure of who it is, my muscles tighten in preparation to flee if I need to. I've never been skittish of strangers, but after my last day, I'm craving familiar faces.

Sensing my alarm, Silas soothes his hand down my arm, but his eyes remain locked on the man approaching. Silas doesn't seem worried about the stranger's presence, and I use that knowledge to force myself to relax. One thing I will never doubt is Silas's judgment of others—especially the people that inhabit his world. It's a world I'm new to and I've yet to meet all the players.

"Do you have any idea how far I had to run after this fucking freak?" A thick Irish accent fills the heavy air. "I fucking hate cardio."

The sound of chains comes again when he drags something through the door behind him. "I stepped in a puddle full of mud; my shoes are absolutely trashed. Don't think I won't be adding that to your bill, Laurent."

The stranger finally steps out into the light. I thought Silas had a lot of blood on him, but this man looks like he bathed in it. The strands of his messy blond—almost brown—hair are caked with it. Smears cover his face like he halfheartedly tried to wipe it off but gave up quickly. His white T-shirt is splattered in so much blood it's like a gruesome tie-dye project. The tattoos on his arm and neck are barely visible because of his skin being painted crimson.

"And he had to make things difficult by refusing to walk himself—like a *toddler*. I had to drag his arse all the way back here." With a final tug of the chain in his hand, he pulls Gideon's bound body across the threshold of the doorframe.

Silas stiffens at the sight of his foe, but he doesn't make a move toward him.

Gideon's hands have been chained to his ankles behind his back. His face has been badly beaten, but he's still conscious. His dark gaze darts around the empty room like he's looking for something, but when he comes up empty, he glances in our direction.

"You brought a friend, Silas. I'll admit I didn't see that one coming." Gideon chuckles to himself like he finds it truly comical. The sound still sounds so forced and unnatural to my ears. "Here I thought all the people in your life who liked you enough to help you were currently indisposed."

The Irishman's face crinkles. "*Like* is a strong word." He shoves Gideon's body with his foot, forcing him farther into the room. "And whether I was here or not, he would have found a way to get his hands on you. One would think you'd know that already since you've been plotting your revenge for a century, but then again, you really aren't the sharpest tool in the shed, are you now, Gideon?"

Gideon's wild eyes clash with mine like I'm the one who insulted him. His lips lift in a snarl, the tips of his fangs exposed. It's the same look he had when he took the knife to my chest, and it instantly makes my stomach drop.

Before I'm able to open my mouth to give a warning, a roar escapes from Gideon and the chains that have been wrapped around his body snap. In a flash of chaotic movement, he's on his feet and barreling toward us.

Everything happens so fast, my exhausted brain struggles to keep up with it. One second, I'm in Silas's arms and the next I've been placed on my unsteady feet. In the time it takes me to inhale my next breath, Silas is colliding with Gideon. Silas's hand grabs onto the other vampire's face and with a movement that looks effortless, he brings the psychotic vampire to the ground.

The back of Gideon's head hits the floor first, followed by the rest of his body. My own bones shake from the collision. The concrete breaks underneath Gideon, and cracks spread out across the flooring in a way that reminds me of a spider's web.

I've seen my fair share of human fights but watching two vampires with their enhanced speed and strength fight is something else entirely. My simple human eyes struggled to keep up with their quick movements. Each blow they take to their bodies makes the entire building rattle. I find myself holding my breath as I'm helpless to watch.

Gideon's foot swipes out, kicking Silas's legs out from under him. Silas appears hardly bothered by the attack. He's back on his feet within a second, but still, I'm worried for him.

Without thinking, I take a step toward the feuding vampires as if I could step in and help Silas. My bare foot just leaves the concrete floor before the tattooed vampire is suddenly standing in front of me, blocking my way. "That doesn't seem like the wisest decision, now does it?"

Unsure of who he is exactly, I retreat back from him. "Someone should help Silas," I argue.

The blond man's head tilts back as he laughs. "*Help him*? Darling, Silas doesn't need help, nor does he *want* help. He's been *craving* this fight since the second you were taken from him. So, we'll let him have his moment." He pauses, his light-brown eyes with flecks of gold appraise my bloody and almost bare form with keen interest. "It's truly adorable you think you can help though. I've seen how much fight you've got in that tiny body of yours, but unfortunately it isn't going to cut it right now." My skin crawls at his admission. The very fact that this mysterious man just confirmed that many other strangers watched the footage of my time here. "A brave little thing indeed."

The fighting stops for a second, the sound of metal scraping across the ground fills the sudden silence. Looking around the Irishman's body, I find Silas using the discarded chain to lash Gideon's body. Each aggressive blow and grunt of pain makes me cringe inside. The tattooed man in front of me, however, doesn't look fazed in the slightest.

Pushing down the unease, I question him, "Who the hell are you?"

"Ah yes, I forgot that we haven't been formally introduced. We've been discussing nothing but you for twenty-four hours. At this point I feel like I know you so well we could be long-lost friends." His perfect white teeth show as he grins at me. "I guess it's only fair I introduce myself. My name is Lorcan, but friends like you can call me Lor."

"I'm not your friend," I remind him immediately.

A cocky grin splits his face. "I suppose we aren't yet, but it's only a matter of time before we are. Besides, officially I'm not Silas's friend either, but he still calls me Lor. Has since I first met him many, *many* years ago."

I should feel more cautious of him, given my latest experience with a vampire that wasn't Silas, but I don't. Even with the alarming amount of blood that coats him, the longer I stand in front of him, the more comfortable I become in his presence.

"Silas doesn't really have friends," I remark as the ache in my chest begins to intensify. The adrenaline from falling and reuniting with Silas is starting to evaporate and the relief it was providing me is leaving with it. I know touching an open wound is never wise, but my shaky hands reach up on their own accord. The second my fingertips touch the torn skin, my stomach rolls and a rushing sound starts in my ears. Looking down at my hand with now fuzzy vision, I find my fingers coated red. I swallow hard, forcing the nausea to stay down before I find the strength to utter, "I think I'm going to pass out."

The sentence isn't fully out of my mouth before my knees buckle and I feel myself falling for the second time tonight. This time, hands catch me under my arms, and I'm lifted back up.

"Falling for me already, Quincey? I won't tell Silas if you don't," he speaks, but his words hardly make sense to me. Lorcan lifts me up and begins to carry me away. I'm suddenly too exhausted to argue with him, and I have no choice but to allow it to happen. Over his shoulder, I watch as Silas, a long metal pole in hand, stalks toward Gideon, who lies on his stomach on the ground.

I blink, trying to keep my vision clear and the darkness that threatens to overtake me at bay. With his fangs bared and midnight eyes full of fury, Silas lifts the pole up above his head before piercing it through Gideon's middle. From here, I can tell it went all the way through the villainous vampire and into the flooring, effectively impaling him in place. I know I should be feeling something about what I just witnessed, but I've suddenly grown numb—I'm too tired to feel anything.

I'm placed gently down onto a stack of empty crates. My body lurches forward, depleted of all strength, but once again, hands are there to keep me upright.

"Silas, stop toying with him and get on with it already," Lorcan hollers, but his voice sounds funny. Like he's yelling through a tunnel. "Your girl is fading fast. She needs a doctor."

My eyes close for only a second before hands are holding either side of my face. I attempt to jerk my head away from the unwanted touch, thinking it's the Irish vampire, but when lips press to my forehead and I hear, "It's okay, my love. I have you now." I relax and lean into Silas's touch.

I feel myself being lifted off the crates before I'm once more cradled in his arms. "He doesn't get to die here," Silas speaks darkly, his chest vibrating. "It's too easy. I want him taken to the church. I'll deal with him there." *The church?*

"You got it," Lor responds, sounding farther and farther away by the second.

"I'm going to pass out," I cut in with a slur, feeling the need to warn Silas so he's not alarmed. He's felt enough of that over the past day. He shouldn't be forced to feel it anymore. Even in this state, I want to do what I can to alleviate his worry.

"I know. It's okay," he promises. "You're safe now. I'm not going anywhere. You can close your eyes, *Mon Soleil.*"

CHAPTER 13

I'm first aware of the murmuring voices all around me, then the hands that touch my broken skin. They prod at my chest and then at my inner arm. My eyes are heavy and I'm too tired to brush away the hands, but when the familiar prick of a needle diving into my vein comes, the exhaustion leaves me and my fight-or-flight response kicks in.

It was just a dream, Quincey. Silas didn't find you and save you from Gideon. He's still trying to drain you of your blood, the small voice in my head whispers darkly as I'm filled with a sudden and unmeasurable amount of adrenaline.

My eyes snap open and instantly collide with an unfamiliar pair of green ones.

Another unfamiliar face... I just want to see his face.

Someone says something off to my right, but I can't hear them through the rushing in my ears. I'm too fixated on the stranger standing in front of me, I can't turn my head to follow the sound either.

Hands wrap tightly around my forearm when I attempt to yank my limb away from the needle. A distraught sound I barely recognize comes from my lips as I pull harder away from the grasp. This time I'm successful, but I don't sit still long enough to examine my surroundings.

My only goal is getting out of this room. I can't be in here anymore. I don't want to die in here alone while each drop of my blood is taken from me.

The adrenaline shoots to my legs and I swing them off the side of the surface I lie on. I've just barely pulled myself into a sitting position when hands come down on my shoulders and I'm forcibly pulled back down.

Desperation takes over as more hands come down on my body. My arms flail about and I kick my legs out at the person who's trying to pin me down again.

I'm vaguely aware of the hot tears and the burn in my throat as I continue to scream. I tried so fucking hard to keep it together and remain strong, but I can't anymore. The cinder block walls made of false bravery have broken and there's nothing holding back the fear anymore.

"Quincey," a voice calls out to me, but I can barely hear it over my own yelling.

"Don't touch me!" I plead in a hoarse scream. "Just let me go! Please let me go. I don't want to be here anymore."

Hands lock down around my wrists, trapping them at my sides just like the metal cuffs Gideon used on me. I ignore the pain that comes from my sore body as I try once more to gain my freedom.

Faces come into view in the chaos, but I'm not really seeing them. They're just blurs in my tear-filled eyes. I have no idea who hovers above me, and I don't care. They're attempting to trap me and that instantly makes them my enemy in my book.

It's like there's a boulder sitting on my chest and the breaths between my screams are becoming more constricted and labored. The air I inhale isn't reaching my lungs, but instead gets trapped in my throat.

"I can't breathe," I sob. "Please let me go, I can't breathe."

My chest heaves, and my body begins to shake as the panic rushes through my veins.

"I need to sedate her," someone shouts out, but I can't locate the owner of the voice.

My head thrashes side to side, but hands grab my face in a gentle but firm hold, halting my erratic movements. "Quincey," he says, his smooth voice cuts through the deafening sound in my ears. "You're safe. I'm here with you."

He's not here, it's just another dream.

"No, you're not. It's a lie. Let go of me!" I cry out while trying to shake my head from the grip on my face. "Stop touching me. I don't want to be touched anymore."

The hand stays on my face while his voice booms through the room. "Stop touching her!"

"But..." someone argues.

"If you don't remove your fucking hands from her, I will feed them to you. I won't ask again, do it now!"

The second the various sets of hands are gone, I'm flying up, but before I can throw my body off the bed, arms wrap around me. I cry and fight against them, but they're too strong and don't budge an inch. "Please," I sob. "I want to go home."

"You're home, Quincey." I make out his voice again. This time, it sounds closer. It sounds *real*. "Open your eyes and look at me." I hadn't realized I'd closed them. "Look at me. Open those beautiful blue eyes of yours and look at me. I'm right here."

I lock on the voice and force it to soothe the turbulent fear racking my body. "*Please...*" I don't know what I'm begging for when I say that word, but it's the only thing I can choke out.

His head drops against mine and he gathers me closer to his chest. "Breathe for me, *Mon Soleil*. You have to breathe. I *need* you to breathe."

I flinch when his hand soothes down my back, but it takes only a second for the unease to morph into comfort. In slow movements, he trails his hand down my spine and after a moment of silence and peace, I'm finally able to suck in a shuddering breath.

"Good girl," he praises softly. "Again. Breathe for me one more time, Quincey."

One more time.

My hands grip the fabric of his shirt as I force myself to bring more air into my lungs. Eyes still squeezed shut, we repeat this until the buzzing in my ears vanishes and the pressure in my chest fades.

Despite all the things I've been put through over the years, I've never experienced a panic attack before, but it seems there's a first for everything. And I'm here to put on record that it fucking sucks.

Not until my heart returns to a normal beat do I pry my eyes open. A large part of me thinks I'll still be locked in the ominous room with the red lights, but I'm proved wrong when I'm met with the warm light of a bedside lamp. A very familiar lamp.

My eyes dart around the room—a room I hated when I first arrived here, but now I'm so thankful to be back inside it. Everything is where I left it and that fills me with an immense amount of comfort. The makeup I'd carefully applied for my date with Silas is still littered across the dresser across the room. The shoe box that contained the new shoes Della had purchased for the occasion still sits open, tissue paper falling out the sides. The towel I'd forgotten to hang up is lying in the middle of the room on the hardwood floor.

Normal. Everything looks normal. The only thing that appears out of place are the two strangers standing beside my bed with worried looks on their faces. Both wear scrubs and their hands are covered in sterile gloves.

Closing my eyes again, I bury my head in his shoulder. "*Silas*," I breathe out, my voice raspy from the screaming.

"I'm right here," he assures me softly. "I'm right here with you,

Quincey. You're home and you're safe. No one can hurt you here—no one will *ever* hurt you again."

Even though I believe every word he says, tears fall down my face, dripping into the fabric of the blood-stained shirt he still wears. "Who are they?" I ask.

"They're here to tend to your wounds," Silas explains. "The... cuts." I swear it sounds like he chokes on the word. "They require stitches."

On its own accord, my head begins to shake back and forth. "No, I don't want anyone else to touch me. Please, no more," I beg him. Anyone's touch but his sounds repulsive. Silas is the only one I trust to not hurt me right now.

"The knife wounds are too deep to heal correctly on their own, Miss Page," one of them tries to reason. "The stitches will help keep the scarring to a minimum."

The other one adds, "You are also severely dehydrated and more than likely in need of some antibiotics and a blood transfusion to get your platelets up. We were trying to place an IV, but you pulled it out when you woke up."

I understand what they're saying and the nurse side of me knows that they're right. I know what I need, but the idea of them coming near me makes my chest constrict again.

"Please let them help you," Silas pleads. "I can help you in many ways, but this isn't one of them. I can't stop your bleeding, Quincey, but they can. Please let them."

Please. When men like Silas Laurent say please, you have to listen and mark the goddamn date, because like a comet, it happens rarely.

"Don't leave me." The only way I'll be able to let them come near me is if he's here with me.

"Never," he vows instantly. "Never again, my love."

With his back against the headboard and my back against his hard chest, Silas held me as they placed stitch after stitch in my skin. Not once while they tied forty stitches in total, did his hand stop creating a soothing path down my arm. Not even when the movement got in the way of the doctor, did he stop. Silas simply expected the doctor to work around it and eventually he found a way.

I stayed there on his lap until the last drops of the IV fluid and blood had entered my veins, and familiar waterproof bandages had been placed over the fresh stitches. They'd carefully examined my wrists, and I'd vaguely heard the words *nerve damage*, but in all honesty, I wasn't actively listening to what anyone was saying.

I was lost in my own thoughts, repeating the events of the last twenty-four hours in my head. Like one does, I played out different scenarios and wondered if there could have been a different outcome. Like, had we not decided to go on our first date, and I hadn't been preoccupied with getting ready, Ira wouldn't have been attacked because I would have been in the room with him, reading by his bedside. Or what if I'd run the other way instead of to Ira's room, maybe I could have hidden from Gideon long enough for Silas to show up and save us. That one was a pointless thought, because I know, no matter how the equation changed, I always would have gone to Ira first. Regardless of my own safety, I never could have left him behind. Even knowing now what would happen to me if I entered his room, I would have made the same decision.

Ira's only wish was that I was there for him when he died. It wasn't how we thought he'd leave this world, but I was still there holding his blood-soaked hand, just like I promised I would be.

When the doctors were done, Silas didn't move to show them the way out, he'd simply nodded his head in a silent dismissal. They left a bottle of pain reliever on the nightstand and quietly left the room.

I'm not sure how much longer we'd stayed like that, but at some point, he'd asked if I'd like to take a bath and my response was immediate. There was nothing else I wanted more than to wipe it all away, to remove the dirt and blood from my skin.

And now, as I sit here in the claw-foot bathtub, with my knees pulled to my chest and my head resting on them, I'm learning it's not going to be that easy to wash it all away. It doesn't matter how many bubbles fill the warm water or how long I sit here, I'm not sure I will ever get rid of the *bad* that clings to my skin. It's penetrated my pores and infected my blood stream. It's a part of me now.

Silas entering the bathroom has me finally looking away from the steady drip of the faucet I'd been fixating on since he left.

It's still covered in blood and torn in places, but the simple black Henley he wears makes my lips twitch. So do the black jeans he wears. "I didn't know you owned anything but black suits." Since the day I met him, he's worn only a three-piece suit. Even when he's home, working alone in his office, he donned a suit and black diamond cuff links. "I'm a little disappointed I had to go to these extreme lengths to see you in a pair of jeans, Laurent," I tease, because that's what's normal for us.

I tease him or I push his buttons and then he makes that dark, scowly look that I love. That's *normal*. And I really want normal right now, but much to my disappointment, that somber look doesn't leave his face when he looks at me.

"I brought you some sweats and a shirt to change into. Or I can find you a robe—I'll have to call Della. I'm not quite sure where she keeps things like that," he rambles. Silas Laurent doesn't ramble and sitting here watching it happen before me is like an out-of-body experience. He is the most sure-of-himself person I've ever met, and right now, my poor king looks like he doesn't know what to do with himself. "I also took the dirty sheets off your bed. Again, I'm not sure where the clean linens are, but Della will—"

No longer able to stand it, I cut him off. "*Silas,*" I plead. "Please, just stop. Don't worry about the bedding or clothes. That doesn't matter right now."

He runs a hand, still stained in blood, over his face. "I just want to make sure you're comfortable. I don't know how—" he pauses, dropping his hand. "I don't know how to *fix* this, Quincey. My only concern for the past twenty-four hours was getting you back. I couldn't think past that—I couldn't *allow* myself to think of anything else. The thought consumed me so much I never once considered what I would do once you were returned to me. How do I make up for the things that happened to you? Clearly, I'm at a loss since I just offered to find you a fucking robe." Midnight-black eyes collide with mine. "I should be offering you the goddamn sun right now."

In this moment, Silas Laurent seems so human it's almost heartbreaking.

"I don't want the sun and I don't need a robe," I assure him. Lifting my hand from the soapy water, I reach out to him like he's my life raft in a turbulent sea. "I just need you."

The sharp angles of his face turn serious as he vows, "You have me." Without hesitation, he takes my hand and allows me to pull him closer to the bathtub.

"I know." I smile softly. "Will you please just hold me for a little while longer. At least until the water runs cold."

His hand squeezes mine once before he drops it and in quick moments, he removes the articles of ruined clothes. He doesn't know it, but I plan on having a bonfire soon where I'll burn those clothes along with the ruined lace panty set I'd been wearing. I don't want a reminder of this day.

Despite his large size, he moves with such graceful and agile movements as he climbs into the tub behind me. Sitting between his strong thighs, his arms gather me up and he pulls me against his chest.

It takes a few minutes, but eventually I feel the marble-like muscles of his body relax against me. Or they relax as much as he's capable of. I'm not sure Silas has ever fully relaxed a day in his life, and the more that I experience of his world, I'm starting to realize why. How can he relax when there are men like Gideon out there scheming on how to hurt him?

Brushing the wet strands of my clean hair off my forehead, he presses a long kiss to my temple. "You are my heart, Quincey Page."

CHAPTER 14

Silas

She fell asleep in my arms before the water had a chance to run cold. Not once did she flinch or stir when I carried her out of the tub and wrapped her in a towel. Still, she remained sound asleep in my arms as I brought her down the hallway to my bedroom.

One of the first things I noticed about Quincey is she always smiles in her sleep. Something I found confusing at the time, given her turbulent upbringing, but now it's something I want to protect. I'd wish on every star in the sky if it meant her dreams remain pure and happy. Even despite what she's endured with Gideon. I never want my dark world to infect the innocent escape she finds in her dreams.

When I'd carefully placed her in my bed, a place I had vowed to never allow a woman to reside in, she'd snuggled herself farther under the dark maroon bedding. I stood over her, waiting, *needing* to see for myself that Gideon hadn't robbed her of this as well. It took only minutes, but eventually her bruised and cracked lips lifted in the faintest smile, and I felt her peace settle in my chest, calming the last of the chaotic winds inside. True to the name I'd donned her, the sun can always cast away the most violent of storms.

Sliding beneath the covers beside her, I'd carefully pulled her closer to my side and wrapped my arms protectively around her. Even with the guards stationed around the estate, the need to shield her with my own body was impossible to ignore. Plus, I wanted to feel her heartbeat against me. I've never been more thankful to hear a heartbeat in my entire life. Each steady beat, and each breath she takes, is an invaluable gift to me.

Counting each beat, I fell into a restless sleep beside her. Every time she stirred or made any noise in her sleep, my eyes snapped open, searching her face for any signs of distress or pain, but each time she remained fast asleep.

Even when my phone started to buzz across my nightstand around sundown, and I'd reluctantly removed myself from the bed, Quincey remained asleep. Her mind needs just as much healing as her body does right now. If she needs to sleep for the next week to make that happen, I will let her. I will wait patiently at her bedside while her sleepy smiles keep me company.

Tying the black towel around my hips, I step out of the shower, but instantly I'm halting in place at the notable silence. My blood runs cold as concern grips my chest and unease settles in my bones.

She's not in my room.

The rhythmic sound of her heart is no longer filling the dark bedroom and the sweet scent of her shampoo isn't as strong as it should be.

Storming out of the en suite bathroom, my stomach drops when I confirm my bed is now empty and the door to my bedroom is cracked open, a thin stream of light coming from the hallway casting onto the dark hardwood floors.

Flashbacks of finding her missing just two nights prior play in my mind as I frantically follow her scent through the hallways of the house.

I go flying by the now vacant room, but skid to a stop just past the doorway when I catch the dark silhouette standing in the middle of the room.

Steeling myself, I slowly enter the shadowy room. The last time both of us were in this room, we were welcomed with a horrifying sight. It's one I wish I could take from her, so she didn't have to feel the weight of it.

Without a word, I flip the light switch she didn't bother to turn on when she entered. Dressed in the T-shirt I'd left for her on the bench at the end of my bed, Quincey's head slowly turns in my direction. The sight of her powder-blue eyes full of tears is like a sucker punch to the gut.

"Quincey…" I just barely get her name out when she begins to whisper.

"It's like he was never here." Her bottom lip wobbles. "All of his stuff—it's just *gone*. Just like that, it's *all* gone."

For months, this room was unbearably hot with the ever-present fire burning in the hearth, but now it feels as cold as it was before Ira moved into it. The heavy curtains he always wanted open so he could see outside are pulled tight, hindering any moonlight from entering now. The place where his hospital bed once sat has been replaced with a queen-size sleigh bed. Where the team of cleaners had found the piece of furniture, I do not know. I pay them a lot of money so I don't have to worry about things of that nature. The blood that had been spilled has been cleaned from the hardwood floors, and the rug that had been stained has been replaced.

"Even his chess board is gone." She points at the empty coffee table in front of the cream love seat. Wiping her face, Quincey croaks, "And his glasses are gone. Why—why would they take his glasses?"

"We were worried the gunfire from that night may have caught the attention of the authorities. Most of them know better than to come here or ask questions, but in my line of work, you can never be too careful."

The police chief and I have an understanding, and for a long time, he's kept his men in line, but there's always at least one brave detective that believes they can be the one to take my empire down. They're too confident for their own good, and in the end, they always learn the hard way that they're wrong. "I couldn't risk there still being evidence of what happened, and I couldn't very well just leave him in here while I searched for you."

Swiping more of the tears that fall, she turns her body toward me. "Where is he now? Did you already get rid of him too?"

Caught off by the harshness of her words, I narrow my eyes at her. She's thrown words at me before like they were daggers, but never have I witnessed the icy ruthlessness in her eyes. Like a camera flash, it's there only briefly before the usual warmth returns to them. "Do you really think I would do that to Ira? That I would simply *'get rid'* of him like he was yesterday's trash?"

Cheeks red and eyes now flustered, she waves her hands around the space, now devoid of any personal touches. "You got rid of his things like they meant nothing!" she shouts, her voice cracking with the emotion she's barely keeping back.

"Quincey." I shake my head as I slowly approach her like she's a skittish kitten. I can't pretend to understand the varying emotions she's experiencing. She's been through more than anyone should have to in such a short period. She tries to look away from me, but I gently grip her chin to keep her in place. Her eyes flutter closed instead. "Look at me," I order. After a moment of hesitation, her eyes finally meet mine once more. "Ira's personal effects have been boxed up and are with him. I thought you would like to be the one to go through them."

As if she'd been holding it, she releases a long breath before leaning into my hand. "How did you know I'd be here to go through them?"

"Because there simply wasn't any other option," I answer without hesitation. "I once vowed to burn down the world for you, and I meant every word. If Rory hadn't discovered the warehouse, I would have turned everything to ashes until I found you." I'd made that promise thinking I'd never have to act on it, but I was minutes away from following through with it. "You were always coming home to me, *Mon Soleil*."

Leaning forward, she drops her head to my bare chest. Her hands, that now have a constant tremor to them, clutch my sides. "How could you have been so sure?"

"I didn't wait hundreds of years to find you, only to lose you. You're *mine*. The angel of death himself will have to take you from me, that's the only way I'm letting go of you now."

She stays quiet for a moment, her head remaining pressed to my silent heart before she finally speaks up. "I knew you were looking for me. There wasn't a single part of me that doubted that for a second, but there were a few moments I really didn't think you'd make it in time. When—" she starts but the words get stuck in her throat. "When he made the first cut, I thought he'd stop there but then he went to the other side of my chest, and I thought about you finding me bleeding out just like I found Ira. I wouldn't ever want you to see me like that, so I found myself, just for a second, hoping you wouldn't find me. I wanted to spare you from that. No one should have to see that."

"That heart of yours is too kind for this world, my love. Even in your darkest moment, you were consumed with thoughts of someone else's well-being." My hand soothes down her back. "I wish there was a way I could make you forget that memory. That's not how Ira would want you to remember him."

"No." Her head shakes instantly. "I don't want to forget it. I want to remember that, even though it was horrible, I was there for him like I promised." Her tears begin to drip down my chest as she speaks in hoarse, broken whispers. "I held his hand and told him everything was going to be okay, even when I knew I was lying." Her shoulders shake as the sobs consume her body. "I *kept* my promise, Silas." She lifts her chin and looks up at me when she stammers, "I really don't want to cry anymore."

"I know," I tell her softly, brushing the hair from her tear-soaked face. "But you can. You can cry, Quincey."

And with that, the woman who's met every challenge I've thrown at her with her head held high and her defiant smirk in place breaks in my arms.

For a week, she remained in my bedroom, while the physical and mental scars inflicted on her mended. When she wasn't drifting off to sleep in my bed, she was shifting between the bed and the chair by the fireplace, one of the romance novels I brought to her always in hand.

I can only hope the places her dreams and those books took her gave her the peaceful escape I didn't know how to give her myself.

Since the beginning, Quincey Page has thrown me off balance, and now I feel even more at a loss when it comes to her. All I want to do is keep her safe and heal the wounds she endured, but I don't know how to ease her pain when I'm the one who caused it.

I may not have sliced her skin with a knife, but I recognize the role I played. While she may be willing to grant me her forgiveness, I'm not sure if I will ever be able to forgive myself.

I'm determined to find a way to make up for it, but I'm quickly learning my efforts are becoming more irritating than appreciated by Quincey.

Sitting with her back against the headboard, Quincey's head cocks to the side as she stares at the far wall where the new canvas hangs. "Why is that there? Where did the other painting go?"

When I purchased the antique Gothic painting many decades ago, I hadn't given the dark depiction a second thought. Not until I found Quincey's sad eyes lingering on the depiction of a man being staked to a stone table did I pay it any mind. Instantly, I felt foolish that I'd left such a blatant and thoughtless reminder mounted on the wall. While she slept, I'd replaced it with a simple red monochromatic painting that had been in storage.

Also looking at the new canvas, I ask, "Do you not like it? I can find another one."

She closes the book she has open on her lap. "I just don't understand why you changed it. The other one was obviously something you enjoyed, or you wouldn't have hung it on your bedroom wall."

"Really? You can't think of a reason as to why I wouldn't want it hanging on my bedroom wall any longer?"

Her lips press into a flat line as she stares at me for a second. The bruising on her face has turned yellow and the cut on her lip is just a faint scab. The stitches in her chest will need to be removed in the next week, but the doctor who's been back to check on her says the cuts are healing well. Unfortunately, the scars will be permanent. Ugly reminders for both of us.

"Silas, I know what you're doing," Quincey finally sighs. "But you don't have to. I'm fine."

Fine. That's the word she's been using since she woke up the day after crying in Ira's room, and every time she says it, I hate it more and more. It's a lie and I despise lies, especially when they come from her.

"You keep saying that."

"Yes, and I mean it. You can stop coddling me now," she smiles reassuringly, but still, I don't believe her. "I want nothing more than to spend time with you, but you've put everything on hold for a week now. I've heard your phone ringing nonstop—I know things need your attention."

Stalking toward the bed, I shake my head at her and cage her between my arms once I'm close enough. "Nothing is more important than you, Quincey. Everything else can wait for me." Just as I don't like her lying to me, I don't like lying to her, but while she continues to recuperate, I'll continue to do so. She doesn't need the added stress of knowing what a shitstorm everything is outside of this house.

Scooting farther up the headboard, she tilts her head up toward mine. "I'm more than capable of waiting for you as well." Her eyes linger on my mouth as she says, "But you know, not *too* long."

She waits patiently for me to bridge the gap between us, but when I make no move to do so, Quincey snakes her hand up and grips my chin, guiding my mouth to hers.

My veins burn with a hungry fire as her lips press against mine. Each time I've been given the gift of kissing Quincey Page, I experience the same rush I had the first time I consumed blood. Her kisses feed my black soul the same way blood fuels my body. My fingers curl into fists on the bed as I force myself to not deepen the kiss like I want to.

I crave to reacquaint myself with her body—to feel her heat until it becomes my own once again—but no matter how much I crave her, I can't bring myself to go further than this.

No matter how many times she says *she's fine*, I don't believe her. She needs more time and I have an endless supply I can give her.

The way the corners of her mouth dip in a frown doesn't go unnoticed when I pull away from her. I'm saved from having to explain myself to her when my phone buzzes in my pocket for the third time this hour.

Disappointment clear in her eyes, Quincey gestures at me with her chin. "You should get that." When I don't reach for the device, she quickly insists. "I'm serious, Silas. Something is clearly going on. I've never heard your phone ring as much as it has this week. Doesn't Duke usually handle things for you?"

Duke.

I kept telling myself I was going to wait for the right time to tell her about Duke, but each time I opened my mouth, I couldn't bring myself to say the words. The thought that the news of Duke's injuries would only add to the pain I'm trying so desperately to soothe stops me.

A truly selfish act, I know, but as long as each day she continues to heal and grow stronger, I'll continue to shield her from what I can.

For now, her believing both Duke and Della are giving her space to recuperate, will have to do.

Reluctantly, I pull the phone from my pocket and glance at the number. I recognize the last four digits and immediately know what the call is pertaining to. While my molars grind in irritation, I force my face to remain impassive. "I don't need to answer this. I already know what they're calling about." Silencing the device, I pocket it once more before reaching for her face. My thumb brushes gently over the faint bruise on her cheekbone. "But you're right, I don't think I can put this off any longer."

Her head turns so she can press a soft kiss to my palm. "I will be fine here, I promise, Silas." The way her heartbeat spikes tells me what I already know; Quincey still isn't fine, and she doesn't feel safe here.

Feeling torn between the two things that need my attention most, I stiffly nod after making the reluctant decision to leave her here for just a short while. "I won't be gone long—two hours at most. And you won't be alone. There are still guards stationed all around the property and Lorcan will remain here as well."

While I've been holed away with Quincey, Lorcan has been acting as my eyes and ears. His wire transfer cleared almost five days ago, yet he remains. He's also been the one overseeing details that are usually handled by Duke. They're tasks I never asked of him, but the Irish vampire has surprised me by sticking around and assisting me.

He'd offered days ago to stay with Quincey if I needed to leave, a selfless act that caught me off guard. But truthfully, while Duke remains in the hospital, Lor is the only person I would leave Quincey with. I know if a situation arises, his particular skill set will ensure her safety.

"He's *still* here?"

"Yes, I'm as surprised as you. He usually prefers a nomadic lifestyle." I'm not sure he's ever stayed in one place longer than three days. "But don't worry, he knows he isn't permitted in this room. He won't bother you."

"For some reason, I very much doubt that."

"If he wishes to keep his head connected to his shoulders, he'll heed my warning."

CHAPTER 15

My fingers shake as I grip the cold marble of the bathroom countertops. I've been standing here, staring at my distorted reflection in the chrome faucet of the sink, trying to find the courage to look at myself in the actual mirror. Correction: I've been trying to find the courage all week to look at my reflection.

I'm afraid of what I will see when I do. It's not just the bruising and cuts I'm afraid of—I'm afraid that I will look as different as I feel. I thought time would give back the piece that Gideon stole from me, but a week later, there's still an empty place in my soul. When they say ignorance is bliss, they mean it. Once that pastel-pink balloon of innocence pops, there's no repairing it.

Silas told me from the beginning his world wasn't safe, but now that I've seen and experienced the harshness of it myself, I learned the hard way just how true his words are. My pink balloon has burst, and it's been replaced by an angry fire that burns in my belly.

And I'm worried that when I look in the mirror, I will find that anger shining in my eyes. That I will *see* how I've changed.

Keeping my eyes down, I pull the oversized shirt over my head and mindlessly throw it onto the black tile floors. Every aspect of Silas's bathroom is dark and sleek—sexy, just like him.

My hair is knotted from going to sleep with it wet. Gathering the long strands, I tie them on top of my head so they're not hindering my view.

My jaw clenches and I force myself to look up.

Barefaced and naked, I stare at the person reflecting at me. She looks like me—maybe a little thinner from a lack of appetite, but I still recognize her. The same freckles line her nose from spending her summers in the sun, and there's still that scar on her right knee from when she tripped over a broken bottle of her mom's tequila when she was eight.

And her eyes... her eyes look as they always have.

She's still me.

I'm... me.

Relief washes over me like a waterfall of warmth. Gideon tried to break me, but in the end, his plan backfired, because that anger he caused is only making me feel stronger. I don't have any more tears left to cry. Each one I was willing to give him has been shed over the past week, but now I'm ready to move forward.

I'm taking back the life he tried to steal from me.

I'm done being coddled and cared for, and I'm definitely fucking over the way Silas is looking at me. He looks at me like Gideon won and he did, in fact, break me. Silas handles me like I'm a fragile piece of glass that will shatter at any moment.

He barely touches me, and when he does, it's so gentle and tender, I find myself resenting it. I don't want him to handle me like I'm damaged goods. I want him to grab hold of me with such passion the bruises he leaves cover the ones left by Gideon.

I would wear Silas's bruises with honor—they're a symbol that I'm his and that's all I fucking want to be.

Holding my breath against the pain, I peel the bandages off the matching wounds below my collarbones. My stomach twists once I finally lay my eyes on what Gideon did. True to his word, he made the Xs symmetrical. For the rest of my life, I will look in the mirror and remember what I've survived.

After redressing the wounds in fresh bandages, I examine my bare body one last time in the mirror. Feeling at peace with what I see, I swipe the discarded T-shirt off the floor and pull it over my head as I leave the bathroom.

I don't know what I'm going to do, but I'm done sitting in this room reading books and staring at the ever-changing paintings. Speaking of paintings, I glare at the boring red one that had replaced the original one. The irritation I felt when I first discovered Silas had switched it out reignites in my chest. It's just another way he's coddling me.

"Good Lord, woman. What were you doing in there? I thought I was going to go gray waiting for you to resurface," a thick Irish accent comes from the bed.

Stopping in my tracks, my head whips in the direction of the voice. "What the hell are you doing in here?"

The blond vampire is reclined on Silas's side of the bed, a bright blue sparkly tumbler cup in his tattooed hand. Shrugging, he takes a drink and dark liquid moves up the matching blue straw. "I was growing bored downstairs and I figured since you're no longer a crying mess, you might finally make for some good company."

Crossing my arms in front of my chest, I look between him and the tumbler. "Are you drinking blood out of a *Starbucks* cup?" Looking closer at the cup, my jaw drops. "*Wait*! That's mine."

Duke brought it to me one of the times he had snuck me another romance novel.

"Is it?" he shakes the cup back and forth. "I found it in the kitchen."

Grimacing, I shake my head. "It's yours now. Consider it my thanks for helping Silas find me."

Lorcan sits up in the bed and crosses his legs beneath him. His shoes are still on, and I just know I'm going to have to change the linens before Silas gets back.

"I must say, this is a really lame present compared to what Silas got me. He got me a shiny check with six figures on it, but I'm open to other forms of payment." His lips pull into a flirty smirk.

My stomach rolls at the knowledge that Silas paid that much to find me, but at the same time, my heart also warms, knowing he was willing to do anything to get me back. I can't imagine what I'd do if the roles were reversed, and Silas was taken from me.

I want to be irritated with Lor, but despite my best efforts, I find myself smiling back at him. "I'm sure you are, but you and I both know you'd be a dead man walking if you touched me."

"I have a feeling it'd be worth it," Lor flicks his light-brown eyes over me. "Silas never did learn how to share."

"Maybe I'm the one not willing to be shared," I point out, but right now, I'm so hungry for Silas's touch, if being shared is what it would take for him to do more than caress my arm or give me a soft peck on the lips, I would do it.

Lorcan rolls off the bed, leaving the maroon duvet wrinkled. "You're missing out, darling." He looks around the room, taking in each corner of Silas's private space—a space I still don't feel totally confident occupying.

"You're not supposed to be in here," I remind Lor, even though I know he knows this.

"I don't much like someone telling me where I can or can't go. In all honesty, it usually only makes me want to do it more when someone tells me no."

I could lie and say I don't relate to what he's saying. I originally discovered what Silas was because I wanted to see what he was hiding in the rooms he told me I couldn't venture into. Of course, my happy ass ignored all the neon red warning signs and marched through the doors that contained his secrets. But I don't regret doing it for a single second.

"So, what do you want to do? Surely you don't want to be holed up in this room any longer. A change of scenery would do you good." His nose wrinkles up in sudden distaste. "It smells like Silas in here."

Without another word, he stalks across the room, leaving the double doors open behind him.

I hesitate only a second before I remind myself I'm not a captive in this room and exit the doors behind him. As we descend the winding staircase, Lorcan looks over his shoulder at me and grins like he's somehow won something.

The second my feet hit the last step, I know something is wrong. Holding on to the railing, I slowly look over the entryway as concern grips me. Just like my bedroom, everything is exactly where it was the night of the attack. Nothing has been moved.

The flowers I'd cut from Ira's rose bushes hang limply over the side of the crystal vase on the entryway table. A thin layer of dust covers the same table, in some places, I can see lines in it like someone has run their finger through it at some point. A trash bag sits by the front door like someone had thought about bringing it outside, but never got around to it.

None of that would have happened if she were here. Consumed by panic and worry for my friend, I chase after Lorcan into the kitchen. "Where is Della?" I demand. The dishes that sit in the kitchen sink confirm that the overly tidy housekeeper hasn't been here in days.

Leaning against the countertop, Lorcan cocks his head at me in confusion. "What do you mean, where is she? She's still sitting vigil at the hospital. I think Silas is overreacting by having her stay there, but who am I to say how he should run things."

My blood runs cold as fear takes over. "What do you mean she's at the hospital?" Silas told me both Duke and Della were giving me time and space to recover.

Light-brown eyes narrow at me as his tattooed arms cross in front of him. "Silas didn't tell you?"

"Tell me *what*?" I all but shout at him. When Lorcan's mouth flattens into a line like he plans on keeping the secret, I march closer and shove at his chest with my weak hands. "I'm so tired of everyone walking around on fucking eggshells around me! Tell me right fucking now or I swear to God, I will leave here and find out myself."

Lorcan's hands fly up in surrender. "Hey! Don't put this on me like it's my fault Silas is pussyfooting around you."

I stop my assault with a defeated sigh. "Just tell me what happened. *Please*."

"Fine," Lor agrees. "Della is fine. It's Duke you should be worried about. He's currently in a medically induced coma. The car he and Silas were in was hit by an explosive. Silas obviously walked away okay, but Duke wasn't that lucky."

There's rushing in my ears as I process this information. Staggering back a step, my hands reach up and grip the strands of my hair. This whole week while I've been holed away, *doing nothing*, Duke—my friend and confidant—was lying in a hospital bed.

The angry ball of fire in my belly grows knowing that Silas would keep this from me—that he would make the decision for me, that I would be in the dark about Duke.

Whirling back to face Lor, I drop my hands and lift my chin as I declare, "I need to see Duke and you're going to take me there."

He stares at me for a second like he's waiting for the punch line of a joke, before his face pulls into a scowl. "No, I am not. Silas wouldn't allow it."

"I don't know much about you, Lorcan, but I know enough to know you've never fully listened to a fucking thing Silas has said." Like a guilty child caught in a lie, the corners of his mouth twitch. "You either take me there or I will drive myself, and then Silas really will kill you for letting me out of your sight."

Completely unfazed by my threat, he lifts the sparkly cup off the counter and takes a long, slurping drink through the straw.

He thinks I'm joking and that my threat holds no weight, but I'll prove him wrong. Spinning on my bare feet, I march toward the front door of the house.

I only get ten feet away before he's calling out to me, "If we're going to the hospital, I'd recommend changing into something where your arse isn't hanging out like that. While I might not mind the view, I'm sure the respectable doctors there might not agree."

Tugging the T-shirt tighter around my legs, I turn to look at him. "You'll take me?"

His shoulders shrug. "Sure, why not? I like the way the vein in Silas's forehead bulges when he's mad at me, and if you're okay with the repercussions of leaving, then I'll gladly be your chauffeur."

Head held high and shoulders back, I simply tell him, "I'm not a prisoner in this house or anywhere else." *Not anymore and never again.*

CHAPTER 16

Quincey

For so many years, I was confident in a hospital. I would walk through those sliding glass doors, and instantly I knew what I was doing. Never did I doubt my skill—I knew I was good at my job. That all changed when every patient I touched started to die.

It took meeting Silas and Ira for me to learn that it wasn't the curse my mom always said I had, but it was, in fact, just a crazy fluke—that it wasn't my fault that they all died.

Even knowing this, as I follow Lorcan through the sterile halls of the intensive care unit, the chaos of a hospital no longer calls to my soul. The woman who used to thrive here doesn't exist and being here confirms that this is no longer my path.

I'm not quite sure where my new path is leading me, but I know without a shadow of a doubt that it will be in the dark world Silas rules. I just need to prove to him that I'm ready to be there. That I'm strong enough to stand at his side.

"Could you look any more suspicious with that hood over your head like that?" Lorcan hisses over his shoulder at me, his handsome face pulled in distaste.

Yeah, I wasn't sure that night in the warehouse if he was as attractive as he appeared to be, but now I know he's even more so. Even under the harsh light of the fluorescent light bulbs up above, Lorcan Reid can fucking *get it*. Just ignore the faint air of batshit crazy coming off him like a cheap cologne, and he's a real winner.

But crazy is fun, and I really appreciate anything that can make me smile right now.

"You look like you're going to rob the place, which would be in poor taste seeing as it's a hospital. Though, if I'm being completely honest, still sounds like fun."

Picking up speed to catch up to him, I whisper harshly. "Would you rather the staff here see my bruises and think I'm your poor battered wife?" I'm more worried about the fading bruises and scabs drawing too much attention to me.

It felt nice to put on real clothes—even if it was just an oversized hoodie and a pair of jean shorts,

"Oh? We're married now?" a dark blond brow raises in question. "I should warn you, darling, I struggle with the concept of monogamy."

"That doesn't shock me in the slightest. You have manwhore written all over you," I respond, rolling my eyes.

Lifting his tattooed arms, he examines them, "Do I? I don't recall getting that tattoo…"

"You're really annoying," I pretend to insult, even though I'm thankful for the easy banter. It's distracting me from the stress and guilt I feel about Duke being in the hospital. I can't believe for a week I had no idea he was here, hurt because he was trying to save me from Gideon.

My fingers nervously twist the frayed hem of my shorts as we near the room in front of us. Instantly, my eyes are drawn to the obnoxiously bright orange tape crisscrossing over the cracked glass of the sliding door.

Confused, I look at Lorcan for an explanation, but all I get is a shrug and, "Don't look at me, I didn't do it. I believe your boyfriend did though."

Boyfriend... I don't know what Silas and I are, but I know that mundane terms like boyfriend or girlfriend don't come remotely close to encompassing all that we are to each other. Right now, it really doesn't matter what our titles are. Either way, I'm really fucking annoyed with him.

Just as we reach the cracked door, the nurse wearing red-framed glasses raises her voice at us from behind the nurse's station. "*He* said there would be only one person staying here with Mr. Greyson." I don't need her to elaborate further. I know the *he* she's referring to is my vampire. "Why do more of you keep showing up here? This is the ICU. We don't exactly have an open-door policy. You can't come in here whenever you please," the bitter woman bites at us, instantly making me come to an abrupt halt.

Spinning slowly on my heels, I turn toward the circular desk she hides behind. "We're just here to check in on Duke. I can assure you, we won't get in anyone's way," I promise her tightly, while pulling the hood off my head. Silas has kept me from seeing Duke all week, I'm not going to allow anyone else to do the same. "If you're going to hinder us from doing so, I have no problem making a phone call. Though, I would really hate to have *him* come here, and sort this all out." Her eyes behind her glasses grow wide at the possibility, confirming what I already assumed. Silas was here and he left a *lovely* impression. "But it's truly up to you and whether or not you're going to make things difficult for us."

Her thin lips flatten and twitch as she thinks over my offer. A couple times, I swear I even see her nose twitch, like she's an angry rabbit or some other rodent. "Fine," she relents. "But don't touch anything."

How stupid does she think we are? "Well, shit, there goes my plan to jump rope with his IV tubing," I mockingly pout before I roll my eyes at the absurdity of her request.

Lor snickers, following behind me when I turn away from the desk.

I'm met by the familiar beep of a heart monitor and the steady sound of a ventilator as I slide the door open and step into the room. The blue curtain is drawn, cutting the space in half and concealing Duke's bed.

Holding my breath, I gently pull it back far enough that I can slip around it.

I've seen many patients in hospital beds with tubes shoved down their throats and IVs stuck in their arms, but I've never seen someone I cared about in this state. The sight of Duke, strong—lively—Duke, like that makes my heart hurt.

This never should have happened to him, I think, just as a small voice comes from the chair in the corner of the room. "Quincey?"

Following the sound, I find Della sitting with a thin blanket over her lap and a half-read book in her hand. I've never seen the older woman without her makeup and hair done. Without it, her dark circles that could rival mine are clearly on display. I wonder if she's slept a wink all week.

"*Della,*" I sigh her name in relief. I'm moving across the small room toward her before she fully has a chance to pull herself out of the chair.

Up until this point, I didn't know if we were close enough to hug each other, but when she meets my embrace with equal enthusiasm, I discover we are.

"It is really good to see you," she whispers, her hand patting my back. "I wasn't sure how he was going to do it, but I knew Silas would find you." Pulling back, she cups my face with gentle hands. "How are you? Are you healing alright? Silas has been frustratingly vague when I've asked for updates on you."

Seems I'm not the only one he's keeping things from.

Della's face falls when she takes in the yellowish bruises and scabs on my face. Collecting her hands with mine, I retreat with a reassuring smile when she attempts to tilt my chin toward the light so she can get a better look.

"I'm okay," I tell her, which only causes her to frown. "Really, I'm okay. The only thing that still hurts are my wrists." And my heart. My heart still hurts for Ira. "If the doctors are right, and I have nerve damage in them, it will probably take some time for them to heal."

That is, *if* they can ever heal—there's some worry that for the rest of my life I will suffer from weakness and numbness in my fingers. I knew as I hung there by my wrists that the damage would be severe, but I really hoped it wouldn't be permanent.

"If you think she looks bad now, you should have seen her when we found her. 'Twas not a pretty sight," Lorcan pipes up unhelpfully from where he leans against the wall. "She looks like a pretty penny compared to that."

Della scowls at the vampire. "Good Lord, are you *still* here?"

Laughing softly, I tell her, "I said the same thing just a little while ago. Silas had to leave and handle something, so he left Lorcan behind as my bodyguard."

"More like a glorified babysitter," Lor mumbles to himself.

Dropping Della's wrinkled hands, I step toward the bed where my sleeping friend lies. "How is he doing? Has there been any improvement?" Lorcan had filled me in more on Duke's status on our way here. I've seen this before and understand what the doctors are doing for him. The hardest part now is the waiting game to see how Duke's body will respond.

Stepping closer to the bed, I wrap my hand around Duke's larger one. His skin feels dry and cracked from the hospital air, but I don't care. My lips twitch at the sight of his overgrown facial hair. Duke has always had a five o'clock shadow, but now there's a visible layer of scruff on his face. There's a bandage on his forehead, presumably from where his head slammed into the steering wheel or window in the crash, but still, he looks as handsome as ever.

Della's face breaks into a watery grin. "They saw a lot of improvement in his last scan. They're going to try and lighten the sedation in a day or two and wake him up."

My breath catches in my chest at the good news. "He's going to be okay," I speak it into existence because I need more than anything for it to come true. We've already lost Ira and losing Duke as well would be unacceptable. *Unfathomable.*

"They won't know if there's any permanent damage until he's fully awake," Della explains, coming to stand on the other side of the bed. I stare at her while she lovingly brushes a hand down Duke's face like a worried mother. I don't know much about Duke's past or family, but I get the feeling that Della is the closest thing he has to a mother figure.

In the end, we've all become a weird dysfunctional family. For a long time, I thought Lucy was the only family I had, but now I have all of them. Which is something I never would have guessed would happen when Silas brought me in.

Shit… Lucy. I haven't reached out to her all week; she's probably losing her fucking mind over my silence. I promised her when I started working for Silas that I would talk to her every day. She's probably thinking the worst right now. For all I know, she has a search party out there looking for me as we speak. Truth is, I haven't seen my phone all week and I haven't made any effort to search for it.

"Della, why don't you leave for a little while. At least go get a shower and something to eat."

Della shakes her head. "The guard who stays here with him while I sleep will be here around dawn. I'll go then so Duke's not alone."

"He won't be alone. I'll stay here. You need a break, and I really want to spend some time with him." I want to make up for not being here all week when I could have been.

Della hesitates for a second, looking torn between caring for Duke and caring for herself. But in the end, she sighs in defeat, "I'll only be gone an hour. Silas booked a hotel room across the street for me to sleep and shower at, that way I was close if anything were to happen with Duke. I'll just run over there really quick and wash up."

"*And* eat something," I insist.

"Yes, that as well." Collecting her purse and sweater from the chair she's been inhabiting for God knows how long, she reluctantly shuffles toward the sliding door. The way she narrows her eyes at Lorcan makes me stifle a laugh.

I can understand how he grates on everyone's nerves, but I'm finding myself quite enjoying his company.

"I'll walk you to the lobby," he offers.

Della's lips purse as she says, "That won't be necessary."

His large, tattooed arm loops around her shoulders, "Oh, but I insist." Looking back at me with a pointed look, he warns, "Don't even think about leaving this room. I will be back in five minutes."

"I'm exactly where I need to be," is my answer to him.

Left alone, the sound of Duke's machines is the only thing keeping me company. As I pull Della's chair closer to the bed, I'm hit with an overwhelming sense of déjà vu when I sit down next to him. I didn't think I would be sitting by a hospital bed so soon after Ira, but here I am doing just that.

"I really wish you were awake so I could thank you for trying to save me," I whisper, clutching Duke's hand between mine. "And I really wish you were awake so I could tell you everything that happened. I'm sure you'll find a way to make me smile—you always do."

The sound of the air being forcibly pushed into his lungs is his only reply.

"I'm really sorry I wasn't here sooner." The anger I feel at Silas surges forward. "He never should have kept what happened to you from me. It wasn't fair for him to make that decision for me." Memories of how Silas has been behaving all week flood my mind. I can feel his tender—almost nonexistent touches—and the way his midnight eyes watched my every move with worry and concern. "I need you to get better, Duke. I can't lose anyone else."

I sit there for another minute, just watching the unnatural way his chest rises and falls from the ventilator. I'm about to get up and ask the nurse if I could get a shaving kit for his beard when I hear the sliding glass door open again.

I stiffen in my chair and my heart starts racing when I hear the soft footsteps. They're too slow—unsure sounding—for them to be Lorcan.

There's a flash of purple from behind the curtain and I jump up from the chair.

Instantly, my mind begins to fill with all the possibilities of what's to come next. Will I need to protect myself? If so, how? Maybe I can get around them and find Lorcan, but I can't leave Duke here unprotected. All I know is that Silas is going to be *pissed* that I left the house and put myself in harm's way *again*.

The chair skids against the tile floor when I take a step back from the stranger that stands in front of me. I don't know what I'm expecting from her, but to find that her eyes are as wide as mine isn't it. She looks as surprised and concerned as I feel.

"Oh shit, you're not supposed to be here." The girl's face pulls in a grimace. "I saw the lady leave and thought the room would be empty."

She takes a step toward Duke's bed, and without thinking it fully through, I step forward, hand raised, halting her movements. "That's close enough," I warn, carefully putting myself between her and Duke. Her dark brows rise, and a bored look crosses her face, but still, I don't back down. "I don't know who you are or what you want, but I know for a fact that you're not supposed to be in here. My guard will be back any second, and he's a lot scarier than I am."

She juts her thumb over her shoulder. "*Your guard?* Wait, are you talking about *Lorcan?*" Her hazel eyes roll dramatically. "I saw him leave with the lady—Seriously? Silas trusted that leprechaun to be your '*guard*'? What the hell is he thinking?"

I know the confusion is clear in my expression as I stare back at her. She knows Lorcan and Silas? Who the hell is this girl? "I feel like I'm missing some key information right now. Let's back up here for a second... Who *exactly* are you?"

Like she's familiar and comfortable in this space, she casually drops her large shoulder bag by the small side table. "I'm the girl who helped save your life, but you can call me Rory."

Rory.

I recognize the name in a second. "You're the hacker girl that works for Silas. You were the one who found out where Gideon was keeping me."

She's shorter than me by a few inches, but her strong personality makes up for what she's lacking in the height department. Her lilac hair falls just above her shoulders in a long bob and her hazel eyes are lined with more makeup than I've ever worn in my life. It's her stunningly beautiful black and gray tattoos that really grab your attention though. Almost every inch of her visible skin is covered, aside from her throat and face.

Her tattooed fingers rise to her forehead before she offers me a halfhearted salute. "That'd be me, and I *worked* for Silas. I don't anymore. I figured working for a fucking vampire might be hazardous to my health." She slowly eyes me up and down. "Clearly, it's worked out really well for you."

Feeling more at ease with Rory's presence, I relax and take a step back. Without needing an invitation, she shifts closer to Duke's bed, but she doesn't make any move to touch him. Her hands wrap around the plastic footboard, and she observes him with worried eyes.

Yeah, this girl definitely isn't a threat to me... or Duke.

"I wasn't taken or hurt because I worked for Silas," I correct, dropping back into the chair. "I was taken because I'm in love with him."

It's odd admitting that to someone when I haven't even told Silas yet. I want to say those three little words to him, but each time I open my mouth to tell him, I can't do it. Not when he's still looking at me like something he needs to coddle or fix. I don't want to look back on the moment and remember the pity he's been wearing on his face.

Rory's head shakes in disbelief. "You're in love with a vampire?"

I shrug casually. "I've never been one to go for the easy or safe option."

Eyes lingering on Duke, she utters, almost as if to herself. "Easy and safe are boring."

When Silas talked about Rory and how talented she is, I didn't expect her to be so young. There's no way this girl is even my age. If I had to guess, she still isn't old enough to legally order a drink at a bar, but there is an air of maturity in her eyes that only comes from having to live through some serious shit. It's something I'm familiar with myself.

Awkwardly shifting in the chair, I clear my throat before saying, "I don't know how to thank you for what you did. I would probably be dead if they hadn't gotten there when they did."

Her painted lips pull in a sort of smirk. "Well, Silas didn't exactly give me a choice in the matter."

"Yeah, I figured as much. He doesn't really take kindly to the word *no*. I could apologize for him, but I don't think either one of you would appreciate that." Speaking on behalf of Silas doesn't seem like a smart move and if he feels inclined to apologize to Rory, he sure as shit needs to do it himself. "Nonetheless, I'm really grateful for everything you did. Thank you for helping me and helping Silas when no one else could."

Rory's face falls and heavy silence fills the space between us. For a second, I'm worried I said something wrong, but finally she speaks up. "I'm kind of in awe of you," she shocks me by saying. "I watched the camera feed and I saw… I know what he did to you." Her head shakes in small, barely noticeable movements. "You were stronger than I could have been—*hell*, I think you were stronger than most people would have been. When you stood up for yourself and threatened him back, I definitely was cheering for you."

"I think you may have been the only one rooting for me." Gideon's voice floats through my head, *you should know you're quite popular, Quincey. I have many people making offers. They're bidding more than I ever could have hoped for.* "I'm pretty sure most of the people watching wanted to see me in pain. If I was in pain, they knew Silas would be too, and that was the ultimate goal."

Rory lets out a low whistle. "They're ballsy—I'll give them that. I don't know much about Silas and his—*role*—but he's not someone I would like to piss off. That was the case even before I knew he was Count *motherfucking* Dracula, but I saw how much they were bidding on your blood. They were all willing to pay more money than I will probably see in my life—so they were highly motivated to hurt him in some way."

The angry burn in my belly grows. The more I heal and feel better, the less angry I am for what was done to me, but instead I'm angry that I was used as a vessel to hurt Silas. I'm enraged anyone would try and hurt Silas in the first place. "They're too afraid of him to face him in person, so like cowards, they hid behind screen names."

"Well, then they're idiots too, because those screen names aren't foolproof. The security on that website was topnotch, but I've seen better. It would take some digging, but if someone wanted to, you could find out who was hiding behind those names," she explains casually while picking at the chipped black nail polish on her fingernails.

I sit up straighter in my chair as a half-baked—probably really fucking dumb—plan comes to me. I don't even have to run it past him to know that Silas wouldn't want me doing it, but that's exactly why I'm not going to tell him. He's keeping his own secrets and I can do the same.

"Rory," I start, pulling her attention back to me. "I know you don't work for Silas anymore, but would you consider doing a job for me?"

Her eyes spark with interest, "What exactly do you have in mind?"

CHAPTER 17

Quincey

I leave Duke's room feeling lighter than I went into it. I know I won't stop worrying about him until he's awake and we have all the answers, but I leave knowing that while we wait for those, he won't be alone. Della will be there. Or Rory, if she's going to continue to sneak in and see Duke.

We didn't talk about what she was doing or why she was there, and we didn't have to. Her eyes when she looked at Duke told me everything I needed to know, whether she wanted to admit it to me or even herself.

Closing the sliding glass door, I find Lor standing against the wall, tattooed arms crossed in front of his chest and eyes closed. He looks relaxed and harmless, but I know differently.

He was listening to everything we were saying and when his eyes partially open and his lips tilt in a knowing smirk, he confirms it.

"I don't need a lecture," I cut him off before he can ridicule me for what I have planned. "I need to do this."

He holds his hands up. "Hey! Don't make assumptions like that.

I'm all for it and was actually going to offer my assistance." He pauses for a beat. "That is if you would like it."

I consider my options for a second before nodding my head. "Fine, but you better keep your mouth shut and not go blab to Silas."

"I'm wounded that you think I would be a gossip, Quincey."

"I think your ego can handle it," I scoff, walking past him toward the elevator.

Before I have time to reach out and push the call button, the silver doors open, and Della appears. Her gray hair has been washed, and it's once again styled in one of her sleek updos, making her appear more like herself. Her face is still devoid of any makeup, but that's okay given she still looks like at any second, she could burst into tears.

"You look better." I smile at her. "Hopefully you feel a little better too."

"The hotel room Silas has me in is nicer than my house. The shower is too." It's not a secret that Silas enjoys the finer things in life. "And I ate something so, yes, I'm feeling better."

Gently clutching her shoulder, I say, "I'm glad. You have to take care of yourself too, Della. Duke wouldn't want you to be miserable."

She releases a long sigh. "I just really hope the doctor's plan works and he wakes up tomorrow."

"He will," is my immediate answer.

Della pats my face softly before she turns to walk toward Duke's room. Before she can get too far, I reach out for her arm and stop her. "Rory is in there right now with him."

Della's eyes narrow and she frowns at the closed door. "Why on earth is she in there? She isn't supposed to be."

"It's okay," I quickly assure her. "She's here for Duke, and right now, he needs all his people supporting him."

"*She's* not his people; *we're* his people." Della looks like a true mama bear about to go protect her cub. It's honestly a really endearing sight.

When she tries to charge toward his room, I pull her back. "Della, just let her be there for him. She isn't going to cause him any harm."

Debating this for a second, she finally relaxes, and I release her arm.

"Fine, but I don't know what I'm going to talk to her about. We don't have any common ground—have you seen her tattoos? And that hair color?"

"Well shit, Della, I didn't think you were so uptight." Lorcan gives her a disapproving look, and I have to swallow a laugh because he does such a good job at mimicking the expression she constantly wears. "We don't talk about your sweater sets and sensible footwear when we sure as hell could. And I have a lot of opinions."

Della's lips pull back in a sneer, but before she can get into a verbal match she's sure to lose, I step between the pair. "*Duke* is your common ground. Go talk about Duke." As an afterthought, I add lowly to ensure no one overhears, "And talk about Silas. Try and convince her that all vampires aren't deranged or evil."

Rory was clearly an asset to Silas and his company. I feel bad that he sacrificed that relationship to save me, but I think with a little nudging, we can get Rory back on his side.

"Well, that won't be easy, considering she met *him*." Della gestures flippantly at Lorcan.

"I'll have you know Rory and I had a wonderful time together."

Like a referee, I lift my hands and separate the two of them. "Okay, you two, that's enough." Ignoring the vampire, I look at Della. "I would expect this from him, but come on, Della. Not you too?"

With one last scowl at Lor, Della walks down the hallway and disappears into Duke's room. The blond vampire has a dumb grin on his face the entire time he watches her leave.

"Had I known Silas surrounded himself with such entertaining people, I would have come here sooner," Lorcan announces, turning back to me. "I thought he was too uptight."

"That's how he wants to appear in the public eye, and I think we all learned this week why." I step into the elevator that's thankfully empty. "Someone is always watching, waiting for him to show any weakness so they can destroy him with it. Keep that in mind the next time you call him uptight, Lorcan. You're only seeing one side of him."

He follows me inside and the doors close behind him. "I'll have to take your word for it." The ding of the elevator fills the momentary silence as we drop three floors. "Are you ready to go back to the house? I bet he'll be home soon."

I stare at my distorted reflection in the chrome doors and think about how Silas will look at me when I get home. My stomach sinking at the thought makes the decision for me. "No, there's one more place I want to go."

For just a little while longer, I want a break from that house and that worried expression on his face.

The familiar music and smell of the club washes over me at the same time Lorcan grumbles, "I think you're trying to sign my death warrant, Quincey. Silas is going to be irate when he learns I brought you here."

"I think he'd be more upset if you let me come here alone." I momentarily forget he's a vampire with superhuman hearing and raise my voice over the thundering bass. When he winces and jerks back, I figure out my mistake. "Which is still an option. You're more than welcome to march your happy Irish ass out those doors," I offer him, even though I know he won't leave.

Lorcan talks a big game, but I'm learning quickly that he's more duty bound than he likes to appear. He told Silas he would watch over me and that's exactly what he's going to do. Even if that means I demand he take me to the nightclub I used to work with Lucy at.

It's Saturday night and packed. I know she'll be here. She wouldn't be willing to miss out on the kind of tips that can be made tonight.

It's been too long since I saw Lucy. The last time I was face-to-face with her is when she helped me pack up my small number of belongings from her apartment.

After the week I've had, I really need to see my friend.

The good babysitter he is, Lorcan sticks close as I weave through the bodies so I can get to the black and gold bar across the room. It's close to midnight and the partygoers are all in different stages of drunkenness. Some look like they're barely staying on their feet, and a little green around the gills. Others look like they're having the time of their lives, the excitement of the city working its magic on them. I find myself jealous of their carefree attitudes.

I don't wish to go back to how things were before when I still believed monsters were just from my drunk mother's imagination, and I will never regret meeting Silas, but just for a moment, it would be nice to walk away and be blissfully unaware of the dangerous world I've found myself in.

A break—that's all I want and then I will happily return to Silas's kingdom of shadows.

Breaking through the large group of people, I slip into an empty spot at the bar and search for my friend.

Lucy stands at the other side, her ever-present scowl firmly in place as she places a cocktail in front of a customer. He tries to talk to her, a coy smirk on his face. With a wicked grin she tells him something I can't hear from here, but I know by the way his face falls and his ego visibly deflates, my best friend just verbally went for the kill. She always does.

Adjusting the high ponytail she wears, she turns away from him with a victorious smirk.

Her observant eyes scan the bar and before I can open my mouth to get her attention, they land on me. The relief she feels is written across her face, but just as fast as it appeared, it twists into anger. She throws her hands up in question as she mouths the words, "*What the fuck, dude?"*

Yeah, Lucy, I've been saying that a lot to myself lately.

I brace myself for her wrath and questions when she scurries around the counter as fast as her high-heeled stilettos will allow her. There are times that I miss working side by side with my childhood friend, but I do not miss the skimpy outfits that are required of the staff here.

"That's her?" Lorcan talks close to my ear so I can hear him over the music. "You should have mentioned your friend is hot, Quincey."

"Don't even bother, she will eat you alive."

He groans, almost like he's in pain. "Promise?" he asks, making puppy-dog eyes at me.

At this point, all I can do is shake my head at him as a final warning. If he wants to try it, that's up to him, but I know it won't end well for him.

Lucy elbows the random guy next to me out of the way. When he looks at her and his lips part like he's going to complain, she silences him with a single look. With his tail between his legs, he shuffles away.

"Quincey *'My mom never bothered to give me a middle name'* Page, where in the fuck have you been?" Lucy shouts once she's standing in front of me. "I have been worried sick about—" I know the second she sees the bruises on my face. She goes from being irritated at me to homicidal in a blink of an eye. "Who did it?" she bites out between clenched teeth. "Who put their fucking hands on you, Q? Where are they? I'm going to fucking *kill* them."

"Luce," I try to calm her down, but it's no use. There's no putting out the fire I accidentally just started. "I'm okay."

Her fingers snatch my chin and tilt my face toward the light of the bar. "The fuck you are, Quincey! Look at your face." As if she's suddenly just now noticing the tattooed man standing next to me, her eyes narrow at Lor. "Did you do this to her?"

Thinking she's joking, Lorcan chokes on a laugh, but stops quickly when he figures out she's being serious. "Excuse me? You think *I* put my hands on *her*? Sorry to disappoint, darling. While I do enjoy living a little recklessly, I don't actually have a death wish."

Looking back at me, she demands. "Then *who*?"

The truth is right on the tip of my tongue, but no matter how much I want to, I can't spew out; *'Holy shit, Lucy. Mom was right, vampires are real and guess what? I let one fuck my brains out, and oops, surprise, I'm in love with him too. But before I could tell him that, I was kidnapped and tortured by another vampire, but don't worry about me, I'm good. Oh, and I now have matching scars on my chest, but it's okay, because X marks the spot, and you and I both know I'm a real treasure'.* Lucy would have me in a straitjacket and matching Velcro mittens at the first mention of vampires.

Instead, I lie. I lie, because I want to keep my best friend safe from this world for as long as possible. "Duke and I were on our way back to the house I've been working at when a deer jumped in front of the car. Duke swerved and we ended up crashing." *Lies, lies, lies.* "I was a little banged up, but Duke hit his head. He's stable, but we're waiting for the swelling in his brain to go down. They're going to try and wake him up tomorrow."

"*What!*" Lucy shrieks, an appalled look on her face. "Why didn't you *call* me?"

Guilt is a lovely thing, isn't it? Makes you feel like you have a thousand-pound weight on your chest, but at the same time, you might puke.

"My phone was damaged in the accident, but honestly, Luce, it's been a really bad week and I was really shaken up from all of it. I just needed a couple days to get myself together before I saw you." They say the best lies are the ones with truth weaved in.

Lucy looks at me, her eyes taking in every inch of my face. I know what she's doing, she's looking for the cracks in my story—and in me—but I came prepared. The entire way over here, I built a wall I never thought I'd have to put up between myself and her.

If she truly believes me or just elects to drop it, I'm not sure, but she releases my chin, and the harsh lines of her face smooth.

"You really scared me when I didn't hear from you, Q. You can't just get some mysterious job and then drop off the face of the earth. That's not how this works—that's not how we fucking work." Her finger points at me. "Don't *ever* do that again."

"I won't," I promise as I wrap my arms around her. There's a twinge of discomfort as my stitches pull, but it's worth it to be reunited with my friend.

"And for the love of God, get a new phone." Lucy grumbles into my shoulder when she hugs me back, making me laugh. "When can I visit Duke? I'll bring him a teddy bear or something. Maybe a bottle of whiskey?"

"He's in the ICU. I'll see if there's a time you can stop by," I tell her after she releases me and takes a step back.

"Good. Once he's up and moving, I want to get a picture of him in one of those sexy hospital gowns." And that's what I love about Lucy. Without having to be told, she talks about Duke like everything is going to be okay—like the alternative isn't even an option. Lucy isn't usually the *glass half full* one of the pair, but she knows I need her to be this one time. "So, what can I do now to help since I couldn't help you this week?"

I feel my face split in a devious grin. "Remember our senior year when we broke into that swimming pool, and we had to run from the cops?"

Lucy winces. "Yeah, I remember."

"Great." I clap my hands together. "I want to be that drunk in the next hour. So, you, my friend, can get a bottle and start pouring the drinks."

Lorcan curses under his breath. "*That's* your plan? Getting drunk alone in some club?"

"Yup."

Slowly, a grin that matches mine grows on Lucy's face. "Who said she's drinking alone?" Waving her hand at the bartender behind the counter, she shouts, "Tequila, top shelf!"

And that's another reason I love Lucy, no matter how stupid the plan or idea, she'll be right there with me, lime and salt at the ready.

CHAPTER 18

Silas

The vindictive monster inside me purrs at the sight in front of me, satisfied with what we've done to our enemy.

The ten-by-ten room is made of nothing but white marble and vampire-proof glass. Each wall of the glorified jail cell is see-through.

Even if he wanted to, there's nowhere for him to hide. The high wattage fluorescent lights ensure there aren't any shadows for him to slink into like the coward he is. He's getting his wish; I can see every deceitful inch of him.

Just like he'd done to Quincey, Gideon has been left exposed and bare in his glass box—like my own goddamn zoo exhibit.

Quincey hasn't talked about her time with him, and I haven't pried for information, too afraid I'd push her too far and I'd inadvertently hinder her healing process, but the few bits of information she'd offered freely were small tidbits about how she thought Gideon's psyche had completely crumbled.

I'd figured that to be true based on what I saw on the video feed but watching the man who was once my most trusted confidant sit in the corner of the glass room with his knees pulled to his chest while he talks endlessly to himself, confirms Quincey's theory.

The final straw for this man's mind was when I took the last thing he had going for him; his revenge plan against me. With that now destroyed, no part of him resembles the man I once knew.

A truly unfortunate occurrence, seeing as I need more information from him.

I need to know who the fuck his partner is because while he's been here in this box, someone is still targeting me.

This time, they aren't damaging the properties or product. They're purposely targeting the employees I have working at those locations. Aside from when he killed my men working at the docks, Gideon hadn't set out to kill my staff. They were simply collateral damage—civilian casualties in the war that Gideon was determined to have.

But that's all changed this past week. Twice now, my businesses have been targeted, and the employees have been brutally murdered. Twenty human lives have been taken so far.

The guard hits the intercom button at my signal. At the loud buzz as the mic connects, Gideon jerks in surprise, but he doesn't stop speaking his mumbled words.

His eyes dart around the small room and stop when they find me standing outside the glass.

"Do you regret it now?" I use the same words he'd asked me at the warehouse. He doesn't answer me, but I didn't expect him to. My head cocks to the side, my face devoid of any expression as I observe him. "I can only assume this isn't the outcome you saw when you formulated this plan." My hands clasp behind my back and I begin to slowly circle the glass cube. "No. You never thought you'd live this long, isn't that right?" I fill in the blanks for him, seeing as he still prefers to talk to himself. I come to a stop just outside the glass wall he sits in front of.

"You thought you could take Quincey from me, then be reunited with your Margret."

I know this to be fact. He's said as much to Quincey when he tortured her.

At the mention of her name, his mouth finally stops forming indecipherable words and his head snaps in my direction. Faster than any human could move, Gideon is on his feet. Standing directly in front of me, his fist slams against the glass. He violently screams, "Where is she? You took her from me!" Saliva flies from his mouth, splattering the clear glass. "I can't see her anymore! What have you done with her?"

"Tell me who your partner is, and I'll let you see her again." It's an offer I have no intention of following through with. The only way he can see her again is through death, and like I've said, he's not getting off that easily.

If he's comprehended what I've said, it isn't clear, the wild—completely insane—look in his eyes disguises any other emotion or thought he has.

"Margret has always been my partner."

"That might be true, but I know there is someone else," I press, unwilling to let this go. There are lives on the line. "Tell me who it is."

He backs away from the glass at an unnaturally slow pace. His fingers twist together, and he turns away. Once again, he begins a conversation with himself that only he can understand.

My patience for the matter begins to wear thin. I told Quincey I would only be gone a couple of hours, and I don't want her to be alone for too long. Though I have a suspicion that Lorcan ignored my warning to leave her be. Like a toddler, he likes to do the opposite of what he's told. He may be over two hundred years old, but he's never used that time to mature.

Just before I'm about to enact my plan B for getting Gideon to talk, he whirls around, a concerning grin on his face. "Bring Quincey here."

My chest begins to rumble hearing him use her name. It's as if he wishes for me to cut his tongue from his mouth.

"That will *never* happen." It's now my personal mission to make sure Quincey isn't in the same zip code of Gideon. I would prefer to keep them states apart, but right now, that's simply not realistic.

The grin remains on his face, unwavering. It looks as fake in person as it did on camera. "If you want your answer, you will bring her here."

"You seem to believe I don't have other ways I can get information from you, Gideon." I *tsk* under my breath. "I thought you would know my ways better than that."

I raise my hand, motioning the guard over to this side of the cube.

"Yes, sir."

"Has he been fed today?" My eyes remain on the crazed man behind the glass.

"Not yet. The last time he was given blood was yesterday, but it was just the allotted amount as you instructed."

For Gideon to suffer as much as possible, he must be fed if he is to live as long as I want him to.

Depriving him of blood for a couple of days won't kill him, but it'll be unbearable.

"Let's see if he feels like talking when the hunger pangs are so intense he can't see straight," I instruct Franco. "Let's see if we can't make you beg for mercy like you thought you could do to Quincey." With that, I leave him and his mumbling alone in the room.

The basement level is cooler than the rest, and as I climb the stone stairs up, the air warms. This is a building I spend as little time in as possible. Usually when I'm here, it means a vampire disobeyed me or broke a law, and their punishment needs to be carried out. Gideon isn't the first vampire in the glass box, and he won't be the last, because they never fucking learn.

This place once was a place of worship, now it's where the council meets when I feel inclined to entertain their incessant demands. It's a taxing task pretending to be engrossed by their words, but if it makes them feel like they have a voice in my kingdom and keeps them in line, I'll bear the boredom.

I purchased this church when I arrived in New Orleans. It was just a decaying building. I restored the inside and ensured the structural soundness of the exterior, but to any human passing by, they'll simply believe it's another abandoned building located off the quarter. There's enough security kept here that if someone does venture through the metal gate around the perimeter, they are taken care of swiftly and efficiently.

My phone rings in my suit jacket, the sound bounces off the stained-glass windows and high ceilings of the space as I walk down the aisle between the pews. Concern instantly fills me that something has happened to Quincey when I see Lorcan's number on the screen.

"What's wrong?" I answer without a formal greeting. When the sound of loud music and joyous laughter comes through the speaker, I stop in my tracks. The concern is replaced by anger in a second. "Where the fuck are you?" I bite out.

"I will be the first to admit that mistakes have been made," Lorcan answers, the regret clear in his voice. "I thought I was helping, but it appears things may have gotten out of control." There's a crashing sound, like glass breaking, followed by a warning growl. "Hey, dumb fuck! Yeah, *you*. If you don't get the fuck away from her, I'm going to put my foot so far up your ass, you will be able to taste the Italian leather of my boot."

"Lorcan!" a female shouts over the booming music. "Dance with us!"

Us?

The anger rushes through me, making my muscles vibrate. "I will ask once more; where the fuck are you, Lorcan?"

"We're at St. Sin."

A herd of deer know when a mountain lion is close. They can sense the danger. It's no different with humans. They might think they're at the top of the food chain, but really, they're prey animals and they know when a predator is among them. They behave accordingly when that happens.

I don't have to push them out of the way or weave through their drunk, sweaty bodies. They simply see me coming and get out of the way, creating a direct path for me to get to her. Their eyes go wide, and their concerned whispers follow behind me, but I don't pay them any mind.

My attention is on the blonde female that dances on the bar top with her childhood friend while men stand below her, cheering her on as if she's their own personal exotic dancer.

I should be relieved to see the smile I adore so much spread across her pretty face, even if it is alcohol induced, but I'm too livid to truly appreciate it. I'm livid at Lorcan for bringing her here when he's fully aware the danger remains and the attacks are still happening. And I'm livid at her for willingly leaving the safety of my home to come *here* where drunk human men can paw at her like they have the right to do so.

Lorcan stands below them, trying to keep the crowd of men that had formed under control, but he's outnumbered and it's evident he's trying to do so without becoming too violent. Violence is Lorcan's specialty, but he's smart enough to keep a low profile when among humans.

It's usually a rule I follow myself, but I can't be bothered to do so right now, especially when a staggering man reaches up to stuff a dollar bill in the back pocket of Quincey's shorts.

Before he has a chance to retract his hand from her body, I've appeared next to him, and his fragile human bones are cracking under my fingertips when I grip his wrist. His head snaps in my direction and he chokes on a pained scream when he looks at me. Whatever he sees written across my face steals his ability to make any noise. The friends that surround him take large steps back, their faces falling.

"I will give you thirty seconds to leave this place." The time allotment is long on purpose. I want him to feel each agonizingly slow tick of the clock. "If you or your companions are still here, I will shatter the bones in your hands so severely, you will never be able to wrap your fingers around your own cock again." My hand tightens around his wrist to enhance my point. "Your time starts now. One… two… three…"

By four, his friends are dashing for the door. He tries to pull from my grasp, but I keep in place until I reach twenty. "You have ten seconds. You better *fucking* run." My fingers loosen and he pulls free, sprinting after the rest of them.

The crowd, having witnessed this, disperses until Lorcan and I are the only ones that remain in front of where they dance.

Lor opens his mouth like he's going to try and reason with me, but I silence him quickly with a warning look. I'll deal with him later, after I've returned Quincey to the safety of my home.

"Quincey," I grit out just loud enough to hopefully be heard over the music. I refuse to stand here and yell her name like another one of those men trying to get her attention. And I know I won't need to; she'll sense that I'm here soon enough. She's always been in tune with me. The alcohol polluting her veins is just hindering that skill right now.

She dances offbeat for another minute before her spine snaps straight and her hands drop from where they were grasping Lucy's hips.

Quincey spins around so fast, I prepare myself to catch her falling frame, but she's steadier on her feet than I thought she'd be.

Powder-blue eyes pin me, and my chest aches when that bright smile is directed at me. There is no remorse for her actions or worry for my anger on her face. She simply looks elated to see me.

"You're here," she sighs happily, dropping down into a squat so we are eye level. Her hands reach out and cup my face. "You're always finding me, aren't you?"

I don't care how angry she makes me, I will always come for her, but right now, I'm not in the mood for sentimental words. "Get off the bar. We're going home, Quincey."

If anyone else heard the seriousness of my tone, they'd follow my instruction for fear of their safety, but not Quincey. Her face hardens and the defiance shines in her eyes like blue flames. "I'm not done dancing."

"Yes," I grit out. "You are."

Completely unfazed, she continues to test my patience. "I want to spend the night at Lucy's apartment."

The alcohol must be making her delusional if she thinks I'd allow her to sleep anywhere else but with me. "Not fucking happening. The only place you're sleeping is next to me in *my* bed. Now get off the fucking bar so we may leave."

Quincey's lips pull back in a sneer. "No."

"It seems you've forgotten how much I despise that word, *Mon Soleil*. Should I remind you what happens when I'm denied what I want?"

I don't know what I expect her reaction to be, but her lips lifting in a sultry smirk and her gaze heating isn't it. "Yes. Why don't you remind me, Mr. Laurent?" Hand still caressing my face, she leans in close so she can whisper in my ear. "If being taught a lesson is what it takes for you to touch me again, I'll happily be your student."

Quincey drags her eyes over my lips and leans in as if she's going to kiss me right here in the middle of this club for anyone to see, causing me to stiffen under her touch. For centuries, I've worked tirelessly to keep my private life a secret because my fear was always that it would be used against me. Gideon is proof that my fear was justified.

Before her lips can touch mine, she pulls back and her face drops. "Yeah, that's what I thought." Her hand falls from my face and she stands to her full height on the bar once more. "If you can't even kiss me like you used to, then you should go home alone, Silas. Come find me when you figure your shit out."

I must really be failing if she truly believes I don't want to kiss her—to touch her body and reclaim it as mine. I would do it right here on this dirty bar top if I felt it was safe. It's clear she's no longer burdening herself with worry for her own safety, but one of us has to. One of us must remain in control.

In a shockingly graceful move, she twirls back to Lucy who's watching me with knowing eyes. I don't know what Quincey has told her, but I know the human is privy to information she shouldn't be, but that is the least of my worries right now.

Quincey's hand reaches out for the bottle of tequila in Lucy's hand, but before her fingertips can brush against the glass, I wrap my hand around her forearm and pull her off the bar.

She stumbles and tries to regain her balance, but it's no use. Quincey falls from the bar with a startled yelp, but as always, I'm there to catch her. She falls over my shoulder with a harsh curse.

Before she can try to shimmy away, I wrap my arm around her bare thighs, locking her in place. When her legs begin to thrash and her hands beat on my lower back, I have flashbacks to one of our first encounters. She was desperate that night to get away from me because she was scared, but tonight she isn't afraid. She's angry and her colorful choice of swear words confirms that.

With a nod of my head toward Lucy, Lorcan understands my silent instruction and begins to help Quincey's friend from the bar top.

Just like when I entered the club, the gathering of people on the dance floor creates a path when I begin to carry an irate Quincey out of the establishment. Worried eyes linger on the blonde woman on my shoulder, but no one dares to try and stop me.

"Put me down!" Her fingernails are raking against my back through my shirt.

"If you're going to tell me no like a petulant child, I'm going to treat you like one by carrying you out of this place since you refused to do so yourself."

There's an irritated growl before she shouts, "Silas!"

Outside of the building, Lucy and Lorcan both meet us on the crowded sidewalk of Bourbon Street. As if she's flipped a switch, Lucy appears completely sober, making me think she hasn't been drinking as much as she wants Quincey to believe.

"I'm taking Quincey home," I inform Lorcan. "Please ensure that Miss Bell here is returned safely to her apartment."

"Put me down. I want to go home with Lucy!"

"More babysitting duty. *Yay.*" Lorcan lifts his hands and mockingly waves them in excitement.

"That won't be necessary. I'm more than capable of finding my own way home." Lucy's arms cross tightly in front of her.

Lorcan's completely unbothered by her blatant disinterest. "You should be more careful. Walking home alone on these streets is unwise. Don't you know about the monsters lurking around corners out here? They're just waiting to get their hands on an ass as sweet as yours." His eyes trail over the tight dress she wears, lingering on her backside just a little too long.

Those knowing eyes of hers cut to me as she says, "Yeah, I'm aware of the monsters in this town. I've seen how bad their bite is, but I'm not afraid of them." Lucy doesn't wait to confirm I'm reading between the lines of her message. She simply knows I am. "My bark is worse anyway, and you're going to find that out the hard way if you don't stop gawking at my ass, Lorcan." Her arm swings out and she backhands him across his chest. "*Enough.*"

Even though it didn't hurt, Lorcan rubs at the spot on his sternum. "You like it rough, darling? That's okay, so do I."

"You have no idea what I like," Lucy snaps. "And if you did, you couldn't handle it."

A shit-eating grin breaks across Lor's face. "Is that a challenge, Lucy?"

Lucy rolls her eyes with an annoyed huff.

Quincey's legs kick violently as she lets out a frustrated screech. "Oh my fucking god! Flirt or fuck, I don't care, but someone make him put me down!"

Lorcan chuckles, but wisely makes no move to assist her.

Lucy grabs Quincey's ankle, giving it a loving squeeze before apologizing to her, "Sorry, Q, no can do. He's caught you and there's no getting free now."

She has no idea just how true that statement is.

Before she turns away to leave, Lucy pauses and looks at me. "I know she's lying to me," she whispers so low that only my advanced hearing can pick up on it. "She spins a good tale, but the restraint marks on her wrists she tried to hide from me gave her away." Her face sets in a deadly glare. "I don't give a fuck who you are, Laurent. If I find out you're the one who hurt her, I will kill you myself." With her parting threat, the human turns on her heels and with her head held high, she walks away from us, leaving the confirmation that she knows more than she should in her wake.

"Lorcan, follow her home."

"Goody, I've been demoted from babysitter to stalker. I'm really starting to forget why I'm still here," he whines mostly to himself, at the same time, Quincey thrashes violently in my grasp.

"Put me down right now or I swear to God, I'm going to donate every single one of your Armani suits to Good-*fucking*-Will!" Her hands slap harder against my lower back.

Lorcan cocks his head, staring at Quincey with raised eyebrows. "Now I remember."

CHAPTER 19

Silas

She climbed into the back of the SUV, opting to sit in the confined third row rather than sit beside me. For the entire span of the drive home, she drank the large water bottle we'd stopped to purchase at a convenience store, and she sobered up.

It was for the best that we didn't talk, seeing as the displeasure still stirred in my chest that she'd be so reckless in the first place. The relief that she was now safe and under my supervision did little to quell the anger.

By the time the car stopped in front of the house, the alcohol-induced haziness had left Quincey's eyes and without a word, she jumped out of the car, leaving me behind.

Her escape is short lived when she discovers the front door is locked. Arms crossed, she stands there now with an impatient look on her face as she waits for me to open the door.

Still scowling, she watches when I press my hand to the black handprint reader next to the door. When Duke was hired years ago, he had each of the doors outfitted with these readers, so we didn't have to mess with keys. And as he said then, locks are easy to pick. It would take someone with a particular background to get through these electronic ones.

The second the dead bolt unlocks, Quincey shoves the door open and stalks inside. She steps out of her shoes as she goes, leaving them in the middle of the foyer before going up the stairs.

"Quincey," I attempt, but she doesn't turn around.

Sighing, I scrub a hand down my face. If I were a patient man, I would allow her time to calm herself down so we can discuss this rationally. Or I can follow her and demand we discuss whatever the hell is going on in that head of hers.

I contemplate my choices for all of ten seconds, but in the end, there really isn't a choice to be made. I don't feel like waiting.

I'm up the stairs and stalking down the hallway before Quincey's even made it to her bedroom door. It's sweet she thinks I'm going to allow her to sleep in a separate bed. I slept alone for the past three hundred years, and I thought I was content with that until I discovered I much prefer having her next to me.

As if she believes a closed door will be enough to keep me out, she slams it shut.

My fingers curl into my palms at her childish behavior.

My fists thud against the wood, breaking the feeble lock. The door bangs against the wall behind it and I saunter inside the room just as she's pulling the hoodie she wears over her head.

Every time I see the bandages on her chest, the uncontrollable monster inside of me rears its head, demanding we spill Gideon's blood the same way he spilled Quincey's.

"Make sure you change your bandages after you shower," I instruct tersely instead. "We wouldn't want you getting an infection."

Quincey whirls around, eyes glaring with anger. "Get out!" she yells, gesturing at the open door behind me. "I can't do this right now—I can't deal with you right now."

"That's unfortunate seeing as I don't intend on going anywhere." I shrug out of the black suit jacket I wear and fold it neatly before placing it on the bed she hasn't slept in since coming home. "It appears that my concern for your health and safety is no longer being appreciated," I observe, while removing the black diamond cuff links from my black button-down so I can roll the sleeves up.

Her hand drops and irritation twists her pretty face. "Your concern has morphed into coddling. You handling me with kid gloves is not *appreciated*." She stares at me and whatever she finds reflected in my expression she must not like because she charges at me, her finger pointing at my face. "And *that*! I fucking hate that look on your face."

She shoves at my chest. If she was anyone else, I'd never allow such behavior, but for her, I try to remain still despite the stirring anger I feel in my veins. "I don't know what you're referring to," I grit.

"You're looking at me like I'm broken and you're treating me like something you need to fix!" Despite her raised voice, not once does it waiver. She remains strong. "I've been treated a lot of ways in my life, but I refuse to tolerate this. I was treated like a verbal punching bag by my mother, and sometimes when she drank just a little too much, I was her physical one too. But I found a way to get through it. I have been used and traded like a goddamn pawn by almost every one of the men in my life. First, my dad traded me to pay a debt, and then you used me in your own way too. But I found a way to get through it."

Her hands drop, stopping their assault on my chest. She steps back, composing herself. Swallowing, she lifts her chin and looks at me as she says, "I was used as a ploy in a war that had *nothing* to do with me. I was kidnapped and tortured because I was viewed as something to be used *yet* again. But I found a way to get through it. It changed me, but I fucking got through it. Whether you want to believe me or not, I'm okay, Silas."

None of this is new information but it affects me like it is. My chest vibrates, knowing that so many people treated her without the dignity and respect she deserves. Myself included. While I don't regret having her in my life, I regret the way in which she was brought into it. I was no better than her father when I paid her debt and blackmailed her into working with me.

"Quincey..."

"And I really need you to believe me because if you keep coddling me and looking at me like I'm damaged, I'm going to scream. That is the one thing I can't get through." She steps forward and her hand grips my chin. "I am not something that can be used or traded. I am not broken and I'm not a pawn. I am a fucking queen." Quincy's hand drops from my chin to trail down my chest. "I could be your queen, Silas, if you'd only look at me as such."

My queen. I've ruled alone for so long. Never have I had a desire to share that responsibility with anyone else, but then came Quincey and her fiery spirit. Could she really be strong enough to stand at my side?

"You have no idea what you're offering, Quincey." My hand snakes up to rest over hers, but the second I brush my fingertips across her skin, she snaps her hand away.

The step she backs away from me further ignites the irritation I'm experiencing. It dawns on me as I narrow my eyes at her that this is what she's been feeling all week. Any amount of distance between us is unacceptable, and all week I've been the one stepping away from her. Even if I thought my intentions were in the right place.

"You're wrong again. I know *exactly* what I'm offering, and I know exactly what I want." Her chest heaves under the simple black bra she wears. "I want the dark king who looked at me with so much passion I didn't know if he wanted to fuck me or kill me. I want the man who touched me without asking permission and grabbed onto me like if he didn't he was going to die. I want that man, but where the hell is he? I haven't seen him all week and I fucking miss him."

Quincey's hands shove violently at my chest again. Even if she's putting every ounce of her strength behind it, I don't flinch. Her palms connect with my sternum, but before she can pull away, my hands encircle her wrists and I pull her closer to me. "He didn't go anywhere, he's been here the whole time," I seethe, dropping my head so we're eye to eye. A fire I've never seen burns in her eyes.

It shines with a level of strength that catches me off guard. Has that been there all week and I've just been so blinded by my own worry I've missed it completely?

She yanks her hands, trying to get free of my grasp. The only reason I release her is because I don't want to cause further strain on her healing nerves.

But what she does next makes me think letting her go may have been a mistake.

"No, he's not. He's not here and I want him back! Give him back to me!"

I didn't think anything could catch me by surprise anymore. I thought I'd experienced it all, but when her palm connects against my cheek in a violent slap, I'm admittedly stunned silent. But the shock is fleeting and replaced with overwhelming rage.

Before she can so much as blink, I've grabbed hold of her and have her pinned by her throat against the wall. A snarl rips through my chest. "Is this what you want?" I question darkly, close to her face.

The last time I had her in this position, she at least had the decency to know she'd lost, but now, she looks at me like she's won. "*Fucking finally*. There he is." Her pink lips pull in a wicked grin and her pulse pounds against my fingers. "This is the man I want. This is the man I fell in love with."

There's been a few times since I met Quincey that I thought I felt my heart beat once more, and this is now one of those times.

Love. I never thought I'd be worthy of someone's love again. No one should willingly hand their heart over to a monster like me, but Quincey, without any fear, is doing just that.

I have collected countless priceless items over the years, each one rarer and more valuable than the next, but all of it is worthless compared to Quincey's heart. Her heart is the most priceless item I have ever been gifted.

It's been over three hundred years since my tongue has strung together the three words I know without a shadow of a doubt to be how I feel about Quincey Page. Yet, as I stare down at those eyes that remind me of a clear blue sky, I can't bring myself to say them. Not because I don't want to, but because they don't feel like they're *enough*.

I cannot truly encapsulate what I feel for Quincey in three simple words.

CHAPTER 20

Silas

Quincey's admission sits heavy between us for only a moment before I'm taking ownership of her lips with my own. She doesn't yelp in surprise or stiffen under my touch, instead she sighs in relief. Relief that I'm giving her what she's needed from me all along.

My gentle touches and tender care weren't aiding her healing—they were hindering it.

Her hand reaches up, covering mine that still collars her throat. She doesn't make any effort to remove the dominating hold. If anything, she signals me to increase the pressure on her delicate throat by squeezing my fingers.

Even after what she's been through, she knows I could never hurt her. While the hands of another man left her with scars, she willingly puts her life in mine.

Her lips part, granting me access when I run my tongue along the seam. I groan when her tongue boldly meets mine. Nothing about this kiss is a well-orchestrated dance. It isn't neat or graceful. It's chaotic and messy. It's full of desperate need.

The fear I've had of causing her further harm vanishes the second her other hand palms my stiffening cock through my slacks. I didn't realize just how hard I'd been suppressing my craving for her all week. It roars to life inside of me like a wildfire. It's just as out of control and unpredictable as a real fire.

"I'm right here," I rasp, biting into her plump bottom lip with blunt teeth. "I didn't go anywhere. I'm still the man you want, but more importantly, I'm the man you fucking *need*."

"*Yes*." She hisses out a breath of pain but doesn't try to escape me. I lick the sting away, making her smile. "I need you. *Only* you."

My hand drops from her throat, but before she has time to protest, I'm picking her up off the ground. In her next breath, we're across the room and her back is hitting the cream-colored comforter covering her mattress.

The four-post bed skids across the hardwood floor from the force of our momentum, making a loud screeching noise. Despite the heated moment, this still causes a breathy laugh.

My hope for us is that no matter how dark things may become, she remains light enough to laugh.

Quincey tries to sit up, but I push her back down flat by pressing a kiss to the center of her chest, right between the bandages that sit there.

On reflex, her hands raise and attempt to cover the evidence of what happened to her from me. I feel her breath hitch and her heartbeat speeds up, but I don't stop. I wish a kiss to those wounds would be enough to heal them, to wash away the memory of them, but I know, like the scars, the memories are here to stay.

I push her hands away with a terse shake of my head. "Don't ever hide yourself from me, Quincey. Bear your scars to me so I may cherish each one of them. They tell your story, and I want to read each beautifully painful chapter of it."

She doesn't say anything in return, but her blue eyes lock with mine and her hands drop back to the comforter, allowing me to see her once more.

Trailing kisses down her chest, I pause at her black bra. Taking the offensive fabric in my hands, I tear it from her body. The clothing isn't fully removed before I'm taking one of her taut nipples in my mouth. She groans, her back arching off the bed when I clamp the bud between my teeth.

I want to savor each inch of her, but my ability to go slow has gone to hell. I need to taste her on my tongue again. *Now.*

My fingers grip the hem of her jean shorts. They fit loose on her hips due to a week of lacking an appetite. I yank the denim off her body, taking the black thong underneath with it.

It doesn't matter how many scars are added, Quincey's naked body will continue to be the most amazing sight for me to behold.

Gripping her ankles, I yank her toward the edge of the bed, so her legs dangle off the side.

I don't give her a warning or build up to it. Dropping to my knees between her spread thighs, her bare feet on my shoulders, I take her in my mouth. At the first swipe of my tongue through her sweet cunt, she calls out my name in a gasp. A sound I will never forget, no matter how many years I live.

My arms curl around her legs, my fingers digging into the soft flesh of her thighs. Bruises are only acceptable on her body if I'm the one who left them. They are reminders that I claimed what is mine.

"The sweetest thing," I purr against her slick flesh. "I love the way your body responds to me. You're already wet for me, *Mon Soleil.*"

Her hands tear at the comforter before she fists it in her grasp and her head thrashes back and forth. "*Fuck.*"

My tongue circles her clit teasingly, making her buck against my face.

"More, Silas," she pleads.

"I'll give you everything you need. Anything you want, it's all yours."

Releasing one of her thighs, I sink two fingers into her heat at the same time I suck her sensitive clit into my mouth. Her hand releases the bedding, and her fingers delve into my hair. She pulls on the strands as I continue to devour her like a starved man.

I *am* a starved man; a week is too long to wait to have her. It's an astonishing thought that I was ever capable of functioning without her.

When her thighs begin to shake and the walls of her cunt flutter around my fingers, I retract away from her, depriving her of the release she was so close to achieving.

Quincey cries out, her hands grappling at me in an attempt to pull me back to her center, but I shake my head slowly at her. "Not yet," I tell her.

She attempts to pull herself up, but before she has the chance, I grab her ankles and violently turn her onto her stomach on the bed.

"Wha—" she begins to ask, but her question is replaced with a shocked gasp when my palm connects with her ass cheek.

"You think you can slap me and get away with it, Quincey?" I narrow my eyes at her when she gapes at me over her shoulder. "You must have forgotten who the fuck I am if you thought that would go unreprimanded." My fingers trace lightly over the pretty red handprint forming on her flesh, but just as she starts to relax, I spank her again. Harder.

She makes a strangled sound, somewhere between a moan and a cry. "Now we're even," she pants.

"No, baby, we're not," I growl, bending down to sink my teeth into the round globe of her ass. She yelps and tries to twist away, but I hold her in place.

I don't bite hard enough to break the skin, despite how my gums burn and my fangs threaten to make an appearance. Besides her pussy, her blood may be the best thing I've ever savored. Depriving myself of tasting it goes against everything the monster inside me knows.

"You went to a club and allowed vile human men to touch you. To touch what *belongs* to me. I can still *smell* them on you." Backing away from the bed, I kick off my shoes and begin to unbutton my shirt. "I'm going to fuck you until all I can smell is myself on your skin."

My clothes join her discarded ones on the floor in an unorganized heap. Her heavy eyes watch me over her shoulder as my fingers work on undoing my belt. They widen when my slacks and briefs fall down my legs and my throbbing cock is finally free.

"Get on your knees for your king, Quincey."

Rolling back into a sitting position, she lazily scoots off the bed. She drops to the floor in front of me without complaint. In every aspect of our lives, Quincey enjoys challenging me, but when she's naked and needy for my touch, she becomes pliant—listening keenly to my every word.

Her pink tongue swipes across her bottom lip and her eyes are glued to where my hand strokes my cock in slow, methodical movements. "Have you ever finger fucked yourself while you thought of me, Quincey?"

Caught off guard, her head jerks up and she looks at me. "W-what?"

"I didn't stutter." My grip tightens on my length, making the muscles in my lower abdomen tighten. "But you don't have to answer because I already know the truth. I heard you." The night I stood outside her door listening to her was the night my resolve began to crack. "While you imagined it was me touching that tight cunt of yours, I stood outside the door, and listened to you cry my name as you came on your fingers."

"I thought I heard something outside my door. That was you?" A gorgeous blush forms on her cheekbones and she shifts restlessly where she kneels.

Smirking, I watch her hips flex. "Does the knowledge that I listened to you that night make you wet?"

She nods her head in answer.

"Want to know a secret about that night? While I listened to you moan and writhe with images of me running through your pretty head, I fisted my cock just like this," I tell her, bringing her attention back down to my dick. "And while I did that, I imagined it was your hand on me, bringing me to my release." She breathes heavier, her bare chest heaving, and her hands flex at her sides like she's trying to restrain herself from touching me. "But I don't have to imagine what that's like anymore. Do I?"

"No," she whispers hoarsely.

"No," I repeat in a praising tone. "I have the real thing now." Taking a step closer, my cock is only millimeters from her face. "Remind me how much better the real thing is than my fantasies." I tap her plump bottom lip with the red, angry head. "Open."

Her hot breath ghosts over my sensitive skin, making me shiver as she parts her lips for me. When her mouth wraps around the tip, I have to clench my teeth and grip the wood post of the bed to steady myself.

Blue eyes clash with mine when her tongue circles me, lapping eagerly at the precum that had started to form. "That's it," I hiss my encouragement.

Quincey brings me in deeper and her small hand wraps around the base. Delving my hand into her golden hair, I take control of her head and help her set a rhythm I enjoy. "I'm going to fuck your mouth and while I do, I want you to touch yourself, just like you did that night."

She doesn't hesitate a second before her free hand dips between her thighs. Her fingers sink inside of her and at the same time, she releases a groan around my cock, forcing me to let out a pained breath.

My grip on the bedpost tightens, my knuckles turning white. I half expect the wood to splinter under my touch. I would buy a hundred new bed frames and break each one of them if it meant I got to experience the ecstasy of Quincey's hot mouth.

Her head pulls back, and she sucks in a lungful of air.

She trails wet kisses down my shaft and on her way back to the crown, her tongue teases me.

I jerk in her hand as the tip of her tongue flicks against the sensitive underside.

"Do you like when I'm on my knees for you?" she questions lowly, lips wrapping back around my cock. Her hips flex and she grinds into the heel of her palm. "Shit," she moans, releasing me with a gasp.

"Are you close?" I ask. The pace we'd set vanishes and our movements become more erratic. Her head nods in jerky movements, but I halt them by tightening my hold on her hair. I press my cock to her lips, forcing myself back inside her mouth. "Suck me, and I'll give you permission to come. You're not allowed to come until I tell you so. This is your punishment for letting those fucks touch what's mine."

"I can't, I'm so close."

"You can and you fucking will."

Without warning, I push in deeper than before, nudging the back of her throat. She gags, and her hand releases me to grab hold of my thigh. Her nails dig into my skin, making my skin shiver as pleasure builds inside of me.

Tears run down her face, but she doesn't make any move to try and push me away. She stays put and takes what I give her. I hold her there, depriving her of oxygen for a moment longer before letting her go.

She takes in a greedy gulp of air.

"Good girl," I praise, wiping the saliva from her bottom lip. "Come for me, Quincey."

On her knees before me, she comes apart on her fingers. It's a sight so stunning it should be photographed and hung on a wall. If I wasn't the selfish bastard I am, I would do it, but I refuse to allow anyone else to see such beauty. It's something I will greedily keep to myself.

She falls forward, resting her forehead against my thigh when the blinding ecstasy is done firing through her nerves.

She's still breathing hard when I scoop her up under her arms and place her back on her unstable feet, facing the bed.

"Hold on to the bedpost and don't let go," is my only instruction before I'm pulling her hips back and lining the tip of my cock at her entrance. "Don't ever doubt who I am again, *Mon Soleil*," I warn close to her ear as my hips flex and I bury myself in her.

My chances of ever entering the pearly gates of heaven burned to the ground when my human life ended and my life as a vampire began. Each life I took, each drop of blood I spilled, solidified my slow descent to hell. I came to terms with my fate a long time ago, but I was wrong in thinking I'd never get to experience heaven.

My heaven is having the walls of Quincey's cunt quiver and flex around my cock.

"Silas!" she gasps as her pussy stretches to accommodate me.

I'm momentarily captivated by the way her heat seeps into my body and becomes something we share between us. I don't think I will ever get used to the way it spreads through me, igniting even the coldest and darkest places. The echoing cavity in my chest warms and I can feel her heartbeat there. I once said her heart beats for the both of us, but this confirms it.

"Because of you, I no longer miss the sun," I rasp once I regain the ability to form words. "And as long as I can fuck your pussy, I will be able to remember what it's like to bask in its rays. My own personal sun, indeed."

"Yes, I'm yours," she promises, her hands flexing on the bedpost. "Only yours."

My hand wraps around the silky strands of her spun-gold hair before I forcibly yank her head back, making her back bow. "Forever yours," I correct as I take her mouth once more in a heated kiss.

She kisses me back with vigor but breaks away to moan against my lips as I pull back and slide back inside of her, giving her that friction she so desperately needs.

Her hand lifts from the bedpost and I snarl, sinking my blunt teeth into her shoulder in warning. "I said keep them there." My tongue laves over the teeth marks I'd created.

"One day you'll really bite me," she breathes out, sounding almost wistful at the idea. Only someone as strong as Quincey would offer her blood to me when, only a week ago, a madman was threatening to drain her dry.

My throat burns and my gums tingle at the thought of sinking my fangs into her. I've tasted her blood, and it's all but ruined all other blood for me. Nothing else compares to the sweet flavor of Quincey.

Snaking my hand around to her front, I slip my fingers through her soaked pussy and begin to massage her clit once more. "You keep offering things you shouldn't be," I scold. "You're so eager to play with monsters."

Her breath hitches in her throat as I create a steady rhythm with my deep thrusts and swirling fingers. "I'm not offering anything, I'm demanding it. Monsters don't scare me, but I encourage you to keep trying." Completely ignoring my order, she releases the bedpost and twists her arm back so she can cup my face. "I'm not going anywhere, so shut the fuck up and get on board, Silas." She sucks my bottom lip into her mouth before biting down. Hard. "I don't have fangs, but I can bite too."

I growl against her mouth. "Are you telling me what to do, *Mon Soleil*?" My fingers pinch her clit and I stroke deep inside of her, bottoming out against her cervix. Quincey groans loudly and her knees begin to buckle from the sensation. Before she can lose her balance, I pick her up and toss her back on the bed on her back. "Do you think that's a wise thing to do? How exactly do you think this will end for you?"

Her legs hook around my hips, the heels of her feet dig into my ass as she drags me back to her center. "There're a couple options, but I'm leaning toward the one where I'm fucked so hard, I forget how to pronounce my own name."

She's not wrong. My only response is to grab hold of her hips and thrust back inside her.

There are no more words or sentiments to be spoken, I take her like a man gone mad. Quincey rises up on her elbows so she can watch my cock disappear in and out of her wet cunt. Her teeth sink so hard into her lip, I'm surprised she doesn't draw blood.

The shivers run down my back, building at the base of my spine and through my thighs, alerting me of my impending release. "Get there," I grunt through clenched teeth. "Touch yourself and come with me."

In a frantic manner, she rubs her clit as I continue my brutal pace inside of her. Her walls flutter around my cock and the muscles of her abdomen tighten.

Blinding white pleasure rips through me, cutting through my black soul, taking all the bad with it. For a blissful second, I'm only aware of the woman who's coming violently around my cock.

She's the woman who holds whatever remains of my heart.

She's the peace in my hurricane, but still a storm in her own right.

And as she's forced me to realize, she's a queen.

My queen.

CHAPTER 21

I didn't wake up in the bed I fell asleep in. No, correction, the bed I *passed out* in. When Silas was done with me, not only could I not pronounce my own name, but I couldn't keep my eyes open. The last thing I remember is the warm washcloth washing my sensitive skin as he cleaned me.

The next time I opened my eyes, I was wrapped in the maroon sheets of Silas's bed and the sun was starting to fall in the sky. He wasn't in bed with me, but I could hear him talking to someone on the phone across the hall in his office.

Coffee is now my best friend while I adapt to my new sleep schedule. Waking up when the sun is setting is an odd adjustment, but it's one I'm more than willing to make. If I'm going to be a part of Silas's world like I crave, I will happily make the necessary adjustments.

It's all worth it to be able to stand at Silas's side. And that's where I belong. I'm not giving up that position without a fight. I don't know if he realizes just how serious I was when I told him I could be his queen.

If he hasn't figured it out himself, I'm going to prove to him soon just how capable I am of taking on that role.

I'm sitting at the kitchen counter, nursing my second cup of coffee, when Lor waltzes into the kitchen, the sparkling blue cup he's claimed as his own in his hand. "Blood bags are boring. This at least makes it festive," he explains when he finds me staring at the cup. "I don't know how Silas goes against our nature and drinks mainly bagged blood. The thrill of the hunt is hard to ignore."

"Silas is too strong to allow those urges to control him. Something you can't relate to, I'm sure." The jab is thrown at him in a joking tone, but instead of taking it that way, his face grows serious.

"Real strength isn't just denying yourself of something entirely. It's still allowing yourself to indulge in those behaviors, but being able to stop like that," his fingers snap. "Truth be told, I don't believe in denying myself anything. Silas and I differ a lot in that sense. He sees being a vampire as a curse. A burden. I see it as the greatest gift, and each day I enjoy it to its fullest because I remember what it's like to feel weak and defenseless. I remember what it's like to be deprived of what my body needs most."

I'm not sure what memory just filled his head, but whatever it is, I can sense that it causes him pain. His eyes blink once, and the emotion is gone just as fast. "But not anymore. Never again will I deny myself what I want. Whether it's blood from a vein or a good ol' fight. If I want it, I will go get it." The sultry smirk I'm accustomed to seeing on his face returns. "Same goes for sex."

As he speaks, I begin to understand the Irish vampire more. Silas was turned and immediately put the weight of managing the vampire race on his shoulders. He took on the burden of keeping them all in line. He never had an opportunity to experience all the joys that being a vampire can bring. Meanwhile, Lorcan has felt nothing but the joys of it.

Lorcan views being a vampire as having endless freedom. Silas sees it as something that's trapped him. The role he took in this world is a lonely one, but I hope that I can help him see it more from Lorcan's point of view. Even if things are still a mess from the Gideon fallout, a little fun and excitement would do him some good.

"Your comment about monogamy not being for you is making a lot more sense now."

Sexy mischief lights up in his brown eyes. "I'm going to live forever, Quincey. Why would I limit who I can fuck? There are so many uniquely wonderful people in this world, it would be such a waste to commit myself to only one of them." He gestures at me with his cup. "I'll leave the monogamy to Silas. He's better at it anyway, which admittedly it's a low bar, but even after all these years, he's kept a shrine to his dead wife. That has to count for something."

I bristle at his words. Silas didn't react well when I admitted to finding the temperature-controlled display cases in the cellar, I highly doubt he's going to react any better when he discovers Lorcan has been snooping around his private belongings as well.

"Lorcan," I start, placing my mug on the marble countertop. "For the love of God, tell me you didn't touch anything."

He rolls his eyes and scoffs, "Of *course* not. Contrary to popular belief, I know *how* to behave, but I simply choose not to. Doing so is rarely the more entertaining of the choices, but I also know when doing something would be a death sentence. Touching those items would have put me in the ground faster than I could have said, *'Silas, your haircut in 1742 was atrocious'*." He lets out a low whistle. "All I'm saying, it's a good thing you met him now when he's hot."

I've seen the paintings and pictures of Silas throughout the years, and while I know it's him, he's not *my* Silas in any of them.

"What were you doing down there in the first place?"

He shakes the blue tumbler in his hand. "I knew he'd have a stash of blood somewhere and it was either I found it or fed off one of the guards patrolling the property." Lor's eyes roam over me. "Or *you*, but once again, Silas is absolute shit at sharing."

It's on the tip of my tongue to admit that Silas has never fed off me, but I stop myself.

Silas has used his tongue to clean blood from my body, but never has he sunk his fangs into me and sipped from my vein. It's never something I thought I'd want or crave but watching him lick the blood off me was so unexpectedly erotic.

Silas told me if it's done right, a vampire bite is one of the most pleasurable things one can experience. Being fucked by Silas Laurent is the best thing I've ever felt but biting me will only increase that pleasure. I want it and, more importantly, how the hell do I sign up for it?

I've already filled out my liability waiver and am ready to go.

It's Silas who's refusing to do it, and while I understand his apprehension, I don't care. It might take some pushing, but I will make it happen.

"You said you were the one who didn't want to share, but you're awfully chill about him keeping all his dead wife's things in the basement like it's a creepy altar to her."

"It's not *creepy*," I defend immediately, even though I *definitely* thought it was really fucking creepy when I first found it. I felt like I'd walked into a serial killer's trophy room, but that's a thought I will never admit. I think it's one best kept to myself. "Cecily was his wife and he loved her. She's still a part of him, and he has every right to want to keep things to remember her by."

That was a very mature and believable response, Quincey, you should be very proud of yourself.

I'm more accepting of the whole thing because I know the reason he keeps her things is mostly out of guilt. He honors her life because he's the one who ended it.

He stands there staring at me for a beat, unblinking, before his head shakes. "*Nope!*" he declares. "It's still really fucking creepy. When you die, is he going to put your knickknacks in a glass box too?"

I feel my face pull in a grimace even though I don't mean to. *When I die... thanks for the reminder, Lorcan.* I love having the reminder that, no matter what, Silas is going to outlive me thrown in my face. While I grow old, my hair graying and my boobs sagging to my fucking knees, Silas will remain completely the same. Forever untouched by the effects of time.

Reading my reaction wrong, Lorcan laughs, pointing at my face. "Ha! See, not so cute when it's your panties he's keeping down there!" His voice raises and my stomach drops, afraid Silas will hear him talking even if he's still upstairs in his office. I still don't understand just how advanced vampire hearing is, but I'm not risking it.

I shove at his arm and place a finger over my lips, gesturing for him to shush. "Shut the fuck up, Lor. He doesn't keep undergarments in there and you know it."

Silas is far more sentimental than that. He has things like Cecily's dresses, wedding bands and empty perfume bottles. The items he kept the most of are the portraits he had commissioned over the years. In the end, him doing that is no different than me keeping old photos from my childhood in a photo album under my bed.

"Just stop talking about it. It's none of our business." I end the conversation with a flippant wave of my hand and at the same time, my phone beeps in my hoodie pocket. I'd found it on the counter where I'd left it the night of the attack. It was dead, but once it was charged, dozens of worried texts from Lucy came through.

There's two from her I received while I was otherwise occupied by my sex coma, but they're not the ones I'm focused on. It's the one from the unknown number that has a wicked smile growing across my face.

I turn the phone around and show the Irish vampire. "Want to run an errand for me? I could use your help picking up a few things."

When he understands the meaning of the text and who it's from, a matching grin forms on his lips and his eyes switch from humorous to murderous in a flash. "This is going to be so fun."

I'm standing in front of the same mirror I stood at the other day, but this time I don't hesitate to look at myself. I stare at the woman reflected in the glass and all I feel is proud. I'm proud of what she's survived.

She had to survive each of those things to become the woman she is now. Each fallen tear and each drop of blood spilled made her stronger.

My finger traces over the medical tape the doctor had placed over the Xs. He told me an hour ago while carefully removing the stitches that he was happy with how they are healing. The lines are still red and angry looking, but he'd assured me they wouldn't always look that way and with time, they'll smooth out.

It was reassuring to hear, but I'm no longer worried about having them or trying to hide them. Not after Silas kissed them and promised to love each scar on my body. I know he thought I was hiding them because I was ashamed of them myself, when really, I was worried what seeing them would do to him or make him feel. I can live with the reminder but was concerned he couldn't. And now I know differently.

With one last look at the mirror, I walk past the closed door of his closet and into the bedroom. The ugly red painting Silas has yet to do anything about still hangs on the wall, taunting me.

"I hate you," I sneer at it. Taking hold of the bench at the end of the bed, I drag it closer to the wall and use it to stand on so I can grab the framed canvas. "You're ugly and you have to go," I continue to talk to it like I somehow owe it an explanation.

I know he's in the room before he even opens his mouth. His stare causes my scalp to prickle, and a shiver runs down my spine. Picture frame in hand, I turn on the bench and grin at him.

His dark brows raise. "Anything I can do to help, *Mon Soleil*?"

In a shockingly graceful movement for me, I jump down and carry the painting toward the door. I stop briefly in front of Silas and rise on my tippy-toes so I can press a chaste kiss on his frowning lips. "No, I think I've got it covered."

His midnight eyes flick between the painting and me. "Do you know how much that painting cost?"

I shrug my shoulder, completely unmoved. "Not a clue, and I don't care. Expensive things can still be ugly." I hold the painting up so I can inspect it one last time before I hopefully never have to see it again. "I know this is your room, but I hate what this thing represents now."

I'm happy to report the expression that's been a permanent fixture on his face since I came back is now gone. Had I known slapping him would do the trick, I would have done it days ago. Hitting Silas isn't a tactic I would *ever* recommend anyone else use, even though it worked *splendidly* for me.

There are fresh bruises on my skin from how he grabbed me, but I like these marks. They let everyone know that Silas has been here, and he's left his literal mark.

While hitting him hadn't been the plan, admitting I'd fallen in love with him hadn't either. That's not how I wanted to do it. It'd just popped out of my mouth during my angry tirade. We haven't acknowledged the slipup yet and he hasn't said it back, but I guess that's okay since I technically haven't said *'I love you'* to him either. Those words hold a much bigger weight to me anyway compared to what I've said already.

Walking across the hallway, I leave the painting leaning against one of the shelves in his office. I have no idea where he'd pulled the thing out from, but he can return it to that spot himself.

Back in the bedroom, I find him standing right where I left him. "I meant what I said, Quincey. The only place you're sleeping is with me—in *this* bed." He gestures at the tastefully made king-size mattress. "This room is as much mine as it is yours now. If you don't like the painting or anything else for that matter, you're more than welcome to change it." I open my mouth, a smart-ass comment about bright-yellow walls and polka dot sheets on my lips, but he stops me by wisely adding, "Within reason."

"I don't want to change anything else," I assure him, wrapping my arms around his middle and resting my chin on his chest. He looks down at me and cups my face in his hands. It's honestly so hard to remember a time that I didn't crave his touch. "Everything about this room—this house—it's all so... *you*. And I wouldn't want to change that."

He tucks a piece of hair that had fallen from my braid behind my ear. "I can appreciate that, but it's not only about me now, is it? This isn't only my house or my room. You live here as well. This is *your* home, Quincey. You have to be comfortable here too."

"No, it's not," I correct him instantly, making his face pull in confusion. "This is just a house, Silas. *You're* my home and I will be comfortable anywhere so long as I'm there with you." Tucking my head into his chest, I add, "Except a tent. Try as I might, I cannot get on board with camping. It's the bugs and peeing behind trees thing for me. I can't do it."

His chest shakes in a silent laugh, making me smile. Who else can say they've made Silas Laurent laugh? I think that's a pretty special and unique skill. "Fair enough." His hand smooths down my back. "Besides a discussion about decor, there's another reason I came in here."

"Oh yeah?" He's been tucked away behind closed doors for hours. He hasn't admitted what's going on yet or what the phone calls are about, and I haven't pushed him for answers. Yet. I will give him a few more days to freely offer the information. We are still figuring out this new balance in our relationship and I don't want to demand answers from him. But I will if it comes to it.

"You said you wanted a rain check on our date, how does tonight sound to you?"

Feeling skeptical, I lean back so I can look up at him. "You want to go on a date? I thought you didn't want me leaving the house?"

"I don't," he confirms. "I want nothing more than to keep you here where I know I can keep you safe and a secret from anyone who might want to cause you harm, but you reminded me of something last night. I'm ashamed that I ever forgot seeing as it's one of the first things I admired about you. You're so strong and courageous, Quincey. Keeping you here is a disservice to you and your character." Silas's eyes heat as he stares down at me. "And as you also reminded me last night, you're not a dirty little secret I need to keep stashed away. You're so much more than that and I think it's time we start acting like it."

I'm not a pawn, I'm a queen. When I told him that, I wasn't sure if he was truly hearing me. I know what I want and what I'm now capable of, but I need Silas to confirm that he does too. "Really?"

"Really," he says without any hesitation or doubt in his eyes. "Now go get dressed. I have everything else planned."

My face falls. "Unless we're going somewhere *really* casual, and since I know you, I highly doubt that we are, I have nothing to wear." One of the suits Silas wears costs more than my entire, albeit very limited, wardrobe. It's never really bothered me until recently. The clothes I have are no longer appropriate attire for the person I want to be. I want to be Silas's equal, and I can't do that in a pair of checkered *Vans*.

Silas's chin nods toward the closed door of his closet. "Don't you though?" His lips twitch like he's fighting a knowing smile. "It's truly a good thing you were sleeping like the dead today, or I never could have pulled this off."

Still confused, he leads me toward the door and when he opens it, my jaw almost hits the fucking floor.

Standing behind me, he holds my arms. "Like I told you, Quincey. This is your room too."

Half of his closet has been filled to the brim with the most stunning selection of clothes I've ever seen. Each item looks like something I would only see in an issue of *Vogue* or donned by a celebrity. It's clothes I could only dream of wearing myself and now they're all in this closet—*my* closet. These are clothes worthy of being worn by the woman on Silas's arm.

"Where did all of this come from? How did you do this?" I stammer.

"There are stylists I hire for my own clothing. I gave them a call and asked them to build you a wardrobe fit for a queen." My heart constricts at his words. He really sees me for what I am. "They brought everything here while you slept. Anything you could possibly want should be in here."

I'm stunned silent and he knows it.

"Get dressed, Quincey," he repeats after pressing a kiss to my temple. "We have a date to make up for."

CHAPTER 22

Silas extends his hand and helps me out of the black SUV once we arrive at our location. When he said we were going on a date, I had a couple guesses as to where we might go, but one of the most luxurious hotels in the city wasn't on my list.

Out of the car, I run a hand down the front of my silk dress to smooth out any of the creases from sitting in the car. It had taken me an embarrassing amount of time to choose an outfit to wear. I don't know how long I'd stood in the closet staring at the rows of new clothes before I finally settled on the champagne-colored dress. It's a far cry from what I'm accustomed to wearing, but I've truly never felt more like myself in an outfit before. I feel confident and the slit up to my mid-thigh makes me feel sexy.

He releases my fingers, only to place his hand on the small of my back. "I'm starting to wonder if this was a mistake," he says lowly close to my car. My stomach sinks, thinking he's about to change his mind about us being seen in public together, but his next words quickly rectify that. "With you dressed like this, all eyes are going to be on you. I don't know how I'm going to tolerate so many people looking at what's mine."

"Let them look." I smirk. "And while they're imagining what it's like to have me, you'll already know because you're the only one allowed to touch me." My fingers trace up the front of his black shirt. "And while they stare at you, I'll smile because I know I also have something they can't have."

Before Silas, I was never a possessive person. Boyfriends came and went, but I never cared enough about them to be jealous when other girls flirted with them. But now, there's a burning sensation in my chest at the thought of someone flirting with Silas. I will stab a rusty fork in someone's throat if they so much as look at him too long.

And *yes*, I'm aware that by thinking this, I've taken on the psycho bitch title. *Hell*, if the title came with a tiara and sequin sash, I'd happily wear them so everyone got a fair warning before they tried to fuck with me.

"No one will ever touch you again," he vows, his voice growing dark at the thought.

"I know," I reassure him, smiling softly when he takes my hand from his chest and raises it to his mouth so he can kiss the pulse in my wrist. It's one of my favorite things that he does.

"Come on." He tugs me toward the grand entrance of the building. "Everything should be set up for us."

Still having no idea what we're doing at a hotel, I tease softly so none of the people milling about can overhear me. "You know, if you wanted to fuck me in a different bed, we didn't have to come all the way here. There's like five other beds at home we've yet to christen."

To me, Silas's house is entirely too big for just two people to live in, but I'm probably the wrong one to ask. His lifestyle is the complete opposite of what I'm used to. The dress I'm wearing is more than a month's rent for most of the population. *Shit*, some of the purses I saw sitting on the shelves in the closet are more than most cars on the market. This is Silas's normal, and I'm trying to get used to it, but some of those price tags made me nauseous.

"While I do appreciate where your head is at, that's not why I chose to bring you here." Stepping into the lobby, I'm shocked by how stunning it is. It doesn't look like a single thing has changed since it was built. The art deco decor is beautiful, and each piece looks authentic, from the gold light fixtures to the dark-green couches in the sitting area. "When I bought this property, I saw it as a good business opportunity, both on and off the books." It's not a secret to me that Silas's money-making ventures aren't always on the legal side of things. "For those years, while prohibition was happening, it was one of the few places in New Orleans where humans could still find alcohol. And when there're humans gathering in one location, my kind are soon to follow."

My high heels click against the polished, ornate white and black tile as we walk toward the gold doors of the elevator. "So, it became a hunting ground of sorts," I fill in. "Drunk humans make for easy prey."

"Yes," he confirms. "And as the years passed, it remained a place where vampires would congregate." The doors open and Silas ushers me inside. He presses the button for the top floor before continuing his story. "To this day, it's still one of the more popular destinations for my kind, which in turn benefits me, not just financially, but information-wise."

"I'm not following."

"The trick to maintaining order is ensuring you're continuously five steps ahead of everyone. This guarantees if there're ever whispers of trouble or thoughts of insubordination, I can put a halt to all of it before it comes to fruition. They come here to relax and when they do that, their lips become lax. They never suspect that anyone is listening and reporting back to me."

I shake my head, almost in astonishment. Silas continues to amaze me in his ways. He's cultivated the ideal location for a vampire. He draws them in and while they're enjoying their time, he's using their conversations against them.

"It's a rarity that things ever get past me. That's why the ordeal with Gideon is so troubling." It's subtle and I doubt he thinks I can see it, but there's a flicker of concern in his dark eyes as he stares ahead at the doors. If I hadn't been so hypervigilant with his expressions all week, I may have missed it. What's concerning for me is the Gideon thing is supposed to be over. When I've asked about the psychotic vampire, Silas has assured me it's taken care of.

"None of that explains why you brought me here though."

He turns to me, head tilting. "Doesn't it? We agreed keeping you away from all of this was a mistake, and if you wish to be part of my world, what better place to make your debut? They will see you enter on my arm, and word will spread like wildfire. By bringing you here, they will all know exactly who you are to me. There will be no doubt in their minds of your significance." Holy shit, my *debut* is literally in the middle of the proverbial lion's den. Vampire den? Either way, am I ready for this? This is what I wanted—no, demanded from him—but now that I›m here, I feel a ball of doubt form in my chest.

Because I can't hide anything from him it would seem, his fist suddenly slams against the red button on the panel. The elevator comes to an abrupt halt as he turns on me. "I will ask you once more, is this what you want? If you have any apprehensions, you must voice them now, because you cannot walk in there with any fear. They will smell it on you." Silas grabs hold of my chin, lifting it up so he can look into my eyes. "We can never show them any weakness, Quincey. They will use it against us, and we've both seen what can happen if they do. That can never fucking happen again, do you hear me? *Never again.*" His tone is hauntingly dark and something about it makes my skin tingle. Not in fear, but in the kind of way that makes me think finding one of the empty beds in this joint might be a good idea. "Unless you can assure me right now that you will face them with the same level of gallantry as you faced me, we won't be doing this. It's not worth the risk if you're not ready."

His dark eyes scan mine and I swear they're looking into my soul as they do. Silas sees every part of me, even the pieces I don't like of myself. His fingers travel down my jaw to wrap around my throat. My breath shudders as his thumb presses into my rapid pulse point.

"I want to do this," I say aloud, mostly to myself.

"I'm aware of what you want, Quincey." His thumb continues to caress the side of my jugular. "I'm only asking if you believe you can be successful at it. Wanting something and actually doing something are two vastly different things."

Irritation flames up and my eyes narrow at the sliver of doubt in his voice. "What? You don't believe I can go in there?" My spine straightens and my face hardens. I shove at his hand holding me, but he doesn't flinch, which only further angers me. "In the past week alone, I've faced far scarier things than a roomful of fucking vampires," I snap. "Maybe it's you who doesn't think I can do this."

I'm not just simply walking into a roomful of vampires and we both know it. While it appears a mundane task, we both recognize that this is a much bigger deal. We're sending a very clear and direct message to the vampires.

Human or not, I'm here and I'm coming for my fucking throne.

An arrogant smirk forms on his mouth. "I know exactly who you are and what you're capable of, *Mon Soleil*. I just needed to remind you because it looks like you may have momentarily forgotten." Silas's head dips down closer to mine. "Take a breath and calm yourself down. Your heartbeat will be a fucking siren call to them if you don't."

I take in a large lungful of air and in a slow measured pace, I exhale it.

"Again."

I repeat this act over and over, and as I do, my eyes remain locked on his. His fingers flex on my throat, increasing pressure. "Good girl."

He nips at my bottom lip with his teeth as a reward.

The praise causes my lower belly to flutter and my skin to grow warm. "Silas," I breathe. "This isn't lowering my heart rate…" my warning is silenced when his lips press against mine in a short, but searing kiss. He licks into my mouth, and I moan at the flavor of the spicy mouthwash he'd used before we left.

"Wrong," Silas corrects against my mouth. "You calm down when I kiss you." His thumb grazes over that spot on my throat. "Your heart is nearly back to normal."

His free hand traces a line down the thin strap of my dress before passing ever so gently over the medical tape on my chest. My breath hitches against his lips when he skims his fingertips over my tightening nipple. "I can smell your need, *Mon Soleil*," he growls. "And they will too. They will know I'm the one who caused it, and in turn they will hate me for it because they will never know just how sweet you taste."

Silas breaks our heated kiss before we reach the point of no return. Feeling pleased with himself, he wipes the corner of my mouth where my lipstick has smudged. "You know who you are, Quincey. Act accordingly," is his last bit of advice before he's hitting the red button once more.

I steel myself as we travel up to the top floor. By the time the gold doors slide open, I'm ready.

CHAPTER 23

It's what you'd expect of a hotel lounge. The only thing that's different about it is the patrons roaming about.

An ornate oak bar sits in the middle of the room, gold pendant lights hang above it. The light reflects into the liquor bottles that line the mirrored shelves that sit on the wall behind it. The same green velvet couches that were in the lobby are up here as well in the various sitting areas. The barstools are also made of the same fabric, but it's not what the seats are made of that is catching my attention, it's the people sitting in them. I can count on one hand the number of vampires I've met, but each one of them have something in common. They're attractive in a way that is almost fake. Their pale porcelain skin looks airbrushed, pores and blemishes are nonexistent. Their movements are graceful and smooth, to the point they look choreographed. And their bodies look like they were perfectly crafted by sculptors. Each line and curve of their bodies are perfectly symmetrical and proportionate.

The vampires that are here are no different, and to me, they stand out like bright neon signs among the humans that also loiter about. I highly doubt that the humans realize they are mingling among the world's top predators, but to give them some credit, I was blissfully unaware of their existence not that long ago.

Which, to be clear, isn't a brag in any way, shape, or form. I'm actually a little concerned the obvious difference in humans and vampires never caught my eye prior to meeting Silas. There is no doubt in my mind that I've crossed paths with a vampire before, and how I never noticed is alarming. It just goes to show what all you will truly see once your rose-colored glasses are ripped away.

And while I can see the vampires now, they too can see me. I can feel their gazes raking over me as we walk through the space. Their eyes lock on where Silas's much larger hand engulfs mine, but never do their conversations come to a stop. Like trained professionals, they carry on like they're not witnessing history being made by their king having a human at his side.

I fight a smirk when we pass a pretty brunette. She's trying to keep her face devoid of any emotion, but by doing so, it looks like it might literally crack like a porcelain doll. The sound of glass shattering echoes in my head like a silent joke to myself.

As Silas walks beside me, a dark, almost palpable energy rolls off him like a thick fog. We leave a trail of it behind us as we venture farther into the room, and it wraps around each of the bystanders in the bar until they're suffocating. Not until I spot the mixture of two emotions in their eyes do I realize something.

This is the first time I'm truly seeing Silas in his element. He talks about how he never would have picked this life for himself, but he navigates all of this with such ease and confidence, I'm not convinced that this isn't the role he was always destined to have.

I'm still not fond of the idea of fate and still think a lot of it is a crock of shit, but for Silas, I truly think he's following the path he was always meant to be on. And I can only hope that if destiny is real, that

I'm also on the right path.

But let's be honest, I'm in so deep that leaving is no longer an option for me. And if I ever wanted to leave, how exactly would I have that conversation with Silas? *Hey, remember when you had to fight to get me back and then I threw that little bitch fit about wanting to be your queen? Well, psych, I changed my mind. You can just drop me off at the closest bus stop on your way home.*

I told him I wasn't going anywhere—that I was in this—and I meant every word. I'm exactly where I'm supposed to be, whether my destiny agrees with me or not.

Fate can go fuck itself for all I care.

A short man with a worried expression scurries around the bar. His cheeks are pink and when he looks up at Silas, there's a mixture of trepidation and respect in his eyes. It's a combination I've seen many of the guests wearing.

"Mr. Laurent," he rushes out. "We are just putting the final touches on your table, as you requested. It should only be another five minutes. I do apologize for the delay. There was an unexpected issue with an electrical element, but don't worry, we got it figured out."

"I'm not worried," Silas answers. The tone reminds me of the one he first used when we met. It's cold, lacking any emotion. "I was very clear about what I needed from you all on the phone. I have no doubt that all of my requests will be fulfilled without issue." Even I can hear the underlying message in that statement. "We have no problem waiting in the meantime."

The man swallows hard before motioning between us, he begins to ask, "Can I get you or—or your…" he trails off, unsure what to refer to me as. "Your *guest* something to drink in the meantime?"

I chew on the inside of my cheek at this question, unsure how Silas will answer it. As comical as I think it would be for him to order up a nice vintage class of O positive, I highly doubt the serious vampire holding my hand would agree. Though I would pay money to see this nervous man's reaction.

Silas, without having to confirm with me, orders my favorite type of wine. "A glass of sauvignon blanc for Ms. Page." It's not very often I hear him say words in French, but when he does, it turns me into a puddle on the floor. His accent has no doubt weakened over the many years, but when he speaks his native tongue, it sounds like he never left his homeland. "Please ensure you select a bottle from my private wine locker."

The man nods his head quickly before dashing back to wherever he'd appeared from.

"*Ms. Page*?" I mimic. "So formal of you, Mr. Laurent."

Dark eyes slide over to me. "I can't very well introduce you as Mon Soleil, now, can I?"

I know I won't get a smile out of him now, and that's okay. I understand that some things will be reserved for when we're in private, even if it's something as simple as a smile.

My shoulder shrugs. "I don't know, I think it has a pretty nice ring to it."

I'm about to change the subject and ask him why a vampire would have a wine locker when a striking pair of vampires begin walking toward us.

Even though Silas doesn't react, I stiffen, worried about their intentions, but when the classically handsome man on the right flashes a warm smile in my direction, I relax.

"Silas," he cheers, a thick accent of some kind evident in his voice. "What a pleasure! I was just telling Bria that it has been too long since anyone has seen you. I was worried that you had decided to become a recluse."

The stunning, shockingly tall woman next to him rolls her eyes. "And I told him that he was being ridiculous as always." Her chocolate-brown eyes turn to me, the corners of her mouth curl up. "How could he stay locked away when he has someone as beautiful as her to show off?"

I'll admit, I wasn't sure what kind of reactions we were going to see tonight, but one as... *nice*... as this one was low on my list of possibilities. I expected hostility and cold shoulders. At the very least, I expected typical high school behavior where people huddled together, whispering their disdain for me.

The man nods in agreement. "This is very true."

"Thank you, that's very kind of you guys to say."

Bria's manicured hand pats the man's arm. When she talks, she too has an accent, but it's different than his. Italian maybe? "I had hoped that Silas would venture out with you at some point. I've known him for many years, and I think it's due time that he has someone on his arm."

When she looks between Silas and I, there's no resentment or animosity in her eyes. Only admiration. It's nice to know there are other vampires out there that follow him, not because they fear him, but because he's earned their respect. I know it's what he prefers anyway.

I smile politely, still confused by their history, while I remind myself that even though all these people have known him longer, I still know him best. They don't know him at all.

As if he can hear me silently wondering, Silas explains, "Bria and I met many years ago when I needed help getting a shipment from Italy across the Pacific. It was at a time that getting your hands on a ship wasn't easy. Luckily, Bria's family background is in importing and exporting."

She smiles fondly at the memory. "It's not very often he needs help moving product since Silas now has his own fleet, but I help wherever I can. Our businesses cross paths every now and then." A look I can't quite decipher crosses her face as she cocks her head in Silas's direction. "Actually, Quincey, would you mind if I stole him away for only a moment? There's a business matter that I need to discuss with Silas. I tried to get in touch with him all week, but understandably, he's been otherwise occupied."

For a moment, I'm taken aback that she knows my name, but then

I remember that Gideon sent links to all the high society vampires. If I had to bet money, I would say all the vampires here tonight saw at least clips of it.

"That won't be necessary," Silas states, leaving little option for debate in his tone. "Whatever it is can wait until tomorrow."

To give her credit, while she does look apprehensive about pushing him further, she sticks to her guns. "It's regarding the events that took place at the eastern port earlier this week. It will only take a minute, but I do think it's best we talk now."

Silas's body stiffens next to me at the mention of the port, and instantly, I know that whatever Bria wants to discuss pertains to the endless phone calls Silas has received all week. He's put so much on hold so he could stay with me, but he needs to prioritize his business again.

My hand gives a reassuring squeeze to his. "I'll be okay alone here for a minute. Go talk to her. It sounds important."

Silas's brows pull in a scowl when he looks at me.

"She will not be alone," Bria's companion pipes up. "I will be her company while you two discuss the business at hand."

Bria smiles thankfully at him, before looking expectantly at Silas.

He remains in place, staring down at me.

"*Go*," I stress, nudging his arm with my shoulder. "I'll be right here."

Finally, Silas releases my hand and he and Bria walk across the room to stand in a shadowy corner where no one can eavesdrop on their conversation.

"She promised that this would be a work-free night, but I knew better," the man draws my attention back to him. "I suspect you can relate to this, seeing as I doubt Silas ever stops working."

"He stops when he has more important things to tend to," I say, not needing to elaborate further. "But I also never want to be in the way of his work. It's finding that balance."

"That's a very wise outlook, Quincey," he says my name like we're old acquaintances. I've never been able to hide what I'm thinking, which is why I'm not surprised when he quickly adds, "I'm sorry, I guess it's only fair that I introduce myself. I'm Álvaro Soto."

My head cocks, "Álvaro?" I repeat to be sure I understood him correctly.

"Yes," he confirms. "Have you heard of me?"

My lips curl into a small smile as I shake my head at him. "No, I'm afraid your name hasn't come up yet, but as you can imagine, I'm still navigating my way through all this. I'll know all your names soon enough."

Just like they all know my name now, I'm going to make it my mission to learn all theirs. I want to know each of the vampires that Silas has dealings with. I want to know their secrets.

His eyes flick to the bandages on my chest, the angry pink lines of my cuts are on full display beneath the clear surgical tape. "All things considered, I think you are handling all of this with great strength and grace. Not many humans can walk away from what you have." Looking down my arm where the bruises on my wrists are still fading, he adds, "It is good to see that you are healing so well from those heinous things he did to you."

I lift my hands in front of me, turning them over so I can trace the yellow bruising all the way around my joint. "I'm fairly certain that not many of your kind would agree with that. Many were eager to watch me bleed out."

Álvaro shakes his head, face turned up in distaste. "Not Bria and me. We are very happy that Silas found you."

I look at the man's perfectly sincere expression. "I'm very glad that we ran into you tonight. I was worried there wouldn't be any friendly faces. I swear some of these people are glaring at me so hard I think they're trying to create fires with their eyes." Since Silas walked away, their stares have become more intense. I can feel their eyes boring holes into my skull.

"Ignore them. Many are jealous and the others do not understand Silas's infatuation with a human." Álvaro explains this like it's information I haven't already figured out on my own.

"That's the good thing about being at the top, isn't it?" I ask, not bothering to keep my voice low. They all can overhear for all I care. Actually, I'd prefer it. "They don't *need* to understand, and Silas sure as shit doesn't *need* to explain himself. All they need to do is accept that I'm not going anywhere, and I suggest they accept it fast. It'll be so much easier for them in the long run if they do."

Álvaro falls silent, his dark brown eyes examining me like he's seeing me in a new light.

Before either of us can say more, an arm wraps around my back and a large hand settles on my hip. Even in an environment where danger is lurking in almost every seat, I don't flitch. I know it's Silas without having to turn my head.

"Did you two work everything out?" I ask as Bria steps back into her position next to Álvaro.

Bria's dark painted lips turn downward. "We discussed what we could tonight, it will more likely entail a much longer conversation, but like I said, I don't want to take him away from you for too long." Her arm wraps around her companion's. "Let's get out of their hair so they can enjoy the rest of their night."

Silas nods his head in dismissal, and I smile politely at each of them.

"I'm sure I'll see you both sometime soon," I tell them as a goodbye.

"Yes, I would love to get to know you better, Quincey." Bria chirps before looking at Silas. "She's lovely, Silas." With that last compliment, she pulls Álvaro away.

Silas waits for them to return to the seats they'd vacated to come talk to us before he coaxes me forward. "They just informed me everything is ready at our table, including your wine."

CHAPTER 24

Silas

To the white cloth over the round table, to the strings of lights crisscrossing above us, the staff here accomplished everything I requested.

When I purchased this building more than a hundred years ago, it was one of the tallest in town. As the years have passed, the buildings around it have grown taller, but somehow, despite that, the view of the surrounding city has remained just as exquisite as it was the first time I stood on this roof.

"Silas," Quincey breathes out as she takes in the intimate dinner I'd had prepared for her. The hotel roof is never used for such a thing, but I wanted to do something more special than a date at a typical restaurant. "This is beautiful."

She moves in a slow circle, head tilted up so she can look at the fairy lights. While I watch her, my lips twitch because she continues to surprise me.

When I picked up on her apprehension in the elevator, I was

worried that she wasn't ready. The only way I was going to allow her to walk into the vampire-ridden bar was if I couldn't sense a single drop of fear on her. It didn't take much for her to collect herself. The doubt melted from her eyes and her fearless mask slipped firmly into place.

Not once did it falter. She met each of the spiteful looks that were sent in her direction with an unwavering confidence that can only be accomplished by someone as strong as Quincey. She stood with her head held high and her shoulders back at my side. Even when I stepped away and she was momentarily on her own, she didn't flinch.

Up here, away from the prying eyes of the public, her defensive walls drop. She becomes the carefree girl that enjoys reading in the garden.

I'm truly amazed how fast she learned how to switch it on and off. It's a skill that took me longer than it should have to develop, but it's one that comes naturally to her.

"As we discussed on the elevator ride up, I wanted to take you somewhere public where you could be seen, but I'm still a selfish man." At my words, she stops her slow spinning and smiles at me over her shoulder. "I can only share you for so long before I need you all to myself once more."

There isn't a state that I don't find Quincey attractive. The shorts she wears used to grate on my nerves when she first arrived at my house, but now I love how they hug her ass and expose her legs. I thought her casual style would always suit her best but looking at how the silk of her outfit clings to each subtle curve of her body, I know I was wrong.

It's not solely the way the dress fits her body that makes me believe she was always meant to wear clothes like this, it's the confidence she's exuded since she emerged from the newly stocked closet. These clothes make her feel good about herself, and for that, I'm a fan of them.

I would stock two more closets if I thought she'd allow me. She hides it well, but underneath the bubbling confidence is an air of guilt.

The man I was a few hundred years ago relates to her humble

upbringings. He knows that Quincey is not yet accustomed to a life of luxury, but the man I am today wants to use every resource he's acquired to shower her in all the things she's never had before.

The corners of her mouth twitch like she's fighting a laugh.

"Is there something you find amusing, Quincey?" I stalk slowly toward her.

Her white teeth dig into her bottom lip. "You just reminded me of something Lor said once. It had something to do with your ability to share. Or more so, your *inability* to share."

It hasn't gone unnoticed that Quincey and Lorcan have become easy friends. It's something I'm not completely surprised by, seeing as I'm convinced Quincey could make friends with a feral raccoon if enough time was allotted. A feral animal would at least have the decency to not imagine her naked as it mauled her to death. Meanwhile, I can almost guarantee that thoughts of touching what's mine have danced through Lorcan's head. He wouldn't have the strength to stop himself.

"He's right. I don't share," I agree without a second thought. "And he's entirely mistaken if he thought I would ever share you." *Maybe it would do him good to be reminded of that soon.*

Quincey's blue eyes still twinkle with humor. "Are you going to pee a circle around me now, Silas?" Her finger swirls in a circular motion. "I want it noted for the record that doing that would be completely unnecessary, but we both know when you've decided something, it's almost impossible to change your mind. You're both selfish *and* stubborn like that."

Since the beginning, Quincey has teased and taunted me like no one else ever has. Even Duke and Lorcan recognize there is a line they shouldn't cross, but Quincey skips over that line with a devious grin on her face.

"I don't see any falsehood in that statement," I tell her while she picks the wineglass up from the table that only has one place setting. "I fight hard for the things that I want and once I have them in my grasp, why would I ever allow anyone else to touch them?"

"I never said those qualities were negative." Her lips that have been coated in a rose-colored lipstick curl at the corner as she takes a sip from the glass. "No one has ever wanted me enough to fight for me the way that you have, Silas. If that makes you selfish, then I'm all for it."

I close the distance between us and trail my fingers down her face. "I will always fight for you, Quincey. Even when you think you're strong enough to face your own battles. I will still fight for you because you would do the same for me."

"Of course I would." Even in her heels, she's still too short and has to rise up on her toes to press a soft kiss to my mouth. Just as I'm tasting the lingering sweet white wine on her lips, soft violin music begins to play.

Quincey grins against my lips and pulls away from me, her curious blue eyes searching the rooftop for the source. "Where is that coming from?"

My enhanced ears follow the sound. "Down on the street below us."

It's a single violin and it plays a beautifully haunting melody that fills the night air. It drowns out the boisterous sounds of the city and muffles the noisiness of traffic.

Quincey dashes toward the brick ledge so she can see. Even though the wall that encircles the roofline reaches her ribs, a trail of concern shoots down my spine at the sight of her being so close to the edge. Watching her fall three stories before has made me wary of heights where Quincey is concerned.

But when she looks over her shoulder at me and her eyes are full of joy, I force myself to relax and join her. Standing behind her, I cage her with my arms.

"Was this your doing? Did you set this up?" she asks, her eyes locked on where the man stands on the street corner. The streets are quiet due to the late hour, but those who remain on the streets stop and watch him for a moment before carrying on their way.

"While I wish I could take credit for this, I'm afraid this is just pure coincidence." While she watches, I brush her long gold strands off one shoulder, exposing her delicate neck.

Her pulse jumps steadily under her skin, making my fangs burn as they threaten to make an appearance. Unable to stop myself, I press a kiss over the point and enjoy the way her breath hitches in her throat at the contact.

Quincey has become my biggest lesson in maintaining control. Her blood is so sweet, and it constantly calls to me. It goes against everything in my monstrous nature to not sink my fangs into her. It's even more difficult to refrain from doing that when she willingly offers her vein to me.

"One day," she promises in a breathy whisper, just like she did the night prior.

"Mmm," I mumble against her skin. "You can keep telling yourself that, my love, but my answer will always be the same."

"Okay," Quincey relents. "I can be patient."

"And you call me stubborn."

We fall silent, each of us captivated by different things. The violinist holds her attention, her fingers tapping softly against the brick as she keeps beat with him. And while she does that, I continue to caress and nuzzle her neck. A neck that will look perfect wearing the gift I had made for her.

While she's distracted, I pull the gold chain from my pocket. The jeweler's work exceeds what I had originally imagined when I requested he make it. Delicately, I place it around her neck so that the pendant is perfectly positioned between the bandages on her chest.

The clasp locks together at the base of her neck, and my lips curl at the knowledge that the only way it can be removed now is by a key that is in my possession. And I have no intention of ever removing it.

Quincey's fingers brush against the pendant and she gasps softly.

"A sun."

She spins in my arms so that she can look at me.

"My sun," I correct. "*Mon Soleil*."

It's roughly the size of a silver dollar, and it's made of yellow gold. In the center of it is a larger round diamond, and in each sharp point of the sun's rays are smaller diamonds.

"You are part of my world now, Quincey." My head shakes and I correct myself. "No, you're more than that, you are my *whole* world now, but my world isn't kind to people like you. It's dark, and its shadows corrupt and decay any light." It swallows people alive and when they finally surface, they're not the person they once were. "You have to promise me you won't allow my darkness to corrupt your light, and that you will remain my sun always."

She fists the necklace in her hand. "I promise, Silas. I will always be your guiding light out of the shadows."

For years, Ira was my moral compass, but when he died, he left that job to Quincey. I know she will correct me when I wander too far off path, just as he did.

I cup her face in my hands and kiss her. It's not a carnal kiss like we often share. It's simply a promise to be what each other needs.

Her arms wrap around me and her head rests on my chest. Slowly, we sway to the soft violin music coming from below. "Be my light, but still dance with me in all my darkness."

And for the next hour, that's what she does.

CHAPTER 25

Silas

"It was a bus this time, sir," one of my guards in charge of maintaining the scene tells me. "Fifteen humans are dead, ten are en route to the hospital now. Two of those are children."

My hand tightens on my phone at this information.

A bus explosion, while notable news, isn't something that would usually concern me. But when said bus explodes in front of my tech company's office and passengers on board were employed by me, my attention is needed.

The attacks haven't stopped all week and now they've started to affect other people's businesses.

Bria DeLuca and I have an agreement. I allow her to move product in and out of the ports I control here, and in return, her family allows me to use the ones located up north around New York. It's an agreement that's served us well for many years, especially seeing as her merchandise is different than mine and we are not competing for business.

We haven't had any problems until this week when the men in

charge of offloading her shipment were found dead. Similar to how my own staff were found dead in one of my cargo containers, hers were eviscerated and left on top of the container for the birds to pick at.

And now a bus exploded in front of Blackwood Technologies and more innocent lives were lost.

"Find out what kind of explosive it was and if it matches the one used on my vehicle," I instruct tightly. If it's the same as the one used on Duke and me, it will confirm that Gideon is still somehow playing games with me from inside his box. "I'm going to put a stop to this."

Bring Quincey here, his request replays in my head. At the time, it had been an unacceptable answer, but each day that I don't have the name of his partner, more lives are being lost.

I end the call and slam the device onto the surface of my desk in frustration. The glass cracks from the force and the metal bends, but I don't care. I can have a replacement waiting for me in an hour.

I care that I'm going to have to do something I vowed would never happen. It's unfair that this would even be asked of her after everything she's endured, but I don't see another option.

Leaving the broken phone behind, I stalk out of my home office and follow her scent through the house. They never lived here, but the house still feels too quiet from the absence of Della and Duke. I'm accustomed to hearing Della milling about, either busy in the kitchen or finding the one speck of dust on a bookshelf somewhere. Duke is always so lively no matter where he is and always finds something to laugh at.

Dealing with these attacks makes the weight of Duke's absence even heavier. If he was awake, I wouldn't have to bring Quincey to Gideon, he would be able to see the piece that I'm missing.

When I find her sitting on the stone bench in the courtyard, I come to an abrupt stop in front of the French doors.

In the past couple of days, Quincey has taken to sitting out there for a few minutes a day. Sometimes she talks to him and sometimes she simply just looks at the roses he left behind, but either way she goes out there alone and mourns Ira.

But tonight, she's not alone. Lorcan is with her, sitting next to her on the bench. He nods as he listens to whatever she says. She speaks in such a hushed tone, I can't pick up on it through the glass.

Suspicion and a tinge of distrust mix in my gut when I push open the doors and walk into the night air.

Lorcan hears me first, his brown eyes looking over his shoulder at me as I approach. His tattooed elbow nudges Quincey, drawing her attention to me too.

A happy smile breaks out across her face. "There you are. I was worried you were going to lock yourself in your office all night." Her lack of guilt or concern for interrupting them quells some of the unease I'm feeling.

"What are you two doing out here?" I ask, still feeling curious about their whispering.

Lorcan leans back on the bench in a relaxed slump. "Quincey was telling me a little about that Ira fellow and how he basically played matchmaker for you two lovebirds."

Quincey was his parting gift to me before he died. I'm thankful to him for a lot of reasons, but I owe him everything for bringing her into my life.

She smiles fondly at the memory while looking at the rose bushes that surround us. "I'm glad that he'll get to spend the rest of his time here where he was happiest."

After having to put everything on hold to tend to Quincey, Ira will finally be put to rest here in the garden. His wishes in his will were for his ashes to be scattered in a place of my choosing. Ira stressed in depth that he didn't want *'his urn to be left on some shelf to collect dust'*, which illustrates how well the human knew me. It was Quincey's idea that they be spread in the soil of the roses. In them, he will continue to live.

Lorcan's head bobs in agreement, but there's an idiotic look on his face that tells me an equally idiot comment is about to be made. "If I ever die, stuff me like one of those deer, but instead of mounting me on some wall like humans like to do, put me on wheels so you can move me room to room. That way I'm still involved." His lips curl in a smirk at Quincey. "You can put me at the end of your bed. You know I like to watch."

And there it is.

Quincey's mouth drops open, appalled, while I feel my face darken and a low growl form in my chest. I think we're both equally troubled by his remark, but when her lips curl into a smile and she begins to laugh, I learn I'm wrong.

"Oh my god. That's brilliant. I could put you on the porch as a Halloween decoration. It'll scare the shit out of trick or treaters and the mailman," she jokes between laughs.

Frowning at this, I remind her, "We don't have mail delivered to the house and we definitely do not have children in costumes coming to our door. It's a safety hazard."

Wiping the laughter-induced tears from her eyes, Quincey looks at me and shakes her head. "Yeah, no shit, baby. It was a joke—I know you know what those are." She and Lorcan share an amused glance before she stands from the bench. "And let's not forget that this house is in the middle of bumfuck nowhere. Not exactly an ideal stop for trick-or-treating."

"I don't like neighbors."

"*Really?* That's a startling revelation and brand-new information to me," she drawls dramatically as her arms encircle my waist. "I never would have guessed that about you."

Lorcan chuckles but doesn't add further to the jest.

Even if her good mood and jokes are at my expense, I'm enjoying seeing her laugh and smile. I hate to ruin it for her, but it must be done.

Observant as ever, she senses my shift and her face falls. "What happened?" All the humor that had just been present in her voice is gone."

Lorcan's relaxed posture also stiffens, and his face becomes serious. He shifts forward, prepared to act if necessary.

"There is reason to believe that Gideon wasn't working alone." This isn't new information to the blond vampire, but it is to Quincey. Her eyebrows pull together in question, but before she can voice her confusion, I continue. "There have been four attacks this week, all of them have been directed at various businesses of mine. It's similar to what Gideon was doing prior to taking you. Before, it was my property and inventory. Now the employees—*my employees*—are being targeted."

Quincey jerks back, her arms loosening from my middle. "*What*? This has been happening for *days* and you haven't thought to inform me until *now*?" Her eyes blaze with anger.

"I was hoping I would have more answers and a better solution before I informed you."

What I truly hoped was that I would be able to get the answers from Gideon myself and she would never have to come face-to-face with the monster who chained her and carved into her. You would think that with all my years on this planet, I would have learned my lesson when it came to wishful thinking, and yet, here I remain.

She stares at me like she's looking for any falsehoods in my expression. "Why are you telling me this *now*? What changed?"

"A bus exploded in front of Blackwood's downtown building today. Many lives were lost." I steel myself adding, "Children's lives were lost."

"*Fucking hell*," Quincey curses under her breath, her hands gripping the strands of her hair. "How do we stop this? How do we figure out who his partner is?"

"I don't believe *we* will be figuring out anything moving forward," I tell her, hatred for Gideon burning through my veins. "That's a job that has unfortunately fallen into your hands, Quincey. Gideon says he will only tell you who his partner is."

Quincey's hands fall from her hair, and she stands there, looking lost. A varying array of emotions crosses her face until she settles on one. Determination. "No one else can die because of him," she declares. "Take me to him. *Now*."

CHAPTER 26

The irony that Silas's supersecret vampire *'Bat Cave'* is located in an old decrepit-looking chapel isn't lost on me.

What better place for a sinful king to run parts of his highly immoral empire than in a place of worship? Seems completely on brand for him if you ask me.

Another time, I probably would have laughed hysterically at it, but my sweaty hands, and the mixture of anxiety and anger inside of me, are stopping me from experiencing the full extent of the humor. It's something I will file away and save for a later, less serious, date.

One thing is clear, it's been a long time since this place was holy ground.

While the outside of the building looks like something fresh out of a demonic horror movie—barbed wire and ominous graffiti acting as the cherry on top of that aesthetic—the inside looks like it's been maintained and modernized throughout the years.

The original stained glass sits in the windows and the wooden pews are still lined up like they are waiting for worshippers to sit in them and listen to a sermon. Except there isn't a preacher standing behind his pulpit at the front of the room.

There's only a large ornate metal chair that sits there like a lonely fixture. It's on the raised platform, so whoever sits in it can look down at the people sitting in the pews. Which I think is the point.

The steady sound of my heels clicking on the modern gray tiles comes to an abrupt stop when I freeze in front of it. It takes everything in my power to keep my face impassive as I gawk at it.

Keep it together, Quincey. You don't want to look like one of those fanny pack–wearing tourists when they lay their eyes on the castle at Disney World for the first time.

I clear my throat and collect myself. "You have a throne," I manage to say, my eyes sliding to where Silas stands next to me. "That's… *neat*."

"No," Silas corrects, face pulled in a scowl. "It's a chair that I occasionally sit in when I'm forced to hold meetings here."

I'm pretty sure that's exactly what a throne is, buddy, but I digress.

"Right. *Sure*. Okay then. Holding meetings, holding court. Same difference." My head bobs and my lips purse as I fight to remain composed.

There aren't any people loitering about in here with us, but that doesn't mean they're not somewhere else in the building listening to us. The last thing I want is for them to witness my impending freak-out in the middle of Silas's fucking *throne room*.

Silas frowns harder at the throne—*Oh*, sorry, I mean *chair*. "It was a gift from a long time ago. It was brought all the way over from Europe, but I never liked it."

"Can't see why…" I comment dryly. "It looks so… *comfortable*. I'm bummed we don't have more of them at the house—they would make such great accent pieces."

I'm vaguely aware of Lorcan covering his shit-eating grin with his tattooed fingers, but his shaking shoulders give him away.

Silas's black eyes narrow at the both of us, but he doesn't comment further on the matter. Which is probably for the best at this point. "Stay up here," he orders Lor. "We won't be long."

I'm not sure if the last part was directed at Lorcan or at me, but either way, I agree. There is no reason to prolong this visit any longer than absolutely necessary.

Silas leads me to a metal door with a keypad on it that reminds me of the one on the front door of his house. His palm lays across the reader and after a buzzing sound, it flashes green. Multiple locking mechanisms can be heard twisting and turning inside before the door cracks open.

Even before I see the stone stairs leading down, I know it's a basement by the cool air that rushes over the exposed skin of my arms.

Opening the door wider, Silas looks at me, waiting for me to walk through myself. He doesn't push or rush me, but instead allows me to set the pace in which I confront my monster.

With a steadying breath, I descend the steps into darkness. Each step I take, I steel myself further. By the time I reach the bottom, I'm no longer anxious about seeing Gideon.

I have a purpose—a job—to do here and that's it. All I need is the name and then I will never have to look at his odd robotic expression again.

Silas takes hold of my wrist in a loose grip and guides me down the dark hallway. There aren't any lights because this isn't a building that humans were ever meant to explore. The good news is I stopped being afraid of the dark a long time ago.

We come to a stop after a brief pause, there's a green flash just like before and a door swings open in front of us.

My eyes burn from the abrupt change of lighting and for a moment, all I can see are spots. I thought the lighting in a hospital was bright, but it pales in comparison to the lighting in this room.

Blinking away the dots, I try to focus on what I'm seeing in front of me and when I do, my stomach drops.

I had grand plans for what I wanted to happen to him. As I lay there on that metal table, I envisioned all the ways I wanted him to suffer. The thoughts brought me comfort at the time and appeased the angry beast that had come alive inside of me.

I thought I was still angry but as I take in the contents of the glass cube in front of me, I realize that Silas is on a whole other level of angry. I'm not sure if we're even playing the same game at this point.

"What is this?" I question even though I don't suspect I'll get an answer. Pulling my arm from Silas's grip, I move closer to the box so I can see the full extent of what's happening.

It's like a car wreck and I'm unable to look away from it.

In slow, steady drops, blood drips from a nozzle in the ceiling, creating a small puddle in the middle of the glass cube. That's not the concerning part. It's the naked man crouched over, licking at the puddle like a man finding water in a desert oasis.

Without paying attention to what I'm doing, my hands reach out and press against the glass. The second my fingers make contact; Gideon's head snaps up and his eyes pin me.

When Silas had found me at the warehouse, I thought Gideon's mind was gone, but staring into those orbs now, I know it was only a precursor for what was to come. Wild and crazed looking doesn't even begin to describe what I see in his gaze. It's like looking into pure, unadulterated madness.

Any sign of the put-together man that he may have once been is long gone.

When he stands up from the floor, his movements even look wrong. They aren't fluid and graceful like a vampire's should be. They're jerky and clunky. Sluggish even.

Silas shifts to stand next to me and when I glance at him, there isn't a sliver of remorse or feeling in his expression. In fact, his face is so devoid of all emotion that when he looks at me, he almost appears bored by all of it.

Without a word to me, he turns his attention back to Gideon. "You got your wish, Gideon. She's here," he coldly says. "Now tell me who your partner is."

Gideon trips on his own feet and falls forward. His hands press against the glass right over where mine rest. On reflex, I rip them away from the cool surface.

"Quincey," Gideon whimpers. "You came. I knew you'd come."

Swallowing hard, I nod my head. "I'm here," *And now I really wish I wasn't.* "Do as he said and tell us who's behind the attacks, Gideon." To my own amazement, my voice remains strong, calm even, despite that being the exact opposite of how I'm feeling.

His fingers shake on the glass, mimicking the way his bottom lip begins to quiver. "Make him give her back to me," he pleads in a broken whisper. "He took her from me again. You're the only person that can make him give her back."

"He's talking about Margret," Silas adds, like he believes I could ever forget the name of the person all of this happened for. No, her name is engraved into my brain like a haunting memory.

"My Margret," Gideon wails. "I can't find her, Quincey. Please help me."

I know what he is, and I know what he's done. And I *thought* I knew how I wanted him to be punished for his crimes.

A week ago, seeing him in this state would have brought so much pleasure to the angry beast inside of me. It would have found joy in hearing Gideon yell for Margret the same way he wanted me to call for Silas.

I'm getting what I thought I wanted, and yet, it doesn't make me feel how I thought it would. I don't feel stronger seeing him weak, and I don't feel happy seeing him sad.

As delusional as it makes me seem, all I feel is pity for the man who stands before me looking completely lost. I can feel compassion for him because while he still shares a name and resemblance with the monster who took me and killed Ira, he's not the same. That man died when his mind broke.

"Okay," I agree. "I'll bring her back to you."

Gideon's body sags in relief. "I knew you would."

I can feel Silas's eyes on me and when he whispers my name in a harsh, almost inaudible warning, I ignore him. "What are you thinking? I don't think dishonesty—" I hold my hand up, silencing him before he can say anything else.

"I know what I'm doing," I snap at Silas, never looking away from the broken brown eyes behind the glass. "Gideon, I will bring Margret back to you, but first you have to tell me who you're working with. The attacks are still happening. People are dying—children are dying."

Gideon's head cocks. "Children? Margret loves children. She would never hurt a child."

"I believe you."

Silas makes an unimpressed, scoff-like noise but refrains from commenting further.

"You do?" Gideon asks me, sounding doubtful. "He never believed me. He took her from me before I could prove Margret was still the same."

I don't know why Silas is still trying to bring *reason* into this conversation—there's really no point. "Gideon, the Margret you knew died when you turned her. Her humanity died with her when her heart stopped. It doesn't matter how much time I gave her; she was never going to be who she once was."

Up until this point, we haven't talked about why he killed Margret. Silas was too occupied with walking on eggshells around me and I was too wrapped up in my mixture of anger and grief to have such a conversation. And now that things are better between us and things are starting to feel normal, I think both of us are afraid of rocking the boat by bringing up the subject.

Even though we haven't discussed it further, my belief and trust in

Silas that he would never kill her without a valid reason hasn't wavered. And listening to what he's admitting now, I know I was right.

If Gideon turned Margret and she came back the same way Cecily did, Silas would have felt like he had no other choice than to take care of Margret.

Gideon surges forward and his fists slam against the glass wall. "Don't talk about her that way. You're wrong!"

"You're delusional—" Silas begins to argue, but I interject by placing myself between his tall frame and the glass.

"I know he was wrong," I lie so I can regain Gideon's attention. We're getting off track from what's actually important. "He was wrong because Margret is fine now, isn't she?" Indulging in his fantasy worked some back at the warehouse, and I can almost bet it will work here too.

The crazed vampire's head nods. "Yes, but he took her from me again." The rage melts from his face and the desperation returns.

"And I told you I can get her back for you, but I need you to tell me who else you are working with. Who is behind the new attacks, Gideon?"

He backs away from the glass and ponders my questions for a second. A thousand different thoughts flash in his eyes but I can't understand a single one of them. Finally, his mouth pulls into a frown. "Going against Silas was always going to be challenging. I thought it would be smart to have a partner." For a split second, he makes me believe we're going to get an answer from him. "But Margret didn't trust anyone, so it had to be just us."

And just like that, my hope for an answer deflates.

"So, no one helped you? What about the person I heard you talking to at the warehouse?" I ask. I never did see who came to the door before the gunfire started. "Who was that?"

"He was in charge of security." Gideon sighs. "I'm almost positive he's dead now too."

With a quick glance in Silas's direction, he confirms this with a nod.

Gideon looks at me expectantly. "I told you the truth. Can I have her back now?"

You know he's truly lost his mind because his only concern is about Margret. Not once has he asked to be released from the glass prison he's being held in.

I can't help but sigh in defeat. If Gideon doesn't have a silent partner out there, that means there's another entity out there who wants to cause harm to Silas. But I think that's the true nature of this world. When you're at the top, everyone wants to tear you down. The game will never end, the players just keep changing.

"Yes, I'll go get her for you now." Silas sends me a look of confusion, still not sure how I'm going to pull this off. "Where are the light switches?"

"Excuse me?"

"Just trust me on this." I'm not really in the mood to have him question me. I didn't question him about how he was keeping Gideon, but now I'm kicking myself that I haven't. "We need to turn off some of the lights to create shadows."

Silas moves to the control panel on the wall and flips a couple switches. On one side of the room, half of the lights turn off. Gideon moves close to the dark corner that now sits across the space. He stares into the shadows and waits with a hopeful look on his face

I know the second he can see her. His lips curl into a relieved smile and the tension melts from his body.

"Margret," he calls to her happily.

I can feel Silas's gaze on me. Without turning his way, I explain, "He can only see her in dark places." The dark corner of the room he was keeping me in may have appeared empty to me, but in his eyes, Margret was standing there, keeping him company.

"Gideon." Hearing me say his name, he reluctantly looks back at me. "If I find out you're lying to me, I will take her away from you again."

Silas may think that the way to break him is by treating him like a caged animal, but I just proved I know better.

Gideon's face drops, looking distraught at the notion. "We don't kill children."

For another minute, I watch as he happily talks to an apparition of Margret.

"This can't continue," I inform Silas in a low whisper before I stalk out of the room, leaving behind the man who was once my monster but is now nothing at all.

Hating someone is easy, but having compassion is hard.

And I seldom chose the easy path.

CHAPTER 27

My teeth are grinding to the point of jaw pain by the time Silas closes the doors to his office behind us.

I'm not sure how many offices this man has, and part of me doubts he knows either.

This office looks plain compared to the one at home. There aren't any bookshelves lining the walls, full of mementos from throughout the years, like at home. Hell, there's barely anything on the walls. Just a few paintings that have probably been around longer than Silas himself. Which means they're *old*.

After my slow perusal through the bare-bone space, I finally turn and face him. He stands there, that same blank expression on his face as he wore in the basement.

"You can take off your mask now," I snap at him. "No one can see you in here, so you can drop the act. Plus, I don't want to talk to King Silas. I want to talk to *my* Silas."

It's a change I don't think most people would notice, but the slight softening of the harsh lines of his face is a glaring difference to me. His dark eyes even shift from cold nothingness to the midnight eyes that haunt my dreams.

Just like that, he's back. *Good.*

My fingers wrap around the pendant hanging from my neck. "When you gave me this necklace, I promised you that if you ever ventured too far into the darkness, I would be your guiding light. I would bring you back and center you." My voice is eerily calm, given the turbulent emotions inside of me. "Whether you want to or not, I need you to hear me when I say you've ventured too far with this one, Silas."

He went from expressing no emotion just seconds ago to his face filling with anger. "You, more than anyone, should be thrilled that Gideon is being dealt with accordingly."

"I *do* want him dealt with, but not like this." My head shakes at him. "I thought this is what I wanted. I thought I wanted him to suffer a slow, painful death for what he did, but when I look at him in that box, I know it's wrong." I take a step toward Silas, but he mirrors it by taking a step back. "And more importantly, I know it's pointless."

"How can you say that to me? After what he did to you, how can you stand here and tell me that this is pointless. That man *butchered* you."

Butchered? I must bite back a wince at his cruel word choice.

"You are arguably the smartest person I know. You can analyze a person or situation and know all the answers in seconds, but you are so blinded by your anger that you can't even see it. The man that's behind that glass isn't the same man who hurt me. Hell, he's so far gone, I would bet he doesn't remember everything that happened in that warehouse." I wish I could forget it too, but I can't. My goal now is to find ways to cope with it. "You think you're punishing him by keeping him in that box? Silas, he doesn't even realize he's trapped in there. If he did, he would have been using his freedom as a bargaining chip—not Margret."

His face twists into a cold smile that most would fear, but honestly, it makes me want to punch him in the nose. "Very well. I will turn on all the lights again."

No longer able to keep my composure, my voice raises as I throw my hands up in frustration. "If you do that, you will just be repeating history." Taking Margret away all those years ago is what got us all into this mess to begin with. "You're punishing someone who doesn't have the cognitive wherewithal to comprehend what's happening to him, and by doing so, you're wasting your fucking time."

"He has to pay for what he did to you, Quincey. I can't allow this kind of behavior to stand. His punishment has to send a message to everyone that you're untouchable—that you're fucking *mine*." When he speaks the last word, his voice is a deadly growl, causing shivers to run down my spine. "And they will all learn what the consequences are when you're harmed."

"You want to punish someone or send a message, Silas? Fine, but send it to someone who can grasp just how truly fucked they are. Gideon is no longer that someone. At this point, you're just prolonging a life that's already over."

Silas's black eyes flare with fury. "You think I should kill him and let all of this be over with? That's what you want?" His lips pull back in a sneer, exposing the tips of his fangs. They're a glaring sign that he's losing his control, but I'm still not ready to drop this.

"I know what Ira would want," I tell him as calm as possible, no longer wanting to match his turbulent energy. "He would want justice for what happened to him, and you're choosing vengeance." An eye for an eye; Ira was simple like that. "What you're doing to Gideon isn't going to bring peace to Ira. Let him rest easy knowing his killer is dead." All my life, I've been focused on saving lives, and now I'm pleading with Silas to take one. It should probably feel more immoral than it does, but I'm completely at peace with it. "I agree that Gideon's actions can't go unpunished, whether he remembers he did it or not, he killed Ira, and for that he has to die."

"Death isn't punishment enough for what he did to *you*." Silas seems even taller than he is when he's in this state. Anger makes him into a bigger, threatening presence. "He hasn't suffered enough yet."

"Yes, he has!" My voice raises again, despite my best efforts to remain the calm one. "For a hundred years, he's done nothing but suffer because you took the love of his life away from him, Silas!"

"And then he took mine!" Silas's admission comes in a deadly roar. It bounces off the mostly empty walls and has me freezing in place, stunned, completely silent.

Standing there, I try to find the right words, but all I can manage to utter is a breathy, "*Silas...*" My head shaking in disbelief. My heart pounds against my ribs like it's trying to free itself from its cage.

Silas's past with Cecily isn't a mystery to me. From the very beginning, I was aware that no matter how many years passed, she would always remain. She was a presence that would always be *here*, whether we acknowledged it or not. Cecily was Silas's first love—his wife—and I never wanted to diminish her importance to him. I accepted that pieces of Silas were always going to belong to her. It was never my wish to replace her.

And I thought Silas felt the same way.

The all-consuming anger that had been taking Silas over just seconds ago, evaporates, taking his sharp fangs with it. "I thought I knew what love was when I met Cecily. I thought I would never break the vows I said to her. *Till death do us part...*it meant nothing to me because I thought, even in death, my love for her would never waver. I thought I could never love another person the way I thought I loved her." His midnight eyes lock with mine, the emotion filling them makes the air catch in my throat. "And then I met you, Quincey, and I learned that I was wrong. The man who made those vows didn't have the slightest comprehension of the word love." I have lost the ability to breathe altogether at this point. "When my time comes and I cross paths with Cecily in the afterlife, I will her owe her an apology because I know

now, I never loved her the way that she deserved. It's a gut-wrenching thing to have to admit, but it's true."

His face contorts as if he's in physical pain. Unable to stop myself, I reach for him, taking his balled fist between my hands. Like it's not enough physical contact for him, his free hand cups the side of my face.

"Cecily was who I needed then, and I am infinitely grateful for those few short years I got with her, but she was never the one I was destined for." His thumb swipes across my cheekbone as his black eyes lock with mine. "Lifetimes I have lived without you, but I would wait a dozen more to call you mine. You are my sun, and you are the love of my life, Quincey Page."

Tears I didn't know were forming in my eyes fall down my face, but neither one of us does anything to stop them. Sometimes allowing emotion to freely fall is necessary, and this is one of those times. There are no walls up between us. Silas's mask is nowhere to be seen, and he's exposing every inch of himself to me.

"These words still don't seem like they're enough to fully encapsulate what I feel for you, but I will say them anyway. I love you, Mon Soleil."

The sad truth is only one person has ever said those words to me. And that was Lucy. She was the only one who has cared about me enough to say such powerful sentiments. Not even my parents. And that's why I will cherish this moment for the rest of my life.

Swallowing hard, I try to rein in the emotion clogging my throat. "They might not seem like they're enough to you, but they're *everything* to me, Silas," I tell him once I can talk. "I love you too, and I'm pretty sure I have since the night you bought Ira's roses. And I—"

Like he's no longer able to resist it, Silas's hand twists into my hair and his mouth collides with mine, cutting off whatever else I was going to say, but it's okay. I already told him what he needed to know.

My body begins to heat from his touch and when his tongue licks into my mouth, my clit pulses between my legs. That's all it takes for my body to want him. One kiss and I'm full of need.

Silas's hands grip the back of my thighs before lifting me off the ground. My legs wrap around his middle on instinct, causing my heels to fall to the tiled floor.

My fingers run through his hair, ruining the perfectly styled strands. Behind closed doors, perfection doesn't matter.

His cock hardens under my ass, and I grind against it, making a growl form low in his throat. "What have I said about teasing me?"

"Can't recall." I smirk against his mouth. "Why don't you remind me?" Just to drive my point home, I grind harder against him until his fingers dig so painfully into my thighs I'm sure they've added to my growing collection of bruises.

My world spins and tilts so fast, I swear my eyes go cross-eyed, but when my back lands on the surface of his large wooden desk across the room, things begin to come back into focus.

His teeth nip at my bottom lip while he tackles the button of my black jeans. "I told you if you continued to do so that I could have you flat on your back with my cock buried in your tight cunt in a matter of seconds."

Stretching lazily below him, I glance at the small clock on the other side of the desk. "Well, you've got me on my back, but there's not a cock in sight and you're running out of time. Tick tock, Mr. Laurent."

"That's where you're wrong, my love," he says between the kisses he trails along my jaw. "We have nothing but time."

One of us has more time than the other, the dark floats through my head, acting as my daily reminder that there's a time on this and one day it's going to run out. Before the thought can fully take hold and drag me under, Silas sucks on the pulse point on my throat, pulling me back to the present. *Which is where I need to remain.*

"Lift your ass," he orders when he begins to yank my pants down. "I would rip them from your body, but you still have to walk out of here and I'd prefer you didn't do it naked."

Because I never learn, I smirk, "I'm sure they'd prefer if I did."

The scowl that crosses Silas's face would make grown men shake in fear, but it only makes my smile grow.

"You think that's funny, *Mon Soleil*?" His fingers grip the thin fabric of my thong, and with a tug, he rips it from my body completely. "You'd permit others to see you naked?" He questions in a snarl that promises retribution. "You'd let others see this pussy that belongs to me?"

"Depends on who's out there—" my taunt ends in a surprised gasp when he delivers a sharp slap to my pussy. "*Oh my god!*" My cry is a mixture of pain and pleasure.

I've never been slapped there like that, and it's something I never would have expected to like, but it only causes the throbbing in my core to intensify.

I rear up into a sitting position, which I figure out was his plan all along when his fingers wrap around my jaw, and he tilts my face up closer to his.

"One day you will push me too far, and then what will you do?"

"Revel in it," I grit out before scraping my teeth across his stubbly jaw. "And reap my reward."

His hand releases me so he can pull the short-sleeved black top over my head. When he finds I went braless today, his nostrils flare, but he doesn't comment on it.

"You think I would reward such behavior?"

I palm his dick through his slacks. "I don't think you'll do it intentionally, but in the end, any way you touch me is a reward."

"Maybe I just need to be more creative."

"Do your worst," I taunt, a wicked grin on my face.

With a heated look of his own, he backs away and methodically removes his suit jacket and his black button-down. His movements are purposely slow to further antagonize me.

I can talk a big game, but Silas knows he's got me right where he wants me. Naked and needy, my pussy all but dripping onto his desk.

"Lie back, spread your legs, and put your feet on the desk," he instructs once the only thing he wears is his slacks. "I want to see every inch of your wet cunt."

I barely have enough time to do as he says before he's on his knees and his mouth is on me. At the first languid swipe of his tongue, I cry out, my back arching while he groans against me, sending vibrations right to my clit.

"Yes," I moan, my hips rising and falling, trying to create more delicious friction.

"That's it," he praises, his lips and tongue working my sensitive flesh, making me feel out of control. "Fuck my face."

His mouth continues to worship my clit as he sinks two thick fingers into me. I squirm beneath him, grinding against his jaw. I'm going to have chafe marks on my delicate skin tomorrow from his stubble, but I don't care.

With each pass of his tongue on me, more air is sucked out of the room. The pleasure inside of me is almost too much, and just when I don't think I will be able to handle any more, a slick finger leaves my pussy and trails backward.

I can't help my reaction. My body tenses as he slowly begins to circle the taut ring of muscle. With each pass, the pressure increases. Sensing my apprehension, Silas turns his head and presses an open-mouthed kiss to my inner thigh. "Relax and let me in," he encourages before returning his attention to my clit.

His tongue flattens against me, creating just the right amount of friction and pressure for me to involuntarily relax. He takes advantage of this and as I shudder out a breath, the tip of his finger presses into a place that's never been breached before.

For a second, conflicting emotions shoot through me, fear and pleasure.

But in the end, pleasure wins. My eyes close and a long, low moan escapes my lips.

He sets an intoxicating rhythm. With each pass of his tongue on my clit, his finger plunges deeper into my asshole.

The orgasm that had been slowly building inside of me breaks through me like an electrical storm shooting through every one of my nerve endings.

His pace doesn't falter and as I ride the waves of my release, he growls against me, "Just as I own your cunt, I also own your ass."

"God," I pant. "*Yes*. You can have whatever you want." My heart, my pussy, and now my ass, they're all his. He can do whatever he wants with them if it means I get to come like that.

"I appreciate the offer, though it's entirely unnecessary," he says after delivering one last stroke through my soaked center, causing my body to jolt from the aftershocks. His finger leaves me, making me feel surprisingly empty, and he stands to his full height. "I don't need permission to take what already belongs to me."

His head bows and his mouth covers mine. Silas doesn't wait for me to open for him. He shoves through the seam of my lips, and he forces me to taste myself on him. I groan, sucking on his tongue.

His dick, still confined to his slacks, grinds against my soaked flesh as he kisses me. "You're going to ruin your pants," I pant.

"On the contrary, I think I'm improving them," he corrects. "When I leave this room, I will be covered in your intoxicating scent and there will be no doubt in anyone's mind that I just claimed something they never will."

"No, never. You're the only one."

I can feel another orgasm starting to build; my body once again is taken over by an untamed need.

"Am I?" Silas questions through gritted teeth and he grinds harder against me.

"Yes, obviously." *What a stupid question.*

"Prove it."

CHAPTER 28

P*rove it.*
I rise onto my elbow so I can look at him in confusion. "What do you mean?" I ask in a breathy pant. Despite the puzzlement I'm suddenly experiencing, his hips never stop their purposeful pace. The wet spot on his slacks is only growing by the second.

"You told me it *'depends on who's out there'*." Silas's heated black eyes hold mine as he reiterates my early taunt. "I know who's out there and I know that while you came on my face, he could hear you."

My tongue swipes over my lips. "W-who?" I manage to stammer out.

Instead of answering my question, his head dips low and he takes one of my pebbled nipples in his mouth. First his tongue caresses it, but when his teeth bite down, I gasp, and my elbows fall out from under me.

My hands clasp his head, trying to hold him closer to me, but he pulls away too soon. I can't help the disappointed whimper that escapes me.

"He might know what sounds you make when you come, but he needs to know that he will never be the one causing them," Silas bites out. "He needs to be reminded that you are mine, and he will only ever be an observer."

His thumb presses into my clit in an effort to really drive his point home. I almost fall right over the edge there, but he once again leaves too soon.

His body comes to a stop, the wonderful friction from his dick also halting. "Do you trust me?"

Silas has asked me this before, and, at the time, all I could offer as an answer was *'I want to'*, but now I freely place my heart and life in his hands. "Yes," I breathe.

The corners of his mouth curl in a satisfied smirk and his finger traces my jaw in approval. "Good girl," he praises before speaking a command I don't think is meant for me. "Get in here."

Not even a full two seconds later, the door of Silas's office opens. My heart thuds hard in my chest as Lorcan walks into the room. His pale brown eyes scan over my naked and exposed body.

I'm expecting a sarcastic comment or flirty remark from him, but it never comes because the humor that is usually in Lor's expression is nowhere to be found. It's been taken over by a look so intense it makes my skin grow warm and flutters form low in my stomach.

Without a word, the heavily tattooed vampire leans against the wall so that he's directly in my line of sight.

Silas looks at Lor as his fingertips trail over my dripping opening. "Lor watching you turns you on, doesn't it?"

I swallow hard, but don't answer.

"It's okay," Silas reassures me. His finger creating tight circles around my clit, making me squirm on the desk. "I already know the answer... I can smell the truth on you but want to hear you say it."

"Y-yes," I stumble over the simple word because I'm no longer in control of my body.

I brace myself, expecting there to be wrath to pay for my honesty, but Silas only nods his head once, his smirk from earlier returning.

"What about you, Lor? Do you like looking at what's mine?" he asks without turning his head toward the other man. Silas doesn't give Lor time to answer like he did me though, instead he answers for him. "I know you do. I've seen the way you've looked at her."

Silas abruptly pinches my clit between his fingers, and I almost come off the desk. "*Fuck!*" I cry out.

I watch as the tattooed columns of Lorcan's throat shift as he swallows, but still, he remains silent and where he is.

"This one time, you're going to watch as I take her, Lorcan." Silas's instruction leaves little room for debate. "And while I do, I want you to remember that all you'll ever be able to do is watch. Never touch." Just like before, when Silas's hand slaps my pussy, I can't contain my gasp. "Isn't that right?" he snarls at me.

"Yes, that's right." I don't know how I manage to string together three full words, but I do. *Someone give me a gold fucking star.*

"And he will never know just how sweet you taste." My front teeth dig painfully into my bottom lip to stop myself from gaping at him when he runs his tongue along his palm, licking away the wetness that had transferred there. "He can only imagine it."

Lorcan, who's been standing like a statue, finally shifts restlessly and his fingers flex at his side.

Midnight-black eyes pin me. "Tell me what you want."

This isn't a hard question, and for the rest of my life, the answer will never change. "You. I want you." *No, I need him.* "I just want you."

A triumphant look crosses Silas's face. "I know."

Silas's hands tackle his belt and before I can fully exhale the air in my lungs, his thick cock is free from the confines of his pants and it's burying deep inside me.

The invasion is exactly what I need to send me over the edge. I come violently around him and my body thrashes against the surface of the desk. My nails claw at the wood and I wouldn't be surprised if I'm leaving permanent scratches in the finish.

Silas stays still, not moving an inch, until the waves of pleasure begin to wane. He waits until the precise second I almost come down before pulling completely out of me and diving back inside. The friction causes more tremors to shoot through me, all the way to my tingly fingers and toes.

My hands reach for him and instead of the desk, my fingernails sink into his perfectly sculpted chest. They rake across his pecs, leaving a faint red line I know will be gone before we're finished here.

But Silas still encourages the behavior. "That's it, scratch me. Leave your mark on me."

My vision clears and I'm able to once again see the vampire that stands across the room. His brown eyes lock with mine and the sexual desire in them makes my pussy quiver around Silas.

Lorcan doesn't look at me the way Silas does. Silas looks at me like he wants to claim and keep every piece of me for himself, and if he doesn't the world may end. Lorcan looks at me like he wants to eat me alive, savoring each bit, but once he's gotten his fill, he'll leave me.

That's the difference between love and desire.

True love is everlasting, desire is fleeting. Knowing the difference between the two is important.

This moment between Lor and I is just as fleeting, but that doesn't mean I can't enjoy the fuck out of it while I have it.

Silas captures my hand in his. He brings it to his mouth and his teeth scrape across my fingertips. "Yes, just like that, look at him while he watches me claim your cunt," he pauses. "You like his eyes on you?"

I manage a shaky nod. My skin feels too hot between Silas's touch and Lorcan's gaze.

"What about you, Lor?" Silas asks, not making any effort to conceal the taunt in his voice. "Are you enjoying yourself?"

Lor's eyes narrow at the back of Silas's head, the muscle in his jaw flexing as his teeth grind.

Silas drops my hand, only to ensnare my ankles in his grasp. My breath catches in my throat as a strangled moan fights to get free when he changes the angle. He yanks my feet off the table and pulls my legs straight against his chest. His arms wrap around them, keeping them in place as he continues to tunnel into me at a daunting pace.

"I didn't hear your answer, Lorcan," he barks harshly, a devious grin forming on his face. "Tell me, is your cock so hard it hurts yet?" Silas looks at me when he asks, "He can't touch you, but should we allow him to touch himself? Should we let him fist his cock while he watches?"

I swear he's siphoning all the oxygen out of the room. I can't breathe when he says things like that to me.

My mouth dries at the thought of Lorcan fucking his hand while Silas fucks me.

A little voice in my head whispers, warning me not to cross the line—that it's not fair to Lorcan, but at the same time, a louder voice replays Lor's earlier words to me.

Never again will I deny myself what I want.

That's what he told me when he explained his outlook on life. If Lorcan didn't want to be here doing this, he would have left the room. Silas didn't have to threaten him to enter through that door, he came through voluntarily and he's staying just the same.

And that's why I'm confident with my choice when I breathlessly whisper, "Yes."

Lorcan waits for Silas's nod of approval before his tattooed hand reaches for the button of his jeans. I can feel his sable eyes on me, but I'm too captivated by how his fingers drag his zipper down. He's moving at such an unhurried pace, like he simply has all the time in the world.

He tugs at his waistband, pulling his well-worn charcoal jeans farther down. It's not at all a shock to me to find that the Irishman doesn't wear any form of underwear. The only thing offering him any coverage are the tattoos that continue well past his pelvic bone.

At the same time Lorcan pulls his impressive length from his pants, Silas's fingers return to my clit. "Oh fuck," I hiss. "More." I'm not sure if I'm asking for more pressure from Silas or if I'm asking Lorcan to do more than stand there.

But I don't have to wonder long because I get both my wishes. Silas rolls my clit between his fingers, making my hips buck off the desk, and Lorcan finally grips his dick. I watch, completely captivated as his hand with the heart and dagger tattooed on it begins to stroke up and down. Each pass is methodical and measured. Nothing about him is rushed or chaotic.

He's completely in control.

Meanwhile, I feel like at any second I'm going to come unraveled from my own skin. Or worse, melt into a puddle of nothingness right here on Silas's desk. As someone who's recently faced death, this is a way I wouldn't mind going out.

Fingers tighten around my jaw, and I'm forced to turn away from Lor. It's not a complete loss, because the look I find on Silas's face is just as hot if not hotter.

His black eyes look down at me with hunger I've never seen before. "Savor each moment of this, Quincey, because this will never happen again. After this, it will only ever be you and me."

He forcibly presses two fingers into my mouth without any preamble, cutting off any response I may have had.

I'm entirely thankful he has the wherewithal to not use the finger he'd used to invade my ass. My mind has turned into a needy ball of mush, and I'm no longer capable of thinking clearly.

He pushes them farther down my throat, triggering my gag reflex, but he still doesn't let up. "Do you wish she was gagging around your cock, Lor?"

"Fuck you, Silas," Lorcan finally grits out, his voice a deadly growl that sends shivers right to my pussy.

Silas releases his hold on my face, and I return my gaze to Lor. His brown eyes are heavy when they bore into mine, and his hand has picked up its pace. He's close.

And so am I.

My walls begin to quake around Silas's length and my breath begins to come in short pants. The pressure that's building between my thighs is almost unbearable. I'm right there, I just need the final push to fall over the edge of no return.

"Silas," I plead, knowing he will understand what I need.

"I know," he grunts. "I've got you, *Mon Soleil*. I'll take care of you."

And he does. All it takes is a few more deep thrusts before I'm being taken over. It's like a tidal wave of pleasure hitting me at full force. My back bows violently and legs shake as my toes curl. Pleasant warm ecstasy moves through veins and nerves, making everything feel like it's short-circuiting.

My pleasure only intensifies when Silas's powerful body goes rigid and his release splashes against my walls. His head turns and his blunt teeth embed into my ankle. It hurts in a way that only adds to my climax.

Still overcome with intense shocks still working through my system, I'm vaguely aware of a harsh curse coming from the other side of the room. My blurry eyes seek out the sound and find Lorcan shuddering. He milks his dick, ropes of his release landing on his simple white Henley and the floor.

His eyes that had been squeezed shut as he came, snap open and collide with mine. My breath hitches at the intensity that resides in them. Seeing him in this state is like meeting someone else entirely.

Like he's flipped a switch, he returns to the man I know. The corner of his mouth lifts in an arrogant smirk and he sends me a playful wink.

"This was fun," he announces while tucking his semihard dick back into his pants. "Truly a shame it was a one-off thing, but if you two change your mind, you know where to find me."

He doesn't wait to be dismissed or even acknowledged by Silas before he slips out the door he'd entered through.

Starting at where he'd bitten my ankle, Silas begins to trail kisses up my leg. "Did you enjoy yourself?" he asks against my too-warm skin.

"*Mmmhmm...*" I lazily murmur, suddenly feeling exhausted. Between the emotional toll of coming face-to-face with Gideon again and then my fight with Silas, I'm mentally drained. But now I'm also physically drained. Every single one of my muscles feels like they've been vigorously worked out.

"I'm glad," he tells me as he gently lets go of my legs, allowing them to dangle over the edge of the desk once more. There isn't any anger or jealousy in his face when he speaks, letting me know that he, too, is content with what just happened.

"It was fun, but it also solidified something I already knew." Weakly, I pull myself into a sitting position. "I only want you and I will only ever *need* you." Even with Lorcan staring at me the way he was, I didn't crave his touch like I crave Silas's.

Silas takes the pocket square out of the suit jacket he had discarded earlier and brings it between my legs. Gently, he wipes away the mess he created. My body jolts at the contact, still sensitive.

He tosses the cloth into the small trash can beside the desk before returning to me.

Silas's large hands hold my face between them as he stares down at me. "And I will only ever want you," he promises, while pressing a long kiss to the center of my sweaty forehead. "A lifetime isn't long enough with you."

Without a second's thought, I ask for something I didn't know I even wanted until the words leave my mouth. "Then change me."

CHAPTER 29

I got the phone call I've been waiting for all week and now my heeled boots are pounding against the sterile laminate flooring of the intensive care unit.

Giddy excitement is working itself through my body and the relief I feel has a permanent smile on my face. It doesn't even falter when the bitch of a nurse glares in our direction as we speed past her station.

Though I do raise a middle finger at her, just to be sure there isn't any confusion on her end about where my feelings regarding her shitty mood lie.

Suck my dick, Nurse Ratched.

The orange tape is still on the sliding door, but this time it's been left open. Which is a good sign all on its own.

Not bothering to make sure Silas is still behind me, I rush through the doorway and rip back the hideous blue curtain.

I didn't know I was holding my breath, but when his hunter green eyes clash with mine and his face splits into a huge smile, I release the air I'm holding captive.

"You're smiling." I don't know what possesses me to state the obvious. Maybe it's because the last time I saw him, his condition was so grim, I wasn't sure if we'd ever get to see his smile again.

"Hey, darlin'." Duke's southern drawl washes over me like an old friend and before I can stop myself, I dart across the room to wrap my arms around him.

Della's eyes water as she watches our reunion from her chair next to his bed.

Relief like none other washes over me when Duke returns the embrace with his arm that isn't still riddled with IV tubing. "Hi," I finally greet after a minute, still refusing to let him go. "It's really good to hear your voice, Duke." I didn't think I would get choked up seeing him, but my throat suddenly feels tight. "I *really* needed you to be okay. I don't know what I would have done if I'd lost you too."

We finally pull apart so we can look at each other.

"I still have a long road to recovery, but I'll get there." The determined look on Duke's face makes me think he's going to prove all the doctors wrong and be back to his old self before they predict he will.

A traumatic brain injury is no joke, but Duke is too strong to let anything get in his way. And I will attend every physical therapy session with him until it happens.

His green eyes examine my face as he says, "Looks like we both made it out okay for the most part." He gestures to the bandage that is still on his forehead. "I heard we both gained some new battle scars though."

My healing scars are hidden beneath the simple white cotton top I wear, but that doesn't stop me from tracing my fingertips over where they reside. "Yeah, I guess we did. We can compare them once we get you the hell out of here."

"Sounds like a plan," Duke agrees as his focus swings to Silas. "I also heard I missed a hell of a fight too."

Silas raises a brow, confused about how he knows anything about my rescue.

Duke nods his head at the woman who hasn't left his side all week. "Della here was catching me up on everything while we were waiting for you two to show up." His eyes flick between Silas and me, and his smile widens. "It's really fucking good to see you guys together."

I glance at the vampire over my shoulder quickly and try to ignore the ball of unease in my stomach when his black gaze meets mine.

The air between us is still thick with uncomfortable tension and it fucking sucks.

Lacking a filter has always been my downfall and now is no different. But the thing is, I don't regret what I said, but I do regret my timing.

Admittedly, I could have planned that one better. Though I don't think there was ever going to be an ideal time to ask Silas to change me. *Hey honey, I used your mouthwash, I hope you don't mind. Oh, and by the way, you should turn me so we can spend eternity together.*

Yeah… that would have gone over *super* well. I'm pretty sure running naked through Easter Mass with *'The devil sends his regards'* written on my left ass cheek would be better received.

Before I said it aloud, it was something I didn't even know I wanted, but now it's all I can think about. The longer my request sits out there, the surer I become of my decision.

I don't want a couple years with Silas, I want all of them.

And being like him would grant me this.

"So, what else did Della tell you about?" I ask Duke, trying to get the attention off Silas and me.

Duke's brows pull and he looks at me, confused by my weird subject change. As subtly as I can manage, I shake my head and beg with my eyes for him to drop it. Luckily, brain injury or not, the plea doesn't go unnoticed by Duke.

"You mean did she tell me about my Irish replacement?"

Effortlessly, he fills the awkward air.

"Replacement?" Silas comments dryly. "*Hardly*. No one could ever replace you, Duke. Your job will wait for however long you need to get back on your feet."

Duke isn't just Silas's right hand; he's also the man Silas was planning on leaving in charge of everything when Silas inevitably must leave town again.

The infinite life of a vampire means you can't stick around too long in one location. The fact he will never age or change is bound to draw attention after a few decades.

Before all the chaos over the past week ensued, Silas admitted his time in New Orleans is once again coming to an end. His plan was to promote Duke as the face of his operations here while Silas sets up in a new city. This was a conversation we had in passing, and I hadn't thought much about it until now.

Careful to not sit on him or any of the leads still connected to his healing body, I perch on the edge of his bed. "I'm sure Della here has painted Lorcan in a *lovely* light," I say sarcastically.

On cue, the older woman scoffs and grumbles under her breath.

"She probably described him as the spawn of Satan himself."

"Was I wrong?" she asks blandly. "I could have sworn I saw horns and a tail on that sociopath."

No, sorry, Della, that wasn't a tail. It was just his giant dick, but I can see how you'd be confused. The words are on the tip of my tongue, but by some miracle, I find the strength to sit quietly. I mentally pat myself on the back for my momentary success.

"Della just doesn't appreciate his humor," I joke instead. "I have a feeling that you'll actually get along with him, Duke. You two can team up and annoy the shit out of Silas."

"I'm pretty sure the only person who can annoy the boss man that much, and live, is you, darlin'."

Even if he's agitated with me right now, Silas nods his head. "This is true."

Duke chuckles, and as he does, his hand catches in the nasal cannula that sits on his face. Old habits die hard and on instinct, I reach out to fix the tubing. I did this multiple times a day with Ira, his horrendous coughing fits always dislodged it from his face.

"So..." I start once I have it settled. "Did Della tell you about anything else? Or just Lorcan?"

Even if it isn't any of my business, my curiosity over the situation is too strong for me to ignore.

Duke frowns. "No, was there something else I needed to know?"

Yeah, there was a cute purple-haired pixie that kept sneaking in to see you. What's that about?

Disappointed I won't be getting any answers about Rory yet, I think quick on my feet and like a fucking magician, I seamlessly pull an alternate topic of conversation out of my hat. "I was just seeing if Della blabbed about my drunken escapades at St. Sin," I say. "I need to know if she butchered the story, and if I need to tell it to you correctly."

Della's lips purse, clearly not amused. "No, I thought I'd do you a favor and allow that embarrassing moment of yours to remain a secret."

While she has a fair point, agreeing with her won't make her face do that funny thing I enjoy so much.

Completely deadpan, I question her, "Why would I keep it a secret, Della? Dancing on top of a bar with a bottle of tequila in my hand is nothing to be embarrassed about."

The corner of Della's eye looks like it's going to start twitching as she fights the look of disgust that's threatening to come through. The pinched expression is exactly what I was hoping would happen.

Duke shifts, the slight wince he makes doesn't go unnoticed. He's awake and breathing on his own, but there is still healing his body needs to do. According to the conversation I had with Della on the phone, Duke is experiencing some weakness on his right side, but with rigorous physical therapy, it should improve.

But true to his character, he masks his pain by grinning at me. "Were Lucy and you getting into some trouble without me? Lucy mentioned it too, that you guys knew how to cause some mayhem."

Lucy was raised by her aunt who worked full time, and I raised myself. That meant we had very little parental supervision. There were definitely a few times things got out of hand. The good news is there was only ever one fire, and it wasn't *that* bad. I mean... Lucy's hair grew back eventually.

I point my thumb at the tensely quiet vampire. "Silas carried me out of the bar before we could get around to starting any real mayhem."

"He carried you?" Duke's brows raise.

"Yeah, he went full caveman on me. Threw me over his shoulder and everything."

Duke laughs, and Della's eyes roll beneath her cat-eye glasses at the same time a big yawn takes her over. I can't imagine how long the past week has been for her.

"Della, let's go get you some coffee," I offer, standing from the bed. "It'll be good for you to get out of this room for a minute anyway."

She hesitates in her chair, but it's Duke's reassuring words that finally get her to stand. "Go get coffee, Del, and if they have one, bring me back a blueberry muffin."

I'm almost positive he knows the hospital still has him on a limited diet, but if a small fib will encourage her to take a break, I'm all for it.

Silas's hand locks around my upper arm when I walk past him. "Go to the coffee cart and come right back here, Quincey," he warns lowly. "I don't want you wandering."

The events that took place after our visit with Gideon may have momentarily overshadowed the original reason we were at the church. But we are both once again very aware of the fact that someone else out there is targeting Silas. We will need to be even more aware of our surroundings for the time being.

He waits for my head to nod in understanding before letting me go.

His midnight eyes peer into mine. It's like there's a thousand different things he wants to say, but instead of saying them, he remains silent.

The knot in my stomach tightens when he turns his head back toward Duke. Dismissing me.

Della and I walk in silence to the elevator. The second the doors close behind us, I slump against the wall and close my eyes.

She remains quiet, allowing me a second before speaking, "You have until we reach the lobby to feel whatever you're feeling, but when the doors open again, you need to pull yourself together."

"It's just never going to be easy, is it?"

"No, probably not," Della simply answers. "Heavy is the heart that loves the crown, Quincey, but that doesn't mean you let the weight of it tether you down."

Heavy is the heart that loves the crown.

Truer words have never been spoken.

But it's because of my love for him that I will continue to fight for what I want. And I will continue to prove he's not the only one wearing a crown.

CHAPTER 30

Silas

Stiffly, I sit in the chair Della had vacated, but instantly the turbulent energy in my muscles screams at me to stand up. I have to force myself to stay still and not pace at the foot of Duke's hospital bed. The man just woke up from a weeklong coma, he needs to heal and not be concerned with my own grievances.

But that doesn't appear to be a concern of his like it is mine. "Are you going to talk about it? Or just sit there and silently sulk."

My face pulls in a scowl. "I don't sulk."

Duke laughs at this. "Yes, you do. It's kind of the hallmark of your personality, Silas."

Refusing to acknowledge his remark, I remain silent and momentarily get lost in my disorganized thoughts. There are too many unanswered questions right now.

The mystery of the attacks, and the trepidation that comes with them, is taxing. At any given moment, I'm expecting my phone to ring and for them to tell me another attack has happened.

When I believed Gideon was still somehow playing a role in all of this, the motives behind the attacks made more sense to me. And there was a clear-cut answer on how to put a stop to all of this.

I don't want to believe a word that comes out of Gideon Rolfe's mouth, but with this, I'm inclined to believe he's no longer involved. The fear of us taking Margret away from him was too strong for him to lie. And frankly, I don't think his cracked mind is strong enough to keep up such a ruse.

Then there's the question of what exactly the future holds for Gideon. I was content with my plan to let him rot in that glass box for his remaining days. As inhumane as it is, it felt like the perfect fate for him, given what he'd done.

I didn't want to hear what she had to say, and I wasn't receptive to her outlook on it at the time, but the longer Quincey's words circulate in my head, the more my stance shifts.

She was right when she said Ira wouldn't wish that fate upon anyone. Even the man who killed him.

And then, not even an hour after admitting to her that she is the love of my life, she asks to become like me—a vampire. That is what's been taking up the most space in my brain.

"Alright, out with it," Duke sighs. "You have this weird, distant look in your eyes and it's freaking me out."

My fingers curl in and out of fists on my lap, and my teeth grind. "Quincey asked me to change her." My voice is barely a dark whisper.

Duke's mouth gapes and he stares at me for a solid minute before shaking his head. "Well, *shit!*" he groans like he's truly disappointed. I relax some, believing he understands my unease, but his next comment has the relief evaporating. "I owe Della money now."

"Pardon me?"

"Della said that Quincey would want you to change her within the first year of being together. I said there was no way, and that Quincey would want to enjoy being human a little longer. So, I bet it'd take two years. I owe Della fifty bucks."

Disgusted they would place bets on something so significant, I scowl at him and stand from the chair. "I don't see how the prospect of me ending Quincey's life is a matter you thought appropriate to wager on.'"

"Technically, you wouldn't be ending her life," he dares to argue. "If it goes right, you'd be adding to her life. By a *lot*."

"And what if it goes wrong, Duke?" I snap angrily. "Then what?"

If it goes wrong, I would be killing her twice.

"I told you before, there is no guarantee that will be the outcome. You and I both have seen how most of them come back with their humanity. You created a whole law because of the slim few that have come back like Cecily and Margret."

"Are you forgetting about Scarlett?" I know my question will cut deep, but it needs to be asked. "It's not just the vampire lives I'm concerned about, it's the humans. Your sister is dead because of the *slim few* you talk of."

Coming home to find his sister in a pool of her own blood is an image I'm sure he won't soon forget.

The pain Duke still carries around to this day flashes in his eyes. "No. I haven't forgotten what happened to Scarlett. I've thought about her every day for the past four years, but that doesn't change the fact I still think your law is too extreme," he reveals. "And I can say this because I'm the one hunting down the vampires that break your law. I have heard each of their pleas and their explanations, and you know what? More often than not, they're not breaking your law to be malicious or to fuck you over. They're breaking it because they're just like you; in love with a human and they want all the time they can get with them."

When I brought Duke on, he was a highly skilled soldier who was highly motivated by the death of his sister. When I offered him the job of hunting down vampires that broke my laws, he jumped at the chance. My trust in him grew over the years, and so did his skill as a hunter. While his job has evolved, he is still the one I trust to handle the problems caused by rogue vampires.

Even though I'm a vampire myself, it is useful to have a skilled vampire hunter on your payroll.

"So, what do you suppose I do? Just allow vampires to turn whoever they damn well please? How will I keep order over that?" Keeping the vampires in line has always been my priority.

"The same way you always have, but instead of putting all the responsibility on yourself to make sure rogue vampires are managed, put it on the vampires that turned them." Duke answers the question like it's something he's spent a lot of time pondering. "If they take on the feat of siring another vampire, they have to be prepared to put down their creation if it comes back a true monster. And if they fail to do so, then the same rules as now apply. Their punishment is death."

No longer able to stand still, I begin to pace the length of the room as I thoroughly think over Duke's proposal. "I can't change a law that's been in place for a century simply because Quincey is here requesting to be changed. They will see it as an incredibly selfish act and there could be an uprising."

Duke scoffs, unimpressed by my worry. "How many attempted uprisings have you had over the years? Each of them has been unsuccessful, it would be cute to see them try. But if you want to avoid blowback, show them you're not changing it for yourself, but for all the vampires like you. Do it for the ones that missed out on the years they could have had with their loved ones if the law hadn't prevented it." His face darkens when he adds, "But make it very fucking clear to them that if they allow soulless monsters to roam free and they can't do what needs to be done, I will fucking come for them."

At least Duke and I remain in agreement on this.

CHAPTER 31

Lorcan's supposed to be with Quincey at the hospital while she spends a couple hours with Duke.

I'd wanted to take her myself, but there was an issue with a distributor that I had been putting off for days now. It was when I left that meeting that I got the message from Lor.

I can't think of one plausible reason he would be texting me to meet him at the church. The calls and messages I've left him in return have gone ignored, which both angers me and concerns me. If he's with Quincey, he knows he needs to be in constant contact with me.

It was my worry that ultimately convinced me to follow his instructions and meet him there.

My confusion only grows when I spot a familiar car parked down the street under a tree. Bria shouldn't be here tonight, and yet, there her car sits. *No one* but the guards should be here tonight.

Leaving the car and my driver behind, I march to the front door, weaving through the large shrubbery that surrounds the property. The lack of streetlights and the overgrown landscaping helps to keep our movement in and out of the building concealed from the nosy humans. Though most of the time, we're moving faster than a human eye can track.

The multitude of voices coming from the other side of the door has my hand pausing just as it's about to wrap around the brass handle. They all sound raised and unhappy, like they're in the middle of a heated argument.

What the fuck is going on here?

No one calls a meeting here but *me*, and even then, the meetings are few and far between. I'm rarely, if ever, in the mood to entertain their grievances.

An angry storm begins to form in my cavernous chest. It sweeps through my veins like a windstorm and lightning all but shoots from my fingertips when my palms slam against the double doors.

They fly open, crashing against the walls that sit behind them. The bang causes the room to fall silent and as I step into the building, two dozen pairs of eyes lock on me. Most are full of irritation and confusion, but some look as angry as I feel.

But the powder-blue ones that lock with mine from the front of the room look completely unbothered. If I didn't know better—and I *do* know better—I would say there's a hint of excitement in them as well.

The sound of my shoes clicking against the tile fills the eerily quiet space as I stalk down the aisle toward her.

Pale pink lips pull into a smirk and her bare legs gracefully cross. The white dress that looks like it's nothing more than a buttoned white blazer hikes up another inch on her thigh.

Her fingers tap on the metal arm of the chair she sits in, in a slow, steady beat.

Until this very moment, I've never viewed it as anything but a chair, but it appears every bit the throne Quincey described it as. Especially with her in it.

Quincey Page entered my bloody kingdom as a prisoner, and now she sits upon my throne like the queen she is.

"Silas," a shrill voice comes from the pews. "What is the meaning of this? I don't appreciate being summoned here by a *human*." Rowena's elfin face is pinched in fury and her dark red lips are pulled in a sneer.

"Honestly, Rowena, take it down an octave, will you?" Quincey winces, her hand holding her ear. "You're making dogs bark two blocks away."

Ignoring the redheaded vampire, I move closer to where Quincey is. "*Mon Soleil*," I grit out once I stand below her. "What are you doing?"

Her lips curl into a grin. "I thought I would formally introduce myself to everyone here," she answers, her voice is calm and collected. Slowly, she stands from the metal chair, her eyes scanning each of the faces in the crowd. "I know for a fact that everyone in this room saw the video, but I thought it was important that they all get to know me when I'm not chained to a table."

Her face remains unmoved, that coy smirk fixed in place, but it's her eyes that send a clear message.

Trust me.

It's not in my nature to sit back and watch as things play out. And it's not in my nature to be in the dark. Information is a large way in which I maintain control, and right now, I know nothing. I'm not sure how Quincey was able to organize this without me as much as catching a hint of it, but despite all that, I do trust her.

It's the vampires sitting in the church pews that I don't trust. Since my arrival, their hateful looks have wisely started to wane. There are a few guests that haven't bothered to hide their contempt, but Quincey looks completely unbothered.

She looks like she's in her element.

"I know you're all confused about what I'm doing here. I know you're all wondering what the hell Silas is thinking. As Rowena so kindly pointed out, I'm just a human." Quincey effortlessly holds everyone's attention as she speaks—each of them waiting for a clear explanation as to what they're doing here. "In your eyes, I'm weak and below you. You're probably thinking of ways to eliminate me as we speak." A wicked grin I'm very familiar with forms on her lips. "This is my warning not to as it will end very badly for you."

The vampires look among themselves, not looking as if they believe her.

"What could you possibly do to us?" one of the men yells out.

A warning snarl builds in my throat, and I take a step toward him, but Quincey's hand landing on my shoulder stops me. Her fingers squeeze once before letting me go.

"I'm *so* glad you asked," Quincey chirps. "I've been dying to show you all for days."

For days? What the fuck has she been up to?

She leans against the metal chair with her ankles crossed. The bite mark I'd left there just days ago remains as a faint bruise. "Remember that website link you were sent? You know, the one you couldn't stop yourself from clicking on, and then when you saw what it was, you couldn't stop yourself from watching it? I mean, don't get me wrong, I understand why. I'm a very entertaining individual." No matter what the situation, her sarcastic mouth remains. Her hand gestures toward the man who's questioned her. "What was your favorite part? Was it when he hung me from the ceiling or when he used his knife on me?"

Quincey waits patiently for an answer, but he remains silent. "It's okay, Pietro, if you won't tell me yours, I'll tell you mine."

The room goes still when she reveals she knows his name. I'm struggling to remember what it was, but somehow, she's managed to figure it out.

"My favorite part was when you were busy watching my pain, the website you had willingly logged into was implanting a virus into your computer. Or phone. Doesn't really matter what device you were using;

it worked all the same. It opened a door to your most private files. Each keystroke you made, every message you sent and every dime you spent were being monitored and uploaded to another server." The lingering displeasure that had been on their faces morphs into concern. "I'm not sure what Gideon was going to do with the information, but we can assume it wasn't good. Don't worry though, I'm the only one who has access to it now."

I'm at a loss for how she managed to pull this off. There is no doubt in my mind that she recruited help, and I would bet my entire wealth that a purple-haired hacker had something to do with it.

"She's bluffing, the website was shut down," Pietro snaps.

"Was it though?" Quincey's head cocks to the side as she stares at the vampire. "Or did it just lock everyone out?" She waits for a second for them to answer her again, but they never do. "Fine, I'll just tell you. You were locked out. This was clearly a big disappointment for you, Pietro, seeing as you've been trying almost daily to log back into it. Were the copious amounts of online porn no longer cutting it? Thought you'd up the ante a little bit?"

"You're lying—" he begins to defend himself, but her fingers snapping together as if she'd figured something out, cuts him off.

"Oh, that's right," Quincey exclaims. "You prefer to make your own movies with the underage girls you smuggle into the country." Her blue eyes slide to me when she shares the next detail about Pietro. "And when he's in a pinch, he likes to bribe a certain dockworker at your port to sneak them in." Before I can react, she shakes her head. "Don't worry, the dockworker has already been dealt with."

"*How?*" I manage to bite out.

"I sent a friend," she answers simply before addressing the group once again. "So, here's the point I'm trying to make, other than the obvious one about Pietro being a child molester." That will be dealt with accordingly when this is over. I'm not a moral man, but I draw the line at children. "I now have a file on each of you. I know all your dirty secrets. I know who you've fucked, and more importantly, I know who you've fucked over. For many of you, those very people are sitting in this room with you."

She pushes away from the chair, her relaxed, carefree posture morphs into one of pure confidence. "I suggest you consider this information the next time those thoughts of eliminating me cross your mind. I'm not as strong as you, but I have each of you by the balls—*well*, some of you I have by your necks."

On cue, the side door across the room pushes open and Lorcan emerges from the doorway. The exhilarated look he wore the night we rescued Quincey is back, giving him a slightly unhinged appearance.

But it's not him that holds my attention, it's the six people who shuffle out behind him. Each of them looks dirty and disheveled, like they've been held somewhere filthy.

"What the hell is going on here, Silas?" Rowena jumps to her feet in dismay. Many of the others follow suit and stand with her so they can get a better look at the new arrivals.

I know each of them and half of them sit on the council. The woman at the front of the line is someone I've been acquaintances with since the first Great War. She looks at me, wide eyed. "Do something. This is insanity!".

I make no move to stop or change anything. "Why would I do that?"

This isn't my show, and I want to see what else my girl has up her sleeve. I didn't think I'd ever feel prouder of her than I did when she held her own against Gideon but watching her take complete control of a roomful of ruthless vampires is on a whole other level.

I'm both extremely proud and turned on by her blatant show of authority. If there weren't so many eyes on us right now, would take her right here on my throne.

Quincey steps down from the platform and leisurely weaves between the prisoners that have been revealed. She smiles at each one of them, but it's a smile that tells everyone that she has something devious planned.

I'm trying to piece together how Lorcan and Quincey have managed to keep control of six powerful vampires. Lor is strong, but not that strong.

Looking at the Irishman, I tilt my head in silent question.

Knowing what I mean, Lor gestures to the silver collars around each of their necks before he mouths a single word... *"Boom."*

Explosives.

Jesus fucking Christ.

While a bomb detonating around a vampire's neck is a surefire way to kill them, the idea of Lorcan and Quincey playing with explosives is a wildly unnerving thought. I barely want to trust Lorcan with a pair of children's safety scissors.

Like he's unable to sit still, Lorcan fiddles with the remote control in his hands like it's a toy to play with, and not something that's connected to multiple explosive devices.

"Some of you may recall that Gideon had planned on auctioning off my blood." I will forever be grateful that we were able to find her before he took too much from her. "Remember how he went on and on about how much money people were bidding? You six were the highest bidders... by a *lot*."

The rage roars to life inside of me at this revelation. It was always my plan to hunt down the ones that participated in the auction, but Quincey's already done it for me.

They're lined up like death row prisoners on their way to the electric chair. Quincey is their warden now, but I'm more than happy to take on the role as their executioner.

"I know exactly how much each of you bid on my blood." She blows out a low whistle of astonishment as she continues her slow weave through them. "I'll admit, I'm a little flattered you were willing to spend that much on me. Makes me all warm and tingly inside." She pauses in front of a bald man and her face darkens. "But it wasn't my blood you really wanted, was it? You wanted what it symbolized. A way to hurt Silas."

I realize now that while our anger is the same, we are feeling it for two different reasons. I'm angry that they would try and steal her blood away from her, but Quincey is angry on *my* behalf. It's become my mission and sole priority in life to protect Quincey, and now she's returning the favor.

Her face pulls in a sneer. "You probably thought no one would ever find out that it was you, but I did." She walks with calm, unhurried movements to the man at the end of the line. His head is bowed in utter defeat. "I knew exactly who you were when you arrogantly stood in front of me, blabbing on about how relieved you were that I was alive and well." Her hand smooths down the dark red silk scarf he wears as she purrs, "I told you I'd see you again, Álvaro."

The Spaniard slowly raises his head and his eyes lock with the distraught-looking Bria in the pews. She stands with her hand covering her mouth in disbelief.

Bria turns from her mate and seeks me out. When her gaze lands on me, her head shakes. "I didn't—I didn't know. I had nothing to do with this." Her voice shakes, something I've never heard from her. Bria's unwavering confidence is what she's known for. "Silas, believe me. I would never…" She can't bring herself to finish the sentence.

"It's true, she didn't." Quincey nods in confirmation. "She was completely in the dark about who she was sharing her life with. Poor girl was so snowed that she didn't even know that for years now, her man has been stealing from her."

There have been multiple instances over the years of Bria's shipments coming up short. She's accused her vendors and, of course, they all denied it, but she never believed them. Bria dealt with them in ways she felt were appropriate, but in light of this new information, she's realizing that she's taken innocent lives and punished the wrong people.

"How'd you do it, Álvaro? My theory is you raided the ships before they could make it to port." Quincey's right. That would have been the time when the shipments were most vulnerable.

The disbelief morphs into hatred, and Bria's muscles wind so tight, she looks like she's going to spring over the pews and attack him herself. "How *could* you?"

Álvaro looks blandly back at her. The passion that was always in his eyes when he looked at his mate is nowhere to be found. He doesn't resemble the man I've known for years. "It was business."

Did he ever truly love her?

"He thought he could use you the same way Gideon thought he could use me as a ploy to hurt Silas," Quincey turns around and addresses the group of vampires that watch with uneasy eyes. "As you can all see, I don't take kindly to such behavior."

"So, you're going to... *what*? Kill them all right here in front of us?" Rowena barks an unimpressed laugh. "You don't possess the gumption to kill something as inconsequential as an ant under your shoe, but you want me to believe you can take a *real* life."

I think killing them all is a great plan. My fingers twitch at my sides, itching to do just that, but it's no surprise to me that my love has other ideas. She's proving she can be as cunning as the rest of them, but she knows when she shouldn't cross the line.

Quincey's nature is to spare lives, not take them.

"No, I don't need to kill anyone. I think I've done a fairly good job at getting my message across."

You want to punish someone or send a message, Silas? Fine, but send it to someone who can grasp just how truly fucked they are. When she said those words to me, I thought she was referring to the situation with Gideon only. Little did I know she was secretly talking about her overall plan.

And the vampires here truly see how fucked they are if the

information Quincey has on them gets out. She scared them without drawing a single drop of blood.

She was right, delivering a message to people who can fully understand it is so much more satisfying. The nervousness and worry coming off the vampires are palpable. And the fact that it was Quincey who caused it makes it all the better.

Quincey told me she was ready for this world and that she wasn't scared. I believed in her then but watching her now prove it to everyone else in this room is one of the most magnificent things I've ever witnessed.

"Killing each of them would mean my message ends here, and that would defeat the whole purpose of this meeting." Quincey takes Álvaro's chin in her hand and forces him to look at her. His lips pull back in a warning snarl, his fangs extended, but she doesn't flinch. "I want you to leave here and spread your cautionary tale. Tell them how bad you fucked up, and how I still had mercy for you even though I had every reason to want to blow off your head."

Quincey shifts to stand next to me, creating a united front. I've never had a desire to rule with anyone at my side and now can't imagine ever doing this without her again. Her levelheadedness will counteract the days that I act rashly, and her fiercely protective side means she will always be in my corner.

"The rest of you should also share what you saw here tonight too. The faster the news gets out that I'm here to stay and I'm not playing games, the better," she tells the people sitting in the pews. "If we're all on the same page, we're pretty much done here. You're all free to go."

The vampires in the pews hesitate like they aren't sure if they're truly allowed to leave. Multiple sets of eyes flick to me for confirmation. "Why are you looking at me? She told you to leave."

A mass quantity of them don't need to be told a third time and scurry to the exit without a look back.

Before one of them can get too far, I call out his name, my booming voice echoes through the vaulted ceilings. "Pietro! You don't honestly believe I'd let you leave this place, do you?"

If it hadn't been children he was trafficking through my port, I would have made his death swift, but now I plan on strapping him to a post and allowing the sunrise to burn him away. It'll be slow and painful. Each second of agony will be payment for every child he ever hurt.

"Sir…" he tries to defend his actions, but I silence him with a single look.

I motion to the guards that have been standing silently by the door that leads to the cellar. In a flash of an eye, they've detained the offensive vampire. "Deal with him at sunrise. I don't want his life to be prolonged longer than necessary," I order them as they drag him past where we stand with our backs to the basement door.

Rowena prowls to the middle of the aisle. Her venomous green eyes glare at us, a look of pure hatred on her face. "You're so blinded by your disgusting infatuation with her that you can't even tell how humiliating this whole thing was," she spits at me. "I don't care what information she may or may not have on me. I will never take orders from a fucking human."

Quincey scoffs, her arms twisting through mine while her head rests on my shoulder. "Let's be honest here, Rowena. You don't hate me because I'm human. You hate me because I have something that you will never have again."

The redhead's lips pull back in a snarl, her perfectly shaped white fangs flashing. "He'll soon grow bored of you, Quincey, and when he does, I'll be there to set him on the right path." The vampire leaves the building in a blur before any more verbal spars can be exchanged.

I'm truly starting to believe that Rowena's days are numbered.

"How the fuck do I get this off?" a vampire shouts in frustration, his fingers carefully patting the collar for a latch of some kind.

Quincey shrugs halfheartedly. "I couldn't tell you, but I wish you the best of luck at figuring it out," her tone trips with false sweetness. "I can only suggest you do it *very* carefully."

Lorcan nods in agreement. "Yeah, the guy I got them from said they were pretty unstable." His palm slams against the man's shoulder in a patronizing pat, making the man's body shake. His eyes grow wide, and he freezes in place, expecting the device to go off.

Lor laughs at the man's reaction. "I would recommend trying to remove it in a tiled space, like your bathroom. That way if you set it off, they don't have to scrub your brain matter from the carpets."

Quincey chokes on a laugh and bumps her fist against Lor's when he offers it. Their lighthearted relationship hasn't changed in the slightest since the events the other night.

The easy smile that had started to cross her face falls when her eyes lock on something. My head turns in time to watch as Bria flies across the room in a blur toward us. On instinct, I tuck Quincey behind my arm, bracing for an attack.

But Bria isn't coming for us, her target is Lor. Or more so what he carries in his hand.

The element of surprise makes Lor's reaction a millisecond too late and the woman snatches the detonator out of Lorcan's fingertips.

Bria turns to her mate with an immeasurable amount of pain in her eyes.

Álvaro barely has time to gasp her name before Bria hits the button that has his name written on it.

"No!" Quincey screams but it's too late.

The sound of the device detonating is louder than you'd expect from such a small bomb. It causes the stained-glass windows to shake but it's not the noise that's most concerning. It's the hot spray of blood and bodily material splashing across everything and *everyone* in a fifteen-mile radius.

Quincey yelps, turning her body into mine, but the damage has already been done. Every inch of her body is speckled in red. The white dress she wears now looks like a crime scene.

Álvaro's headless body crashes into an empty pew, and it lands awkwardly over top of it.

For thirty seconds, everyone is too stunned to make any noise or move an inch.

It's Bria who moves first. With a final look at her deceased mate, she holds the blood-covered remote out to Lorcan.

The Irishman plucks it from her fingers and offers her a very sardonic, "*Thanks.*"

She simply nods once and walks away; her blood-soaked heels leave a trail of footprints to the exit.

"Bria," Quincey tries to call to her, but it's no use.

I truly do not know how Bria is going to cope with such a rash decision. I know firsthand what it feels like to end the life of your significant other, and I wouldn't wish that crushing weight on anyone.

The other vampires wearing collars look rightfully petrified, and one by one they stiffly leave the church after Bria.

"Holy *fuck,*" Quincey curses harshly from behind the blood-stained hand she holds in front of her mouth. "Good call about the tile, Lor."

The pair shares a look, and as if they'd had a telepathic conversation, they look at me and at the same time declare, "I'm not cleaning this up."

Shaking my head at the two of them, I pull the pocket square from my suit. Part of it has blood spray on it, but it's clean for the most part. Holding Quincey's face, I begin to wipe what I can away. "You have a lot of explaining to do, *Mon Soleil.*"

"I know."

Not caring if there's still blood on our faces, I dip my head a press a kiss to her mouth. "I'm proud of you, Quincey."

For the first time in days, the thick tension that's been sitting between us is absent, but Lorcan ruins the moment by grimacing at Quincey.

"Darling, I'm not quite sure how to tell you this," he starts. "So,

I'm just going to come right out and say it. There's a molar in your hair."

CHAPTER 32

"And once Rory had all the names, she sent them to me," I explain as I wring the last of the water from my hair. It took two *thorough* shampoos for me to finally feel like my hair was clean. I don't think the visual of Silas removing a tooth from my hair is one I will soon forget. Or ever forget. Pretty sure it's been seared into my brain. "Lorcan's been gathering them all week for me, since I'm pretty sure that's where my area of expertise ends and his begins. He actually had a lot of fun doing it, which let's be real, is not a huge shocker."

Silas stands with a black towel around his waist and his arms crossed in front of him while he listens to me explain how I pulled everything off tonight. He doesn't interject or ask questions, he just allows me to talk. His face is doing that thing where it's completely blank, but you know there's about six hundred thoughts flying through his head.

"I thought I had everything planned, but I don't think anyone could have predicted the finishing touches Bria put on the night." My fingers grip the towel that's around me tighter as I shiver. I worked in a trauma room. Gore doesn't usually faze me, but having it splatter on me with chunks—yes, I said chunks—getting stuck in my hair is a whole different ball game that I wasn't prepared for.

He moves to stand behind me and we both look at each other through the reflection of the mirror that hangs over the vanity. His fingers brush my clean hair off my shoulder, and he leans down to kiss me there. "I wish you felt like you could have told me your plan, Quincey," he says lowly against my skin. "I would have helped you."

"That's the thing, I didn't want your help," I admit to him. "This was something that I needed to do alone. If you were part of it, they wouldn't have taken me seriously because they would have been looking at you. I needed them to look at me and *really* see me for who I am."

"They saw you," Silas confirms. "And I see you, Quincey. I see how fucking strong and resilient you are. There are very few people that can go through what you have and make it through with their empathy intact." His eyes lift from my shoulder to look back at my reflection. "I would have killed every single one of those fuckers that participated in the auction, but you let them live."

"You once told me that you will rule with fear, but you prefer to rule with respect. Had I just killed them, the others might have feared me, but they wouldn't have respected me. They wouldn't have seen me as someone smart enough to play the long game." As a human among vampires, it will already be borderline impossible to gain their respect. "And it's a *very* long game, Silas."

It makes my heart physically hurt to think that I'm only going to be part of his world for a limited time. One day, I will physically age past him, and then what will we do? *Hi, this is my lover, Silas. What? No, I'm not his grandmother...* Yikes, that is a nightmare.

"You're very smart and you don't let your emotions get the best of you. You see reason in things that I sometimes miss." His fingertips trail down my arms soothingly. "Like Gideon." He surprises me by saying.

This time, instead of looking at him through the mirror, I turn my head up at him. "What about Gideon?"

Silas turns me completely around so my lower back hits the marble of the vanity. "You were right that keeping him held captive isn't doing any good. It's not helping you or me feel better. And Ira would be disappointed in me."

Silas Laurent is admitting he was wrong, someone grab a pen and mark the fucking date.

"I can't allow him to live, but I don't intend to keep him in that box any longer. I will do what needs to be done."

Feeling incredibly proud of him, I cup his face with my hands and pull him down to me. "Thank you," I whisper before kissing him.

As it always does, our kiss starts off gentle—sweet even—but at the first brush of his tongue against mine, it switches on a dime, and everything becomes heated.

His fingers dig into my hips and before I can process what he's doing, he's lifted me off the ground and placed me on the vanity.

When I touch his skin, it's warmer than usual from his shower, but it feels as perfect as it always has under my fingertips.

He untucks the towel I have wrapped around my breasts, leaving me completely bare to him.

There is no slow steady buildup with this one. Our kiss becomes messy, even painful at times when our teeth collide. We suck, we bite, we ravage each other until my skin becomes too hot and my heart beats too hard against my rib cage.

I tear away the black towel from his waist and take his thick length in my hand. He growls his pleasure into my mouth, encouraging me further.

Abruptly, he breaks the kiss and replaces his lips with two of his fingers. "Suck," he orders darkly without any further instruction, but I don't really need it. Or want it.

My tongue flicks teasingly along his fingertips, as if they were the head of his cock, before I languidly bring them into my mouth. My tongue swirls around the digits, thoroughly coating them in my saliva.

When he's satisfied, he removes them from my mouth with a *pop*.

My eyes close and my head falls back as he slowly sinks them into my pussy. They stretch me and tease me in preparation for what I really need from him.

"I'm ready," I pant. "I want you inside of me."

Silas's free hand grips my chin, and he pulls me forward so he can kiss me again. "I want six more years," he confuses me by saying against my mouth.

"W-what?" I choke out as his thumb begins to massage my throbbing clit.

"I want to spend six more years with you as a human. Give me those years, and I will do it."

The erratic heartbeat I had just seconds ago freezes in my chest, along with every other one of my muscles. Locked in place, I gape at him. "*What?*" I repeat like an annoying parrot that only learned two words.

Silas releases my chin so he can gently cup my face. "You'll be thirty-one... the same age as I was when I turned."

My hand releases his swollen cock and grips the countertop so I don't fucking fall over.

"You'll do it? You'll turn me?"

"Yes, *Mon Soleil*, I will turn you."

"What changed your mind?" I ask, my head tilting.

"It's more of a *who*. Duke pointed some things out to me, one of the biggest ones being that I've been allowing what happened to Cecily to control my life—but also many others' lives. There will be a memo going out in a few hours that describes the revised law." Silas rests his forehead against mine. "It still scares me to death, but I love you, Quincey, and I want more than one lifetime with you. I selfishly want to claim all your years as mine."

"I love you too, and that's why I don't want to wait six years for our eternity to start."

Silas kisses my forehead before pulling back so he can look at me. His hands slowly trace lines down my body. "No, this is the only offer you're getting. As selfishly as I want your years, I also want your warmth for a little while longer." His fingers brush against the sun pendant that I can't figure out how to remove—not that I'd want to. "I miss the sun, Quincey. You will always be mine—human or not—but I want you to be able to enjoy the sun for a little while longer before you're confined to the night like me. I want you to enjoy the thrills of being human for a few more years."

"You know, I'm quite fond of the moon myself."

His lips twitch like he finds humor in that. "Good, because the moon will be your constant companion six years from now."

My body jumps when his fingers trail downward once more. "You're not going to budge on this six years thing, are you?"

"No," he says simply. "I will give you everything you could possibly want. *Anything* else, I would do it in a heartbeat, but this is the one thing I cannot."

He's given me everything I could ask for and this is the one thing he's asked of me. I can wait for him. "Six years really isn't that long, is it?"

Silas takes hold of my thighs and drags me to the edge of the counter. "Those few years mean nothing when I'm promising you eternity." The head of his cock glides through my wet center, bumping against my clit.

"And I promise to love you each and every one of those days."

He slowly sinks inside of me, filling me until he's completely stolen my ability to breathe.

It's okay, though.

Silas has already stolen my heart; he might as well take my air too.

But is it really stealing when it's freely given?

CHAPTER 33

Nothing has been calm or tranquil since I first met Silas. There was always something happening, but for the last three weeks, everything has been peaceful.

Eerily quiet.

And while that seems like a good thing and something I should probably be thankful for, I find myself feeling anxious. Like I'm waiting for the other shoe to drop.

Or more like I'm waiting for the next attack to happen.

Since the impromptu meeting at the church, there haven't been any more deaths at Silas's properties.

At any given second, I'm expecting a bomb to go off somewhere in the city or for armed men to show up at the house again. I just know in my gut that something bad is coming.

"What's wrong with your face?" Duke asks, pulling me away from my dark thoughts.

"Nothing is wrong with my face," I argue, catching the orange ball he tosses back at me. We've been doing this for an hour and while it seems like a mundane task, the repetitive motion is helping Duke with his balance and coordination. "I'm just thinking."

After getting out of the intensive care unit, he was moved to a rehabilitation center close by. They've been doing physical and cognitive therapies to help him regain his strength and mobility on his right side.

I've tried to come by every day to spend time with him, and if I can't make it, Della is here. We're all doing our part to make sure Duke knows he's not alone. There are days that I can see the sadness and doubt in his eyes. Those are the days that I cheer him on most. If he can't believe in himself, I will do it for him.

I toss the ball back and his right arm's response is delayed just enough that he can't grasp it. A look of frustration cuts across Duke's face as he watches it bounce across the room.

He reaches for the cane he's been using for the past week to get around, but I stop him. "It's okay, I'll get it."

Duke's quiet for a second, waiting for me to bring the ball back, but once I'm standing back in my spot across from him, he asks, "What are you thinking about?"

I catch the ball and hold it against my stomach as I sigh. "Do you ever get a really bad feeling in your stomach, and no matter what, you can't ignore it? It's just *there*, screaming at you to pay attention."

Duke looks at me. "Yeah, a few times."

"Were you right? Or did you ignore it long enough and it went away?"

I'm hoping for the latter.

His face falls. "I ignored it once, and I learned the hard way never to do that again." We don't talk about it, but like me, Duke's seen a lot of death. His time in the military was a dark one. "A lot of the time your gut is trying to tell you something that your brain isn't seeing. Trust that feeling, Quincey."

"The attacks have stopped. Gideon is dead, and Silas and I are finally on the same page. Everything should feel fine—*great* even—but I know something is coming."

Twenty-four hours after Silas agreed to turn me—in six years—Gideon Rolfe was executed for his crimes. It took a hundred years too long to happen, but he was finally reunited with Margret.

I breathe easier knowing my attacker and Ira's killer is no more. I'm more relieved that it's finally behind us and the weight of it isn't on Silas's shoulders anymore.

This time Duke catches the ball with ease. I love the small victorious smile on his face when he does.

"I'm sure you're right. It's never quiet in Silas's world for long. That's part of what makes it so exciting. It always keeps you on your toes." He bounces the ball on the ground a couple of times, dribbling it like a basketball. "I'm going fucking stir crazy in here. The beige walls and constant routine are making me want to pull my own goddamn hair out."

Shaking my head at him, I laugh softly. "You're just like Lor. You can't sit still to save your life." I thought the two of them would hit it off, and much to Silas's dismay, I was right. It all started with them bickering over the word *'darling'*. Duke argued that he used it first, but Lor claimed it didn't count because Duke butchered the sweet endearment with his *'dumb'* southern drawl. It went on for an hour before they finally decided they can both use it. I found the whole thing hilarious. Silas, however, was not amused. "I'm a little disappointed that my company hasn't been entertaining enough for you." I mockingly pout, like I'm truly offended. "Shall I bring a sexy brunette with me next time? Or perhaps a tattooed cutie with a knack for computers?"

Is it fair to put him on the spot with this question? Probably not, but I've waited three weeks to talk to him about it. My patience for the subject is officially gone and I'm feeling nosy.

Duke stares at me, nothing in his face giving anything away.

"Come on!" I throw the ball at him with a little more zing on it than usual, but he still manages to wrap his fingers around it in time. "Give me *something*, Duke. You have two equally amazing women crushing on you. I want to know where you stand on that."

Duke drops the ball in his hand but doesn't bother to try and go after it again. "What?" He looks absolutely lost. Poor guy. "Rory doesn't have a... *crush* on me."

I swear to God, men can be so fucking dumb.

"Jesus, Duke, I know you were in a coma for a week, but you can't seriously be this dense."

Duke is unmoved by this and continues to insist that I'm wrong. "She doesn't have feelings for me—hell, I'm not convinced she even *has* feelings. And Lucy...we agreed to not bring emotions into it."

My best friend would deny it until she turns purple in the face, but I know she has some feelings for Duke. She would never admit to doing something as *'lame as having a crush'*—her words, not mine—but I can hear it in her voice when we talk about him.

"If you say so." I shrug in defeat. "I suppose Rory must have been sneaking into your hospital room for another reason then."

Sorry for telling your secrets, Rory, but I think a gentle kick in the ass would do you both good.

Duke's brows pull together in confusion. "She did what?"

I grin at him as I repeat something Silas says often, "I didn't stutter." Bending down, I scoop up the ball that rolled under the massage table. "But for what it's worth, Duke. I like her." I like Rory *and* Lucy, but in the end, it doesn't matter who he picks. All that's important to me is that he's happy. "And *holy shit,* I love how vindictive she can be. When she found out Pietro was trafficking girls, she cleaned out one of his offshore accounts and donated every penny to a nonprofit."

I had told her to keep some of it herself to compensate her for the time she spent working on it, but she refused. She said helping me get back at the assholes who bid on my blood was payment enough. Plus, she said she wanted to help me stick it to the rest of the vampires.

"He's lucky that's all she did to him. I've seen her record and let's just say it's *extensive*."

"Yeah, I can tell she's been through some shit," I tell him as my phone starts to buzz in the back pocket of my jeans. Pulling the device out, I add, "But it just made her stronger." Checking the caller ID, I find Lucy's name written across the screen.

"No, it gave her a fucking attitude problem," Duke corrects.

I'm laughing at that when I put the phone to my ear. "Hey, Luce! I'm still with Duke, but I'll be here a little while longer if you want to swing by. Maybe you can bring him dinner since the food here is crap."

Lucy's come by a couple times with me to hang with Duke. She doesn't participate in the exercises like I do, but instead sits in a chair, sucking on a lollypop, while she judges Duke's progress. She's gone the tough love route. Everyone but the confused nurses finds it hilarious, Duke included.

There's nothing coming from the other side of the line, so I try again. "Lucy?" Maybe she butt-dialed me?

Ice-cold fear runs down my spine when she finally speaks. "Don't react, Q. You have to keep it together. Don't let Duke know anything is wrong. Do you understand?" I can count on one hand the number of times that Lucy Bell has ever been scared, but when she talks now, I can feel her distress through the phone.

And that is why I know it's very important that I listen to her. It takes every ounce of strength in me to keep the lighthearted smile I'd been wearing with Duke on my face. I subtly let out a long breath and force my muscles to relax, despite the overwhelming tension.

"Sounds good to me," I respond. To keep up appearances, I nod my head like I'm truly enthralled with what she's saying. Looking at Duke, I point at the phone. "Lucy says hi, but she won't be able to make it tonight. She says she'll come by in a couple of days instead."

Using his cane, Duke ambles over to where there's small hand-weights. "What, does she suddenly have something better to do? Are we not exciting enough for her?" he teases.

By some miracle, I find the ability to laugh at this, even if my fingers are starting to tremble around my phone. "She says she's headed home to crawl into bed. Probably a good idea, since she sounds exhausted. Maybe she's getting sick. Are you feeling okay, Lucy?"

There's whispering, but I can't make it out. After a pause, Lucy reluctantly says, "She wants to talk to you."

Who's she?

"Hello, Quincey." A familiar voice replaces Lucy's. "I sure hope you're enjoying your visit with Duke."

Rowena.

And like that, the moment I've been waiting for happens. The other shoe drops and it's way worse than I thought it'd be. I was expecting more attacks on Silas's employees, but it's hitting way closer to home than that. Rowena has Lucy.

"Say something so he doesn't get suspicious," Rowena snaps.

My mouth opens and closes once, my mind drawing a momentary blank. I finally manage to respond. "Yeah, Duke's improving. You'd be proud of him."

"Good," she almost purrs. "Here's what you're going to do, Quincey. Without signaling for help, you're going to get out of that building and come to me. If you don't, I'm going to rip your beloved best friend's heart from her chest."

My stomach turns and nausea tightens my throat, but still, I keep my face impassive.

"And then I'm going to go after Duke—he'll be easy since he's defective right now. Then I'll go after sweet Della and that idiot Lorcan. I will save Silas for last, and I will keep you alive to watch each of them die. Do I make myself clear?"

I lick my dry lips and choke out, "No, you didn't cut out, I can still hear you."

"You have twenty minutes to come to St. Sin. If you're a second late or you foolishly bring someone with you, I will kill Lucy before you can so much as scream for help. Leave your phone there so you can't be tracked." There's pure evilness in her voice when she talks. "On your mark... get set... go, Quincey."

The line goes dead, and my heart stops in my chest.

Fear cements me in place as I think over my options.

I know I should call Silas but doing so would put Lucy's life at risk. That cannot happen, and that's why, in the end, there's only one option. Lucy has been the one constant in my life for the better part of two decades, and I refuse to jeopardize her life.

She's my family.

Pretending to read a message on my phone, I frown at Duke. "Silas just texted. He finished with his meetings early tonight, so if it's okay, I think I'm going to head out."

Duke smiles at me as he does a slow bicep curl with one of the small weights. "Of course, darlin'. I appreciate you spending time with me. I know you've got your own things on your plate, but it means a lot."

Walking across the room, I wrap my arms around him and squeeze tight. "I told you I would come here until you're better and I meant it. You'll be back out there with Silas before you know it."

"Fuck, I hope so," he says once I release him. "Go, get out of here, just because I'm trapped here doesn't mean you need to be."

I gather my belongings off the small table I'd left them on, and I leave my phone next to Duke's

I feel like I'm holding my breath when I move to the doorway. Looking over my shoulder at him, I say, "Everything's going to be okay, Duke. I'm sure of it." It's a lie, but I feel like it needs to be said.

"I sure hope so, Q." Even now, his smile is as contagious as it's always been.

Smiling back, I wave before leaving the room.

Lorcan is with Silas visiting some business partner or something and couldn't come with me to see Duke. Two of Silas's guards are with me tonight instead. One is downstairs in the car watching the entrance while the other waits outside Duke's room in the hallway.

He pushes off the wall he's been leaning on when I shut the door behind me. He's a giant and he doesn't talk much, so when his head cocks, I know he's asking me if I'm ready to leave.

"I'm going to go use the bathroom, and then we can leave." I point to the door that's at the other end of the hall. The one that's close to the stairwell door.

His huge head nods once in understanding. "I'll wait here."

As calmly as I can muster, I walk down the quiet hallway. When I reach the bathroom door, I place my hand on it like I'm going to push it open. Looking back at the guard, I find him thankfully looking at the opposite end of the hallway.

As quick as I can, I turn and push open the stairwell door and slip inside before he can turn back to me.

The second the door closes softly, I jump into action. I take the stairs two at a time. At some points, I feel like I'm going to lose my balance, but my grip on the chipped railing keeps me upright. The sound of my shoes clanking against the cement stairs echoes through the cavernous space.

Down the two flights of stairs, I have to slow down so I don't draw attention to myself as I move through the lobby of the facility. People mill about, completely unaware of the turmoil I'm feeling. My vocal cords beg me to scream and ask for help. I bite my tongue to make sure that I don't do just that.

My plan for how I'm going to get to St. Sin is up in the air until I see the black SUV sitting in the parking lot where we left it. A plan—albeit a *poor* plan—comes to me. I don't have time to second-guess myself or really think it over.

I must commit to it and hope that the guard sitting in the driver's seat believes me.

Taking a deep breath, I release all the emotion I'm holding inside. My eyes start to water, and pure panic takes over my features.

Like someone is chasing me, I dash toward the idling car. "Help!" I scream, my palms slapping dramatically on the tinted windows. "Oh my god, you have to help him!"

The guard swings the door open and jumps out, his gun already drawn. "What's wrong? What happened?" he demands, his observant eyes scanning the parking lot for danger.

Through the theatrical sobs, I spin a lie. "There's someone in there! He has a gun. He shot the other guard." My hands pull at the sleeves of his black blazer. "Please, you have to go get Duke out of there."

Bringing Duke into this lie isn't fair, but I know it will work. As loyal as these guards are to Silas, they're just as loyal to Duke. Part of Duke's job is overseeing all the hired guns. Many of them have military backgrounds just like Duke and I know that bond runs deep. They won't leave a man behind.

He pushes me toward the back door of the car, and I don't fight him. "Get in and lock the doors. I'm calling for backup now." His arms wrap around me and he all but throws me into the back seat.

Before he slams the door, I tell him, "Please be careful!"

I stay where I am until he reaches the entrance to the building. The second he disappears through the doors, I ungracefully climb over the middle console and into the driver's seat.

Looking at myself in the rearview mirror, I wipe away the tears that stopped falling when the door shut. I compose myself as much as possible, putting on my own version of Silas's granite mask.

I know what Rowena wants and I'm not going to give her the satisfaction of seeing my tears.

With one lass steadying breath, I throw the car into gear and peel out of the parking lot.

And while I drive, I wish upon every star in the sky that the kiss Silas gave me before he left tonight wasn't our last.

CHAPTER 34

I know something is wrong when I approach the entrance of St. Sin. The yellow neon signage is turned off, and the front door is locked. It's a club that sits on Bourbon Street; it's never closed.

A pair of drunk partygoers walk up to the dark windows and tap on the glass. "Hello? It says on *Yelp* that you're open," one of them slurs, making the rest break into laughter.

With my sweaty hands balled into fists, I turn away from them and run to the alley. The manager, Ray, was always forgetting his keys when I worked here, and I know where he stashes a spare for the back door.

On my tippy-toes, I pry the loose brick out of the siding and retrieve the brass key hidden inside the cavity. I glance down the dark alleyway to make sure no one is watching as I open the door. It's funny, the last time I used this key was the night I first met Silas. This very alleyway I stand in is where our story started.

It would be a neat, full-circle moment if I wasn't about to try and save my friend from a malicious redheaded bitch.

The inside of the building is just as dark as the exterior. Only the emergency lights remain on. They grant me just enough visibility to not trip over my own feet or into something.

When I walk into the main room, and the heeled boots I wear slip through a puddle of something, I begin to really wish the lights were on.

In an ungraceful manner, my legs go out from under me, and I land on my ass in the same puddle I'd originally stepped in. My hands slide through the sticky liquid when I put them out to steady me. As it coats my fingers, I figure out what it is I'm now sitting in.

Blood.

After the past month I've had, I'm very familiar with what it feels like to be covered in blood. It's a sensation I'd prefer to not recognize so easily.

An indescribable fear wraps around my chest and squeezes until I can't breathe. Is this Lucy's blood? Did Rowena already kill her? "Oh god," I groan, the nausea from before returning at full force.

My muscles shake as I climb back to my feet. It's just dark enough in here that I can't make anything out. It's all just dark shapes and shadows.

Wiping my hands on my jeans, I stumble across the space toward the bar, where I know there's a light switch behind the counter.

I need to see whose blood I'm now drenched in. Like a mantra, I repeat, *'you don't know if it's hers, you don't know if it's hers.'*

My fingers just brush against one of the barstools when some of the overhead lights are flipped on.

"You made good time, Quincey," Rowena's disjointed voice comes from behind me, making my heart skip in my chest. "That's good. I've grown tired of waiting."

Whirling around, I find her sitting on the raised platform where the DJ booth sits. She looks as regal as ever with her shin-length silk skirt and her lace top. Her red hair is curled into perfect ringlets and her ever-present, dark-red lipstick is perfectly in place. Everything about her is polished and perfect. Except for that devious fucked-up head of hers.

With the lights on, she's not the only thing that's now visible.

The more my eyes scan the space, the more faces I recognize. Various staff members of St. Sin lie in haphazard heaps on the floor. They look like they've been torn apart by a wild animal. The black tiled floor is made mostly of blood pools now. I worked with most of these people during my short stint here as a bartender and now they're collateral damage from the war Rowena started.

I look at each and every one of their faces, but don't find my friend among them.

"Where is Lucy?" I demand, my anger gives me the confidence to stalk toward her. "I did what you said. I'm here. Now let Lucy go."

Rowena's green eyes roll in her head with an unimpressed scoff. "Your friend is fine—she has a very crude vocabulary—but she's fine." Her hand gestures at the door that leads to Ray's office. "See, I'll prove it."

A tall skinny man exits the office and, in front of him, he pushes a gagged and bound Lucy in a wheeled desk chair.

Even if her mouth is taped shut, her eyes reveal everything Lucy is thinking. She's still scared, but it's slowly being eclipsed by a blazing rage.

"Lucy," I sigh in relief. "Are you oka—" the question dies on my lips when I spot puncture marks and dried blood on her neck. "What the fuck?" my voice is a murderous growl when I turn back to Rowena. "What did you do?"

Dramatically, Rowena wipes the corners of her mouth even though there's no longer evidence of her action on her lips. "What? I got peckish. I worked up quite the appetite doing all of this." She points flippantly at all the dead humans around us.

The skinny vampire tears the tape from Lucy's mouth.

"Motherfucker!" she cries in pain once the silver tape is off her face. Panting, my friend looks at me, "Q, she's a fucking *vampire*."

There's no point in trying to lie or deny it. "I know."

She gapes at me. "What do you mean, you *know*?"

"Silas is one too," I admit. I have a sinking suspicion that I may not be making it out of this club, so I don't see any harm in sharing a few secrets with my best friend before I go. "I've learned all kinds of things from him."

I expect Lucy to freak out and ask all kinds of questions, but instead her eyes narrow. "I know," she shocks me by saying. "I wasn't sure if *you* knew."

It's my turn to gape at her. "What? How did you know?"

"Come on, Q. You think you're the only one good at keeping secrets? I know all kinds of things." Lucy's attention swings to the redhead. "Although, I'm still really confused about what we did to piss *her* off."

I have *so* many questions for my best friend.

Rowena raises a brow at her. "What *you* did?" she repeats. "You didn't do anything, Lucy. You were simply bait. Thank you for playing your role so wonderfully."

"I aim to please," Lucy spits at her. The skinny guard cuts the zip ties off Lucy's wrists and motions for her to stand from the chair. Once she's free, she pushes at his boney hands. "Get the fuck away from me, *Skeletor*."

I don't know what Rowena's grand plan is, but it makes me uneasy that she'd so willingly allow Lucy to be free.

Rubbing her wrist, Lucy shifts closer to me.

Standing from the stage, Rowena begins to weave through the small tables placed about the room. "You're here because Quincey had to come in and *fuck* everything up. You see, I had a plan. I was patient for *eighty* years. I bided my time, but then he met you, Quincey, and you destroyed all of that hard work."

"So, that's what all this comes down to? A fucking cliché? You didn't get the boy, so you lost your ever-loving mind over it?" I knew she wanted Silas, but I didn't think she'd go through such drastic extremes over it. "Rowena, I have to believe that you're above such juvenile behavior."

"It's not about a boy!" she shrieks, sounding almost witchlike. Which, given the current vibe of the room, is fitting. "That's what makes you so wrong for him. You're with him because you *love* him. Love is a useless emotion that will only get in your way and hinder you." She paces between two tables like she's too restless to stand still. "I have no interest in love. Only power. Specifically, the kind of power Silas could have granted me. All he had to do was see me and see how good we are together, but no." Her eyes lock on me like a predator looking at its prey. "All he sees is you. All he wants is *you*. A pathetic, weak human."

As she paces, I continue to move my body so that I remain a barrier between Lucy and her. I'm not sure exactly how I will stop Rowena if she lunges for my friend, but I know I will do whatever it takes for Lucy to walk out of here.

"You think he will have any interest in you if you kill me?" I question. "Killing me would automatically enroll you into a life of torture." I won't be here to act as his moral compass. If I thought what he was doing to the man who *failed* at killing me was bad, I can't imagine what he'd do to the woman who succeeds at killing me.

Rowena lets out a loud cackle-like laugh. "Silly girl, I no longer care if he willingly hands me the power. I'm well past that. Like I said, I'm done waiting. I'm taking what I want." From the pocket of her skirt, she pulls out an ornate dagger. The green gems that are embedded in the hilt reflect in the soft light of the room. "But I'm going to destroy him on my climb to the top. I've already started by wounding Silas's businesses, but the final nail in the coffin will be when I take you from him. That will surely wreck him. I mean, honestly, who will want to listen to him when he's an emotional wreck over a worthless human? I warned him that he was embarrassing himself by being with you."

I think of all the humans that died because Rowena didn't get her way. Each one of those deaths was so pointless. I watched the news reports about the bus explosions after I was told about it. The footage was devastating. The same anger I felt watching it is the same anger that flares up inside me now.

"I think your behavior right now is embarrassing, Rowena." I never take my eyes off the dagger she wields. "What will happen when word of what you've done gets out? You think the other vampires will respect you enough to follow you?"

Her lips pull back in a sneer. "You seem to be under the impression that I plan on leaving witnesses." Her green eyes lock on Lucy. "They will believe whatever tale I decide to spin them."

"They'll see through your lies," I warn her. "They will smell the crazy on you and they will—"

My threat dies on my lips when the back of her hand connects with my face with so much force it sends me flying backward.

I land on my side on the unforgiving tile floor and skid through several feet of spilled blood. Dazed and concussed from the blow to my face, it takes me a second to pull myself back into a sitting position.

With slightly blurry eyes, I look up at Lucy and my heart turns to ice when I find her being held in place by Rowena's guard. She's fighting him, her body thrashing harshly against his to get free, but it's no use. She will never be strong enough to break free.

Rowena gleams at me as she stalks toward Lucy with her dagger held up. "I told you I'd make you watch them all die," she sneers.

I know what she's going to do, and because of it, my world slows to a crawl.

My blood rushes in my ears so loud it's deafening and adrenaline shoots through my veins, giving me the strength and speed I need.

I don't think twice about my next moves. Even if there was time to thoroughly examine each of my choices, I would make the same decision. *Every time* I would choose this.

Silas calls me recklessly fearless, and I guess in this instance he's right. I don't feel a single drop of fear as I race toward them.

"*Quincey!*" I hear Lucy scream, but it's too late.

Acting as her shield, I throw myself in front of Lucy at the same time Rowena's blade thrusts forward.

I'm still not sure if I believe in fate, but if it does exist, I think I'm okay with this being mine.

My entire life has revolved around saving people. It only makes sense that it would end that way too. If dying is the price I must pay to save the life of someone I love, I will do it without fear in my heart and a smile on my face.

CHAPTER 35

Silas

"**D**uke?"

"Silas, something is really wrong."

One phone call and five words. That's all it took for my world to come crashing down. *Again.*

She's missing. *Again.*

And this time she wasn't taken, she left voluntarily.

Her dramatics were convincing enough to trick my guards, and by the time they discovered she was lying about the gunman, she was gone. Along with the vehicle.

Duke's phone call solidifies my decision; after tonight, I'm no longer going to own a phone. Each time the fucker rings, I get bad news.

The last time Quincey went missing, I was overwhelmed with an immeasurable amount of helplessness, but this time is different. This time I'm prepared because I anticipated something like this happening.

I don't allow myself to be incapacitated by the news because I know where she is. Or at least I know where the necklace is.

The gift had two purposes, but one was more important than the other. While I liked the idea of her wearing something that represented her namesake, the tracker the jeweler had implanted in the pendant was my main reason for giving it to her. There's a reason the clasp can only be opened with a key—I needed to be sure that it could never be taken off her neck. I needed to know that I could *always* find her.

It was a decision I made from fear of losing her again, but now, as I stare at the red dot on the GPS, I know my fear was valid.

Fear is an emotion I went centuries without feeling, but since Quincey danced into my life, it's one I find myself feeling frequently. It's the kind of fear that wraps around you and squeezes you so tightly you can't breathe without it hurting.

"Stop the car," I order Lorcan. "This is close enough."

Leaving the vehicle in the middle of a one-way road on a busy Bourbon Street is bound to cause a lot of problems for people, but at this time, it's not my problem. Getting to Quincey is.

I'm still unsure why Quincey escaped the guards, but I know with certainty it has something to do with Lucy. Quincey's last phone call was with her friend, and now the necklace is transmitting from St. Sin.

Lorcan keeps pace with me as I sprint down the crowded sidewalk. Until this point, I wasn't convinced that Lorcan possessed the capacity to care about another being. His motives in life have always been sexually or monetarily driven. The look of concern on his face proves that Quincey is special and can make even the most twisted of souls care for her.

The club that is usually lively and bustling with people is quiet and dark. But the scent of blood seeping out from the structure is so strong, I taste it on my tongue.

Lorcan looks at me, but I shake my head. "It's not Quincey's. There's a door around—"

The panicked scream calling out Quincey's name has the sentence dying on my lips. Cold fear snakes down my spine and dread pools in my stomach.

Refusing to waste precious time by running to the back door, I crash through the blacked-out window. The glass shatters around me, falling to the ground in sharp shards.

My feet land inside the building just in time to watch Rowena's blade sink into Quincey's chest.

Powder-blue eyes lock on mine as her body jolts. A choked gasp comes from her lips and blood begins to blossom around the hilt of the dagger, soaking her already stained shirt.

Lucy tries to get free of the man holding her, but she's powerless against him. Fat tears fall down her face, and she repeats Quincey's name over and over again.

I want to go to her, but I need to eliminate the woman standing between us first.

There will be no long, drawn-out death for her, or the glass box. No, she will die here. The idea of spilling Rowena's blood has my monster side growing excited. With each passing second, the chains on my control are snapping until my chest begins to vibrate with untouched power.

Rowena's wicked smile grows on her face when she looks at me over her shoulder. "It's a shame, isn't it, having to mourn the things you wanted but could never truly have?" With a harsh yank, she pulls the dagger from Quincey's chest. "Long live the queen," she snarls.

"No!" I thunder.

With the blade still embedded in her, it was slowing down the bleeding, but with Rowena removing it, the wound now bleeds freely.

Quincey's shaking fingers probe at the wound and when her hands come back bloody, her knees give out and she crashes to the ground.

"Lorcan!" I don't have to elaborate further. He knows what I'm ordering. He charges toward them with his fangs bared in fury. The man holding Lucy tosses her to the side and boldly matches Lor's attack with one of his own. They clash together, but I don't watch what happens next.

My attention turns to my own prey.

With a violent roar, I rush at Rowena. She's quick and able to dodge my arm when I reach out for her. I expect her to turn and fight me, but instead, she attempts to escape through the broken window. This action proves what I already know about her—she's a coward. That's why she prefers to work in the dark corners of our world. She talks a big game about wanting eyes on her, but the second she's faced with true confrontation, she flees instead of fights.

Catching up to her, I grab hold of her long red hair and pull her back by it so hard she flies across the room. Her body crashes into the ceiling-high glass shelving of the bar. The bottles and glassware smash to the ground with her.

I'm standing over top of her before she has a chance to stand to her feet.

Drenched head to toe in various liquors, her wet hair sticks to her skin when I yank her to her knees. Her fingernails claw at the hand that holds her in place while my free hand scoops up one of the half-broken bottles from the ground.

"Silas—"

I will never be able to confirm if my name was a plea for me to have mercy or if it was the beginning of another taunt. The shard of glass I shove through her neck silences her. It slices through her pristine ivory skin and rips through her jugular, severing her vocal cords.

It's not a life-threatening injury, but it does create the access I need. I tear the severed bottle from her throat and drop it to the glass and alcohol–covered ground.

Before she can try and run from me again, my fingers plunge into the gaping wound I'd created in her neck. With my free hand on her shoulder for leverage, I begin to rip her head from her body.

It's brutal and it's messy, but it feels so fucking good. She earned each agonizing second of this. My only wish is that I could have prolonged it further. The bloodthirsty beast inside of me purrs as her blood coats my fingers.

Her mouth opens in a strangled scream as her skin tears, and her vertebrae come apart. With one final tug, I sever her skull completely from her shoulders.

I release her head and it falls into the piles of glass. It lands face down in the mess with the strands of her red hair splayed out around it. I don't think Rowena Morgan has ever looked better than she does now. It's like a work of art.

"Quincey... *Q*! No, you have to keep your eyes open!" Lucy's hoarse pleas fill the now quiet space. "Look at me, Quincey."

In a flash, I'm over the bar, and kneeling on the blood-soaked floor next to Quincey.

The sight of her causes frigid tendrils of terror to snake around my throat until they suffocate me.

Her skin that's usually golden from spending days reading in the sunshine has turned a ghastly gray, and her wobbling lips have a blue tinge to them.

Her head rests in Lucy's lap and as tears fall from her friend's eyes, they land on Quincey's face. They streak through the smears of blood on her cheekbones.

Lucy's fingers press against the wound, but the blood pools over her fingers. "I can't get it to stop," she chokes out as she fights a sob. "It won't stop. Fuck, Q, what were you thinking? Why did you do that?"

"It's okay," Quincey manages to whisper. With each passing second, her breathing is becoming more labored. She has to fight for each breath she pulls into her lungs. "It doesn't hurt."

Lucy turns her head and wipes her tears off on her shoulder. "Okay, that's good," she manages to say. Her jaw trembles so hard, I'm surprised she can speak at all. "That's really good, Q. Everything is going to be okay."

Swallowing down my own emotion, I reach for Quincey. Lucy

looks at me and shakes her head. "No, I have to keep pressure on the wound."

"Not anymore, Lucy," I tell her. "It's not helping."

I suspect the knife nicked an artery in Quincey's chest. No amount of pressure is going to stop the bleeding now.

This time when I try to gather Quincey in my arms, Lucy reluctantly lets me.

Her skin feels cool to the touch, and I can feel the way her muscles tremble from the shock. "Quincey," I murmur against her temple.

Her heavy eyes follow the sound of my voice, and when they connect with mine, there's an excruciating pain in my chest. The light that has always shone so brightly in those powder-blue orbs is fading. Just like the life inside of her.

Her lips twitch, but she doesn't have the strength to fully smile at me. "Silas." My name on her lips doesn't sound like a lullaby this time, instead, it sounds like a somber goodbye.

She promised me she would always be mine and now she's trying to leave me.

"You're always finding me," she stammers, the same words she told me the last time I found her in this club.

"Always and forever, *Mon Soleil*." Always will I catch her, always will I find her, and always will I love her. "That was my vow to you."

Her eyes flutter closed, forcing the tears that were forming to drip down her face. My thumbs wipe them away.

"Kiss me," she pleads in a soft whisper. "Kiss me one more time."

Dipping my head, I do as she asks. Her lips feel cold against mine and when she breathes out, it's barely a whisper across my skin. "That wasn't the last time I'll kiss you, my love," I say lowly close to her ear. "I told you I want to spend lifetimes with you, this is not where we end, Quincey Page."

She can't respond and I can only hope that she can still hear me.

I asked for six more years, but that plan vanished the second the dagger pierced her chest. Our timeline may have been forcibly altered, but that doesn't change what I already know.

I want Quincey forever.

Before Quincey, I couldn't comprehend how someone could feel desperate enough to turn someone they love. This world is dark and unforgiving. I thought death was the better fate, but now as I hold her as she slowly dies in my arms, I finally understand the desperation.

And for the first time, I understand Gideon's pain, but the comprehension does little to quell the expanding distress in my chest.

Lorcan kneels in front of me, his hands coated in the blood of the man he fought. "Silas, if you're going to do this, you need to do it now. Her heart is slowing."

I know what I need to do, but I still find myself locking in place. The internalized fear I've had for so long keeps me from moving. I don't think six years of preparation and acceptance would have made this any easier for me to do. I still would have felt the same polarizing fear.

I haven't prayed in a very long time. Not since I was baptized by the darkness and corrupted by the sins of this world, but looking down at Quincey's pale face, I pray to whoever will listen.

Don't let her end up like Cecily or Margret.

"What is he going to do?" Lucy questions but she sounds so far away.

"He's going to change her," Lor answers her, but his eyes remain locked on me. "But he needs to do it now if we have any hope of it working. *Silas!*" he snaps my name with more urgency, his bloodied hand shaking my shoulder. "You have to get your blood down her throat while she can still swallow it. If you don't get enough in her, it won't work."

I stay where I am, staring at the woman who somehow found a way to warm the coldest places of my soul. She effortlessly became my heart when I was resigned to the fact I'd never have one again.

"Why isn't he doing it?" Lucy's voice raises as the panic takes her over. "If he won't do it, you can, Lorcan. Do not let her die."

"I can't, darling. It has to be him." Lorcan releases my shoulder so he can grab my face in a hold I'd never allow, but now I can't be bothered to pull him away. "You once made me promise to kill you if Quincey died. I told you then I would do it, but now I really don't want to. Please don't make me fucking do it. I don't want to kill my friend."

I knew the damage I'd cause if Quincey died would be catastrophic and someone strong would need to put me down. That's the promise he made to me that night in the parking garage. I thought he was detached enough to do what needs to be done without any qualms.

In my arms, a low wheezing breath escapes Quincey.

Do it now! A voice inside my brain roars at me.

"Okay," I murmur aloud, mostly to myself as I push the fear down. "Okay, my love. I've got you. I'm going to fix this."

Lifting my arm, I pull the sleeve of my suit jacket up so I can expose the veins underneath. Never have I shared my blood with anyone else, but I will give her every drop if it means Quincey stays here with me.

My canines lengthen when I bring my wrist to my mouth. I bite down hard, tearing through my flesh and opening my veins for her. If there's discomfort, I can't feel it.

Holding my arm over her mouth, I allow the blood to drip through her parted lips. I relax some, thinking that she's going to ingest it without any complications, but on her next pained exhale, she chokes. Blood sprays from her mouth as she weakly coughs.

"*Fuck*," I harshly curse.

"We have to help her." Lucy scrambles closer, crawling through Quincey's blood. "Lorcan, hold her face and keep her mouth open."

Lorcan does as he's ordered, but there's skepticism in his eyes. For the sake of my fading control, I must hang on to whatever sliver of hope remains that this will work. The second I lose that sliver, there will be no recovering from it.

Holding my wrist above her lips, blood steadily pours into her mouth. Lucy runs her fingers down the column of Quincey's throat, coaxing her body to swallow every crucial drop.

"Keep going," I order them both through gritted teeth. "Come on, Quincey, you have to keep your heart beating for me." As long as it continues to beat, it will push my blood through her system. The vampire blood cells will take over her human ones and trigger the change. But only if there's enough vampire blood in her veins. "I know you're tired and want to rest, but you can't yet. Stay with me a little while longer, my love."

We keep forcing the blood down her throat, even when her breathing becomes infrequent and so shallow, her chest barely moves.

Lucy's cries are drowned out as I focus only on Quincey's slowing heartbeat. I commit the sound of each beat to memory so I will never forget it once it's forever silent.

Though I highly doubt I will ever forget a single thing about her. My memories of her are engraved so deeply in me, I will wear them like scars.

"I love you, Quincey." I don't know how this will end for us, but I know that I need her to hear those words once more while she's here. If she leaves me, I will follow her into the afterlife so I can tell her again and again.

Her heart stutters a few more beats, and with one last ragged exhale, it goes as still as mine.

The silence that follows is deafening.

EPILOGUE

Silas

When we lose people, we do what we can to preserve their memory. We cling so desperately to whatever we have left, afraid that if we let go, we will forget them entirely. I would argue forgetting the departed is worse than losing them. Forgetting them would mean there wasn't any evidence they were here with us in the first place.

It falls on the ones left behind to remember them and tell their story.

I thought by keeping her things exactly how she left them when she left me was a way of remembering her. The guilt that I am the reason she died to begin with also kept me from parting with any of the items. I worried by letting go of them, I would somehow forget her and the important—albeit—temporary role she played in my life.

The guilt I felt over her death was already heavy. I didn't think I could bear to forget her as well.

I know now this isn't the case, and I have my sun to thank for that.

BLOODY KINGDOM

Letting go of the past doesn't mean you forget it, Silas.

It's taken me a long time to figure out I don't need the trivial things she left to remember. She is the reason I am here today and for that, I will always remember her and be eternally thankful for her.

Sometimes our loved ones' stories have bitter ends, but there are still lessons in their pages. It's our job to listen to them—to learn from them.

I will keep her lessons with me until my last breath, but it's time I part with her things. She wouldn't want me to keep them around anymore than she would want me to hold on to the guilt.

With one last fleeting look at the belongings, I tell her goodbye and let go of *all* of it. My fingers drop the match and in seconds, everything is aflame. The flames eat through the material I've worked so hard to preserve, and as they do, there is no remorse. Only peace.

The same peace I can only hope she has.

This is something I've been putting off doing, but my impending move has finally persuaded me to do it. It wouldn't be the fresh start that is needed if I still insisted on carting around artifacts of the past.

I stand there until the flames wane, and the past has returned to dust.

Leaving the ashes, I walk back to the house I have called home for the better part of a century. In fifty years, I may once again call it home, but for now, it will sit empty, waiting for my return.

To ensure the property remains standing all those years, Della will be tasked with maintaining the interior and a hired company will oversee the landscaping. When Della's old bones are no longer capable of such labor and she finally retires, I will find someone else, but until then, I wouldn't trust the estate in anyone else's caring hands.

I had offered to bring her with me, but New Orleans is Della's home, and she has no desire to leave her city. She won't be alone, though. Duke will remain here in my place as we planned.

Five months of intensive physical therapy finally got the soldier back on his feet. In the months since the accident, I've watched a fresh wave of determination wash over him, and now he's ready just in time.

To some extent, it's as if he's the prince preparing to take the throne. It's in title only, of course, since I have no intention of surrendering any power. He will simply be the face of my human dealings, like Blackwood Technologies and many more.

All decisions will still come through me.

I will still occasionally have to come to town to handle vampire dealings, but for the time being, everything has been calm. Word traveled fast about what happened to Rowena, and everyone has fallen in line once again. It will be interesting to see how long this period lasts. With vampires, it's never long.

The air is heavy with the scent of Ira's red roses when I walk through the courtyard. Like every time I'm out here, I pause in front of the plaque Della had ordered to commemorate his final resting place. *'In memory of Ira Friedman'*, it reads. The years of his life are engraved underneath and each time I look at that short line between those dates, I'm reminded of just how fleeting a human life really is.

I also know it doesn't matter how long the line might be, it will never be enough time. In the end, you will always beg for one more minute—one more second—with the one you love.

I know I did.

After so many years alone, I never thought I'd be in a position where I'd care deeply enough about another being to beg for them to live. It's because of Ira and his puppeteering that I know what it's like to be so desperate for *one* more minute.

One more minute is how long I needed for her heart to keep beating. Sixty seconds. That's it.

I am thankful to Ira for pulling his strings because if he hadn't, I never would have received that last minute. I also would have missed out on the lifetime I craved.

Ira always knew what was best for me, and it was no different with Quincey. He knew before I did she would be the piece my dark soul always needed. He may not be here with us anymore, but it's okay because he left the most invaluable gift in his place.

Arms snake around my waist and, as they do, the same warmth that has always accompanied her works its way through the cold fibers of my being. I worried when her heart stopped beating she would lose her warmth, but to my utter relief, it's remained.

Her heat never stemmed from her body temperature, it was always her sunshine-like soul.

Whether she's a human or vampire, Quincey will always be my sun, and that will never change.

"Are you telling him thank you again?" she asks against my back. Even without seeing her face, I can hear the soft smile in her voice. While things have changed, she's as observant as always. Nothing gets past her now.

Raising my hands, I weave my fingers through hers and hold them against my sternum. "Something like that." *Thank you* will never be a strong enough sentiment for Ira. "Figured I'd have one last conversation with him before we leave for New York."

Admittedly, I wasn't completely sure about spreading his ashes in the garden when Quincey first suggested it, but now I know it was absolutely the best place for him to be. He was never as content as he was when he was tending to his garden.

Quincey, keeping her arms around my torso, twists her body so she can move to my side. "That's ridiculous, Silas. Just because you won't be here in *this* garden doesn't mean you won't still be able to talk to him when you want." Tilting her head, she pins me with her eyes. Just like her warmth, the softness in her eyes hasn't left. "You'll carry him with you wherever you go. Plus, I was planning on taking a cutting of these roses with us. I figured we could plant more at the new house."

'House' is putting it mildly. I've found another sprawling estate in upstate New York that's far enough away from other houses to ensure

our privacy. The updating and modifications that are needed for vampire residents are being completed in the next month, but in the meantime, we'll live in the penthouse I've owned in the city for many years. New York has always been a city I've had business in, but it's never been one I've lived in for long stretches of time. I'm looking forward to the change.

After the events at the church, Bria has taken a hiatus in her business dealings, and for the time being, has left me the rights to her docks. It's a region I haven't had the chance to conquer to its full extent and this opportunity she's giving me is one I intend to profit heavily from.

"I think that's a great idea."

She smiles at me once before her nose scrunches up in distaste. "You need to change—you smell like smoke." For most, the hardest part of becoming a vampire is the bloodlust, but not Quincey. It's been the enhanced sense of smell. The scents she used to enjoy as a human now are too strong for her. Almost immediately, she went through my colognes and body washes, throwing away the ones that made her pull the same face she has now. "Don't pack this suit with the rest of your clothes, you don't want them all to smell."

In all my years, I've never seen someone adapt to being a vampire as fast as she did. I worried about keeping her contained away from humans for some time, but within the first two weeks, she was spending time with Lucy and Duke without a problem.

"Might be easier if I just threw it away," I offer, partially teasing, but the humor seems to have been lost on her. "What's going through that head of yours?"

My hands wrap around her shoulders, and I force her to stand in front of me.

Every time I look at her now, I'm overwhelmed with so much gratitude that she made it through. There was a period I really thought I was too late, and not enough of my blood had made it into her system. After removing her lifeless body from the floor of St. Sin, I took her home, and I paced at the end of the bed where she lay. And as much as I wanted her to wake up, I dreaded it in the same breath. I was afraid she would not wake up the Quincey I know and love.

When her eyes finally did open and she looked at me with the same level of emotion she always has, I knew her humanity was intact. The amount of relief I felt took me to my fucking knees, and that's where I stayed until she wrapped her newly strengthened limbs around me in a tight—borderline painful—hug.

There was a learning curve at the beginning where she adapted to her new body. While there are many things that have remained the same, like her eyes and her soul, similar to every person who's turned, she experienced a few physical changes as well.

Her hair is longer and silkier. It also appears to have lightened a few shades—something I didn't think was possible. The golden glow to her skin is no more and is now perfectly porcelain, just like mine. There isn't a single flaw in her complexion. The freckles that sat across the bridge of her nose and upper cheekbones are gone, but so are the scars she acquired during her human years. This means the Xs Gideon carved into her chest were completely erased from existence. She swore she was okay with them, but I know she felt some reprieve to not have to carry those around as a reminder.

"Did you burn Cecily's things because of me?" I hadn't discussed my plans with Quincey, and I wasn't sure if she'd seen me carry the items out of the house, but of course she knew what I was doing. "I just want to make sure you know I would *never* ask you to do something like that."

I take her face in my hands. "I know you'd never ask me to, my love." Knowing her, without having to be asked, she'd offer to help me get the items ready for transport. She's that generous and understanding. "It was just time. I can't let the objects from the past hold me back when I have a beautiful future with you in front of me."

True to her nature, she's not wearing any shoes, and she has to lean up on her bare tippy-toes to press a chaste kiss to my mouth. "Lifetimes," she says against my lips. "We have lifetimes."

Lifetimes.

I was prepared to face those endless years alone, but now I'll never be alone again. For the rest of my infinite days, I will have her by my side.

"That we do." I thought I wanted six more years with her as a human, but there's a peace in knowing our eternity has already started. "I'm looking forward to each second."

"Me too." She pulls away with a sly smile on her face. "You're probably not going to look forward to the next couple hours though…"

My brows pull in confusion. "And why's that?"

Her eyes roll. "Silas, you can't put this *giant* ring on my finger and expect them to not want to celebrate with us." Quincey waves her left hand around and the rather large emerald-cut diamond glints in the moonlight. Call it old-fashioned, but of course I wanted to marry the woman I will share a bed with the rest of my life.

She attempts to teasingly back away from me in the house's direction, but I snag her fingers before she can get too far. I pull her to me and trap her in my arms. "What if I wanted you all to myself tonight?"

Her perfect white teeth bite into her bottom lip. "I'd say you can have your wicked way with me when they leave."

"I'm not a patient man, Quincey."

"I know," she breathes, her pupils dilating. "But try to be, for me. I want to spend time with everyone before we leave."

"Quincey, it's not like you won't ever see them again. Duke will visit New York frequently to keep me up to date on things here, and Lucy and Della have already booked multiple flights for the coming year."

"I know this, but when is the next time we'll all be in the same room with each other?"

"Lorcan is coming with us." For *now*, anyway. Lor claims working with me for some time will be a refreshing change for him, but his nomadic lifestyle will catch up to him and he'll be disappearing into the shadows soon enough. "We'll be in the same room with him more than I'll probably like."

She pats the side of my face patronizingly. "Stop acting like you still can't stand him. Everyone knows you're friends. The only person you're lying to is yourself, and at this point, it's just sad."

"*Lucy* and *you* are friends. Lor and I are..." I trail off, unable to come up with an accurate term. All I know is it's nothing similar to what they have.

Lucy and Quincey's relationship has changed little, if at all, since Rowena's attack. It's only grown stronger now that Quincey no longer feels like she must keep secrets from her friend. Though Lucy still hasn't been as forthcoming with her own secrets. It's something Quincey has elected to not push too hard on, opting to allow Lucy to tell her in her own time. Meanwhile, I haven't been as patient. I had Rory—who is finally back working for me—investigate Lucy's past. It came as no shock to me she was able to find some *curious* information about Lucy. The most glaring of which being *Lucy Bell* didn't exist prior to twenty years ago. There is no information or paper trails for the first five years of her life.

It appears Miss Bell might be a better secret keeper than even me, but that didn't stop me from offering her a job.

After the massacre at St. Sin, Lucy quit her long-held job there. After a few months of not working and thinking over her next moves, she said it was finally time she set her sights on something bigger. Which is exactly what I was hoping she'd say. I had a role I needed filled, and I thought someone with Lucy's demeanor and knowledge of vampires would be good for the job. With Rowena dead, the underground vampire club she ran was shut down, and I took the opportunity to purchase the property. It will continue to be a place for vampires to convene, but no longer will it be a place for them to feed. Under Lucy's watchful eye, there will no longer be blood slaves at that establishment. I've also added vampire security as additional muscle if things get out of hand, but before I informed Lucy of their roles and employment, she wasn't afraid. She seemed excited at the opportunity.

Reluctantly, I sigh, "As if I could ever say no to you." Lifting her hand to my mouth, I kiss the ring I'd placed there two weeks prior. The pale-yellow diamond reminded me of the sun, which made it perfect for her. "So, we are celebrating our engagement tonight?"

She nods her head in confirmation, the corners of her mouth twitching in a knowing grin.

"Even though we're already married?"

The grin she'd been fighting spreads across her face, her eyes lighting up with joy. "Yes, because they still don't know you whisked me away to Paris an hour after you finally got on your knees for me." Her prediction had finally come true. It may not have been in the context she'd expected, but I'd argue it was even better. "Which I think is because of your aforementioned lack of *patience*."

I gave her my blood to keep her alive and now I've given her my last name.

"I've waited for you long enough, Quincey. Why would I want to wait any longer to claim you as mine in yet another way?" I have her soul, her love, and now her hand. "You are my sun, my heart, my mate and now you are my wife."

I'd taken her as my vampire mate almost immediately. She'd begged me for so long to bite her and this time she got to return the favor with her own set of fangs. With the midnight moon streaming through the windows, we exchanged bites and created a bond only death can break.

Cupping her face, I claim her mouth as well. She kisses me back and breathlessly whispers, "My king."

"*Ma reine.*"

My queen.

ACKNOWLEDGEMENTS

I will never be able to thank my readers enough for their patience with this book. It was never my intention to take this long, but this story needed more time to fully develop. Thank you for your endless encouragement while I took on this story. I hope that Silas and Quincey's ending makes you as happy as it made me!

As always, I need to thank my family for their love and support while I embark on this crazy career. Mom, thanks for letting me ramble on and on about plot point, when I know none of them make sense to you. Thank you, Dad, for being proud enough of me to send my books to your clients. Thank you, McKenna, for letting my cry when I'm overwhelmed and taking my phone when my attention span is majoring lacking. Thank you, Cooper, for standing over me and asking over and over again if "I'm done with my book *yet*." Look buddy, I'm *finally* done.

I never could have done this without Greer. Not only is she my best friend, but she is my forever cheerleader. Whenever I felt like I couldn't do it, she was there, reminding me how capable I am. G, I'm so endlessly thankful for you and our friendship. I can't wait to come visit you and work on all the *top-secret* things. *wink wink*

Cat, my magical fairy. Babe, I don't even know where to start with you. I adore everything about you. Thank you for making me all the pretty things. You are so incredibly talented. I love you so much, little kitchen.

Lee! Girl, thank you for being my accountability partner. I loved loved loved your check-in texts and even though it made me cower in shame, I loved when you used your mom/teacher voice with me. Thank you for telling me to *'get my shit together'* when I needed to hear it most.

Aundi, my dear, thank you for helping me with this story and hyping me up when I needed it. Your advice and encouragement are so appreciated. Thank you for being the president of the Lorcan fan club!

Ellie and Rosa, you two are the dream team. Thank you for working with my crazy schedule and making my words pretty. Ellie, I owe you soooo many tacos.

Thank you, Christina. Your ability to deal with my bullshit should be celebrated. I want to tell you that I'll be better organized next time, but we both know that will be a lie. I can disappear into my writing cave because I know you'll be there to pick up the slack in my absence. You're a rock star.

To my street team, thank you for taking the time to share and read all my things! I love seeing your excitement for all my books and your love for my characters! You guys keep me going.

ABOUT THE AUTHOR

Kayleigh lives in Denver Colorado, just two hours away from some of the best skiing in the world. A luxury completely lost on her considering she avoids snow at all costs. Well, she avoids *outside* at all costs—she's what you'd call an 'indoor cat'. She much prefers to sit inside on her computer all day drinking massive amounts of caffeine. She'd have an IV drip of the stuff connected to her if she could. When she's not writing, you can find her binge-watching Netflix like it's her job. Or at the local Mexican restaurant, because the girl loves tacos and margaritas.

instagram.com/kayleighkingwrites

goodreads.com/kayleighkingwrites

amazon.com/author/kayleighkingwrites

facebook.com/kayleighkingwrites

ALSO BY KAYLEIGH KING

The White Wolf Prophecy
Wolf Bound
Soul Bound
Shadow Bound
Fire Bound

Made in the USA
Columbia, SC
06 December 2021